House of Refuge

Also by CJ Murphy

frame by frame

The Bucket List

Five Points Series
Gold Star Chance
Forever Chance
Redemption's Road
Sovereign Chance

House of Refuge

CJ Murphy

Desert Palm Press

House of Refuge
(Five Point Series – Book 5)

By CJ Murphy

©2023 CJ Murphy

ISBN (trade) 9781954213593
ISBN (epub) 9781954213609

Desert Palm Press
1961 Main Street, Suite 220
Watsonville, California 95076
www.desertpalmpress.com

Editor: CK King, Raven's Eye Editing
Cover Design: Murphy's Law Ink

Printed in the United States of America
First Edition February 2023

Note from the author:

Rhebekka Deklan and her sister Ellie are fictional characters, though the religious and spiritual abuse they experienced exists in real life. My first book with these characters, Redemption's Road, came to me after watching a PBS Maker's documentary on Lutheran Pastor Nadia Bolz-Weber. My own pastor showed me that understanding the light of grace changes everything. Nadia showed me that the larger the cracks of understanding are, the easier it is for grace to make its way in. Someone just has to turn the light on so we can see them. In addition, I was driven to bring these characters to life after watching a special investigative series on the Oxygen Network called The Witnesses. That investigation revealed the heart-wrenching abuse stories of numerous former Jehovah's Witnesses and how that abuse had been and continues to be hidden. Redemption's Road and House of Refuge were written so that I could be one of the people that turned the light on.

For anyone wondering, the story is not written from a personal experience as a victim of sexual abuse. My pain came from years of emotional and physical abuse. Many other people that I personally knew or knew of were true victims. My experience revolved around twenty years of spiritual manipulation that led me to believe I was unworthy while I was immersed in a world carefully constructed and conscripted. My worth was measured by compliance. The fact that I was attracted to women meant I was anything but compliant and, by default, completely unworthy of grace in their eyes. In her book Shameless: A Sexual Reformation, Nadia Bolz-Weber said, "We can only really know and be known when we show how life has marked us."

No one comes out of this life without marks, visible and invisible. As an author, opening myself up to other's opinion of my work feels a great deal like seeking worthiness and grace again. The big difference is my eternal soul isn't in question. As you read the next chapter of Rhebekka's journey and those she meets on her path, I beg you to remember we are all worthy of grace no matter how we identify or who we love.

CJ

Dedications

This book is dedicated to those who carry the burden of the truths hidden in notes, files, and blue envelopes. May the lambs silenced by false truths find their voice and roar like the lion they are.

Character Index

Rev Rhebekka Lynn Deklan- Retired Rock Star and current pastor of a nondenominational house of worship. She grew up as a Jehovah's Witness in an abusive home and may be referred to as Bek/Bekka.

Rev Naomi Rainelle Deklan-. After a long separation, she and Rhebekka reconciled and married. She Co-pastors with Rhebekka and is a musician in her own right.

Ellie McNally- Rhebekka's sister who co-founded their band Regal Crimson. Retires to Tucker County after a bout with cancer.

Siobhan O'Broin- (Pronounced Sha-vonne) Former Irish special forces soldier who owns a bar in Elkins and plays in an Irish Folk Band. Dating Ellie.

Lucian Altovice- Runaway from the Elkin's orphanage. He's a trans boy with musical talent.

Laura Sandestro-A nurse at the Elkins orphanage and a member of Rhebekka's congregation.

Tank (Tancy) Raines- Rhebekka's best friend and former bodyguard. Chief brewmaster and operator at Redemption's Road. She has a military background and was in the foster system in Tucker County until she turned eighteen.

Dr. Amy Halston- ER doctor at Garrett Memorial Hospital and is Tank's girlfriend.

Karmen Washington- Owner of a café and bakery in Thomas. Close friend of Rhebekka. She is in a relationship with Zandra.

Zandra- Graphic novel illustrator and Karmen's girlfriend.

Chance Fitzsimmons- Tucker County Sheriff with K9 Zeus. Foster mother to Hunter. She has scars from an accident as a smoke jumper and lost her law enforcement father on duty.

Jax Fitzsimmons- Veterinarian and horse enthusiast. Married to Chance and is Hunter's other foster mother.

Hunter- Six year old deaf boy that was orphaned when his birth mother died of an overdose. He has an educational assistant named Julia.

Maggie Fitzsimmons- One of Chance's two mothers. Owns a successful real estate company.

Dee Fitzsimmons- Chance's other mother. Basketball coach and calls Chance by the nickname Five Points.

Kendra Fitzsimmons- Maggie and Dee's other adopted daughter. US Marshal and avid archery enthusiast.

Brandi Antolini- Veterinary student and girlfriend of Kendra.

Taylor Lewis- Chief Deputy of the Tucker County Sheriff's Office partnered with K9 Midas.

Penny Lewis- Tucker County Sheriff's Department Office Manager and is married to Taylor. They have a little boy named Jace.

Chapter One

RHEBEKKA WATCHED THE SCREEN with rapt attention. The sharp, agonizing pain in her heart was surely the ripping away of the arteries and veins that connected it to her body. She was lightheaded. Her eyes stung from the tears that poured over her cheeks and dripped steadily from her trembling chin. One phrase repeated over and over in her thoughts. A sardonic chuckle bubbled up from her chest as she spoke them aloud. "Wolves in sheep's clothing."

Naomi snuggled closer and pulled Rhebekka into her arms. "That's why you're different, why we teach of a God of love, not one of fear. They manipulated both of you for twenty years."

The program continued with one story after another. Those stories had been recorded, sealed in special blue envelopes, and kept out of the hands of the authorities. Young girls were forced to recount their molestation, face-to-face with their male abusers, in front of a group of elders more concerned with protecting the organization than the child. The stories were horrific. It was wrong and immoral by any definition. Those children were now adults and fighting back, fighting to bring the abuse into the light. Those same women, and some men, were being labeled apostates by their former religion for daring to reveal the truth.

Rhebekka looked over at her sister. Ellie sat ramrod straight, mouthing the words to a song they hadn't listened to in over two decades. Music is a powerful trigger, and it was obvious that Ellie was just as affected as she was. Rhebekka needed to be close to her sister. "Come over here." Ellie didn't move, and Rhebekka watched as Naomi gently touched Ellie's leg.

Ellie startled and looked over at Rhebekka. "That's what we are now, isn't it? Apostates? How many times did we see those groups on the sidewalks as we were ushered into the conventions?" Ellie was on her feet now and pacing. "I can hear Mom telling us not to look at them, not to even acknowledge them. All along, those protesters were telling the truth."

Rhebekka couldn't take it any longer. She paused the television and went to her sister's side. "Do you remember how they hammered on John 8:32? 'You will know the truth, and the truth will set you free.' None of them are free, because they intentionally promote falsehoods. We know the real truth. The people who shield child molesters within their congregations are perverting the message of God by caring more for their own reputations than the safety of the children they're responsible to protect. They hide behind rhetoric to justify their actions. I thank my God every day for letting us get away."

Naomi joined them. "I knew it was bad from all the things you both have told me about your childhood, but I could never have imagined people so bent on mind control that they would ignore claims of child abuse to protect an organization. I can't understand."

The three of them had been watching an investigative report on the Jehovah's Witnesses organization and the systematic concealment of thousands of pedophiles within their congregations, worldwide. They returned to the couch, where they curled around each other, seeking shelter and comfort like tiny kittens huddled in a corner. Rhebekka stared at the still shot on the television. The familiar logo was on every piece of literature from the organization. A fortress to keep out worldly influences, their watchtower provided the seclusion needed to brainwash the victims within. From the stories being told, it also kept the abused inside as prey for those who sexually violated children without fear of repercussions.

Naomi stroked her back. "I think we've watched enough of this today. Both of you are reeling from these revelations. How about we go for a walk and clear our heads? On the way back, we can stop by Karmen's and pick up something sinfully chocolate."

Christmas was less than two weeks away, and preparations were underway for the Christmas Eve service at House of the Rising Son and a party at Redemption's Road later that night. Rhebekka loved Christmas and wished more than anything they hadn't marred the season by stumbling on this documentary. These days were normally filled with joy and anticipation, something they were denied as children. She took a deep breath and turned off the television before looking at her sister. "Feel like a walk?"

Ellie sat there, still staring at the blank screen. "A walk isn't going to clear my head. What I want is a strong drink and a piano."

Rhebekka reached out and grasped hands that felt like ice cubes. "Ellie, you're freezing. I'm not even sure your fingers will bend without breaking off." She cupped one in her hands and rubbed vigorously.

"Then a glass of Crown Royal is just what the doctor ordered to warm me up from the inside." Ellie pulled her hand from Rhebekka's and headed for the bar in the corner. "Can I get you one?"

Rhebekka shook her head. "A drink won't clear your head either, little songbird."

"Probably not, but it will temporarily help me forget what's in there."

Naomi got up and slipped on her coat. "I'm going to run to Karmen's and pick something up." She walked back over to Rhebekka and kissed her before whispering in her ear. "Tread lightly here. I get the feeling there's more to this than meets the eye. You two need a few minutes to talk. I'll pick something up and wait for you to text me to come back." She walked over and squeezed Ellie's arm. "Anything in particular you want?"

"Chocolate, anything and everything chocolate."

"You got it. I'll be right back."

Rhebekka watched Naomi go, beyond grateful for her wife's intuitiveness. She grabbed her Gibson from the studio and strummed the chorus of a song she and Ellie had been working on for the last few days. Ellie downed one shot and was pouring another two fingers of the peach liquor blend, Crown Royal's latest release. It wasn't so much that Rhebekka was worried about Ellie's drinking. Her concern lay in the frame of mind that convinced her sister a drink was what she needed. When Rhebekka could stand the silence no more, she began to sing. "Ice-cold wind whips through my soul..."

Ellie joined her singing, "...and the long cold nights exact their toll."

The sisters sang in perfect harmony about finding shelter and security away from the things that hurt them. As they continued through the unfinished verses, Ellie grabbed a pad and began trying out lyrics, using one phrase, then a different one, scratching out a word and replacing it until they had three verses to the song tentatively titled Storm Shelter.

Rhebekka let the last notes of the final chord fade away and smiled at her sister. The storms they'd survived were small in the grand scheme of the world, but monumental in their own lives. "We've still got it, you know."

Ellie smiled. "Thank God for that, or we'd all be going hungry. I'm starting to really like this as a single for Strings and Silk." Martina and Myranda ended up in the foster system when they were twelve and thirteen, because their mother and father were drug addicts. Their extended family was incapable of taking them in. They were fortunate to land in the home of two exceptional men, who raised them as their own in Vermont. Both Vince and Benny were music teachers and encouraged the girl's ambitions. Ellie walked to the keyboard and began pecking out the bridge of the song.

Rhebekka strummed along. "Wouldn't it be nice if all foster kids ended up in loving homes? Look at how far little Hunter has come, living with Chance and Jax."

Ellie's eyes danced. "He is adorable."

"He's flourishing. They've been able to dial in his hearing aids so that he can hear some speech, and he has a fantastic interpreter. I can only pray they will be able to formally adopt him."

Ellie sipped her drink. "Is there a problem?"

Rhebekka put her guitar down and stepped over to the windows that overlooked the main drag in Thomas. There were signs of life up and down the street, where people dressed in colorful ski jackets roamed the small shops. "There are some that are opposed to having a lesbian couple gain permanent custody."

"Are you telling me that they're good enough to foster him, but not good enough to be permanent parents to someone whose only blood family overdosed and left him on his own?"

With a calloused finger, Rhebekka drew a heart in the window condensation. "Unfortunately, yes." She turned to Ellie. "Once again, the priorities of society are screwed up. Children aren't protected but instead used as political pawns. We have children in cages, children being thrown out of their homes for being gay, agencies preventing children from being placed in healthy homes, and religious leaders protecting pedophiles in the name of God."

Ellie looked away. "Let it go, Bek. I just can't right now."

Rhebekka swallowed hard. There was something Ellie wasn't telling her. Whatever it was, she would let her sister reveal it in her own time. It didn't mean she wouldn't continue gently prodding, but for now, she'd let it drop. She picked up her phone and texted Naomi, then spoke softly to her sister. "Okay, El, but we're going to talk at some point. Count on it."

Ellie sighed and looked at her. "I know, just not today."

Before Rhebekka could slip her phone back in her pocket, it lit up with a call from one of her parishioners. "Hey Laura, how are you?"

A deep sigh came over the phone. "I'd be better if I knew what to do."

Rhebekka made her way to the office, looking up to see Naomi come back in the loft with a box from Karmen's. Pointing to the phone she waved Naomi over and put the call on speakerphone. "Maybe Naomi and I can help. What's going on?" Ellie joined them.

"Do you remember Lucian, from here at the children's shelter?"

Rhebekka thought back. "The transgender boy?"

"Yes, and he's run away. They say they have people out looking, but I've got to be honest, I'm really not sure how hard the institution is looking. Lucian will be eighteen in three weeks, and he'll age out. He's had such a struggle. They refuse to call him Lucian and continue to deadname him by referring to him as Lucy Ann. I believe they've contacted the Tucker County Sheriff's Office and Sheriff Fitzsimmons."

Rhebekka was outraged. "That's ridiculous."

"It's like they're trying to force him into compliance, and I think he's just had enough. Even the girls at the home aren't incredibly supportive. Some have even made unfounded accusations against him. I've watched him withdraw further into himself. I've been trying to talk to him, but lately, he's completely closed off. The only time I ever saw any joy in him was when you and Naomi would visit to play music. Pastor, I'm terrified for him."

Rhebekka clenched her phone so hard that her fingers started to hurt. She forced herself to relax. "Do you have any idea when he left or where he might go? How about what he was last seen wearing?" She knew she was peppering Laura with too many questions. Rhebekka closed her eyes and took a deep breath. Her ears were ringing slightly, a sign that her blood pressure was rising.

"I wish I did. They took the kids on a field trip to skate at Canaan Valley State Park. When it was time to get back in the van, Lucian wasn't there."

She'd had several conversations with Lucian, trying to comfort him and assure him that there was absolutely nothing wrong with him. Now he was out there somewhere, hopefully still in Tucker County. She looked at the clock and noticed it was two in the afternoon. Temperatures would be dropping, and night would be on them before they knew it. She needed to contact Chance. "Laura, I'm going to make some calls. If there is a search underway, I'll try and gather my folks and the kids from the after-school program, if they're willing. If you hear anything let me know. We'll find him. We have to believe that."

Rhebekka hung up and had started to call Chance, when Naomi grabbed her hand.

"Let's ask for a little extra help first."

She didn't have the words. Her heart knew what she needed to say, but it was as if her mouth was frozen. Yielding to her wife's skills and powers of perception, she bowed her head and listened to the voice that had brought her back from the depths of despair more times than she could count. She let her mind quiet and listened to the comforting pleas Naomi asked of God. Their God was one of love and compassion. When Naomi finished, Rhebekka's mind immediately went to a passage in Matthew. *Not a single sparrow can fall to the ground outside your care. Please be with Lucian, for I know he is even more precious to you.*

Rhebekka dialed Chance's number. When she answered, she could tell the sheriff was in her vehicle.

"Rhebekka, what can I do for you? I'm on my way to investigate a missing person."

"If it's about a transgender boy named Lucian, he's who I'm calling about."

"I was told it was a girl named Lucy Ann dressed in boy's clothing. I'm guessing there's more to this story than the children's shelter gave me?"

Rhebekka sighed and rubbed her temple with her thumb. "Yes, there is. Are you coming by here? I'd like to go with you. I've talked with Lucian several times and likely have some insight to share."

"I'll be there in fifteen minutes."

"Thanks, Chance. Just in case no one ever tells you this, you're a good sheriff."

Rhebekka hung up and went to the closet to find her warm snow boots and parka. Naomi came around the corner and pushed a beanie down over Rhebekka's dark locks.

"Promise me you'll call when you know anything. I'll go ahead and make some preliminary calls to the troops to get a feel for how many volunteers I can round up."

Rhebekka leaned in and put her hand around the back of her wife's neck, drawing her in for a deep kiss. "You're pretty amazing, you know that?"

Naomi kissed her back and wiped a small smudge of lipstick off the corner of Rhebekka's mouth. "That's what you keep telling me. Take your collapsible ski poles. I know you've adapted to your new leg, but let's not take any chances."

Rhebekka smiled. A top-of-the-line prosthesis, and many hours of grueling rehab, had allowed her to recover from the accident that took her leg. "They're at the bottom of the stairs. I'll grab them on my way out, along with my hiking pack. I love you."

Naomi zipped the heavy ski jacket and wrapped her arms around Rhebekka. "Whatever you do, promise to come home to me."

Rhebekka drew her close and sighed into the top of the shorter woman's hair, knowing Naomi was still haunted by the memory of Red Creek's freezing water that nearly took more than a leg. "A promise I willingly make and fully intend to keep. See if you can use your skills to get Ellie to open up. My gut is churning. There's something she hasn't told me. If it's what I'm thinking, God almighty will have to hold me back."

Naomi released her. "Go. I'll handle things here. She'll talk about it in her own time and maybe not even to us. Siobhan is who she leans on differently than she does you. Ellie knows we're here for her, no matter what."

Rhebekka kissed her and turned for the stairs. "I'll call when I can."

* * * *

Rhebekka slid into the passenger seat of Chance's Suburban and buckled her seatbelt.

"Good to see you, Rhebekka. Thanks for coming out."

"I'm always happy to see you and Zeus. I wish it were under better circumstances. I don't have to tell you how worried I am."

Chance glanced her way. "What can you tell me about the person reported missing?"

Rhebekka tightened her fist, anger bubbling inside her at the transphobia the children's shelter was perpetuating. "I know they told you that Lucy Ann is missing. That's the deadname of Lucian, a trans boy from the children's home. He's been having a tough time with them over his coming out. Physically, he looks a lot like me, though much leaner and two or three inches shorter. The last time I saw him, he had dark hair that swept over his eyes." Rhebekka shook her head in disgust. "Unfortunately, no matter how much things have changed, West Virginia is still less than welcoming to those who don't conform to the traditional sense of gender or sexuality. Do you remember Laura Sandestro from church?"

Chance nodded. "I do. She attends services with us and works at the children's shelter, doesn't she?"

"Yes. She approached me about Lucian Altovice some time ago. I've gone over there for music programs and tried to engage him.

Unfortunately, everything Laura's told me leads me to believe that he's lived hell since announcing he's trans and wants to be called Lucian."

"Did he open up to you at all?"

Rhebekka stared out the window. "Lucian told me he entered the system at age twelve, after his caretaker grandmother passed away. There was no other family. There were a few trials with foster families, but he was returned to the system when he wouldn't conform to being the little girl they were looking for."

Chance turned onto the road that would take them to Canaan Valley State Park. "I can't imagine the rejection he felt. I'd hate to think where I'd be if Maggie and Dee hadn't taken me in. I'm not much of a conformist myself, as you know."

"The world would be a much better place if there were more families like yours. Look what you've done for Hunter. He's thriving despite the many things he's gone through and had to adapt to. Seeing him smile is one of the highlights of my Sundays."

"I hope you know how much he loves coming to church. The more they dial in his hearing aids, the more he can actually hear. I don't know how much he understands, but he always tells me God made him special just for us."

Rhebekka's heart warmed at the sentiment. "We are all wonderfully made. How's the adoption going?" She looked at Chance and noticed her hands tightening on the steering wheel.

"It always seems like there is one more hurdle we need to jump, one more opinion to get. We're good enough to foster him, but there seems to be some debate as to whether Jax and I are good enough adoptive prospects. I don't understand it all. We have a lawyer who specializes in same-sex adoption working on it. It's Hunter's first Christmas with us, and he's come so far. I can't even imagine him not being with us. It would kill Jax, and I'm not sure Zeus would survive either."

"Something tells me it would hurt you just as deeply." Rhebekka spotted the lodge coming into sight. The ice rink was a little farther past. Deep snow covered the ground, and she looked at the dashboard display that showed the time and temperature. *Three o'clock and twenty-one degrees. Lord, help us find him.* Rhebekka spotted a familiar face standing with a taller man in front of the skating rink's office. "There's Laura."

Chance put the vehicle in park and reported to the dispatch center that she'd arrived on scene. Rhebekka grabbed her backpack as Chance released Zeus from the back. Laura walked to meet them.

"Sheriff Fitzsimmons, it's good to see you. I wish it were under better circumstances. Rhebekka, thanks for coming." Laura sank into the hug Rhebekka offered.

Rhebekka held on tight for a minute. "It's going to be okay."

Laura nodded, then turned to Chance. "That's our activities directory over there, with a member of the lodge's security. He likely has what little info there is. Sheriff, there's something you should know about Lucy Ann."

Chance squeezed Laura's arm. "Pastor Rhebekka filled me in on Lucian. Finding him is now my department's top priority." Chance walked over to the man on a phone that Laura indicated.

Rhebekka held Laura's hand. "What else can you tell me?"

Laura looked away, then back to Rhebekka. "As I told you on the phone, other than the paperwork, I don't think Ken over there is upset that Lucian ran away. There were seven of the kids that came over today for the outing. From what I gathered from the girls, they remember seeing Lucian skate for about twenty minutes or so. They don't remember seeing him after that. Around one, Ken bought hot chocolate for everyone. My alarm bells would have gone off when he didn't show up with the group, but Ken's didn't until about two."

"Did anyone think to look for his shoes to see if they are gone?"

"I have no idea. Lucian is always by himself, so everyone is used to him doing his own thing."

Rhebekka looked up to see Chance walking back to them. "Anything we can go on?"

Chance adjusted her hat. "The security officer has agreed to let me examine their video footage to see if we can find him on camera leaving the rink area. That will give us some indication as to which way he might have gone. Once we have a starting point, we can begin a search. Rhebekka, do you want to come with me? I have a basic clothing description, and two sets of eyes are better than one."

Rhebekka looked at Laura. "You have my number. Keep in touch with me on anything you hear from the children's shelter."

Chance wrote something in a notebook and turned to the distraught woman. "Laura, I've asked the adviser to get me a piece of clothing that Lucian recently wore. Unfortunately, I'm not confident it will be high on his priority list. If you can, will you go for me, maybe grab a bedsheet? That should have a strong scent mark for the dogs."

Laura's eyes lit up. "I certainly can. They don't change the beds until tomorrow."

Rhebekka pulled Laura to her. "We will find him. Remember, we have a loving God to help protect him and lead us."

Rhebekka followed Chance and Zeus to the Suburban, and they followed security back to their operations room.

"We've only got a few hours of daylight left, so I've called Sarah to start getting the search and rescue team together. All I need is a starting point and they'll do the rest."

Rhebekka looked skyward and said a silent prayer that God would drop a few breadcrumbs for them to follow to the missing sparrow named Lucian.

* * * *

A bank of monitors blinked in an eerie black-and-white panorama of the resort. The amount of activity at the resort made it challenging to determine which of the hooded figures was the one they were looking for. When the group had exited the van, the video showed them as nothing more than a mass moving toward the skating rink check-in. Security had backed up the tape to a few minutes before the credit card receipt registered in the system.

Rhebekka sat glued to the small, closed-circuit monitor, watching for anything that would distinguish Lucian. Unfortunately, none of the cameras offered any closeups of the patrons. She could pick out several of the others, but Lucian had become a master at blending into the background. "If only this was like the crime scene shows that let investigators zoom in and use facial recognition."

Chance chuckled but nodded. "If I had a dime for every time someone used the phrase 'but on CSI.'" She used her fingers to indicate quotation marks. "That damn show has made the public have an unreasonable expectation of police work. All the forensics they portray are greatly exaggerated. I'd love it if all my suspects confessed in under an hour."

Rhebekka sighed. "I imagine it's a lot like how people expect God to perform miracles whenever they ask."

"I never thought of it that way, but yes. We're doing everything we can to find him. Nothing is ever easy. That's the reality of the job. It's a lot of hours doing things like this."

Rhebekka jumped up and her chair rolled back and crashed into a filing cabinet. "There! There he is."

Chance turned to the security guard. "Can you back up the tape on that camera?"

They sat staring at the lone figure that walked out a side exit of the rink, the face hidden in a hood and hands deep into jacket pockets. The person looked left and right before slowly walking around the closed pool area and disappearing into the woods.

"We know where to start. I'll get Sarah and the crew over there." Chance stood and grabbed her cell phone from her coat pocket.

"I'm going down there. If there are tracks, I'll avoid them, I promise. I need to go look. He's got too much time on us, and daylight is fading far too quickly."

Chance pointed at her. "Do not get lost. I don't have time to look for both of you."

Rhebekka saluted and held up her GPS unit as she pushed the door open with her shoulder. As fast as her leg would let her go, she found the closest exit and traversed the long steps leading to the skating rink and pool area. The landmarks from the video led her to the area near the woods. She blinked her eyes against the heavy snowflakes falling on her face that had already covered any trace of the footprints Lucian might have left. Inside her backpack were the collapsible hiking poles and a headlamp. She pulled the headlamp on and extended the poles before she marked a home flag on her GPS unit. With a final thought of her promise to Naomi, she started into the woods.

It wasn't long before the buildings were no longer visible. Tree branches heavy with snow surrounded her. She was no tracker or first responder by any stretch of the imagination. All she had was a burning desire to find a young man in trouble. She was trudging through snow up past her calves. Grateful for her thermal boots, she realized that even after all this time, her mind still tricked her into thinking the toes on her amputated foot were cold. She needed to pay attention to how cold she was getting. When she'd had her accident, she'd suffered from severe hypothermia. That made her very susceptible to a reoccurrence. *I'll never put Naomi or Ellie through that again.*

Rhebekka stopped and listened. There was activity nearby. That must be search and rescue. On a spring day, the roar of Blackwater Falls would be echoing around her. She pulled up a layer map of Canaan Valley State Park on her GPS. The thick copse of trees around told her that she'd veered away from the marked trail. The map revealed she was headed in the general direction of the main road that went through the valley. Her ability to see was diminishing, even with her headlamp. It was time to admit defeat, for now. *I won't give up, Lucian. I promise I'll be in your corner if you'll just let me find you.*

* * * *

Naomi approached their garage and activated her turn signal. The tightness in her chest had finally dissipated when she answered Rhebekka's call to pick her up at the lodge. Rhebekka had said she wanted to work on a plan for volunteers if the search continued into tomorrow. Chance had to remain at the state park while searchers were in the field.

Her wife's pants were soaked all the way to the waistline from walking in the deep snow. Even with the heat on as high as it would go, she watched Rhebekka shiver all the way home from the valley. *Good thing our garage is heated.*

"I'm sorry, Naomi."

"You don't have to be sorry, honey. I just worry about you." She reached up and touched the opener attached to the sun visor of the Land Cruiser. "How did your leg hold up in the snow?" She pulled the keys from the ignition once she was parked.

"Surprisingly well. I kept thinking it would pop off when I tried to take the next step, but it never did. I'll be honest and tell you it's aching. When we get inside, I'll take it off for a while and use the knee walker."

Naomi knew that it had to be bothering Rhebekka significantly to admit to needing a break. Typically, she had to cajole Rhebekka into resting. Getting in the house was step one. "For now, you can make calls and recruit volunteers if they don't find him first. I'm asking you to let someone else do the heavy work of the actual search. It won't do Lucian any good if his few advocates are out of service." Naomi pulled with both hands at the stubborn door that creaked and complained as it scraped across the concrete. "We need to do something about this door. It gets worse and worse."

"I'll take a look at it later." Rhebekka pulled with her, then joined their hands together. They made their way down the garage steps to the house door.

Naomi's fear of losing her wife still hadn't faded with time. Rhebekka's near-death encounter still rattled her. They'd been married less than a year after their long separation, and winter's shadows were growing long. She pushed her key into the lock. "Let's get you inside and into a hot shower."

She felt Rhebekka press her flat against the door from behind.

"I'd rather have a really hot bath and company."

Naomi pushed the door open. She turned and grinned at her wife. "I think we can arrange that. I also saved you a few of Karmen's ultimate brownies."

"Now you're just talking dirty."

She turned and rose onto her tiptoes. She wrapped her arms around Rhebekka's neck and kissed her soundly. "Good thing I can pray for forgiveness. Come on."

Naomi watched Rhebekka slowly climb the stairs and wondered if there was a way to create an elevated passageway from the garage directly into the apartment. It was evident that the fatigue was more significant than Rhebekka was confessing to. *I'll bet she's gritting her teeth against the pain but damn if she'll admit how much she hurts.* Inside the apartment, Naomi walked to the bathroom and turned on the hot water in the large, clawfoot bathtub. Rhebekka went into their bedroom to strip out of her wet clothes. Naomi texted Ellie that they were home and gave a quick update on her sister's condition.

Ellie: *She always overdoes it. Good thing she has you. Give her a hug for me.*

Naomi: *I will. She always puts herself last. That's something we can't change. Call you later. Love to Siobhan.*

Naomi poured a tumbler of Scotch and took a sip before taking the time to calm her nerves with a few lines in her journal. It was something she'd taken to doing when her emotions were high years ago, after the breakup. It was a way to release the thoughts that kept her up at night. Sometimes it was nothing more than a prayer, and sometimes it was much more.

Rhebekka is home safe. She sometimes scares me to death, but I couldn't love her more for why she was out there. Lord, I know you're listening, so I ask that you watch over Lucian and bring him home safely as well. Everything is within your power.

She picked up the tumbler and carried it into the bathroom, where heat from the bathwater steamed up the mirrors and condensation droplets ran down the cold glass of the window. She poured in some lavender-scented oil before testing the temperature. Perfect. She walked into the bedroom to strip out of her clothes.

Rhebekka was pulling her shirt over her head, leaning heavily against the wall, her prosthetic sitting on a chair beside her. Silent tears left trails on her cheeks.

"Let me look at your leg. You can't always see the pressure spots like I can." Naomi knelt and removed the liner that helped hold the socket in place. Angry red splotches covered the skin. "This is irritated, honey. You need to go without your prosthetic for a bit."

Rhebekka shrugged and balled up the shirt. "We'll see what it looks like later. Lucian is out there all alone. It's nothing compared to what he's going through."

"That doesn't mean he or anyone expects you to destroy months of progress. We'll find Lucian, and when we do, you need to be able to walk."

Rhebekka dropped her head back against the wall, her shirt still in her hand. "This didn't have to happen." She angrily threw the T-shirt into the laundry basket.

Naomi stood and handed her the crutches off a shelf. "Go on. Get into the bath and I'll join you in a minute." Rhebekka took them without complaint and made her way out of the room. Naomi steadied herself on the closet doorframe and choked back a sob. There was no denying how much emotional pain her wife was going through. The agony was born of an abusive childhood and a restrictive religious upbringing that condemned and ostracized anyone who fell along the LGBTQIA+ spectrum. No doubt, Rhebekka was reliving her own past in Lucian's plight. Naomi stripped off her own clothes and walked to the bathroom. Rhebekka was reclined in the tub with her head against the back as water dripped off the hand that held the tumbler of Scotch. Naomi took it from her and swallowed a generous swig.

"Come join me."

Naomi nodded as she stepped gingerly into the tub while holding Rhebekka's hand. She slowly lowered herself until she could relax with her back against Rhebekka's chest, then handed the tumbler back. "Are you warming up yet?"

Rhebekka nodded to the Scotch. "This is helping as much as the hot water is. Though I have to say, I definitely got much warmer when I looked at you."

"Sweet talker."

"Is it working?"

"Of course it is." Naomi gently lifted Rhebekka's residual limb and began to massage gently. "I don't see any skin tears, so we've got that going for us. I think you'll be fine if you give it a day's rest."

Rhebekka sipped the Scotch. "I'll try, but no promises. There is a seventeen-year-old boy out in the cold and dark. He has no one to turn to, and that's not okay."

Naomi knew when not to push, so she let it drop. "We'll find him. Relax, and let me take care of you right now."

She continued to gently knead Rhebekka's leg, slowly working her way higher until she could detect a slight rocking of Rhebekka's hips. She continued, knowing her touch was turning Rhebekka on.   `She turned and knelt before Rhebekka, her dripping torso rising above the water line. She ran a hand up Rhebekka's leg and detected a noticeable tremble. "I want you."

Rhebekka groaned, and her hips rocked forward again, causing a small wave in the tub. "You make me crazy."

Naomi placed her hands on the edges of the tub and leaned forward. She captured Rhebekka's lips in a sultry kiss, delving her tongue deep inside her lover's mouth. "I also keep you sane and satisfied." She dropped her hands down and let her fingers seek Rhebekka's nipples. Her eyes were drawn to the tops of Rhebekka's small breasts rising above the water line with every ragged breath. "You are so beautiful, my love."

The second she made contact, Rhebekka's eyes fluttered shut, and her hips rose once again. "Don't tease me, please, Naomi. I need you to touch me."

"Oh, I plan to touch you everywhere, starting right here." Naomi let her hand trail down Rhebekka's body. When she reached the juncture between Rhebekka's legs, she separated the lips of her lover's center and slid her thumb through the wetness that had nothing to do with the hot water that surrounded them. She stroked Rhebekka's clit. Moments like this joined them on a level only achieved by genuine trust and intimacy.

"Harder."

That one word stirred Naomi to lower her body and grant the request by quickening her pace and rubbing the hardened ball of nerves. Rhebekka's neck arched back, revealing corded muscles and tendons. "You're so beautiful." She continued moving her thumb until her hand started cramping with every stroke. She could feel Rhebekka tremble and instinctively knew her wife's orgasm was building. She used her other hand to pinch Rhebekka's nipple as she stroked. Over and over, she stroked until she could see the last threads of control break. Finally, Rhebekka let go with a guttural cry.

Naomi slowed her hand, relishing the aftershocks her touch continued to bring forth. She leaned forward and kissed a path from Rhebekka's chest to just below her collarbone. She lingered there, nipping before continuing her kisses up to her jawline. She kissed the corner of the open and panting mouth before her. "I love you, Rhebekka, more than you will ever know."

"I think you're trying to drown me."

Naomi smiled and moved her fingers. "Maybe just giving you a baptism in my love."

"What a way to go."

"Indeed. Now, how about we finish this bath and find you something to eat? First, you need to rest, and then we'll formulate a plan. You've gotten much better, but your 4:00 AM bedtime is still your norm more than not. If you take a little nap with me, we'll map out our next steps to help find Lucian."

"I'm too tired to argue with you."

Naomi soaped a loofa sponge and began bathing her lover. "You wouldn't win the argument anyway."

"No, but the makeup sex is great."

Their laughter created ripples in the water, as Naomi rinsed the soap away. "Honey, you never need to argue with me for great makeup sex. Come on, let's get out of the tub."

Naomi stepped out and attached the two handles to the bathtub. It had taken them some time to perfect a system that safely allowed Rhebekka to enjoy a bath instead of a shower without fear of falling or injuring herself. She stood with a towel, ready to wrap around her love when she exited. "You know there is nothing about your accident that I'd ever want to relive, but I enjoy the way you let me pamper you now."

"From the minute I left home all those years ago, I never wanted to depend on anyone or anything. Anything could become something that could be taken from me or used against me."

"That's in the past, baby. It's not dependence. It's mutual trust and a sharing of the load." Naomi moved the towel over Rhebekka's chest and shoulders. "Two become one."

"It's hard to believe I ever thought I could live without you."

Naomi's heart pounded in her chest. The memories of the weeks on end of lonely nights without seeing or touching Rhebekka, had been one of the most painful periods of her life. The separation did affirm that there was no one else for her. No matter how often well-meaning friends tried to tell her to move on or arranged for her to meet someone in the hopes of sparking an interest, she would remember how it felt to touch and kiss Rhebekka. "Being apart from you nearly destroyed me."

Rhebekka leaned against the vanity and pulled her close, and Naomi melted into the embrace. No words were needed. The feeling of Rhebekka's naked skin against her own chased the shadows of yesterday away.

Naomi leaned up and kissed Rhebekka's jaw before handing her the crutches that stood against the wall. She drained the tub and led her wife to their bedroom. Marley and JJ, the two cats they'd rescued from the shelter, lay curled together in the window seat. She turned back the sheets and waited for Rhebekka to lie down before crawling into bed beside her. Rhebekka's skin was warm as she snuggled in and pulled the covers over them. Naomi was relieved Rhebekka was no longer shivering, and her chattering teeth had quieted.

"Rest now, baby. The world will still be waiting for us in a few hours."

Chapter Two

RHEBEKKA SAT AT THE kitchen table with her cell phone to her ear. Her pen traced and retraced the letters in Lucian's name. It was almost ten before Chance called to update her. The search crews had made their way to the canyon's edge through the woods. Another group had started from the bottom, and the two teams met up without any sighting of their missing person.

"I do have a reported sighting of an individual matching the clothing description walking along Appalachian Highway near Canaan Valley Store. I wouldn't be surprised if some local gave him a ride. I'm going to go check on some security cameras from that general area."

"Did Laura bring you anything for the dogs to pick up a scent from?"

"She did. Unfortunately, the dogs had trouble in the deep snow and lost the scent."

Rhebekka rubbed her eyes. "I'll try tapping into a few of my sources and see if anyone in Davis saw him. He wasn't prepared to stay overnight outside in the elements. I'm sure he would try to get to someplace he could shelter."

"The temperatures are going to dip into the negatives tonight. My officers will continue to canvas the area while they patrol. We'll find him, Rhebekka. We have to believe that."

Naomi sat a cup of something that smelled like hot chocolate by her notebook and sat down beside her.

"Naomi and I are going to start working on gathering some volunteers. Laura sent me a picture so we can make up missing person posters. This kid feels like he is completely alone."

"You always tell us in your services that we are never alone. I have to believe that God is watching over him."

"True enough. Call me if you need me to do anything. I'll keep you informed of our efforts from here."

"Get some rest, Rhebekka. You hiked about five miles in deep snow."

"I'm feeling every mile. Be careful, Chance. I'll talk with you tomorrow." Rhebekka hit the red button on her phone and raised the mug to her lips, blowing on it before taking a sip. She could taste the

Baileys Irish Cream mixed in with the real chocolate Naomi had melted into warm milk. "This hits the spot."

Naomi leaned over and wiped some foam off her lip. "Chocolate is God's gift to the worried."

"Then you'd better make this by the gallon. They didn't find him. I talked to our youth group, and they'll be here tomorrow to help make posters to put up. I want to make sure our phone number is on there in case he happens to see one and wants to get in touch with us. I have to believe he has some plan in mind, more than just a moment of opportunity. He's far too smart for something as half-assed as running away in a wilderness area filled with rivers and canyons."

"I tend to agree. What did Laura say when you talked to her?"

"They discovered a few of his things were missing from the children's shelter. A picture of his grandmother is missing from the table by his bed, and some of his toiletries are gone. He'd been working at The Wright Note music store for a year, but the home's administration spoke with his boss and found out Lucian put his notice in last week."

Naomi sighed. "Sounds like he's been planning to run for some time."

"Which is a bit scary. Where could he be?"

Naomi studied a map sitting in the middle of the table. "It's about fourteen miles between the valley and Davis. Not impossible to walk, but in this weather, not likely. So, I'm betting he hitched a ride. We'll put posters up in Thomas and Davis, especially in the convenience and grocery stores. He'll be looking for something to eat or drink if he has money. Those are the places he'd likely stop."

Rhebekka wrote notes on her legal pad. "Good thinking. We should let Karmen know. Her big picture window looks right out onto the main drag. Maybe she'll spot him." She grabbed her guitar and began strumming chords, trying to focus her scattered thoughts. "When Ellie and I took off, I'd saved every dime from my job to give us enough money to survive on for a while. Unless I miss my guess, he's probably done the same. We were just trying to put as much blacktop between our father and us as possible. Lucian doesn't have a car. He can't have gotten that far unless someone gave him a ride." She continued to play and relive that first night of being on the run after Ellie turned eighteen. They'd just wanted to disappear into the crowd. *Ellie was so terrified he'd find us.*

That thought brought her back to Ellie's reaction to the documentary again. She turned to Naomi. "You haven't told me why Ellie freaked out at the documentary we watched."

Naomi clasped her hands around her mug. "She would only say that your father wasn't the only thing she was running from all those years ago. I tried to press her, but she wouldn't say anything. I texted my concerns to Siobhan and she said she'd watch over Ellie."

Rhebekka's breath caught in her throat at the implication there were other things beyond the abuse they'd suffered at the hands of their father. She searched her memories, flipping through them like a photograph album until something clicked. She pounded her fist on the kitchen table, startling Naomi. *Ellie used to go stay with Carrie when things got too bad at home.* Carrie's father was an elder, a member of the local governing body of the congregation. It was odd she couldn't remember the circumstances as to why, but Ellie had abruptly stopped visiting Carrie. *Why would she just stop?* She even remembered the time when her mother had forced Ellie to go to a slumber party at the girl's house. Her sister had nearly become defiant before finally submitting to their mother's wishes. "That son of a bitch."

"What's wrong?"

"I think I know what's wrong with Ellie, and if I can prove it, it will take all your powers of persuasion for me not to commit murder."

Naomi grabbed her arm. "What are you talking about?"

Rhebekka filled her in on what she suspected. She was sure there was something to her memories. "I've got to talk to Ellie."

"Honey, I think you need to let Ellie tell you in her time. Pushing someone to reveal or relive painful moments in their life is unkind and even harmful. We can be here for her when she's ready, but we can't force her to tell us on our timetable. Have faith that she can tell you when the time is right. Ellie is thriving and has a meaningful life. She has you to thank for getting her out of there."

Rhebekka put down her guitar and opened her arms. "Come here."

Naomi sat in her lap and wrapped her arms around her neck. "I know how hard this is for you."

"I've always tried to protect her. Somehow it feels like I failed."

Naomi's gentle touch as she ran her hands through Rhebekka's hair soothed the ache for a moment. "You didn't fail. She's happy and has found someone who treats her like a queen. She's a successful singer and now a producer. There's no failure in that."

Rhebekka could feel her heart rate dropping with every word Naomi said. There was such a melodic quality to her voice. "You could have been a successful singer in your own right if you'd have accepted my offer."

Naomi laughed and snuggled into her shoulder. "It wasn't what I wanted, though I did enjoy my moments with you in the spotlight. I wouldn't have wanted to do it without you."

While Regal Crimson had been on tour, Rhebekka invited Naomi on stage with her and Ellie. Naomi's harmony gained cult fame during live shows after that. The minute the crowd knew Naomi was at the show, their chants crescendoed until Rhebekka played the beginning chords of Don't Let Me Forget. One of Regal Crimson's biggest hits, the song was born out of a memorable night together and was one of the few ballads she wrote back then.

Rhebekka smiled at her wife and sang the opening line. "After tonight, don't let me forget how it feels to hold you, to kiss you, to breathe in only you."

"Silver-tongued devil."

"Is it working?"

"Always and forever. Those days were exciting, but I wouldn't trade them for the life we have now. Before, I had to share you with the world. Your heart was mine, but your time wasn't."

"It's so hard to believe the life I lived then. Probably harder to believe I'm still alive after it."

"You're living proof that prayer helps. I think I wore out my welcome asking God to protect you." Naomi shifted, then reached down and grabbed the guitar.

"Your prayers changed my world."

Rhebekka watched Naomi place her hands in an odd position on the frets. "Oh, we haven't done this in a while." She put her left hand slightly above Naomi's, then slipped her right arm over her wife's shoulder until her fingers rested over the sound hole. She was grateful for Naomi's small stature in moments like this. They hadn't done this in years, but it was as familiar as touching her.

"You choose the song. I just wanted to feel your arms around me."

Rhebekka thought for a second, then began picking out the chorus to Eric Clapton's Change the World. Naomi joined in a bit, and together they played through the melody a few times. Rhebekka broke off into something they'd been working on together, and their music filled the loft. Her mind kept drifting to the two significant areas of concern in her life, Ellie and Lucian. She couldn't help either one if they wouldn't let her in.

"Where'd you go?"

Rhebekka jumped slightly at the sound of Naomi's question. "Huh?"

"I couldn't keep up with you."

Rhebekka wrapped her long arms around Naomi's shoulders. "I was thinking about Ellie and Lucian. They're both running, one from the past and one from the present. I want to help both of them, but they have to let me."

Naomi put the guitar down. She shifted in Rhebekka's lap and cupped her cheek. "When we broke up, do you remember what you did?"

"Naomi, I—"

"I don't mean the action that broke us up. What did you do after? Did you come to me so we could work through it?"

Rhebekka leaned into Naomi's touch. For so long, she'd forced herself into cold isolation far from the woman she loved. "No. I ran away."

"Our nature is to run from painful things. I think Lucian and Ellie are doing exactly what you did; they're running from things that hurt."

"I understand. It doesn't make my desire to help heal the wounds any less."

"That's because you're a pastor, honey. It's part of our calling to see people through rough waters."

Rhebekka sighed and tightened her hold. "Sometimes it feels like we're navigating Class III rapids."

"I can't think of anyone I'd rather be in a raft with."

"Just keep rowing." Rhebekka knew there were many perils that could lie on a river. An experienced guide was critical and invaluable. *Lord, help us keep this thing afloat.*

* * * *

Naomi yawned as she flipped the grilled cheese sandwiches on the cast iron griddle. Rhebekka had roamed the loft until well past her regular 4:00 AM bedtime. Naomi had watched for hours as her wife worked through a repertoire of technically challenging pieces. It was stunning to witness Rhebekka's skills as a musician.

Rhebekka accepted the plate Naomi handed her. "I'm sorry I kept you up. I'd hoped my headphones would silence the noise so you could sleep."

Naomi smiled and leaned across the bar to kiss Rhebekka. "It wasn't your playing that kept me awake, honey. My concern was more with your well-being. When you're troubled, so am I."

Rhebekka took a huge bite and hummed with pleasure.

"Don't choke yourself. I promise I'm making you another one." She slid the second sandwich onto Rhebekka's plate and one onto her own. "I have tomato soup made from what we canned last summer."

"Thank you for a perfect winter lunch."

Naomi stirred the soup before ladling it into blue-glazed clay bowls and joining her at the bar. "You're welcome. Oh, Karmen told me she wanted us to settle on our Christmas Day menu. They'd talked about going back to Cleveland, but the café is so busy this time of year it's hard to get away."

Rhebekka nodded. "I'm good with anything you two decide. You know me, as long as there isn't peanut butter in it, I'm good with it."

"Noted. So, what's the plan for today?"

Rhebekka blew on her spoon. "I want to go over to Davis and look around to see if we can spot Lucian. Maybe even ask around a bit if anyone has seen him."

"We don't have anything on the schedule. We just need to be back in time for the after-school program. I made sure we had supplies yesterday."

"What would I do without you?"

Naomi leaned over and kissed Rhebekka. "The best part is you'll never have to find out again. Eat up. Let's get started." She finished the rest of her sandwich and slowly sipped her soup. Naomi watched Rhebekka crutch her way over to the couch to begin putting on her prosthesis.

"Wait a minute. Your skin was still red this morning. Knee walker or crutches, but no leg."

Rhebekka frowned. "That's going to slow me down."

"So will a week at the wound care center." Naomi chuckled as she loaded the dishes into the dishwater. "Would you like me to call Allana?"

Rhebekka grabbed her crutches and made her way over to the knee walker that rested against the wall. "No, I'm good. Knee walker it is."

"You are so much more reasonable than you were years ago. I'll get my phone." Naomi chuckled as she walked back to the bedroom and pulled the phone from its charger. *She'll never admit it, but she comes by that stubborn streak honestly.*

* * * *

Rhebekka struggled through the snow up the steps to the garage. "I should have shoveled these first."

"Honey, we hired the neighbor boy to do that. This snow fell after he went to school. He'll get it again when he gets home. I think we should consider hiring someone to build something like a bridge to the house. These steps keep us in shape now, but it's not going to be fun going up and down them when we're eighty."

Rhebekka watched Naomi try to push open the door with little success. "Let me try." Even with both of their efforts, the door wouldn't budge. "Damn it! First, we need to get this door fixed, then we'll see about your idea. Hit the remote on your keyring. We'll go through the big garage door instead."

"It's okay. I know you're worried and frustrated. We'll find him."

"I'm sorry. I don't mean to let my temper get the best of me. You're right; I am frustrated. When I talked to Chance this morning, she told me they have so little to go on." She opened the car door for Naomi. "They haven't given up, but there's been no sighting of him."

With a warm palm against Rhebekka's cheek, Naomi reassured her, "We'll find him. Let's go."

Rhebekka made her way around the vehicle, put her crutches in the back seat, then climbed behind the wheel. "I pray you're right. The temperature is supposed to get below zero tonight."

* * * *

That evening, they climbed the stairs to the loft, tired and worried. They'd spent the afternoon driving around Thomas and Davis for two hours without a single lead on Lucian. The only true bright spot of their day was watching their after-school kids create hundreds of missing person posters.

Rhebekka rubbed her hands through her hair. "I can't believe they gave up ArchAngel time. That never happens," Rhebekka said.

"We have good kids, honey. They see someone in need, and they want to help. You've shown them that example time and time again. Each of them took some posters to put up in their home areas. Come on, let's see if Tank and Amy are up for some pizza and a movie."

24

"And beer. We're low." Rhebekka pulled herself up the last few steps. Her leg was bothering her. She was grateful Naomi had pushed the issue about not wearing her prosthesis.

Naomi pushed open the door and pulled out her cell phone. "What do you want on the pizza, and what beer?"

"Everything but the kitchen sink. I'm starving. Please ask them to bring some Savior's Red."

Naomi kissed her. "You got it. Go sit down. I can tell you're in pain. I'll bring the Advil."

"Married less than a year and you can read my mind. How lucky could I get?"

Naomi raised an eyebrow and smirked. "Very lucky if you play your cards right."

Rhebekka saluted and crossed her heart. "I'm planning on a royal flush."

"Go, you nut."

Rhebekka watched her shake her head and walk away. She fell into the couch and groaned as she removed the knee walker. *It could be worse, Bek.* She pulled out her own cell phone and texted Ellie. *Just wanted to tell you I love you.* She watched the stairsteps go up and down, indicating Ellie was answering her.

Love you too, big sis. I promise I'm okay. Siobhan and I are in Elkins working the bar at Beanders. Talk with you tomorrow.

Rhebekka was using all her restraint not to push Ellie, even though it was eating her alive. She dialed Chance and listened to it ring.

"Hey, Rhebekka. Did you have any better luck than I did today?"

"Unfortunately, we didn't. We'll have the missing posters up by tomorrow. We stopped in at a few of the stores, but the clerks said they hadn't seen him either. He's got to be freezing and hungry by now."

"Rhebekka, he could have caught a ride completely out of the county. We just don't know. I'm in contact with the children's shelter, for what it's worth."

"Unless I miss my guess, they're more worried about the paperwork for a missing child than the actual child that's missing."

"You could say that."

"It feels like I should be doing more, but I don't know what else we could do."

"For now, nothing but get the word out. My folks scoured the woods, and he's not there. We'll keep looking for him. I promise you that. While I have you on the phone, I need a favor."

"Anything, Chance, you know that."

"Would you be willing to be a character witness for Jax and me in Hunter's adoption?"

Rhebekka's heart swelled. She'd known the couple was working toward this but hadn't considered she and Naomi might be asked to speak for Chance and Jax. "Without question, we would. Whenever you need us to do anything, don't hesitate to ask. You've been there for me in ways I can never begin to thank you for. This would just be one small way to say thank you."

"Remember, you're the one who legally bound me to the woman I've loved for more than half my life. I'd call it pretty even."

"Not even close, but who's keeping track? Tell Jax and Hunter I look forward to seeing them Sunday."

"I will definitely do that. You two have a good evening."

"You, too."

Rhebekka disconnected the call and smiled as she said a little prayer. *Let this come to be, Lord. They deserve to be a family.*

"What are you smiling about?"

Rhebekka accepted the beer Naomi held out to her. "I was talking to Chance. She didn't have any updates but asked us to do something for her."

"What?"

"They'd like us to be character witnesses in the adoption request."

"Jax always wanted children, but her former relationship wasn't good. Her dream had always been to have a child with Chance."

"How do you know that?"

Naomi snuggled into her arms. "Girls talk, you know."

It wasn't hard to see that Jax was meant to be a mother. Rhebekka had seen her with Jace many times before Hunter came into their lives. She also knew that Naomi would have been a fantastic mother had things been different. "Did you ever want kids?"

Naomi turned to her. "With Aaron?"

"Not necessarily. I guess I'm asking if you've ever thought about it."

"There was a time, but not really when I was married to Aaron. How about you?"

Rhebekka contemplated the question. She certainly had maternal feelings for the kids in the after-school program, but she wasn't sure she'd ever truly contemplated giving birth to one. "I have no doubt there was an expectation of children when I was engaged to Sam. His parents wanted grandchildren, but Mom wanted us to be pioneers or become Bethelites."

Naomi squinted in question. "Bethelites?"

"The organization owns a huge complex in upstate New York. Everything was moved up there somewhere around 2016. They used to have complexes in some of the most sought-after real estate in New York City, which they sold for millions. Bethel is where they print the literature and where many young Jehovah's Witnesses are housed. The people that live and work there are called Bethelites."

"That sounds creepy."

"I won't say I disagree. From the former Bethelites I've been in contact with, it's all very controlled. I visited when I was about fifteen. It all looked very impressive, exactly as they wanted it to appear so they could inspire young Witnesses to apply."

"Bait and switch?"

"Something like that. After you're there, you have very little control. They tell you when to get up, when to eat, when to sleep, and when to do just about anything."

Naomi leaned up and looked at her. "When to have sex?"

Rhebekka cracked up. "Or at least how. If you get pregnant, you're out of there." She used her thumb to make the gesture. "They aren't set up for children, and their care would take away from the work they expect the residents to do. And you're always under surveillance. I don't know if they have cameras in the apartments, but there are people on the cleaning staff who go into the rooms with instructions to look for inappropriate movies or other entertainment."

"You're kidding."

Rhebekka raised her hand as if in oath. "I swear. One guy said he was admonished because they found a DVD of *The Bad News Bears* in his room. They told him it was because it had inappropriate language in it."

"That's a little beyond controlling."

"You know what word I use for it, and no one can convince me it isn't. When a group of people controls every aspect of your life, who your friends are, what you can and can't do, and what social structure you will have, it's no longer a religion. Add on that they protect pedophiles, and it becomes criminal."

"Why your mother can't see it for what it is still shocks me."

"It's all she has. She's had such an unhappy life that she clings to the hope that the life she's been living isn't all there is." Rhebekka shook her head. "What she doesn't realize is her life could be better. She chooses for it not to be."

Naomi rubbed her back. "Remember, all of us deserve grace. I know what she did is wrong, but we can't sit in judgment of her and not expect to be judged on our mistakes just as harshly."

Rhebekka relaxed into the touch. "I'm working on it. I'm nowhere near as judgmental about her as I used to be. You know that. I'm a work in progress."

"Not to sound too cheesy, but you've come a long way, baby."

"Oh, look at you pulling out the 1960s advertising slogans."

Naomi giggled and kissed her. "I couldn't help myself."

The doorbell rang, and Rhebekka checked the Ring camera they'd installed to see Tank and Amy standing at the bottom of the stairs holding up a pizza box and two growlers. She hit the button on their new security system to let them in.

"I'm starving. I'll get the paper plates." Naomi got up and walked toward the kitchen.

Rhebekka met their guests at the door. "Welcome to our humble abode."

"Can't you two find a house that doesn't require two flights of stairs to visit?" Tank grumbled as she walked through the door.

"Don't mind her, she's cranky because I told her she was only allowed two slices." Amy kissed Rhebekka on the cheek as she came in.

Tank growled. "I'm starving to death and she's worried about my cholesterol."

Rhebekka turned to Amy, worry building inside her. "Is it that bad?"

"No, but I don't want it to get that way, either. It's borderline, so if we get it under control now, there won't be an issue."

"But two slices wouldn't feed a bird, and I'm a full-grown woman." Tank put down the growlers, walked over to Naomi, and kissed her. "You wouldn't do this to Rhebekka, would you?"

Naomi wrapped Tank in a hug. "In a New York minute if I was worried about her. Now be good. I made a salad. That should help fill you up."

"Rabbit food."

Amy stood with her hands on her hips. "Tancy, stop acting like I'm depriving you of anything. If you want to cry about it, I'll put you on a low-cholesterol diet. Then you'll have something to whine about."

Rhebekka nearly bent over in laughter. She pointed to Tank. "Let me help you out. Thank you, dear. Yes, dear. I appreciate that you care enough to worry about me." She zipped her fingers across her lips with a big grin.

Tank raised her hands in defeat. "Can we eat now?"

Amy wrapped her arms around Tank's neck and kissed her. "Yes, I love you. I want you around for a while. Is that too much to ask?"

Naomi made her way to Rhebekka. "Aren't they cute?"

"I'm not sure about cute, but right for each other? Absolutely. Are you two going to fuss all night, or can we eat?"

Tank flipped Rhebekka the bird and set off laughter from the entire group as they pulled slices from the box and poured beer into frosted glasses.

* * * *

They were sitting in the living room watching a generic detective show on TV. Naomi leaned forward. "This stuff fascinates me."

Tank agreed. "I know. We just had my DNA tested through one of those companies."

"I told her I thought that it wouldn't be a bad idea since we didn't have any background information on what health complications her biological family might have. We put her information on a few of those family tree sites. You never know who might come forward. Her records were sealed at birth, and we haven't been very successful in getting any information."

Naomi perked up. "I didn't know you were interested in finding out about your family."

Tank scoffed. "I wouldn't go so far as to call them family. Relatives, maybe, but family is something else completely. You and Rhebekka are family to me. The two people that contributed to my genetic profile are far from family."

Amy rubbed her back. "I wanted to know what we might have to watch for. There are certain diseases that people can be genetically predisposed to, like diabetes or Parkinson's. The more we know, the more we can prevent." She leaned in and kissed Tank's cheek.

Tank leaned into the touch. "And I appreciate it, though I do wish I could have another piece of pizza."

Amy rolled her eyes. "One. One more piece."

Tank jumped from the couch and practically climbed over everyone to get to the kitchen.

Naomi reached across and grabbed Amy's hand. "She'll eventually get used to someone caring about her the way you do."

Rhebekka joined in. "She's never had anyone except us to want the best for her." She pulled Naomi close. "It's a tough thing for us hardheads to swallow."

Amy watched Tank heat up the pizza in the microwave. "She's easy to love, once you break through that Marine-turned-bodyguard exterior. She's mushy in the middle."

"Don't I know that one." Naomi kissed Rhebekka before settling back to finish the show.

A few hours later, Tank and Amy headed home. Naomi tapped Rhebekka's temple. "I can see the gears turning in your head. What are you thinking about?"

"I feel bad. Tank went from foster home to foster home before she aged out and went into the military. There are so many kids out there like her and Lucian. I can't imagine what would have happened to Hunter if Chance and Jax hadn't stepped up."

"There are far too many kids in the foster system, and those who are less than perfect don't stand a chance most of the time. When I was teaching, I had a student that went through six homes in three years."

"Unreal. I hate this for Lucian. He has to feel so alone."

"Well, tomorrow is Saturday. We'll spend the day putting up the posters and looking for him. Until then, we'll ask God to protect him and guide us. That's all we can do."

"Thank you, Naomi, for always being my voice of reason."

"That's my job, and I love my work. How about we go jam together for a while? I know you aren't ready to go to bed anytime soon."

"Good idea. It will help me wind down."

"Oh, I have other methods for that." Naomi kissed her and led her to the sound booth. "But I'll save that for later."

Chapter Three

CHRISTMAS WAS TWO DAYS away, and the mountain towns were bustling with visitors as the snow accumulated on the ground and the slopes. Some were coming home to visit family for the holiday. Others were visitors here to ski and take advantage of other recreational opportunities in the valley. All the new faces complicated Rhebekka's search for Lucian. *He's a master at fading into the background.*

It had been nearly two weeks since Lucian disappeared. Rhebekka couldn't imagine him being all alone at this pivotal time in his life. The day after Christmas, he would turn eighteen and legally be an adult. She'd taken to driving up and down the streets of Thomas and Davis every night instead of prowling her studio. She prayed that she'd spot him on one of those trips.

Rhebekka checked her phone after she filled up with gas at the convenience store, then texted Naomi that she was on her way home. Her phone rang a few seconds later. "Taylor, nice to hear from you. What can I do for you?"

"Are you someplace we could meet up? I just dropped off a young woman at the Conner Boarding House, and I need some advice on how to proceed with something."

"How about you meet me at my place? I'm a few streets away. Naomi's there, and she's dishing out some homemade chicken gumbo. Not something you want to miss, I assure you. Bring Midas up with you."

"That sounds great. See you there."

Rhebekka pulled out onto the road, wondering what Taylor needed help with. The streets were freshly plowed but grimy with dirt and cinders. The forecast called for several inches of snow over the next few days. When everything was covered in a fresh layer of white, it reminded her that grace truly is like the verse in Isaiah. *'Though your sins are like scarlet, they shall be as white as snow...'*

She hit her garage door opener and parked the Tundra inside. She missed her Tacoma, but it hadn't been salvageable after the accident. She wasn't sure Naomi could have stood the reminder anyway. "Shit!" The side door opened unexpectedly, and nearly sent her flying into the fender. *What the hell? That thing has been hard to open for months.* She opened and closed the door a few times in wonder. "Did the building shift? Naomi will be happy. She hates this door."

Once inside the apartment, Naomi greeted her with a kiss. "Still no sign of Lucian?"

Rhebekka shook her head. "No. With all those posters out, I really had hope that he'd call me. Good to see you, Taylor. How's the family?"

Taylor raised her cup in greeting. "Everyone's good. Jace is growing far too quickly. It's hard to believe he's almost a year old."

Rhebekka joined her at the table and Midas gave her a friendly nudge. "Well, hello to you too, Midas. Such a good boy." She turned to look at Naomi. "I assume the feline girls are in hiding?"

"No, they came out to visit, turned up their noses, and went back to the bedroom," Naomi said with a smile.

Rhebekka tilted her head toward Midas. "Don't mind them. They're a bit snooty."

Naomi set bowls of gumbo on the table, along with hot bread fresh from the oven. Rhebekka said a short prayer of thanks before they dug in.

"So, you had something you needed advice on, Taylor?" Rhebekka slathered the bread with softened Amish butter.

Taylor finished her first bite and let her eyes roll back in her head. "Yes, but Naomi, you have to give me this recipe for Penny. She's going to be sorry she missed this."

"I'll be happy to send a bowl home. I make enough to feed an army and freeze what we don't use."

Taylor wiped her mouth. "I'll let this cool a bit and tell you my tale. I was on my way back from Elkins, when I nearly ran over someone walking in the road."

"In the dark? That's suicide." Naomi looked shocked.

"I know. About an hour ago, I was driving back from Elkins in near white-out conditions. I came around a blind turn and spotted a hunched figure walking along the guardrail. I almost put the cruiser into a slide to avoid them." Taylor took a sip of her coffee. "Anyway, I picked up this woman wearing a desert camo winter coat and carrying a duffle bag. You know, the kind they travel with in the army?"

Rhebekka nodded and ate a few bites while listening to Taylor.

"This woman was headed to the Connor house and planned on walking there. She had this little puppy in the bag, all wrapped up in a fleece blanket. I told her it was a long way up the mountain, and it was far too dangerous for her to be walking the roads in this weather."

Taylor continued with her story, eating as she went. "She says her name is Kierlynn Raines."

That got Rhebekka's attention. "Raines?"

"I know what you're thinking, and it struck me as well. I only know one Raines. I asked her if she was related to anyone around here. She immediately perked up and asked if I knew of anyone with the same last name. She was cagy up until then and didn't want to give me an answer as to why she was in town. All she would say was the area was close to her objective. When I questioned her more, she clammed up."

Naomi poured everyone more tea and rejoined them at the table. "Did she ever tell you more?"

Taylor nodded. "It took her a bit of encouragement, but she revealed that she was looking for someone named Tancy Raines. I know what Tank's real name is, but I didn't reveal anything other than there are some in Thomas. She told me that she did one of those commercial DNA tests and that she and a woman named Tancy Raines might share some familial ties."

Rhebekka sat up and leaned toward Taylor. "Tank told me a few weeks ago that Amy talked her into doing the same thing. They wanted to see if they could find any relatives to check on medical history."

Taylor shook her head and chuckled. "Well, according to this woman, they're sisters. Rhebekka, this will be a hell of a thing for Tank to find out. It might be better coming from you. As I said, she's staying at the Conner Boarding House."

They finished their dinner, and Naomi packed a takeaway meal for Penny.

"Thank you, Naomi, this will get me out of the doghouse for getting called out while I'm supposed to be on vacation. I'm also thankful my Penny's folks are here."

Naomi and Rhebekka walked her and Midas to the door. Rhebekka shook Taylor's hand. "How's that relationship coming?"

"Better than you would believe, given our history. They've come a long way since Jace's birth. We're getting there."

Naomi hugged her. "Some people take longer than others to come around. Will they be joining you for the Christmas Eve service?"

"That's the plan for now. Thank you both. Merry Christmas. See you soon."

Rhebekka wrapped her arms around Naomi as they watched Taylor and Midas make their way down the steps. "Looks like I need to call over to the boarding house. Maybe I can get this Kierlynn to meet us at the coffee house."

"I'd say invite her here, but she might not be comfortable coming into a home of people she doesn't know."

"Agreed." Rhebekka took out her phone and dialed, placing the call on speakerphone. There were several rings before the proprietor answered.

"Conner Boarding House, how can I help you?"

"Agnes, this is Pastor Rhebekka down the street. Chief Deputy Lewis stopped by and said she gave a ride to your new guest. Is it possible for you to get a message to Kierlynn Raines?"

"Sure, let me get her. She's in the lounge looking through our book collection. Hang on."

Rhebekka could hear muffled sounds before a cautious voice came on the line.

"I'm Kierlynn Raines. Can I help you?"

"Kierlynn, my name is Rhebekka Deklan. My wife Naomi and I are pastors down the street from where you're staying. Chief Deputy Taylor Lewis asked me to get in touch with you about an introduction to a very close friend of ours, Tank Raines. You likely have the name Tancy. There is a little coffee shop down the street from you. We can meet you there in a few minutes if you have time to talk."

The pause on the line stretched out for a few uncomfortable seconds. "Yeah, I can do that. How will I recognize you?"

"I'll be wearing a black bomber jacket and my wife will have on a long, tan, duffle coat with a hood. We'll try to get the table by the window."

"Okay, let me feed Digie, and I'll be there in about twenty minutes."

"See you then."

Naomi walked over to the couch with her boots in hand. "Sounds like she's a bit reluctant."

Rhebekka grabbed the soft leather coat lined with wool before she helped Naomi into it. She slid on her own before pulling a beanie from the pocket and jamming it down over her ears. "She did. I can imagine she's nervous. Are you ready?"

Naomi nodded and grabbed her purse. "Let's go."

* * * *

The coffee shop was busy, but they snagged the table at the window as a couple got up to leave. Naomi flagged down the waitress and ordered a carafe of black coffee, a variety of sweeteners, and a small pitcher of cream. They unbuttoned their coats as another group at a table next to them asked about borrowing the chairs they weren't using.

"We need one of them, but help yourself to the other one." It made Rhebekka happy to show kindness to people in any situation. She wasn't sure what she could do to help the woman they were about to meet.

"Think she'll show up?"

"Your guess is as good as mine. It's almost freaky how recently we talked about this with Tank."

"They say God works in mysterious ways. This might just be another one of those miracles."

Rhebekka smiled as she looked up. She recognized the waitress that put the tray down on their table. "Hi, Holly. It looks like the new job is working out for you."

Holly blushed and placed the carafe in the middle of the table before removing the cups and saucers. "It's just Friday through Sunday, so it doesn't mess with my schoolwork. I like it. Any word on Lucian?"

Rhebekka shook her head. "No. I talked with the Sheriff's office today. We'll keep praying for his safety."

"I'll keep an eye out for him here at work. You just never know. Let me know if you need a refill on the carafe."

"Thanks, Holly. I appreciate it. I'm proud of you."

Holly blushed again and waved.

"Those kids think the world of you." Naomi squeezed Rhebekka's hand, then stirred cream into her coffee.

"It's the closest thing I'll experience to having my own."

"And no stretchmarks required." Naomi smiled as she took a sip. "I think our guest has arrived."

Rhebekka stood and waved the stranger over to them. When she pushed down her hood, Rhebekka immediately took stock of her appearance. *Same jawline and odd-shaped ear cartilage. She put out her hand as the woman approached.* "Hi, you must be Kierlynn. I'm Rhebekka, and this is my wife, Naomi. Please, sit down and join us."

Kierlynn unzipped her coat and ruffled her hair. "Nice to meet you."

Naomi held the carafe. "Have some coffee. Do you take anything in it?"

"Just black. Thank you, ma'am."

"You're welcome, but you can just call me Naomi. Ma'am makes me feel like my mother."

A slight grin broke out on Kierlynn's face. "Forgive me. After twenty-five years in the military, it's a habit." She held up a hand. "Please, don't say thank you for your service."

Naomi nodded. "That wasn't what I was going to say, but duly noted. I was going to say welcome to Thomas."

Rhebekka listened to the conversation, taking mental notes. *Her military service is apparently a sore subject.* "Chief Deputy Lewis tells me you're looking for a family member."

Kierlynn took a sip of her coffee. "I am. It's a long shot. Please excuse me, but I'm a private person. I don't share my business with just anyone."

"If I said the person you might be looking for is my best friend in the world next to my wife, has protected my life for many years, and is in business with me, would that make you feel any better about opening up?"

Kierlynn sat back and took a deep breath. "Probably. I guess I should start from the beginning. You already know my last name is Raines. I'm originally from California. My mother, Alice, was briefly married. According to her, when she got pregnant, he took off."

Rhebekka watched as Kierlynn developed a nervous tick of bouncing her knee while explaining how she came to find out who her father was.

"Once my mother died, I realized I had no family left in this world."

"Why do you think your sister's here?" Rhebekka looked at the woman before her. She seemed to be contemplating how much she'd just revealed.

"I found a picture of a woman holding a baby. There was a first name and a year on the back."

"I'm guessing the child in the picture wasn't you?" Naomi asked.

Kierlynn shook her head. "No. I don't know who the woman was, but the name on the back was Tancy, with the year 1969. I wasn't born until 1975. I started trying to find the person in the picture right after I found it. I bought a subscription to one of the family tree sites and put some feelers out. It was almost six months before I got a hit. I couldn't believe it when the birth year and name from the picture matched. It's not definite, but there's almost a 50 percent DNA match. It's the best shot I've got, even if it's a long one."

Rhebekka curled her hands around her cup. "I'm sorry about your mother."

"Thank you."

"Tank's story is hers to tell. She's a private person as well."

"Tank?" Kierlynn's face held questions.

"That's what I've always known her as. Yes, her name is Tancy, but there's only one person in this world allowed to use that name without totally pissing her off."

Kierlynn smiled for one of the first times since she'd sat down. "I'll keep that in mind. Can you help make an introduction?"

"This news is best coming from the two of us." Rhebekka nodded toward Naomi. "I know where you're staying, and I can pass that along. Do you have a cellphone number?"

Kierlynn provided the number and drank more of her coffee. "You said the two of you are pastors just up the street. You wouldn't happen to know anything about that giant Jesus, would you?"

Rhebekka and Naomi burst out in laughter. They explained everything and invited Kierlynn to Christmas Eve services. They finished their coffee and made small talk as other customers came and went. Rhebekka reflected for a moment on how miracles seemed to happen around Christmas time. *Let's hope Tank feels the same way.*

* * * *

They drove to Tank's and knocked on the apartment door attached to the brewery at Redemption's Road. It was almost ten, and the snow was still falling steadily. Amy opened the door and ushered them in.

Rhebekka hugged her. "Good to see you again, Doc. I'm really glad you're off duty and here with Tank. She's going to need you."

"She texted me that you were on your way. The bar is hopping tonight, but she's mostly supervising since there's extra help on tonight."

Rhebekka nodded. "I called in some favors because I don't think she'll be going back down. It's nothing bad, but it will be a shock."

"What kind of shock?" Tank came into the room from another entrance that led down to the bar.

"Let's let them take off their coats and head to the living room." Amy held out her hands for the garments. "Why don't you pour us all a drink, and we'll get comfortable."

Tank looked skeptical. "This must be something I'm not going to like if she's telling me to pour a drink, not beer. Come on. Not like I haven't had bad news follow me around like a head cold before."

Rhebekka shook her head and went to the wet bar to help get the drinks. "Relax. It's nothing bad. At least, I don't think so. A tad shocking, as I said."

Amy threw another piece of wood in the fireplace and sat on the couch. "What's this all about?"

Rhebekka sipped her drink. "Do you remember telling me, recently, that you had your DNA done and put it on a family tree site?"

Tank sat down beside Amy and nodded. "I do."

"I just had a conversation with someone who might be related to you." Rhebekka sat up a little on the couch as Naomi held her hand.

"Related to me? How?"

"We had coffee with a woman named Kierlynn Raines from California. She believes you might be her sister."

Tank looked slightly confused and overwhelmed. "How in the world would she know that? Hell, I don't even know who my parents are."

Amy rubbed her back. "Don't shoot the messenger, honey. Let's hear Rhebekka out."

Naomi added more information. "Taylor Lewis stopped by to tell us she'd given Kierlynn a ride up the mountain."

They relayed the story Kierlynn had told them, trying to fill in what details they could as Tank asked questions. Tank stood and began to pace.

"I know I should have expected this with the test, but finding out I might have had family all this time pisses me off. I know it wouldn't have changed my childhood. If it weren't for you and Naomi, I wouldn't even know what a family is. Now I've got Amy in my life, and that's better than I could have even imagined. Still."

Amy made her way over to Tank and threaded their fingers together. "My life is better than I ever thought it could be, too, but that doesn't mean you aren't allowed more in your life. Let's hear her out. What do you have to lose?"

Rhebekka handed Tank the drink she'd abandoned. "You've always been like another sister to me. We've had our ups and downs. Hell, it's no secret I owe you my life. You've been there for me through the out-of-control music fans and my out-of-control habits. Let me be here for you as you see who she is and what she wants."

Naomi stood and hugged Tank's neck. "We've always said that family of choice loves each other sometimes more than the family we're born into. We do that when it's easy and when it's hard. There is always room for new family to come into our lives. If not, you wouldn't have Amy. From what little Kierlynn's told us, I don't think she's had an easy life either. She's all alone after the death of her mother. Our arms are big enough to wrap around another person."

Tank hugged Naomi back, then turned to enfold Amy in her arms. "My fucked-up life is probably more than you bargained for, but I couldn't ask for a better family than you and these two knuckleheads."

Amy kissed her. "My life is so much better because you're in it. I'll take whatever comes along with you, no matter what's ahead."

Tank turned to Rhebekka. "Where do I go from here? Is she staying in town?"

Rhebekka nodded. "She's at the Conner House. I have a cellphone number for her as well. I can tell you she has some of your physical characteristics." Rhebekka pointed at her own ear.

"She has the same auricular malformation?" Amy asked.

Tank looked at Amy as she played with the top rim of her ear, which was visibly folded down. "If that means my weird ear, how's that possible?"

Amy turned to her. "A constriction of blood supply can cause the malformation of the baby's ear during fetal development, or it can be an inherited condition. Do you know if she has the same preauricular pit?"

Rhebekka squinted at Amy. "Doc, you're talking Greek to me when you use medical terms. Layman's terms, please."

Amy grinned at her. "A tiny hole near where the ear meets the temple."

Again, Tank rubbed her ear. "I used to tease everyone that hole is where my brain pushed out the extra junk I didn't need."

Naomi chuckled. "I think she does, but I can't swear to it."

Amy turned to Tank. "Both of those things would be indicative of genetically inherited traits. If your birth father had those same physical characteristics, I'd say you got your adorable ears from him."

Tank blushed. "I've never thought they were adorable, but I've been stuck with them. So glad you like them."

Rhebekka took a deep breath. She'd known the news would be difficult for Tank to hear. She was taking it much better than she'd expected. "Let's sit down and plan how to make introductions."

Naomi offered her thoughts. "What do you think about meeting her at our place for breakfast? That way, you won't have to worry about clearing a table for other customers that want to be seated. It will be private, and she can walk to our place from where she's staying and bring her dog."

Rhebekka nodded at the suggestion. "We have Christmas Eve services tomorrow, then the party here later that night. If it goes well, you can invite her to join us for Christmas if that's something you both would like. No one should have to be alone on Christmas unless they want to be."

"After we open gifts on Christmas morning, we're going to the nursing home to play and sing for them," Naomi added.

Amy stroked Tank's arm. "It would be in a safe location where neither of you will feel overwhelmed by prying eyes. We'll eat, then disappear down to the church to get things ready."

Tank rubbed her hand through her hair. "I just don't know. My whole life, I wanted to know where I came from and who my family was. Now, it's terrifying."

Rhebekka knew that the real question on Tank's mind was why. Why was she given up in the first place? Why did she have to grow up in foster care? Why wasn't she good enough? Those feelings of abandonment and self-consciousness had haunted Tank her whole life. They'd had so many discussions about it with few answers. The bad thing was that Rhebekka knew she would likely end up with more questions than answers. What she hoped would come out of this was a connection on a different level for her, one like Rhebekka shared with Ellie. Only time would tell. "So, nine in the morning, our house. Do you want to make the call, or do you want me to?"

Tank rubbed her forehead. "I'd appreciate it if you did. I don't want the first time I talk to her to be over the phone."

Amy smiled. We'll be there around eight to help cook."

Naomi hugged Amy. "I'll be happy for the assistance. See you in the morning."

* * * *

Rhebekka opened the passenger door and climbed out. "That went better than I expected."

Naomi stepped toward the garage's side door and braced herself to jerk it open. She nearly fell back when it swung open with ease. "Whoa!"

Rhebekka caught her before she fell. "Damn, I meant to mention that to you, but I completely forgot after hearing Taylor's news."

Naomi steadied herself. "I've been using the big door, because I was so tired of jerking or pushing this open. That door hasn't swung that easily since I moved here. I'm not complaining, just surprised."

"I need to check the foundation and check that nothing has shifted."

"You didn't mess with it?"

"Not a bit. I've been doing the same thing as you've been doing. I hate leaving it open too long, because it lets out all the heat." Rhebekka looked at the hinges. The old brass was dull with an aged patina. There were fresh scratches on the screw heads, and the hinges appeared to be moved slightly. *I wonder if maybe Siobhan worked on it? Ellie wanted to borrow the truck the other day to move some equipment into the studio.*

"Well, whoever fixed it, I'm grateful. I thought it was going to pull my arm out of its socket the other day, and the screech it made was like fingers on a chalkboard."

"I won't argue that." Rhebekka looked around the garage. Nothing was missing that she could see. *Genius, what kind of thief stops to fix a stubborn door before they leave? Get a grip.*

Back inside the loft, Naomi yawned. "I know you aren't close to going to bed, but I'm beat."

Rhebekka kissed her. "Go to bed. I'm pleased that Kierlynn agreed to come for breakfast. Tomorrow will be a big day. I'll come to bed when I get tired."

She watched the woman who had changed her world rub her eyes and walk back to their bedroom. She pulled out her phone and called Daniel. *It won't hurt to do a little checking.* Her former techno-wizard, who had handled all sound and visual equipment for her former band, was also a night owl. She texted to see if he was free for a video call. He replied immediately, and she headed for her sound booth with her laptop in hand. She pulled up her video call app and started a connection with her longtime friend. She smiled when she saw his face. "How are you, geek?"

"Fat and sassy, since I'm retired and designing virtual reality games for a living."

"Like ArchAngel?"

Daniel nodded his head. "The same kind of platform but with aliens, bad guys, and fantasy worlds. After Christmas, I want to load the enhancements into ArchAngel. The kids will freak out."

"Those kids think you are one of the coolest guys in the world."

"As they should."

"Modesty is one of your best qualities." They laughed and talked about a few more inconsequential things before Rhebekka broached the real subject of her call.

"Tank has a sister?" Daniel's tone was a bit flummoxed.

Rhebekka put the phone in a bracket so she could pace around the sound booth. She picked up her guitar. It was her way of centering her thoughts. "It seems so on the surface. There is much to be discovered. Which is one of the reasons I called."

"Ah, I know where you're going with this. You need my other skills."

Rhebekka nodded. "Can you do a little digging and see what you can come up with on a Kierlynn Raines, born in 1975? When we talked, she mentioned she's recently retired from the military with twenty-five years of service. She said she's originally from California, but I have no idea if that's where she's been stationed or not."

Daniel turned to his bank of monitors, his fingertips moving over a virtual keyboard projected on the desk in front of him. He turned on a second camera so she could see the information he was scanning through.

"From what I can see, she's a decorated soldier. Here's a story about her in the military paper *Stars and Stripes*. Her last tour of duty was in Afghanistan." He continued to sift through information until he came across an online story on a Truckee, California news site. "Damn."

Rhebekka picked up her phone. "What?"

"She was a medic assigned to a group of female soldiers acting as an engagement group. The article says they were dubbed Female Engagement Teams. They were supposed to interact with the women and children to hear their concerns." Daniel turned his face toward Rhebekka. "She was part of a group that survived a brutal attack by insurgents. Their male counterparts were apparently interviewing men suspected of being Taliban soldiers in another part of the village compound. Five women fought to keep a group of women and children safe and avoided their own capture. She's been through hell, Bek. This says it was a horrendous firefight. She was nominated and awarded the bronze star for her actions that saved the lives of two of her fellow soldiers and three of the Afghans they were interacting with."

"Was she wounded herself?"

"Kierlynn has the purple heart, so I would bet she was. It will take a deeper dive to discover the details, but this is a good start."

"Keep digging. Tank's meeting her in the morning for the first time. Everyone is meeting here for breakfast as an icebreaker."

"I hope this will be a good thing. Tank has always felt adrift."

Rhebekka took a deep breath. "I've prayed many times, over the years, that Tank would get some of the answers that have haunted her. I can only hope this will give that to her. While you're digging around, see what you can find on a Tance Raines. He's supposed to be their father. Unfortunately, I don't have any information on him at all."

Daniel pointed to the screen. "You got it, rock star. How's Ellie doing?"

Rhebekka smiled. Daniel had been her go-to for information on her sister as they toured worldwide. Her attempt not to appear as a worrying older sister had led to a deep friendship with Daniel. She'd seen him through his decision to live his most authentic life as Daniel instead of the Daniella he'd once been. "She's terrific, man. I've never seen her this happy with anyone. Siobhan was just what she needed, a stable presence in her life. The production company is going well and she's mentoring some real talent. Ellie was born for this role."

"How's her health?"

"All her scans and bloodwork show no abnormalities. There are medications she takes regularly, but that seems a small price to pay for good health." Rhebekka visibly shivered at the thoughts of the cancer that could have ravaged her sister had it not been for the early detection and treatment she'd received. She knew that there were things emotionally that were locked inside, and she'd done all she could to get Ellie to let her in on them. Naomi had urged her to let Ellie bring them to light in her own time. It had been extremely difficult not to push. "Thanks for taking care of her all those years, my friend. Come and visit soon."

"I'll try to find some time. You two are the sisters I never had. You know I'm not close to my parents or four brothers."

"You're always family here. I may need another favor from you, if we ever find Lucian."

Daniel's face turned serious. "Still no sign of him?"

Rhebekka shook her head. "None."

"When you do, and I'm saying that because I believe you will, I promise to be there for him."

Rhebekka's heart swelled. Daniel's transition had taken time and understanding. "He'll need a friend like you."

"He'll need people that can walk him through the emotional and physical aspects of being trans." Daniel ran his hand over his mustache and goatee.

"And you are certainly the man to help him with that. I'm blessed to have you in my life." She looked at the clock. It was close to midnight. "I'd best get to practicing for my Christmas Eve service."

"If I find any red flags on Kierlynn, I'll try to get them to you before the big intro. Otherwise, I'll send it as I put the information together."

"Good enough, man. Thanks."

They signed off, and Rhebekka began playing a version of O Holy Night. These weren't the songs she'd grown up with as a child. She'd heard, and learned to play, the original versions of every song of joy and anticipation at her grandpa's knee. These were songs of wonder at the child to be born, who would save the world and offer a grace like no other. For the next few hours, she played and worked through her message for the service. She leaned into every note as tears rolled down her face at the joy Christmas now brought her. Her parents had denied that joy to her and Ellie, putting an organization above the true message of Christ's birth and the promise fulfilled. She looked around her studio, out the window into her loft, and finally, down at the ring that sat comfortably on her finger. *You are blessed, Rhebekka. Truly blessed.*

* * * *

Naomi worked her way around the kitchen like a professional chef, preparing comfort food for those sitting down at her table soon. They'd decided on a later time of ten, to allow Tank and Rhebekka to get Redemption's Road ready for the Christmas Eve party they had planned for after the service.

She loved quiet mornings, with time to collect her thoughts. This day would be busy. By eight in the evening, she planned to be dancing with Rhebekka and celebrating their first Christmas as a married couple.

Her journal lay on the bar, and she picked up her pen to jot down her thoughts about Kierlynn.

Tank has a sister! We don't know much about Kierlynn Raines yet, but I sense a troubled soul searching for something she's never had. Tank has never had any family beyond the one of choice. I can only pray that their bond will go far beyond the adorable ears they both share. As in every one of these entries of late, Lord, watch over Lucian. We still haven't found our lost sheep, and my heart grows heavy that we never will. Be with him and guide him to safety. I also ask that you bring Rhebekka comfort. She's taking this very hard. Somehow, she blames herself for not getting him to open up to her during their talks at the children's home. We know that isn't the truth, but help Rhebekka see that, too.

She closed the journal and stirred the sausage gravy before peering into the oven. She loved the smell of the golden-brown biscuits and wondered if she might have been a chef in another lifetime. Warm lips grazed her neck, and Rhebekka's strong arms came around her. Naomi turned and ran her hands through her wife's wet hair. "Good morning, my love. I didn't think you were ever coming to bed."

"My brain wouldn't kick off. So many things were flipping through my head. Do you remember those View-Masters we had as kids? Each tiny square on the disk had a different scene. That's what my mind does, only it's a different worry flipping to the next one, without even a push of the lever."

"I remember those. I wish I could take some of that worry from you. Today's going to be fine. Awkward, but fine. Tank has always thought she was alone in this world. From the sound of it, she and Kierlynn have more in common than not. Interesting that they both went into the service."

Rhebekka nodded. "Tank would have stayed in for the duration had she not been discharged for being a lesbian. Ridiculous. How does a person's sexuality affect their ability to serve?"

"Not one single bit. We don't know anything about Kierlynn's life, but I hope we find out more today."

Rhebekka looked a bit sheepish. "I might have a little information already."

"Oh, really? What have you been up to?" Naomi moved back to stir the gravy. She cracked eggs into a bowl and watched Rhebekka pour herself a cup of coffee.

"I called Daniel last night and asked him to do a little digging. Nothing illegal. He just has more sources and bandwidth than we do."

"Did he find anything?"

Rhebekka filled her in on the minimal information Daniel had gathered. Naomi listened as she stirred heavy cream into the eggs. Once blended, she poured measured amounts into muffin tins and placed them in the oven. The biscuits were done and moved to the warming tray. Naomi wondered if Kierlynn's animosity about her military service centered on the incident that made her a decorated soldier.

"Daniel said he'd try finding out more before they were to meet today. I don't expect anything that would give me pause, but it can't hurt to know."

"Daniel is such a talented man. I know Ellie misses having him working all the studio technology."

Rhebekka sipped her coffee. "I'm hoping, when we find Lucian, Daniel will come and visit."

"That would be a great idea. I wonder where he is? It's so worrying to think about him out in these elements, or worse."

"I pray to God every night that we'll find him."

Naomi leaned over the bar and squeezed her hand. "You know God hears our prayers. Sometimes we get answers in ways and times we don't expect." She looked at the clock on the wall. "Everyone will be here in about twenty minutes. I'll finish cooking, if you set the table."

"Deal."

"Teamwork makes the dream work, baby."

The minutes ticked by without notice, each of them busy with their tasks. They heard the doorbell ring at the bottom of the stairs, and the camera showed a visibly nervous Kierlynn with a small dog in her arms. Naomi wiped her hands. "I'll go get her."

She had a gentler presence than her wife. There were times the tattoos that covered Rhebekka's arms gave off an edge. Once people got to know her, they could see beyond the ink to the incredibly kind woman Rhebekka was. They often tag teamed like this, each with their own strengths and talents.

Naomi reached for the door and greeted Kierlynn with a wide smile. "Welcome. It's nice to see you again."

Kierlynn shifted back and forth from one foot to the other. "Thank you for inviting me and letting me bring Digie. She's not used to being alone."

The small dog poked her head out of Kierlynn's jacket and yawned.

"Oh, she's adorable. Come on in." Naomi led her up the stairs.

Rhebekka held the door and waited for them. "Good morning. I see you found the place even without the help of the giant Jesus."

Kierlynn grinned. "I did."

Levity was always the best way to break the ice, and Naomi was grateful for Rhebekka's ability to talk with almost anyone. One of the few things Rhebekka credited to her childhood.

Kierlynn sniffed the air. "Whatever that is smells amazing."

Naomi held out her hands. "Can I take your coat and hang it up for you?"

"What you smell is my wife's phenomenal biscuits and gravy."

"If it tastes anything like it smells, I'm likely to eat way too much." Kierlynn worked her way out of her coat while holding the small, black and brown terrier pup.

Naomi hung the desert camo coat on the hall tree. "How old is Digie?"

Kierlynn shrugged. "I'm not sure. I rescued her from a box I found on the road outside of Clarksburg. I'd say no more than three months from the sharpness of her teeth. Those little things are like needles."

Rhebekka tentatively held her hand up. "May I pet her?"

Kierlynn nodded. "She loves being petted."

Naomi waited until Rhebekka had greeted the puppy, then took her turn. "Hey, little girl. You're so soft. I put a little bowl of water in the kitchen and even a pee pad over there. One of our cats had surgery a few months ago, and I had some left."

"That's really thoughtful. Thank you. I fed her earlier, so she should take a nap while we eat if there's a place she can curl up near me."

Rhebekka pointed to the kitchen. "I put a basket with a blanket right by a chair."

"Great, thank you."

Naomi pointed to the kitchen bar. "How about a cup of coffee before Tank and Amy get here?"

"I'd appreciate that."

"I can tell you're bit nervous. What are you worried about?" Naomi filled a mug near her with a dark brew she and Rhebekka had fallen in love with.

Rhebekka sat down beside Kierlynn and raised her cup. "This stuff has a little caffeine kick in the pants."

Naomi leaned into Kierlynn. "Which she often needs for more than one reason."

The grin across Kierlynn's face made Naomi feel their guest was beginning to relax.

"Sometimes, we all need a kick in the pants. Thanks for putting me at ease. I'm a ball of nerves." Kierlynn stroked Digie's ear.

Naomi put her hand on Kierlynn's arm. "Tank is just as nervous. Don't worry so much. Her bark is worse than her bite. It's a former Marine bark, so it can sometimes get loud and obnoxious."

Rhebekka swirled her coffee in the mug. "Which works out pretty good at the bar."

"I worked with my share of jarheads back in the day. So, she works in a bar?" Kierlynn handed a wiggling Digie to Naomi, who held her hands for the pup.

"She's the chief brewer and operator of Redemption's Road just up the road from here." Rhebekka indicated the direction with her mug.

Naomi cuddled Digie, who made contented sounds as she snuggled up under her chin. "You'll also get the chance to meet Amy, Tank's girlfriend. She's an emergency-room doctor over in Oakland, Maryland."

Kierlynn stared at her coffee. "This is all a bit overwhelming for me. I honestly didn't know if I'd find Tancy."

Rhebekka patted her on the shoulder. "Remember that she didn't think she had any family. Tank grew up in foster care until she entered the military. I met her after she'd been discharged, when she came to work for my sister and me."

Naomi returned to the stove and stirred the gravy while checking the small egg cups in the oven. "My advice is for you to call her Tank. Her girlfriend, Amy, is the only one that gets away with Tancy without her growling. Take things slowly and get to know each other. The heavy lifting will come little by little. If this is what you think it is biologically, then you will be a part of Tank in a way that no one in her life ever has been."

"Tank. I'll try to remember," Kierlynn said sheepishly.

Naomi stood stroking the puppy, who yawned and stretched in her arms. She could see stress rolling off Kierlynn as she stretched and clenched her right hand unconsciously while her knee bounded up and down. Naomi hoped the visit would go well and said a small prayer for guidance. It was Christmas Eve, the time of miracles. *Let's hope we can experience one of those today.*

* * * *

The doorbell rang, followed by the clumping of boots on the stairs. "That will be Tank and Amy. I can tell by the sound of her boots." Rhebekka put her hand on Kierlynn's forearm before heading to the loft door.

Kierlynn stood, and Naomi came to her side as Rhebekka opened the door for her friends. Amy stepped in first, with her hand in Tank's. Rhebekka could almost hear Tank's heart pounding. She squeezed Tank's arm as she came through the door.

Naomi stepped up for the introductions. "Tank, this is Kierlynn. She's come a long way to find you."

Rhebekka watched the two women study each other. Tank unconsciously reached up and touched her ear. Kierlynn smirked and mimicked the action.

Tank chuckled. "I'm guessing you've probably endured a million 'let me bend your ear' jokes."

Kierlynn shuffled from foot to foot. "If I had a dime for every time, I'd be rich."

The two women approached each other and continued to stare. Rhebekka wondered if Tank could see the other similarities, like the jawline and cheekbones.

Tank held out her hand first, and Kierlynn took it. Their eyes locked. "If you'd have called me on the phone and told me, I might not have believed it. All I have to do is look at you, and I see parts of my own face. Hell, we even have the same build." She patted her gut, "Though I've put on a few pounds since my younger years."

Kierlynn stopped fidgeting. "It's just as strange to me. I never looked much like my mom, other than the color of my hair and eyes."

The timer went off on the egg muffins, and Tank's stomach rumbled loudly. Rhebekka laughed. "Some things never change."

Naomi moved to the kitchen as Tank introduced Amy to Kierlynn. After everyone petted and cooed at Digie, Kierlynn put her in the basket. Everyone washed up and carried food to the table, where they all sat down. Rhebekka held out her hand for Naomi, who took Amy's in hers. Amy entwined her fingers with Tank, who hesitated slightly before holding her hand to Kierlynn, who clasped hers, then took Rhebekka's, closing the circle. Rhebekka began to pray and give thanks for the food and friendship gathered at the table. "Lord, guide Tank and Kierlynn as they get to know each other. Heal old wounds and form new bonds as we welcome another into our family. Amen."

Rhebekka watched as Tank squeezed Kierlynn's hand. They were off to a good start. *Lord, smooth out the edges and straighten the path so neither one crashes into the unknown.*

Breakfast conversation centered on Kierlynn's travels and Tank's adventures in brewing and barkeeping. Kierlynn had been traveling the country by train where she could and bus where she couldn't.

"I had enough of airplanes in the army." Kierlynn sat back and patted her stomach. "I'm so full, I could bust."

Rhebekka reached over and squeezed Naomi's hand. "I've put on ten pounds since I got married. Naomi is a fantastic cook."

Everyone helped clean up from brunch before they moved to the living room for deeper conversations about the family connection.

Rhebekka patted Tank's back on the way to her seat. "I'm glad you both are comfortable with having us with you."

Kierlynn let Digie get adjusted in her lap before looking up. "I thought I might be a bit intimidated not having anyone squarely in my corner, but you've shown me more kindness than I've seen in a very long time."

Tank rubbed her hands over her jeans. "How did you even find me?"

Kierlynn explained the family tree website and showed them the printout of the DNA statistical match. She told them she'd caught a train out of San Francisco, choosing a rail route that took her through Salt Lake City, Denver, and into Chicago. "I wanted to see parts of America I'd never had a chance to." She removed a photo from her shirt pocket and handed it to Tank.

Tank looked at the image for a long moment, then turned it over in her hands. "I can't believe I can still read the writing. *Tancy 1969.*"

Amy rubbed Tank's back. Rhebekka knew this was an emotional moment for her friend. It was likely the first time she'd seen any picture of her mother. Rhebekka leaned in. "Same ears, same stubborn curl that sticks up in the back."

Tank unconsciously smoothed down the stubborn shock of her hair.

Kierlynn took a shaky breath. "Mom was diagnosed with cancer last year. By the time they found it, they only gave her a month to live. She had lucid moments near the end and told me who my father was. A man named Tance Raines. When he found out my mother was pregnant, he screamed something about already having one kid he didn't raise. He left that night. From then on, it was just the two of us."

Tank held up the picture. "How did you get this?"

Kierlynn's reflexive motion was something so much like Tank, it was eerie. She tugged on the folded part of her ear as she spoke.

"When I cleaned out her apartment, I found a wallet stuffed back in a dresser drawer. It didn't have anything other than an old driver's license, a 1963 newspaper clipping about a tourist train opening in Cass, West Virginia, and that picture." She pointed to the Polaroid that looked like it had been cropped and laminated at one point. The colors were fairly muted, but the image was still visible.

"I was born in 1975, and that's not my mother. That picture probably hadn't seen the light of day for a long time until I found it."

Tank stared at the picture. "You said there was an old driver's license in it too?"

Kierlynn passed that over to her. Rhebekka leaned in with everyone else. The image on the license was also faded, but the features, including the bent ear, were still visible.

"I'm the spitting image of him." Tank said softly.

Rhebekka took in the moment for what it was. They were witnessing the first time Tank had ever seen one of her parents.

Amy examined the license. "This has a Cass, West Virginia address. I wonder if that's where you were originally from?"

Tank shrugged as she rubbed her thumb across the picture of her mother. "She looks so young, like really young. I'll bet she isn't even eighteen."

Kierlynn spoke with a very soft and timid voice. "My mom said she was seventeen when she got married and had me."

Tank looked up at her. "It appears our father tended toward young women."

Kierlynn nodded. "Seems so."

Naomi leaned into Rhebekka's side. "Regardless of how either of you came into this world or what happened since, that man fathered two strong women. Kierlynn, I don't know you well yet, but both of you chose a life of service to your country and others."

Tank huffed. "Mine was more out of necessity than duty."

Kierlynn nodded her agreement. "Mine was the same. I was eighteen with no skills and no future prospects. Mom cleaned vacation homes for a living. I was too poor to even think about going to college. An army recruiter came to my high school and made military service sound like this huge adventure." She dropped her head. "Mostly bullshit, but I somehow made it through twenty-five years of it."

"I only made it fifteen years before they gave me the boot for being gay." Tank stood and walked to the window overlooking the main drag of Thomas.

Rhebekka shook her head. "So stupid. What the hell does the gender of the person you love or are attracted to have to do with your ability to defend your country?"

Kierlynn's knee had started bouncing again, disturbing Digie. The puppy sat up, yawned, and licked Kierlynn's neck. "Sorry, girl." She pulled her into her arms.

Naomi moved next to her and placed a hand on Kierlynn's forearm. "You've both been on your own too long. We're a ragtag bunch, but you won't find better."

Tank turned and came back to stand in front of the woman who was her biological sister. "Kierlynn, I've never had any blood family I've ever known. I don't remember my mom, just a revolving wheel of one foster family after another. I moved so many times, I couldn't tell you even half of the family names I lived with. I'd like a chance to get to know you, and maybe we can learn our history together. Amy convinced me to take that DNA test to see if there were any medical issues I needed to be aware of. We might not know any more about that yet, but it brought the two of us together." She waved a finger back and forth between the two of them. "I don't know what your plans are, but if you stick around, maybe we can do some research together."

Kierlynn sat Digie in Naomi's lap and stood to face Tank. "I'd like that. I've got no place I call home and nowhere to be. This looks like a good stopping point. I might need to find a new place to stay if the Conners place needs the room, but for now, it's pretty comfortable." Kierlynn held out her hand in Tank's direction. "It's at least a starting point."

Tank grasped her forearm and pulled Kierlynn into a semi-hug. "More than a start. We're family."

Amy joined the two. "A little Christmas miracle."

Rhebekka pulled Naomi into a gentle hug, cradling the puppy between them. "Speaking of Christmas, our service starts at seven this evening. Will you join us?"

Kierlynn scratched her neck. "I've never been much of a religious person, but this will be my first Christmas back in the States for a long time. So if these two are going, I'd like to come."

Amy squeezed her hand. "We're definitely going. I have the day shift at the ER tomorrow so my colleague can enjoy Christmas morning with her kids, but I wouldn't miss tonight for the world. I'm going in to relieve her around four in the morning to give her time to get home."

She turned to Rhebekka. "Isn't Hunter doing something for the program?"

She couldn't hide the smile that burst forward. "He is, but I'll save that surprise for tonight." She thought about the hours Jax said Hunter had been practicing with his aide, Julia. His speech was still developing, but the Fitzsimmons family was wholly dedicated to his progress.

Amy invited Kierlynn to dinner at their place before the services and to the Christmas Eve party at Redemption's Road. Their guests gathered their things, and Naomi handed a sleeping Digie back to Kierlynn, who tucked her inside her jacket.

"I can't thank you enough for helping make this introduction so painless. I'm sure it was evident how apprehensive I was." Kierlynn zipped up her coat.

Naomi stepped forward. "In Hebrews, there is a verse that tells us not to neglect to show hospitality to strangers, for we may entertain angels unawares."

Kierlynn blushed. "I'm far from being an angel, but I appreciate it."

Tank patted her on the shoulder. "Get used to it. These two are truly living examples of their faith."

Rhebekka joined in showing the group to the door and wishing them well until that evening. With the loft empty, she sat heavily on the couch with Naomi beside her. "That went much better than I thought it might."

"Have a little faith, honey."

"Very true, my love." Rhebekka held Naomi and remembered what the Bible said about faith. "Truly I tell you, if you have faith as small as a mustard seed, you can say to this mountain, 'Move from here to there,' and it will move. Nothing will be impossible for you."

Chapter Four

THE MURMUR OF THE crowd seated around the stage area was encouraging to Rhebekka. She never expected a full house but was pleased to walk around and see so many familiar faces. Chance, Jax, and the entire Fitzsimmons clan were present, now that Kendra had graduated from the U.S. Marshals Academy. Brandi, her girlfriend, sat with Hunter on her lap, who signed animatedly to Maggie and Dee. Jax's father and uncle rounded out the last of them.

Rhebekka looked around the place she'd started with nothing more than a dream. The aged wooden floors now saw more foot traffic than they'd seen since the building housed a working theater. The walls were adorned with greenery and tiny, white Christmas lights that twinkled randomly. A live tree sat in a large pot in the corner, adorned with all the trappings of Christmas, including homemade ornaments from the after-school program. The seats were filled with people she loved from all parts of her life.

Her longtime friend and tattoo artist, Roman Talon, and his husband, Andre were there, and Rhebekka watched them chat with Karmen and Zandra. From her Salvations and Libations trivia team, Tom Roland sat beside Laura Sandestro, who looked like she hadn't slept well since Lucian's disappearance.

Naomi was crouched beside little Jace Lewis while his mother, Penny, desperately tried to keep his shoes on him. Taylor pulled him into her lap, and Penny's mother and father laughed at his antics. Rhebekka's attention was drawn to the door as Sarah and Kristin Ryker came in behind the rest of the Parker family. Sarah's eyes reflected as much trauma as the patients she treated on the ambulance. That worried Rhebekka. *Something to think about later.*

Sydney and Lynn sat down near where their daughter, Amanda, was set up. After her injuries healed, Sydney was reclassed as permanently nondeployable for medical reasons. Before that, Rhebekka had been incredibly proud to attend her promotional ceremony to the rank of Lieutenant Colonel, where Lynn pinned the silver oak leaf on her wife's collar. Amanda had been at House of the Rising Son most of the afternoon, working on the technical side of the night's gathering.

Rhebekka had hoped Ellie and Siobhan could join them, but they were still heavily involved in the business over in Elkins. They'd be joining them for Christmas morning. Tank and Amy were deep in conversation with Kierlynn. *She looks more relaxed than earlier.*

With the larger numbers in attendance, she was grateful they'd knocked out a section of the wall last year and opened more of the former opera-house floor. Amanda Parker took her new role seriously as she adjusted the equipment she'd run an extensive sound check on hours earlier. Ellie had also hired her at her production company. The teenager glanced at her watch and nodded to Rhebekka. With one deep calming breath, Rhebekka pulled on her guitar and moved to the stage.

"Merry Christmas, everyone. If you'll find a seat, we'll get started." She strummed through *The Holly and the Ivy* while everyone not already sitting down found a comfortable spot. Naomi took her place at a keyboard near her. "On this night, Mary and Joseph were desperately seeking shelter. The town of Bethlehem was full of travelers as the Romans were taking a census and forcing everyone to report to their familial city. There was a nefarious reason for this order, highlighting the miracle of the baby's survival to become the cornerstone of a new covenant. The child, the promised Messiah, would be born and laid in a manger. This innocent baby became the greatest Christmas gift ever."

Naomi started playing *O Little Town of Bethlehem* with a contemporary beat as a backdrop to Rhebekka's words. Her message was one of hope and grace. A grace she'd never felt in all the years she'd spent as a member of her previous religion. Peace washed over her. "And unto us, a child was born."

Amanda bathed the center stage, where Rhebekka stood, in a bluish glow, while shading the audience. Rhebekka could detect movement in the back as a shadow crept along the wall. She moved her hand into position on the neck of her Martin guitar and began an intricately beautiful version of *What Child is This*. Naomi began to harmonize, and together they let their voices join in perfect harmony, the notes effortlessly floating into the audience. She and Naomi were so in tune with each other, instinctively knowing how to play off the melody until the final chord finished.

The audience was silent for a moment before breaking out into applause. Hunter stood exuberantly stomping his feet. *He feels the music.*

Her sermon was intentionally brief, centering on promises made for the salvation of all and that no one was exempt because of who they were or who they loved. "All are precious in the eyes of God." She took a deep breath and centered her thoughts. "In Romans, it says, "Accept one another, then, just as Christ accepted you, in order to bring praise to God." She reminded them of grace equally measured for all humankind. As a congregation, they sang *The First Noel* together, followed by more Christmas songs.

Julia Gerard, Hunter's educational aide, had come in a little later than everyone else and now joined Hunter at the edge of the stage. His eyes were bright and shining. He nearly vibrated with excitement. Rhebekka stepped over to him as Naomi read the passages from Luke that detailed Jesus' birth and the gathering of the shepherds to witness the prophesied miracle.

Not being fluent in sign language, Rhebekka enlisted Julia to translate. "Are you ready?"

Hunter's head bobbed up and down. It made her chuckle and reminded her of the *Marvin the Martian* bobblehead she owned. His hand made the sign for yes. She smiled and held her hand out to him as she walked back to center stage.

"We have a special treat for you. Hunter has been working with Julia on something for his family and all of you." Rhebekka played a few bars from In *the Bleak Midwinter*, allowing the simpleness of the refrain to resonate with those in attendance. Rhebekka sang the lyrics, until they reached the final verse. She nodded to Hunter.

The small boy raised his hands and mimicked Julia in signing a simple version of the words often sung by a child.

"What can I give Him, poor as I am?
If I were a shepherd, I would bring a lamb;
If I were a wise man I would do my part;
Yet what I can I give Him —
Give him my heart."

She looked out into the audience and watched as Jax clung tightly to Chance. Hunter's hands signed the word heart, drawing the easily recognized shape in front of him. Rhebekka began to cry with joy as the audience raised their hands and waved them back and forth in the deaf clap, something Hunter had taught them all. She joined in and knelt beside him. His face was glowing with pride as she held her fist out to him. They bumped them together and pulled back with an open hand as if there had been an explosion. He stepped forward and hugged her before jumping off the stage and running straight to the two women who held their arms out to him. *Chance and Jax are no less his parents than if he'd been born to them.*

Naomi stepped to her side and put an arm around her. "Christmas miracles."

Rhebekka wrapped her in a hug. "Miracles indeed." The sound of the front door closing caused her to turn. *I wonder who had to leave.* She looked first to where Amy had been sitting. *Did an emergency call her away? No, she's still there.* One by one, she looked at those she knew were in attendance and found all still present. *Who was here but didn't want to be seen?* It puzzled her, but the service demanded her focus.

Small electric candles were passed out as everyone put on their coats. As a congregation, they went outside to the courtyard where the giant Jesus stood projected against the brick wall. Snowflakes as large as she could remember fell gently from the darkened sky as they stood in the crisp air. Each person interlocked their arms and they formed a circle.

Rhebekka calmed her beating heart as Naomi began the carol that needed no instrumental accompaniment, only the sound of clear and reverent voices. Naomi turned the bulb on her candle to light it. All around the circle, individuals lit their candles as they sang the lines from *Silent Night*. The candles shone brightly and illuminated the faces of those gathered. Outside the courtyard, a crowd stopped on the sidewalk to listen as Naomi carried the melody and Rhebekka added the harmony. The many voices blended to lift an acapella version of one of the most beautiful Christmas carols ever written. The final lines rang out, and Naomi and Rhebekka allowed the power and harmony of their two voices to rise above the rest. When they'd finished, the crowd that surrounded them clapped in appreciation.

Rhebekka waved to them. "Please, join us for our final song of the night as we sing Joy to the World and ring in the birth of the Christ Child." Many of them did just that. Another Christmas miracle came to be as black and white, gay and straight, joined together as one in the spirit of Christmas.

* * * *

It was nearly two in the morning when Naomi and Rhebekka made it back to the loft. The party at Redemption's Road had been a lively family affair, a private gathering of all their friends. Those who could play took turns adding music for everyone to dance to, allowing Rhebekka and Naomi to join in on the fun.

"What a night." Naomi sat on the side of the bed, releasing her braid and brushing out her hair.

Rhebekka agreed. "It was pretty magical from start to finish."

"I thought I'd absolutely bawl like a baby when Kendra got down on one knee and asked Brandi to marry her."

Rhebekka climbed under the covers and stretched. "I know. That family certainly loves making big commitments at Christmas time. From what I heard, Dee asked Maggie to marry her on Christmas Day many years ago."

"And you told me Chance and Jax got married on Christmas."

Rhebekka laughed. "On horseback, no less."

"I'm exhausted." Naomi put down her brush and climbed under the covers. She snuggled up to Rhebekka's warm body and entwined her leg with her wife's.

"I have to agree with you there. Could you imagine having to wake up in a few hours to watch kids open packages?"

"Mmm." Naomi didn't comment. She remembered waking up as a child full of excitement, knowing Santa had delivered colorfully wrapped gifts. There was never a thought about tired, bleary-eyed parents. A part of her wondered what it would have been like to have children with Rhebekka. How would it have been to see Christmas as a mother, watching the joy on her children's faces as they wrote letters to Santa? She imagined seeing the childlike wonder of Rhebekka and their children opening packages.

"You got quiet on me. What's going on in that beautiful mind?"

Naomi snuggled in closer and kissed her neck. "It's silly."

Rhebekka rolled Naomi on top of her. "Nothing you ever think, or feel, is silly. Talk to me."

She rested her chin on her hands as she looked into Rhebekka's eyes. "Sometimes I think about what it would have been like having kids with you. I nearly cried when I watched you with Hunter on the stage this evening. You are so good with our after-school kids that I know you would have been a great mother."

Rhebekka leaned up and kissed her nose. "It's you that would have been the incredible mother. I saw you playing with Jace tonight. He kept reaching for you."

"He wanted my necklace."

"I beg to differ. I've seen you hold him many times, and that boy lights up." Rhebekka rolled them over and braced herself above Naomi. "Nothing says we can't have kids."

Naomi ran her hand through Rhebekka's hair. "Honey, I love you, but I am way past the age of being pregnant, and I'm fairly certain you haven't suddenly realized the desire to do so either."

Rhebekka lay down on her side with her head propped in her hand. "No, you're not wrong about that. Adoption is always an option. We have the means to give a child everything they need and certainly enough love for one. Or we could foster, like Chance and Jax. Maggie and Dee did it for years."

Naomi leaned up and kissed her. "It's worth discussing, but can we do it at a decent hour of the day? Right now, I'm drained. My only Christmas wish is to feel you curled around me."

Rhebekka obliged the request and spooned in behind her, kissing her shoulder. "I love you, Mrs. Deklan."

Naomi turned off the light. "I love you, Mrs. Deklan. Merry Christmas." She lay there for twenty minutes more, watching the red numerals on the clock tick over. *Could we?* She drifted off, securely wrapped in Rhebekka's arms and the promise of discussions to come.

* * * *

Rhebekka yawned and grabbed two cups of coffee from the tray Siobhan held. Naomi was nestled between her legs, lying up against her chest as they sat on the floor. "You are a godsend."

"Sounds like you had a long night as well. We didn't leave Beanders until almost three. For the first time in a year, I didn't regret still having ma flat in Elkins." Siobhan handed Ellie a cup and sat down beside her.

Ellie snuggled under her arm. "I won't disagree, but it's the first time we've stayed there since the Forest Festival. The main reason it's a nightmare to try and park."

"Ah, very true." Siobhan kissed the top of her head.

Rhebekka smiled at them. It'd been years since she'd seen Ellie this happy. Her sister was an avowed bisexual, but her relationships with men had always been tumultuous. She always seemed to pick absolute jerks. Ellie seemed at peace and finally healthy as well.

Ellie narrowed her eyes at Rhebekka. "What are you puzzling out, dear sister?"

Rhebekka sipped her coffee. "Nothing really. I was just thinking about how happy you look, even with all the changes over the last year."

Ellie nodded. "I was completely burnt out. It just wasn't fun anymore. Night after night, I had to have someone remind me where the hell we were as I went on stage. The last few years were just a blur of audience faces, tour buses, and an endless rotation of hotel rooms. For the first time in many years, I own a home and a business that I'm completely content with."

Siobhan leaned over and peered at her. "Is that all, lass?"

Ellie grinned. "That's the very least of it. Finding you was like hitting the high note that you've struggled with your whole career."

Siobhan put their foreheads together. "I'll take that."

"They are so cute," Naomi said, sipping her coffee.

Rhebekka took in the moment. It was Christmas morning, and she had everything she'd ever dreamed of. Not one thing under the tree could make her any happier than she was. Thoughts of Lucian crept in. *Where is he? Please, Lord, I pray you keep him in your protection. Tell him he can trust me. We'll figure it out if he'll just come to me.*

"Bek? Are you okay? This is the second time you've spaced out on us this morning." Ellie leaned over with a gift in her hand.

Rhebekka shook her head and took the package. "I'm fine, just thinking about Lucian. It's Christmas. He shouldn't be alone."

Siobhan looked down and away. "Sometimes being alone is better than being with those ya know." Her Irish brogue was deep and thick.

Ellie slid closer and kissed Siobhan. "Well, I'm glad you've decided we're the exception to the rule."

Siobhan smiled. "Truth."

There was so much more to know about Siobhan. Little by little, her story was coming to light. The places she'd been and the things she'd been through weren't pretty. The wide, leather cuff bracers on her wrists covered the physical reminders. Rhebekka shook herself. *It's Christmas. Think happy thoughts, Bek. Happy thoughts.* She looked at the tag on the package. "From your songbird." She looked at her sister. "Thanks, Ellie."

For the next hour, they exchanged gifts, munched on Christmas cookies, and shared memories of their favorite Christmases.

Rhebekka looked at Ellie. "Do you remember our first Christmas in Pittsburgh?"

"We played some Christmas party." Ellie entwined her fingers with Siobhan. "That was the year after we left home."

"Some little cocktail lounge, but I don't think it's there anymore. We were taking any gig we could get. Anyway." She moved the wrapping paper that covered her lap and sat cross-legged on the couch, staring at the Christmas tree by the window seat. "The place had an attached motel, one of those little places you didn't stay in unless you had to. We were living off Ramen noodles, day-old bread, and the thing I won't mention and will never eat again."

"We did eat a lot of peanut butter in those years."

Rhebekka shivered. "There was this little thrift store we went in a few days before we played. You found this tiny ceramic tree with bulbs that lit up when you plugged it in."

Ellie scratched at her neck near where the surgeons had removed her tumor last year. "I remember."

Rhebekka turned to Siobhan. "I'm sure Ellie told you we didn't celebrate as kids, so we constantly looked over our shoulder whenever we'd break some rule that fell into the forbidden territory. We were about as dirt poor as we could be, but Ellie was determined we buy that little tree. It was only a couple of bucks, so I gave in. We got to the room that night, and she plugged it in before we'd even brought in our suitcase."

"It was the cleanest thing in the room. I just…"

Ellie faded off, and Rhebekka filled in the rest.

"We'd always heard from everyone that Christmas was a time of joy and peace. Two things we sadly lacked our entire childhood. Something warmed inside me when she plugged that tree in, and I could see it in her too. Something about the promise of Christmas resonated with us."

Naomi kissed her temple. "You were making decisions for yourselves. A present of choices that you gave each other."

Ellie nodded. "I think you're right, Naomi. Our whole life was lockstep obedience to someone else's choices. This one was of our own making." She was silent for a few seconds. "I still have it, you know?"

Rhebekka felt her heart leap a little. "You do? How in the world did it survive all these years?"

Ellie smiled. "It was the first Christmas gift we ever gave ourselves."

Naomi wrapped her in a hug. "Some things are worth protecting."

Rhebekka looked around at the room scattered with presents. New guitar strings, vintage T-shirts, and a new pair of Chucks were piled up with other gifts. She pulled Naomi closer. "The best gift doesn't come with ribbons and bows. It's being with the people you love. Merry Christmas."

"Now, we'd better get a move on or the nursing home will think we've forgotten them," Naomi reminded them.

Siobhan volunteered to load their instruments and gear in her vehicle while the others tidied up.

* * * *

Naomi looked around the kitchen counter after everyone brought the dishes from the table. "Karman, you guys have to take some of this food home. There is no way we can eat this much in a week."

Rhebekka snapped her fingers. "How about we package some meals up and put them in the refrigerator down at Loaves and Fishes?"

Naomi vigorously nodded her head. "That's a fantastic idea. Franklin has worked incredibly hard to keep that up and running." Franklin Middleton was a promising young man with aspirations to be a pastor. Currently, she and Rhebekka were mentoring him. He'd come up with an idea for a needs room at the back of House of the Rising Son. The room was supplied with basic necessities like new socks, new and gently used winter wear, and a refrigerator where local restaurants often placed leftovers for the taking. Loaves and Fishes also offered a shower room with hygiene items. Many people donated things like sleeping bags and coffee vouchers that helped the small homeless community in the Davis and Thomas area. Most of them moved on to areas with more resources in the winter. A few diehard souls lived in the community year-round and made do with what was available. Naomi and Rhebekka helped make sure the fridge was well stocked. Franklin had gone home to his parents for Christmas this year.

Karmen pulled down the recyclable food-grade paper boxes and began assembling generous portions. "I'm so glad I found these through my supplier. Less plastic going in the landfill."

Zandra handed her another box. "Now, if you can convince the other restaurant owners to use them, it could have a big impact."

Karmen leaned over and kissed her. "One step at a time. We'll get there." She wrote the contents on the top of the box with the date. "We'll take these over on our way home."

Zandra grabbed their coats. "Thanks for having us. We've scheduled a video call with all the nieces and nephews in an hour, so we need to get home."

Naomi hugged her. "You two are family. That's what Christmas is supposed to be, the family gathered together. Plus, I'd never have been able to pull off this meal without Karmen's culinary skills."

Karmen slipped her arms into the coat Zandra held for her. "Give me a break. You're a fantastic cook. I just happen to specialize in the dessert department. I wonder if Tank and her sister would like one of these?"

Rhebekka held up the canvas bag with the dinners. "Tank and Kierlynn were planning on pizza, beer, and conversation. Amy ordered a few partially baked specials from Sirianni's a few days ago." She looked at her watch. "She's supposed to be home in a few hours from the ER."

"I'm happy for Tank. She's felt adrift for a long time. Now she has Amy and a sister she never knew existed." Karmen hiked her purse up on her shoulder. "She's more settled than I've ever seen her."

Naomi put her arm around Rhebekka's waist. "Aren't we all?"

Ellie and Siobhan joined them in seeing Karmen and Zandra off before the four of them went into the living room to relax. Rhebekka threw another log on the fire and joined Naomi on the couch.

"I'm miserable." Siobhan patted her stomach.

Ellie tickled her. "It wouldn't have anything to do with that second piece of pie you had, now would it?"

"Hey, I'm a growing lass. Besides, who could choose between pumpkin and coconut cream?" Siobhan captured Ellie's hands and held them.

Rhebekka chuckled, and Naomi pointed a finger at her. "Don't laugh. I saw how many of those white chocolate, macadamia nut cookies you ate. You'll be on a sugar high for hours."

"Totally worth it."

Ellie looked at Rhebekka. "Did you get a Christmas card from Aunt Dinah?"

Rhebekka nodded. "I did. We sent one to her as well. Mine had a letter in it."

They spoke about the contents while Naomi watched the two sisters. News from home always stirred up bad memories. In a few months, their father would be gone an entire year—a year of burying old hurts. There were daily indications that Ellie was nearing the point of telling Rhebekka something likely to throw them into chaos. Naomi hoped the true healing could begin once they had everything out in the open. Rhebekka harbored great resentment about the way they'd grown up and the abuse they'd suffered. The revelations Ellie would unearth were likely to cut deeper than any physical wound Rhebekka had ever endured.

"Okay, I want to watch *How the Grinch Stole Christmas*." Rhebekka grabbed the remote.

Ellie settled back into Siobhan's arms. "The cartoon or the movie?"

Naomi raised her hand. "Oh, I vote for the cartoon. It's a classic."

Rhebekka pulled up the DVR menu. "Classic, just like you."

"Watch it there. I might think you're calling me old."

Rhebekka lay down with her head in Naomi's lap. "Not a chance. You are classically beautiful in heart and mind."

Naomi pulled her hair. "Nice save. Start the show."

Rhebekka arched her eyebrows up and down.

"Pervert, not that show."

Ellie and Siobhan chuckled from their side of the couch, and Naomi was as content as she'd ever been at Christmas. She was married to the only woman she'd ever loved and related to a woman she'd considered her sister long before marrying Rhebekka. Life was good, and there were many things to be grateful for. So why was it that, deep down inside, there was a longing she couldn't explain?

* * * *

Rhebekka lay in bed holding Naomi. One of the Christmas gifts she'd given her was a promise to allow Naomi to fall asleep in her arms each night. She'd thought about the countless hours she had spent longing for moments like this over the years. Having this woman in her life had changed everything for her. Naomi lay against her, tracing each line of the name branded into her chest. She remembered taking Naomi's signature to Roman. He'd hesitated to create the branding stamp, worried about the implications of branding a name into flesh.

"I still can't believe you did this."

Naomi's voice brought her into the present. "I was just thinking of how hesitant Roman was to do it."

Naomi sat up, her hair draping down her naked chest. "I can see why. We weren't even together when you had this done. Were you that sure you'd never love anyone again? What if you had? Some women would never have stood for seeing a former lover's name branded into their partner's skin."

Rhebekka stared at the woman she'd loved for so very long. She knew every curve and angle intimately. Beyond the name on her skin, every minute they'd spent together was intimately entwined in her memory. The internal imprint would always remain even if you cut away the scarred skin. She pulled Naomi's hand to her mouth and kissed the finger that bore her ring. She slightly slid the ring up to reveal her name, which had been tattooed around Naomi's finger. She tapped it with her own finger. "The same way you didn't hesitate to tattoo my name here."

"Yes, but we were together when we did that, married even."

"True, but the sentiment is the same. You've been written into my elemental being. Branding my body with your name was just my way of holding on to how much I loved you. There would never have been anyone but you. I'd made my mind up."

"You'd brand it into your skin but wouldn't take steps to live your truth?"

"Stupid pride. I was punishing myself."

Naomi leaned over and placed her mouth on a nipple, immediately bringing it to painful erection.

"Oh my God, that feels so good." She placed her hand on the back of Naomi's head, urging her to suck harder. "Merry Christmas to me."

Naomi continued sucking, licking, and gently biting her nipple, switching to the other, then back. She slid on top of Rhebekka, straddling her hips. "You were the best present I ever got. Now I want to enjoy my gift."

Rhebekka melted against the silken sheets, feeling the pulsing of her center with every teasing nip. "I need you."

Naomi slowly shifted positions, kissing down her body until she was nestled between Rhebekka's legs. Rhebekka bucked when Naomi softly kissed her center and spread her legs wider.

There was a euphoric feeling in being touched intimately by the person you trusted above all others. Not even the first time she'd tried cocaine could compare to these moments. "Yes."

Rhebekka felt Naomi slowly draw her tongue along her folds, flattening it out, then pointing it when it reached her clit. She bucked against the bed but was held in place by Naomi's strong arms. Warmth and lust suffused her, as the gentle licks became insistent. Naomi wrapped her arms under Rhebekka's legs, fingernails digging into her thighs, and pressed her mouth harder on Rhebekka's center.

The sensations at her center stopped, and Rhebekka found Naomi looking at her intently. "You are so wet."

"Only you do this to me."

"For a lifetime." Naomi lowered her eyes and once again surrounded Rhebekka's center with her mouth.

Rhebekka lay trembling with pleasure, grasping the sheets and trying desperately not to crush Naomi's face between her legs. There was no turning back; she was at the crest of Blackwater Falls, ready to go over. "So close!" Naomi settled on her clit, sucking hard. Rhebekka's eyes were tightly closed, as waves of color curled over and crashed, carrying her along until she was floating in a blissful pool.

Naomi gentled her strokes, pulling out the last shivers of pleasure before resting her cheek against Rhebekka's thigh. She was silent for a few minutes as Rhebekka breathed heavily. "So beautiful."

"Shit, Naomi. I'm like Jell-O."

"Just the way I like you, relaxed and sated."

"Sated is an understatement of your talents, and relaxed is a temporary state." Rhebekka reached down and pulled Naomi up until she was lying on top of her. She kissed her deeply, tasting herself as Naomi drove her tongue deep into her mouth. Rhebekka rolled them over and reached between Naomi's legs, finding her hot and wet. "So ready for me."

"Please, baby."

Rhebekka answered her lover's call by driving three fingers deep inside her. Naomi lay there openmouthed and panting at each powerful stroke. She pulled a nipple into her mouth and bit down, pulling a groan from Naomi, who spread her legs farther apart. "Turn over." Rhebekka felt a long shiver come from Naomi, as chill bumps erupted over her lover's skin.

Naomi rolled and pulled herself up onto her knees, grabbing the headboard with both hands. Rhebekka slid in behind her and placed a hand on the small of Naomi's back, as she used her leg to move Naomi's knees farther apart. She plunged three fingers into Naomi's wetness, drawing a guttural keen from her lover. Naomi moved with her, backing into each stroke and driving her fingers even deeper.

"Don't stop!"

Rhebekka leaned over, wrapping an arm around Naomi's waist, locking their bodies together. She drove harder and faster until she felt Naomi go rigid, her chin tilted to the ceiling in an openmouthed cry of ecstasy. Rhebekka gentled her strokes, drawing out the orgasm until Naomi's legs began to shake. She lowered them both down to the bed and pulled a panting Naomi into her arms. "Shhhh. I'm right here." She stroked Naomi's back and felt her shiver again.

"Holy shit, Rhebekka."

They lay there, the streetlights' glow illuminating their sweat-dampened skin. "I love you, Mrs. Deklan, with everything in me."

"You're everything is pretty spectacular. I love you too, Mrs. Deklan."

Rhebekka held her close, reveling in the afterglow and counting her blessings. She'd loved this woman for so very long. Her entire world was better with Naomi in it. All things seemed possible. *She's the best Christmas present I could have ever asked for.* She gave thanks to all things in and under heaven that made her happiness possible. Then, in another Christmas miracle, Rhebekka fell into a deep sleep wrapped in Naomi's arms.

* * * *

The day after Christmas dawned clear and sunny, the temperatures still ranging below zero. A fresh layer of snow had fallen the night before, bathing everything in bright white. Rhebekka carried a stack of cardboard boxes they'd broken down after opening gifts. The crisp air burned as she pulled it in with a deep breath that made her cough. Her breath wafted through the air with every exhalation in a white stream. *As MaMaw used to say, you can see your breath.*

She climbed the stairs to the garage and unlocked the door, marveling at how the door swung open with ease. Inside the warm garage, she flipped on the light and shed her gloves on her way to the recycling bin. The smaller boxes she had in her hand would fit along the sides if she removed the large box sitting on top. When she pulled it away, she noticed something that gave her pause. Under the larger piece of cardboard sat one of the meal boxes Karmen and Zandra had dropped off at Loaves and Fishes last night. The date and the words Merry Christmas stared up at her in her own handwriting. She became slightly uneasy and continued to move boxes around, while her eyes searched the room.

Nothing seems out of place. Her eyes were drawn to the back corner. The string to the loft ladder was dangling across the top of the shovels and rakes that hung on the wall. She'd seen it happen when she'd put the ladder up quickly instead of holding onto the string and guiding it. *What the hell?*

Rhebekka walked by the Land Cruiser and opened the door as if she was searching for something, as she continued to look around the room. Near the workbench was a window no one had used in some time. She wasn't even sure it was capable of being locked. The sills were free of dust. *Someone's coming in and out of the garage by the window.* She popped the hood of the Tundra and moved around the front, hoping whoever was in there would think she was doing maintenance.

She pulled her phone out and hovered her finger over Naomi's number, as she moved to the hood and opened it while looking stealthily around the room. Stuck on the rough-cut framing was something that definitely didn't belong. A black glove with red accents that formed a skeletal hand hung at an awkward angle as if it had been snagged without notice. The glove caused a niggling feeling in her brain. *I've seen that glove, but where?* Her finger was still hovering over the speed dial. She searched her memories until one clicked. *Lucian wore a pair like that on the video from the ice rink the day he ran.*

Her heart was beating fast. Please, Lord. If he's still here, let him trust me. She closed the hood and put the phone in her pocket. "You know, the house is a lot warmer, and it has a kitchen where we could make you a hot meal." She waited in the silence of the garage. When no answer came, she tried again. "Happy Birthday, Lucian." Again, she paused, and was rewarded for her patience.

A trembling voice came from above her. "You can't send me back. I'm eighteen now."

Rhebekka clasped her fingers together in a silent prayer of thanks before speaking again. "Very true, though Ms. Laura is worrying herself sick about you. I think we owe her a call, at the very least. A bunch of people have been very worried about you."

"Not from the home, don't bullshit me."

Rhebekka took a deep breath. The next few minutes were crucial in establishing trust. "I can't speak for them, but I can speak for Naomi, me, Ms. Laura, and even Sheriff Fitzsimmons. We've spent weeks looking for you, hoping and praying you were okay."

The voice was more defiant now. "I can take care of myself."

Rhebekka rubbed her forehead. "I have little doubt you can, but even the most independent person could use a little help from their friends every once in a while. I thought we were friends. If I promise to stay right where I am, can you come down here so we can talk face to face?"

The seconds ticked by like hours as Rhebekka's heart pounded out a staccato beat. Slowly, the stairs lowered. A second later, a pair of worn, black boots appeared on the rungs. A bedraggled looking Lucian stood at the bottom like a rabbit about to bolt. Rhebekka held up her hands. "I'm not coming any closer, so relax. Are you hurt anywhere?"

Lucian shook his head. "I told you I can take care of myself."

"You also look like you could use a hot cup of coffee and a change of clothes."

Lucian brushed at the dirt on his pants. "Your storage area is a little dusty."

"I'm sure." She aimed her thumb at the door. "Your handiwork?"

A slight shoulder shrug was the only answer for a few seconds. "I saw both of you almost bust your asses trying to open it. It didn't take much to fix it. I just moved the hinges a bit."

"That's where the fresh brass scratches on the screw heads came from. Thank you." Another shrug followed, and Rhebekka leaned back on the Land Cruiser. "I assume you've been coming in through the window. Why didn't you just knock on the door? We'd have helped you. You know that?"

Lucian balled up his fists. "No one could help me. They'd have made me go back, and I wasn't doing that for another day. I'd been planning my escape for a year. I didn't know when I'd go, so the skating trip was just an opportunity I couldn't pass up."

"Ms. Laura was devastated. I heard what you said, but I want you to talk to her. We have to let the Sheriff know, and she'll probably want to talk to you too. You're an adult now, but we can go get the rest of your stuff."

He looked around the garage, then back up to the loft. "Can I stay here a while longer, just until I can get a place?"

Rhebekka folded her arms over her chest. "Absolutely not. Naomi would have my ass. We have a guest room with its own bathroom. You're welcome to stay with us for as long as you want. We just need to make sure everything, legally, is finished up with the children's shelter."

He jammed his hands deep into his pockets. "How'd you figure it out?"

"Huh?" Rhebekka was confused.

"That I was here. I tried to be so careful."

Rhebekka smiled. "How was the ham?"

Lucian's eyes got huge and he smacked his forehead. "The food box."

"If you hadn't been so environmentally conscious, it might have taken me a bit longer. Oh, grab your glove there on the wall." Rhebekka pointed to where his glove was snagged.

Lucian pulled it off and tucked it into his pocket. "I wondered where it went. I thought maybe I'd lost it on the way back here last night."

Rhebekka pointed to the loft. "Go get the rest of your stuff. I'm going to let Naomi know we have company."

Lucian scrambled back up the ladder, and Rhebekka listened as he scuffled around. She dialed Naomi.

"Hey, you. Did you get lost between here and the garage?"

"Not exactly, but I did find something in the garage you'll be happy about."

"Did you find that garage remote I lost?"

Rhebekka chuckled as Lucian climbed back down the steps and put up the ladder. "Even better, I found our lost sheep."

Chapter Five

NAOMI STOOD AT the bar, her journal before her. Her thoughts were chaotic and pinging around inside her skull like a BB shot into a metal box.

Your lost sheep has found the flock! In you, all things are possible. My heart is filled with love and compassion. Please help us convince him to stay. He's so young, too young to be on his own. Last night we celebrated the miracle that would save the world. Today, we celebrate that what was lost is found. Lucian made his way to us but was too afraid to let us know. I don't know how, but Rhebekka and I will do everything in our power to change his life in a good way. He deserves that.

She closed the journal and placed a bowl of steaming soup down on the counter. Beside it, she sat an equally monstrous sandwich and a Coke. She turned to see Lucian walking down the hall from the room they'd put him in. He ran his hands through his still damp hair and pulled at the waist of the pair of jeans she'd found for him that were slightly too large.

"Looks like I need to find you a belt too." Naomi smiled. He was close to Rhebekka's height, though noticeably thin. *Too much time without proper meals.*

Lucian gave her a sheepish grin. "Thank you for the clean clothes. I tried to wash mine in the shower at Loaves and Fishes, but it was pretty hard. Drying them was even worse. The garage was warm, but not enough to dry wet clothes quickly."

"I wish you'd have just come to the house. We'd have figured something out. Sit down and eat. It looks like I could feed you for a month and not get you to fill those pants out."

Lucian held on to the belt loop as he climbed onto the bar stool. "This smells so good." He leaned in and sniffed at the steam rising from the hearty chicken noodle soup Naomi made.

Naomi watched him close his eyes for a moment before digging in. *Did he just pray?* She returned to the bedroom and found a wide webbing belt with a buckle that used friction to adjust the size rather than belt holes. "This should do the trick."

He'd been barefoot, even though she'd found socks for him. She picked up the basket he'd put his clothes in. It was obvious he'd tried to wash them, as they didn't smell nearly as bad as she'd have expected. He was on the run for almost three weeks. Once she'd put everything in the washer, she noted the feeling in her chest. It had always been her nature to be a giving person, and helping in this small way filled her with love. She'd helped him get clean, fed him, and now was doing an act of care in washing his clothes. *Just like a mother would.* Back in the kitchen, Rhebekka had joined Lucian at the bar, and the two were deep in conversation.

"See if this helps." Naomi handed him the belt.

"Thank you, ma'am."

Naomi smiled. "Enough with the ma'am, Lucian. Please, call me Naomi."

He quirked a smile. "I suppose, if you're willing to call me by my name, I should try to do the same. Thank you, Naomi." He finished the soup. "Can I have another Coke, please?"

Rhebekka sipped at a glass of iced tea. "I called Sheriff Fitzsimmons and Ms. Laura. Both are on their way over here."

Lucian stiffened and put down his spoon. "Are they going to make me go back?"

Naomi could see the tension rolling off him in waves. "You don't have any shoes on, so cool your jets. Your running days are over. Sheriff Fitzsimmons and her friends spent days scouring the woods for you, and Ms. Laura has been worried sick. You owe them nothing less than an apology and a conversation. If I'm not mistaken, you are eighteen. Legally, that makes you an adult. I don't know all the legalities, but I am fairly confident that, as long as you aren't a danger to yourself or others, you can decide where you want to go."

Lucian looked up, shock on his face. "I'd never hurt a living soul." He dropped his head. "At least not physically. If I had wanted to hurt myself, I'd have already done it. I'm not a violent person, never have been."

Naomi pulled a Coke from the fridge and sat it in front of him. "I never said you were. That criteria would put the sheriff in a position to take you into custody to keep you from harming yourself or others. Ms. Laura will attest to your nonviolent nature."

Rhebekka pointed to his food. "Start eating, or she'll start feeding it to you. I expect you'll get an earful from them about the danger others were in while we looked for you. You had us worried sick."

Lucian chewed his last bite of the sandwich and swallowed. "I never meant for anyone to worry. They couldn't have cared less about me at the home. I was nothing more than a weirdo and a problem to them. The staff didn't know what to do with me, and the rest of the kids were just assholes. I honestly didn't think anyone would even bother looking."

Rhebekka sighed. "Ms. Laura cares about you, and I know she doesn't think you're a weirdo or a problem. She was the one who continually urged people to call you Lucian. Do you know she's the one who contacted me when you went missing?"

He wiped angrily at a tear that trickled down his cheek. "She's the only one."

Naomi came around the bar and wrapped him in her arms. "That's in the past. This is the present. You're safe here. Our home is your home until you figure out what you want to do."

Rhebekka reached out and held his hand. "You're no longer alone. There is plenty of room at our table, and you can be exactly who you are. We'll figure this out together."

The doorbell rang, and Naomi felt him tense up. She squeezed him. "It's going to be okay."

Rhebekka looked at the camera feed from her phone. "It's Laura. I'd brace myself if I were you, Lucian." She quirked a grin and buzzed Laura through the door.

The sound of quick footfalls up the steps put a smile on Lucian's face. "See. Someone is anxious to know you're okay." Naomi moved to his side as Rhebekka let Laura in the loft.

A frazzled-looking Laura shot through the open door and made a beeline for Lucian, tears running down her face. "Lucian! I don't know whether to hug you or kill you for making me worry like that." She wrapped him in a tight hug.

He dropped his forehead to her shoulder. "I'm sorry, Ms. Laura. I didn't know what else to do."

She pulled back, keeping her hands on his shoulders. "You could have talked to me. We'd have figured something out. Disappearing into the snow was about as irresponsible as I've ever known you to be." She pointed to her eyes. "Do you know how much sleep I've lost worrying about you being eaten by a bear or falling into some deep canyon?"

He grinned. "Ms. Laura, the bears are hibernating."

She smacked his shoulder and pursed her lips. "Smart ass. You know what I mean." Laura took a deep breath. "You scared me."

"I'm so, so sorry. That was never my intention. I just had to go."

Laura sighed and looked at Naomi. "Kids."

Naomi grinned and used her head to indicate Rhebekka, who had come to stand at her side. "Kids."

Rhebekka protested. "Just because I tried scuba diving in a blizzard once. One time!"

Naomi pointed to the living room. "Let's go sit where we'll be more comfortable. Lucian, grab your Coke. Laura, can I get you something to drink?"

Laura shook her head. "I'm not sure it would go down."

Naomi nodded and poured herself a cup of coffee before joining everyone in the living room. The fire burned brightly as she sat down beside Rhebekka. Lucian sat in front of the fire as if needing to be near the warmth. *Like a moth to a flame.* She looked him over critically. He had dark circles under his eyes, and he was thin, but overall, it seemed he'd endured his time as a runaway reasonably well. She leaned over to Rhebekka. "I wonder how long it took him to find Loaves and Fishes?"

Rhebekka wrapped an arm around her. "I'm guessing we'll find out more when Chance gets here to question him formally. I don't think he did anything illegal, unless running away is somehow a crime in itself. Thank God for Franklin's idea to start Loaves and Fishes. He always said it was a way to help locals without them being ashamed of coming in and facing anyone. Perhaps there was a little divine intervention in its creation. Remind me to thank Franklin when he gets back."

Twenty minutes passed as they all talked before the ring at the door came again. Rhebekka went to let Chance and Zeus in. Naomi looked at Lucian, whose face had gone completely white with fear. "It's going to be okay, Lucian. Chance is a personal friend. She understands the issues associated with being different than everyone. There isn't anyone better I'd want to help navigate these waters."

Lucian didn't look at her, his eyes shifting to the doors and windows as if he was in fight or flight mode.

Naomi moved over beside him on the hearth and put her arm around him. "Close your eyes for a minute." She watched him turn to her, the desperation pouring out of him. "Trust me." She waited until he complied, then caught Rhebekka's gaze and began. "The Lord is my shepherd." She continued praying using the words of the 23rd Psalm.

She felt, more than heard, Lucian join in with her. Slowly, the other voices in the room joined in, praying through the verses that offered comfort in the storm. When she finished with "Surely your goodness and mercy will follow me all the days of my life, and I will dwell in the house of the Lord forever," Lucian whispered a barely audible, "Amen."

Chance had moved into the living room within arm's length. Zeus sat at her feet. Chance held out her hand. "Lucian, it's nice to finally meet you. I'm so thankful you're okay. You gave us quite a scare."

Lucian slowly came to his feet. He wiped his hands down his jeans before extending his hand and accepting the greeting from Chance. "Sheriff. I'm sorry I worried everyone. I honestly didn't think anyone would care."

Naomi's heart nearly shattered at the hopelessness in Lucian's voice. He was still a child in so many ways, jaded by his interactions with those who couldn't accept him for who he was.

Chance smiled at him and looked around the room. "Well, I hope you now know that isn't anywhere close to the truth." Zeus licked Lucian's hand, causing him to jump a bit. "See, even Zeus was worried about you."

"Can I..." He paused. "Can I pet him?" Lucian asked.

"I'd say Zeus has already answered that, but yes, you can." Chance sat on the couch as Lucian knelt before Zeus and stroked his head.

Lucian sat back on the floor and Zeus lay beside him. "What happens now?"

Chance pulled a notebook from her pocket. "I need to ask you some questions. It's important that you give me honest answers, okay?"

Lucian nodded.

"Lucian, did any adult coerce you into leaving the skating rink with them?"

The young man adamantly shook his head. "No, Sheriff. I left all on my own. I didn't tell anyone what I was doing or where I was going."

Chance wrote something down and looked up at him. "Did you run away because someone was abusing you at the children's shelter?"

Lucian looked at her, his jaw jumping. "I'd rather not say."

Laura had been sitting quietly until Lucian answered. "Lucian, if someone hurt you, I want to know. It's not your fault."

When Lucian looked away, Naomi moved back in beside him. "Lucian, you're safe. No one is going to hurt you again. We are on your side, and the only way we can hold those accountable for what happened is for you to tell us."

He'd begun to cry and angrily wiped at his tears. "I doubt it."

Laura came to sit cross-legged in front of him. "Lucian, look at me. I can't change what's gone on in the past." She put her hand on her chest. "I can change how we respond to it and what we do about it."

Rhebekka had been leaning against a wall. Naomi could see her boiling agitation. The one thing she knew for sure was that Rhebekka had suffered at the other end of her father's belt. The pain inflicted at such a young age scarred her. There was little doubt about the amount of emotional pain Lucian had endured. Her fear now was that not all of it had been emotional.

He stood and walked to the window that overlooked the street. "I'd been working about three months at the music shop. With my school schedule, I could only work evenings. So I told the manager I'd work every hour I could. With the money I earned, I could buy what I wanted and dress how I liked." He sat down in the window seat. "That's how I got my leather jacket at the second-hand shop. It was a great find. It's too big in the shoulders, but exactly what I wanted."

The group sat silent, willing to let Lucian tell his story in his way, in his time.

He shook his head. "Anyway, I was coming back to the shelter one night when someone grabbed me right before I got inside. I just remember hands pulling on my arms and legs. I kicked and tried to scream, but I got a glove shoved in my mouth. It was too dark to see anyone, but I knew who it was. I'd been warned enough. They tried to get my pants off, telling me they would show me how much of a woman I was. My leather belt had a complicated buckle." Lucian crossed his arms and held his sides.

Chance gave him a moment, then stepped up beside him. "Lucian, I promise you I will do everything I can to arrest whoever it was. It's mandatory that I investigate."

Lucian looked at Chance with defiance flashing in his eyes. "Like Mr. Jones did? It was probably mandatory for him to do something about it too, wasn't it?"

Laura jumped to her feet. "Lucian, did you tell Mr. Jones what happened?"

"I didn't have to. He was there. He broke it up before they could figure out how to get my buckle open." Lucian's hands were balled into fists.

Chance put a hand up to Laura. "Lucian, I need you to tell me everything. I can promise you I will take this to the ends of the earth to bring those responsible to justice."

Tears ran down Naomi's face. She covered her mouth with her hand to stifle the outcry about to break forth. *No wonder he left. What the hell is wrong with people? Is there no decency anymore?* She listened as Lucian recounted the rest of the assault. Mr. Jones had pointed the finger at him instead of the boys in question.

"He said I wouldn't draw so much attention to myself if I weren't such a freak." Lucian used his sleeve to wipe at the tears dripping off his chin.

Chance had her notebook out, making copious notes on everything Lucian said. "There will be a formal inquiry, and you'll have to testify, Lucian. I realize it's dragging it all up again, but without the victims stepping forward, the hands of law enforcement are tied in an instance that isn't witnessed by an officer. It also happened in another county, so I'll have to contact someone I trust over there to do the actual investigation. I promise, I will be with you every step of the way."

Naomi took one of Rhebekka's hands in hers and joined one with Laura's as well. "We'll be right with you. If they would do those awful things to you, then I have no doubt they're abusing others."

Lucian nodded. His shoulders drooped. He relayed the story to Chance, including the details of Mr. Jones and his continued taunts. He was breathing fast, but it didn't seem like he was getting any air. The way his words were squeezed from a constricted throat was evidence of how heavily the emotional scars he'd been carrying weighed on him.

"Sheriff, I can't go back there. I won't. If you make me, I'll run again, and this time, you'll never find me."

Zeus had moved close to Lucian again, resting his head on the troubled young man's leg.

Chance pointed to her partner. "I think Zeus is trying to tell you that his partner is trustworthy. I won't make you go back. As I said, we need to clear things up with the shelter. What about school? Don't you graduate this year?"

Lucian's head whipped up to Chance. "I'm not going back there. I'm dropping out. If I have to, I can get my GED, but I'm not setting foot back in that hell hole."

Naomi moved over to him. "We can talk about that later. There are plenty of options, and you won't get far in this world if you don't have at least a high school diploma. For now, if the Sheriff agrees, you can stay here with us. What do you think, Chance?"

The sheriff pushed her Stetson back on her head and scratched at her scalp with her pen. "I have to check with the Department of Health and Human Resources on all the legalities, but I think Lucian has reached the age of majority in comparison to being a minor. He was legally a ward of the state or, in some legal terms, a ward of the court. He turned eighteen today, and that's when the legal system considers him an adult." Chance put her hat back in place. "It's going to be hard to get in touch with anyone with it being the day after Christmas. I'm sure there's a hotline, so let me make some calls."

Lucian clasped his hands together and squeezed them between his knees. "So, what now?"

Chance looked to Rhebekka and Naomi. "If it's okay with these two, I'd like you to stay here until I get an answer."

Naomi reached out and covered Lucian's hands with hers. "I can speak for both of us. He's welcome to stay here for as long as he wants."

Chance turned to a new page in her notebook. "If you can give me a place to make some calls, we'll get the ball rolling."

Rhebekka pointed to her studio. "You'll have the quiet and privacy you need to work."

Naomi turned to the young man, whose knee was bobbing up and down. "I'm a worrier by nature, Lucian. One of my favorite verses from Matthew says, 'Can any one of you, by worrying, add a single hour to your life?' The answer is no. In fact, worrying can actually shorten our life. If you give us a chance, we'll figure everything out. You deserve to live life as who you really are. We'll help you do that however we can." She held out her hand to him. "Deal?"

Lucian looked at her, his eyes welling with tears threatening to spill over. He raised a shaky hand and put it in hers. He started to speak, then cleared his throat. "Deal."

She pulled him into a hug and held him, as the tears finally poured out like a dam overflowing. Her thoughts went to the book of Psalms and the power of prayer. Softly, she whispered to him. "Be with us, Lord. As the Psalm says, 'Answer me when I call to you, my righteous God. Give me relief from my distress; have mercy on me and hear my prayer.'"

* * * *

78

It had been an extremely long day for all of them. Rhebekka had sat with Chance as she made phone call after phone call, leaving several messages and reaching very few people. Laura left to try her own connections. The phone calls to the children's home had been the most interesting. The center's director was out of state on holiday, and the assistant director was unreachable. Chance's voice rose more than once before she finally reached out to a local legislator, who then made contact with someone in the Department of Health and Human Resources.

"I thought she was going to threaten someone if she didn't get an answer." Rhebekka put her feet on the coffee table as she sat down on the couch beside Naomi. Lucian was stretched out on the floor, with Marley and JJ snuggled up against him.

Naomi kissed her cheek. "Chance isn't someone to get in the way of."

Lucian scratched Marley between her ears. "She seems like a straight shooter, if you forgive the pun."

Rhebekka laughed. "She is that. She's a great person to have on your side. I can promise you, Lucian, she is on your side."

He dropped his gaze and continued to stroke the purring cats. "So, what happens now?"

Naomi yawned and covered her mouth. "Oh, excuse me." She shook her head. "First, we get a good night's sleep. One that isn't in a second-hand sleeping bag on a wooden floor."

He dropped his head. "Do you know how grateful I was for that sleeping bag?"

Rhebekka nodded. "I'm sure. You can personally thank Franklin when he returns from Christmas with his parents. The needs room was his idea."

"I was running pretty low on supplies, when I saw that poster you put up in the public bathroom at that park with the fake rocks."

The boulder park was a rock-climbing simulator in Davis, funded by donations. *Thank God we put those things everywhere.* Rhebekka felt Naomi slide down until her head was resting in her lap. She let her fingers sift through Naomi's luxurious hair, knowing it would relax the woman she loved and likely put her to sleep. "Good to know our outreach hit the mark. I missed the part about how you got from Canaan to Davis."

"I caught a ride in a Jeep from a group of women from Ohio. They'd been skiing and were on their way home."

The rhythmic rise and fall of Naomi's shoulder let Rhebekka know she'd fallen asleep. She continued her caress. "That explains why no one local came forward with having seen you or given you a ride."

"I walked to the tube park and waited to find the right group to ask. They had out-of-state plates, and their skis were strapped into racks. I thought they might be leaving, so I asked. Apparently, I'm not intimidating, so they gave me a lift."

Rhebekka nodded. "You thought of everything." It was obvious Lucian had considered his personal safety and used as much caution as he could in his choices. They talked about the places he'd slept for the first few nights.

He shrugged his shoulders. "I bought a few essentials from the sporting goods store, like a fire starter, an emergency blanket, and a water bottle with some purification tablets. That natural spring pipe that sticks out of the hillside near the Davis grocery store was a good find, too. On our way to the skating rink, I saw people filling gallon jugs there. I figured if they weren't afraid to drink it, I'd just put a tablet in it to make sure, and I'd be good to go. When I found the food at Loaves and Fishes, I'd gone through most of my peanut butter crackers and beef jerky supplies."

She watched him move a bit before he stifled a yawn, disturbing the cats, who glared their annoyance. "You're a pretty resourceful young man. Go to bed and take those two with you. Tomorrow is another day. I'm going to try and get this one there as well. Would you mind helping me out tomorrow?"

Lucian smiled. "Anything you need. I don't have much to offer, but I'm pretty strong."

Rhebekka pointed at him. "No more of that. The first thing you need to realize is that you do have much to offer. We all have our talents, and we're supposed to use them for the greatest good. See you in the morning, Lucian. I'm glad you're here."

He smiled. "Thanks for letting me stay."

Rhebekka watched both cats follow him to his room. She gently shook Naomi. "Come on, sleepy head. Let's get you to bed."

Naomi sat up in alarm. "Where's Lucian? He didn't run again, did he?" She frantically looked around the room.

"Easy, momma bear. No, he didn't run away. I don't think the cats would let him. He went to bed, and they went with him. So let's do the same." Rhebekka stood and pulled Naomi up off the couch. "Go to bed. I'm going to fix the coffee pot, and I'll be right in."

Naomi rose on her tiptoes to kiss her. "I love you, Rhebekka, but I know tonight you need to play. It's okay."

"My mind is going a million places."

Naomi patted her chest. "I know. There are only two ways to make it stop, and I'm not sure Lucian is ready to hear you scream out my name. Go play. I'll be there when you've let it all go in the music."

Rhebekka sighed and pressed her forehead to Naomi's before her wife headed to their bedroom. It made her heart swell with love as Naomi stopped and peeked in on Lucian. Rhebekka finished the coffee preparation and glanced at a picture on the side of the refrigerator. It was taken the first summer after she and Ellie had escaped. Ellie's hair was sun-bleached and lay in a long braid over her tanned shoulders. Her own locks had been cut short for the first time in her life, and she wore jeans with the knees ripped out. *Rebel without a clue.* They were sitting on the hood of the Subaru that had carried them away from Virginia and laughing at something she couldn't remember now. She took down the picture and held it in her hand. This photo symbolized the first time they'd found happiness on their own terms. They'd fled because of the abuse to face the unknown instead of staying in misery, just like Lucian had.

When they left, she'd had some semblance of a plan, a small amount of money for essentials, and a car to carry them away. Lucian had only himself to rely on and minimal resources. That he'd figured out a way to survive alone amazed her. She closed her eyes and said a prayer of thanks that he'd made his way to them safely.

She clipped the picture back to the refrigerator and flipped off the light switch on her way to her studio. Sleep likely wouldn't come for hours, but she needed to lose these feelings in her guitar strings and the music that healed her soul.

* * * *

Inside her studio, Rhebekka picked up her Strat and slung the strap around her neck. She plugged in the headset that allowed her to play without disturbing others. She pulled the pick from her back pocket and strummed through a few chords, before settling into Guns N' Roses, "Sweet Child o' Mine." There was a raw emotion to her playing. Her long, calloused fingers glided over the frets as the guitar became an extension of her nerves leading straight to her soul. Each note pulled from her instrument released something inside her that only music could.

Her anger over Lucian's assault and general mistreatment pushed her through Pat Benatar's "Hell is for Children" and several other songs. Sweat dripped off the ends of her hair, dotting her shirt as liquid exertion ran between her shoulder blades and down her spine. Playing the guitar was physical for her, and her corded forearms were the visible testament to how much she still played, even years after she'd left the touring schedule behind. The song's final notes faded in her ears, and her body screamed for water. *I need a drink.* She pulled the guitar off her shoulders and turned to set it in its stand. When she stepped out of the studio, she nearly jumped out of her skin finding Lucian sitting with his back against the wall.

He stumbled to his feet and began to step backward. "Sorry, Rhebekka."

She put her hand to her chest. "I nearly had a heart attack. I was just going for a glass of water. You want to join me?"

Lucian pushed the hair out of his eyes. "I didn't mean to disturb you. I'll go back to bed."

She reached out and put a hand on his shoulder. "You didn't do anything wrong, Lucian. I'm just not used to having anyone else in the house besides Naomi. She's no stranger to my midnight jam sessions. Let's get something cold to drink. I'm parched."

In the kitchen, she flipped on the light over the sink as he climbed onto the barstool. She used the hem of her T-shirt to wipe her face and fixed them both a glass of ice water. "Naomi went to bed. Sorry if I woke you up. All those years of touring screwed up my sleep schedule. It's hard for me to go to bed until three or four. She's so used to it. I didn't even think about someone else being in the house."

"Honestly, it didn't bother me. I couldn't sleep, and I could tell you were playing."

"I thought playing in the studio with the headphones would keep anyone from being disturbed. I need to upgrade the soundproofing a bit."

"It was like I could feel you playing."

Rhebekka looked at his hands wrapped around the glass. "You play, don't you?" There were visible callouses on his fingers. Not as dramatic as her own, but they were there.

Lucian dropped his head. "Nowhere near as good as you do."

"Hey, I'm a good bit older than you are and have had years of practice. You'll get there. You worked in the music store, right? Did you have a lot of opportunities to play?" She watched his face take on an excited glow.

"Every chance I got."

She pulled out a stool and sat opposite him, giving him enough space not to feel crowded or hemmed in, but close enough to see her expressions and interest. "What's your favorite instrument?" The change in his posture and demeanor was immediately noticeable. He was excited to be talking music.

"Bass guitar."

That surprised Rhebekka. "Bass guitar is fantastic. The ability to set the rhythm and framing of the song is underappreciated. Some of the most memorable songs happen because of the bass."

His hands flew up. "Exactly. One of the first ones I ever learned was "Another One Bites the Dust." If you take out John Deacon's riff, that song isn't the same."

Passion, in all its forms, was powerful medicine. Rhebekka watched him light up as he automatically put his hands in position, holding an invisible bass guitar, his thumb and forefinger plucking imaginary strings. Proverbs have it right. *'A cheerful heart is good medicine, but a crushed spirit dries up the bones.'*

He stopped and took the glass back in his hand. "Have you ever heard of Carole Kay? She's been playing bass for over fifty years on all kinds of popular songs and commercials as a studio musician."

Rhebekka chuckled. She indeed knew Carole. "I met her once."

Lucian's eyes grew wide. "You met her?"

For the next twenty minutes, they discussed the various bass players that Rhebekka had worked with and how she'd found Casey Destro, the bass player for Regal Crimson. Lucian's fascination with the music world was endless, and he peppered her with questions. She looked at the hands on the clock that told her it was a little after midnight. She was still wired, and it was obvious that Lucian was too.

"Are you up to a little late-night jam?"

Lucian looked back to the bedroom area of the loft. "Won't we wake Naomi up?"

Rhebekka stood. "Not where we're going. Grab your shoes."

He looked at his sweatpants and the baggy, hooded sweatshirt Naomi had given him to wear earlier that day. "Do I need to change clothes?"

"Can you play in what you're wearing?"

Lucian practically ran down the hallway and came back, nearly stumbling, as he jammed his feet into his boots.

Rhebekka pointed to his feet. "The first thing we need to do tomorrow is go shopping. You need something else to wear other than winter boots."

"Honest, I'm good. I don't need anything."

She smiled at him. "Need is the subjective word. You are correct that you do have footwear. The difference is that there are shoes for varying occasions. You can play basketball in boots, but they aren't the optimum footwear."

Lucian dropped his head. "I have some at the shelter. I couldn't carry everything with me and not draw suspicion. I had to make choices." He pointed to his boots. "For what I was planning, I figured my boots were what I needed."

She smiled at him. "Again, need being the subjective word. You needed boots for the snow. We're arranging to get the rest of your things from the shelter. Until then, how about we go shopping and let you make some choices for yourself, not based on what you can carry?"

He scuffed his toe a bit. "I don't have the money to do that."

Rhebekka put her hands on his shoulders. "Lucian, look at me." When his eyes met hers, she spoke. "I understand the meaning of independence and not relying on anyone. I truly do. I promise you; this is different. Nothing we get you obligates you to us for any reason. If you had the means and I didn't, would you want to help me?"

His spine straightened. "Of course, I would. I'd give anyone anything I had to help you."

"Then how can you be upset if I do the same? We've all been asked to do that for those in need."

"I don't understand."

"In Matthew, Jesus said, 'For I was hungry and you gave me something to eat, I was thirsty and you gave me something to drink, I was a stranger and you invited me in, I needed clothes and you clothed me...' The disciples asked when they'd done this for Christ, and the response was that if they'd done it for anyone, they'd done it for Christ. You see, Lucian, I put into practice the things I tell my congregation. I live my faith. In as much as I believe you would do any of those things for me, why would I do less for you?"

Lucian put his head down. "I guess you wouldn't."

"Nope, now let's go jam." She led him toward the door of the loft.

"Where are we going?"

"Do you remember where you watched the Christmas Eve service?"

"Downstairs in the church?"

She turned to him and pointed. "Gotcha. I thought I saw someone hiding in the back. I just didn't know who it was. I wish you'd have come to me then and not left."

He grinned. "Busted, huh?"

"Definitely. House of the Rising Son is there for everyone, believers and those who question faith alike."

They walked down the stairs, her prosthesis reminding her she'd been on her feet a good bit of the day. The floorboards of the ancient opera house creaked and popped with every step as they made their way into the sanctuary. Rhebekka stepped onto the stage and pointed to the instrument corner where a black, five-string Yamaha and a Fender Ultra Precision bass sat. "Pick your poison."

She watched as Lucian wrapped his arms around himself and tentatively stepped closer.

He turned to Rhebekka. "Are you sure? I've never played anything that expensive, and trust me, I know what they cost."

"I want you to imagine you've played every bass guitar out there, and you walked into a store to try those two out. Which one do you start with?" Rhebekka picked up the Les Paul Studio electric guitar Naomi had bought her for Christmas.

The ache in her leg reminded her to get the pressure off it. *Forgive me, Naomi, and don't kick my ass too hard tomorrow.* She moved off the stage and onto one of the couches her congregation usually sat in. With her leg elevated, she put the beautiful Smokehouse Burst guitar into a comfortable position and began picking out Queen's "Under Pressure." Her mind had zero doubt that this iconic riff would be too much for Lucian to resist. It worked like a charm. He grabbed the Yamaha, adjusted the strap, and familiarized himself with the instrument.

His hands in place, he began to strum the pedal riff over and over. "You know, Vanilla Ice totally ripped this off."

Rhebekka laughed. "A court of law agreed with you. He couldn't hold Freddy Mercury's leather pants. Today we'd call that sampling. Many artists do it, and some take the chance to steal someone else's artistic content. Some acknowledge others' work, get permission, and pay them accordingly." She watched as he grew more and more comfortable, his shoulders beginning to sway with the riff.

They played through the song, then went right into "Cumbersome" by Seven Mary Three. Lucian relaxed into the music, closing his eyes during some tracks and letting the musician inside him travel out to the strings and frets. She led him into several songs, amazed at his ability. He was far too humble in his assessment of his skills. A musician existed inside the boy taking his first steps toward the man he would become.

Hours later, she saw him yawn and look up to the clock that read three fifteen. She stood and wobbled slightly on her sore leg.

"Are you okay, Rhebekka?" Lucian took a quick step toward her with a worried brow.

"I'm okay. I probably overdid it on the leg today." She held a finger to her lips. "Shhh, don't tell Naomi."

A voice in the darkness startled them both.

"Too late for that." Naomi stepped forward in a long silk robe. "How about you two rock stars find your way to bed? I promise you can play a world tour tomorrow." She walked up and put her arm around Rhebekka's waist.

"Looks like I got busted twice in one night." Lucian stretched after he put down the Fender he'd switched to an hour ago.

Rhebekka nodded to Lucian. "We both did. Which bass did you like better?"

Lucian's grin lit up his face. "The best thing is I don't have to decide. They're both absolute perfection. I like Fenders though."

Rhebekka kissed the top of Naomi's head as they walked to the steps. "This one would agree. She had a Fender in her hands the first time I saw her."

Naomi kept her arm around Rhebekka's waist. "Quincy Jones said there'd be no rock-n-roll and no Motown without the Fender bass, so you're in good company, Lucian."

Upstairs, they walked back down the hall to the bedrooms and stopped at Lucian's door. "Thanks for tonight, Rhebekka."

"First, how about you call me Bek? Sometimes, Rhebekka is way too formal. Second, you're very welcome. It's been a long time since someone played late into the morning with me."

Naomi yawned. "Better you than me, Lucian. Sleep in, and we'll see you when you get up."

Lucian approached them. "Could I hug you guys?"

Rhebekka felt her throat choke up. Naomi answered for them.

"I could certainly use a hug." Naomi opened her arms, and Rhebekka did the same.

Lucian melted into them, his body trembling. They stood there for a long, extended embrace before Lucian wiped at the tears that had fallen on his cheeks. "I can never say thank you enough, but I'll sure try." He turned and went into his room. Both cats were stretched out on his bed. "Night, guys."

"Good night, Lucian. See you tomorrow." Rhebekka limped toward the bedroom.

"What am I going to do with you?"

"Scold me tomorrow. Tonight, how about you hold me tight?" Rhebekka closed their bedroom door and accepted a long, slow kiss.

"With both arms, my love." Naomi pulled off her robe and climbed into bed.

Rhebekka sat on the bed and removed her leg, then her clothes, before she snuggled under the covers. She sighed into the warmth of Naomi's body, as her wife wrapped her silken arms and legs around her.

There would be time to digest everything that had happened and deal with each problem presented to them as it came. *Tonight, Lucian is safe and warm.* And she was wrapped in the arms of the woman she loved. Her mind quieted, and she drifted into a deep sleep, secure in the knowledge she'd be given the strength to face each trial ahead.

Chapter Six

NAOMI FOLDED THE LAST of the laundry and placed it in the wicker basket. She was sure Lucian would prefer his own clothes to wearing Rhebekka's. She sipped her coffee contentedly and wrote in her journal as she listened to one side of a conversation between Rhebekka and Ellie. Over the last few weeks, she'd watched Rhebekka tiptoe around Ellie's refusal to talk. They are both so stubbornly protective of each other.

It's cold and blustery today. Rhebekka is trying to draw out things that Ellie seems to want left alone. The two of them went through so much. I get the feeling they are about to go through a lot more. On another subject, Lucian is one hell of a bass player. Mental and physical note to myself: Go visit the music store he used to work at. My gut tells me he had his eye on something. It might be time to add another axe to the family.

Rhebekka sat on the couch talking on the phone, her elbow resting on her knee, her hand on her forehead. "Let's go for a ride today. I promise good company, and I'll even bring you a large coffee from TipTop."

Naomi waited to see if Ellie would agree or blow her off again. Unfortunately, it didn't take long to tell that Ellie was still hedging.

"Lucian is fine. Naomi is here with him. Please, Ellie?"

A few more seconds and Naomi breathed easier as she saw Rhebekka's face light up. The two women made a few more plans before Rhebekka disconnected the call. Naomi considered Ellie a sister in all ways but DNA. The two had a close relationship, even through the years she and Rhebekka were split up. She'd broken down with Ellie after finding out about Rhebekka's infidelity. Ellie had been a rock and ready to kill her sister for the pain that had been inflicted. Ellie also begged her not to give up on her stubborn sister and called her when their father died. When Naomi showed up at their hotel door, her presence had brought the last of Rhebekka's fortress down, allowing them to get back together. She closed her journal and waited until Rhebekka turned to look at her.

"Did she finally agree?"

Rhebekka rubbed a hand down her face. "Yes, but not without a good bit of diversionary tactics."

"The two of you are more alike than you even realize."

Rhebekka turned to her with scrunched brows. "You think?"

"Not to bring up a dead and buried subject, but she came to stay with me a lot when we were broken up. She's as bad as you at not sleeping well and getting so far inside her head that even a thousand-foot lifeline isn't long enough. She buries things, compartmentalizes them so they can't hurt her. Her emotions are locked behind tiny doors like in an Advent calendar, though what lies behind the doors is anything but a treat."

Rhebekka sat back on the couch with a deep sigh. "That sounds familiar. How do I reach her now? If my suspicions are correct, there is more pain to come. I've learned, over the years, that ignoring something doesn't make it go away."

Naomi pointed to herself. "Case in point."

"You were never just something. You were always everything. Everything I'd ever dreamed of and never thought I deserved. Sometimes I wonder if I didn't deliberately hurt us in order to protect myself."

"Like leaving me before I could leave you?"

Rhebekka nodded. "Something like that. You didn't deserve the hurt and the anger I caused you. You were the best thing in my life, and it was as if I couldn't stand the anticipation of it going south like things always did."

"So, you imploded our world instead of believing the words in Corinthians that say love 'is not easily angered, it keeps no record of wrongs. Love does not delight in evil but rejoices with the truth. It always protects, always trusts, always hopes, always perseveres.'"

"There was always a small ember of hope that burned inside me. One that said there would be no other in my life. Even if I were unworthy of your love, I would never betray it again."

Naomi leaned over and kissed her. She let the depth of her devotion flow from her lips to the one she'd loved so very much. When she pulled back, they were both breathing heavily. "I knew you were worthy of both my forgiveness and my love. I still think much of it comes back to your childhood and never believing you were worthy of the grace freely given."

Naomi thought of the McNallys, and the childhood Rhebekka and Ellie had endured. In contrast, she thought of Chance and Jax with Hunter, Taylor and Penny with Jace, and even Sydney and Lynn with Amanda. She knew how vital loving parents were to their children's well-being. Her own had been mostly supportive of her life until she came out to them. It wasn't as if they abandoned her, but they weren't thrilled with her choices and had grown distant and less communicative. When she and Aaron divorced, they'd managed to hold their opinions to themselves for the most part. She chuckled to herself. *After they met Rhebekka, in her tattooed, leather glory, I thought their heads might spin off.*

Her current relationship with them was little more than yearly birthday and Christmas cards. Every few weeks, Naomi would call and check on them. The conversations were brief and shallow, if they answered her call at all.

"Hey, where'd you go?" Rhebekka touched her cheek.

"Sorry, sometimes when I think about your parents, it makes me think about mine."

"They didn't care for me from the minute they met me."

Naomi kissed her. "They couldn't see beyond the rock star to the amazing woman I knew. Totally their loss."

"At least, by the time they met me, I'd straightened up considerably. Can you imagine if they'd met me when I stumbled into your church with that massive hangover?"

They turned at the sound of yawning and watched Lucian walk down the hall, JJ and Marley on his barefoot heels. He was dressed in a pair of Rhebekka's sweatpants and an oversized red-flannel shirt.

"Good morning, sleepyhead. Can I get you some breakfast?" Naomi rose and headed to the kitchen.

With another yawn, Lucian pushed his wet hair behind his ears and said a mumbled good morning. "You don't have to fix me anything. I'm good with cereal if you have it."

Naomi smiled and pointed to Rhebekka. "I'm fixing eggs and bacon for that one. If you'd rather have cereal, that's okay too."

She watched him shift back and forth on his feet.

He quirked a smile. "If you're already making some."

"I am. Do you drink coffee, or do you prefer juice?" Naomi pulled out the pancake fixings as Rhebekka grabbed the cast iron skillet from the rack hanging above the stove.

"Coffee, please, lots of sugar and milk." He took a seat at the bar.

Rhebekka passed him a cup of coffee and moved the milk and sugar near him. "Sorry for keeping you up so late."

Lucian sat up, alarm on his face. "You didn't, honest. After we jammed, I was dead to the world. I can't tell you the last time I slept that hard."

Rhebekka nodded. "There's something about letting it all go in every chord that is better than any sleep aid I've ever tried."

"I never slept soundly at the shelter, especially not after what happened." Lucian poured milk over the mound of sugar he'd put in his coffee and stirred.

Naomi could feel her blood boiling as she stirred the pancake batter. No child should ever fear they will be sexually assaulted in their bed. Chance had promised them there would be a full investigation.

The State of West Virginia had once run the shelter home. In what was presented as an increased access to adoption paths, a nationwide company had bid to oversee several of the children's homes. To Naomi, it seemed more like a cost-cutting measure and a shift away from liability. *Out of sight, out of mind.* She laid slices of bacon on the skillet and listened as Rhebekka and Lucian conversed back and forth about music. Her wife sounded as excited as Lucian did. They drifted from favorite styles into the best guitar solos.

Lucian accepted a plate from Naomi and gave it an appreciative sniff. "Thanks for this."

Naomi looked at him and placed one of her hands over his. "You're welcome. Whether it's a simple meal to sustain you or something more, trust that we will always do everything we can to keep you safe and happy."

"I wish I could say the same thing about something I'd cook for you, but it might do the opposite." Rhebekka squinted at him. "So instead, I'll just tell you that our home is your home. I'll do all I can to make your life better than it's been in a very long time. I hope you'll trust me to do that, and I'll trust you to stick around. Deal?"

Lucian's eyes were glassy with tears he struggled to hold back. He cleared his throat. "Deal on one condition."

Rhebekka turned her head sideways. "Conditions? There really is a teenager in there. Okay, let's discuss conditions." She put her hand flat on the counter.

He sat a little straighter and turned to Naomi. "I'll let you feed me, if you promise to let me do cleanup for you. I'll let you do my laundry, if you assign me some chores."

Naomi quirked a smile and nodded. "Okay, deal."

He turned to Rhebekka. "I'll stay if you let me help you somehow. I don't care if it's cleaning the church or shoveling the sidewalks and steps. I'll stay if you promise to keep playing music with me."

Rhebekka rubbed her hand across her chin and folded her arms across her chest. She looked at Naomi. "Think I'm getting a good deal here?"

Naomi raised an eyebrow. "Sounds promising, though I'll add one more condition." She looked directly at Lucian. "We figure out a way for you to graduate. You have to have a high school education, at the very least. After that, you have time to explore what you might want to do, whether college or trade school."

Lucian dropped his head a bit. "I'm not going back where I was before. I'll pack my bags now if that's a deal breaker."

Naomi came around the island and lifted his chin in her hand. "Lucian, look at me." When his eyes met hers, she continued. "No, you do not have to go back where you were. There are options we can look into. That's why I said we figure out a way for you to graduate. I wouldn't put you through hell for anything. You've already been there and bought the T-shirt with singe marks."

He wiped at a tear. "I'm sorry."

"Education is important. As a former teacher, I had many promising young people pass through my life. Some of them came from the worst living arrangements anyone could imagine. Kids were sleeping in cars and eating out of restaurant garbage cans. I watched the desperation in their eyes as to where they'd get the basic supplies for school, a warm coat for the coming winter, or food for their siblings. A good portion of my meager salary ensured that no one who walked into my classroom had a growling stomach."

He angrily wiped at flowing tears that wouldn't seem to stop.

She continued. "Hey, it's okay. I don't tell you this to make you feel bad. I tell you because there is a happy ending for many of them. I worked with them to get scholarships and grants. I haven't forgotten how to do that. There isn't anything Rhebekka and I won't do to make sure the rest of your life is easier than the first eighteen years have been. You have a family now, if you want to be a part of it." She cupped his cheek. "So, Lucian Altovice, will you trust us enough to know we accept you as you are and promise us to stick around long enough to see who you will become?" She held out her hand and waited.

He ran the sleeve of his shirt across his face, then held out a trembling hand. In a small voice, he sealed their pact with a hand that slid into hers. "Deal."

Naomi hugged him, then reached back and pulled Rhebekka into their embrace.

Rhebekka wrapped them both up. "We're a package deal from now on. No running away, and when something hurts, we heal it together."

Naomi's eyes met Rhebekka's. *Oh, how I love you.* The love shining back was as much of a solid promise as Lucian's pact with her. They would stand beside Lucian for all the things that were to come. Whatever battles lay ahead, he'd face them with two people who were completely on his side.

* * * *

Rhebekka balanced a tray of large coffees in one hand as she opened the door of the Land Cruiser with the other. Unfortunately, there was no key fob to open the locks, and the coffees jostled in the tray as she slid the key into the lock. "Shit!"

Hands steadied the tray and prevented the cups from ending on the ground.

"Easy there." Taylor Lewis clasped the tray and smiled at Rhebekka.

"Thanks for rescuing those. My sister would have cried. I might have too, since I asked for them to be extra hot."

"Happy to be of service."

Freed of the coffees, Rhebekka greeted the K9 at Taylor's side "Good morning, Midas." She turned her attention back to Taylor. "How's the rest of the family?"

Taylor's face lit up at the mention of her family. "Everyone's good. Jace got way too many toys, as expected, but in the end, he enjoyed the box his riding toy came in as much as he did the tiny Jeep."

Rhebekka laughed. "Typical. Any time you need a babysitter, don't hesitate to call on us. That little guy is fun to be around."

"We will definitely take you up on that. As much as I love him, there are times I need an hour to finish a project. That tiny human has learned to say 'momma up,' which tends to throw a wrench into the plans."

"You know our number. Use it."

Taylor nodded and patted the phone on her side. "I have you on speed dial. Good to see you. I'm headed to Karmen's for a sandwich ring. We've got an in-service for our department, and it always goes better if we feed them."

"What's the old saying? Feed them, and they will come?"

"Something like that. Tell Naomi hi for me, will you?"

Rhebekka got the door opened and took the tray from Taylor. "I will definitely do that. Be safe."

Taylor waved as she and Midas walked away. "Always, you do the same."

Rhebekka climbed inside and placed the tray on the floor before buckling her seatbelt and starting the vehicle. She checked her mirrors and saw nothing coming on the snow-covered streets. *Naomi would love to play with Jace. Who am I kidding? I love playing with him.* She drove to the stand-alone building in Davis that Ellie and Siobhan had purchased. It afforded them a small production studio downstairs and a renovated living space above it. There was little doubt Ellie's company would soon outgrow the space. She'd never seen Ellie this happy in a relationship. Siobhan gave her the freedom to be who she was without labels, without judgment, and without an eye on her bank account. *Best thing that ever happened to her.*

She stopped at the building and texted Ellie that she was outside. Within a few minutes, her sister climbed in and closed the door behind her.

"Hey, songbird."

Ellie buckled her seatbelt and grabbed one of the coffees. "Hey, back. Where are my cookies?"

Rhebekka put the Land Cruiser in drive and chuckled. "Cookies plural?"

"For this conversation, you'd better get a dozen." The smile left Ellie's face, and she turned her gaze out the side window."

Rhebekka put the vehicle in drive and headed to the deli. After a brief conversation at the counter, she returned to the Toyota with a white bag in her hand. The smell of chocolate and sugar filled the interior.

"Best air freshener ever." Ellie opened the bag and sniffed appreciatively. "As much as I love you, I'm not waiting." She pulled out a saucer-sized cookie and took a huge bite.

Rhebekka suspected Ellie was filling her mouth so she couldn't be compelled to start talking. She planned to drive around, though she avoided the tourist areas. Many that came from East Coast urban areas had little experience driving in snow and tended to overestimate their abilities.

"No one makes those quite like Summer. She's an exceptional baker and a real spitfire."

"Her soup and sandwich combinations are to die for. Siobhan is addicted to her Rueben."

Rhebekka drove on and patiently waited her sister out as she fiddled with the satellite radio and found a station that featured bands with female leads. They sang along as Ann and Nancy Wilson belted out "Who Will You Run To." With every song, their old dynamic came out. Rhebekka began to slide more into the lead, as Ellie's smooth harmonies filled in all the gaps. *She's still so good.*

"I miss those days."

Rhebekka turned slightly to take a quick look at her sister and smiled. Ellie was relaxed, her head resting against the seat. "When we were on stage?"

"Not so much the stage. I mean the days when it was just the two of us driving from place to place when we were trying to break into the business. Life wasn't so complicated. E, S, S, D."

"Eat, sing, sleep, drive. Rinse and repeat." Rhebekka laughed.

"Sometimes the eating thing was a bit iffy. I'm not sure I ever thanked you."

"Thanked me for what? You thanked me every day."

Ellie rolled her head toward Rhebekka. "You know what I mean. I know there were days you didn't eat and told me you did. I know you went without to make sure I had what I needed. You thought I didn't notice, but I did. You always had my back."

"That's what family does."

"Not all of them."

"Yeah, we got the short end of the stick on the parent part, but we had MaMaw and Grandpa."

Ellie reached for her coffee and took a long drink. "I can't imagine how we'd have turned out without them."

Rhebekka continued to drive until she reached Centennial Park. The views were breathtaking. Each hill and valley was clearly delineated with the snow, while the light painted the contours in shadows. They sat sipping their coffees and munching on the cookies. Rhebekka was willing to wait her sister out but was determined to have the truth revealed. They talked about Ellie's work and the bands she was bringing along, before they moved on to Lucian.

"I'm so proud of you for taking Lucian in. It sounds like he's had a tough life."

Rhebekka nodded. "He has, and we didn't know how bad it was. He survived a near attack by other individuals at the shelter."

Ellie went quiet. "Why do others feel they have the right to take what isn't offered?"

Rhebekka's heart stopped in her chest. *How do I answer that question?* "I wish I knew. There is a power dynamic that unscrupulous people take advantage of. They prey on the defenseless for their own benefit, without any consideration of the damage done."

"Sometimes the scars are visible and sometimes not. Sometimes the trauma is buried so deep it has a paralyzing effect that follows you for years to come."

Rhebekka turned to her. "I know you're speaking from experience, little sparrow, and I think it's time we talk about it."

Ellie stared off into the distance. She sighed. "It's hard, Bek."

Rhebekka turned her hand over on the console and opened her fingers. "You won't be alone. We'll face this together, wherever the journey will lead us."

Ellie put her hand in Rhebekka's but continued to stare off into the distance. "I'm sure, by now, you've scoured your memories and figured some things out."

"Was it Carrie's dad?"

Ellie nodded. "He knew how mean daddy was to us, and he used that to get close to me. He was very affectionate, always hugging me. At first, it felt nice. More than once, I had nightmares when I was staying with Carrie. He'd come and get me. We'd sit in his big chair, and he'd hold me. Then it got weird."

"Weird how?"

"He started rubbing my back, and eventually, he'd be rubbing my ass, then other places. I didn't know what to do. He'd put my hand on top of his dick." Ellie described everything he made her do as tears poured down her face.

Rhebekka leaned over and took Ellie into her arms. The console made it uncomfortable, but her sister's emotional pain was far greater. Ellie broke down into sobs, crying into Rhebekka's shoulder. For the next fifteen minutes, Ellie told of the increasing abuse that eventually led to her being raped at the age of twelve, not only by Carrie's father but also by her brother.

Ellie hiccupped through her tears. "They did it to Carrie too. Tom and Dave kept telling us that we couldn't say anything, that it would bring reproach on Jehovah, and that it was our fault for tempting them. Carrie and I knew no one would believe an elder would do anything like that. It happened, Bek. No matter how much they deny it, it happened."

A roaring in her ears warned Rhebekka that her blood pressure was spiking. She could feel the blood pulsing in her temples with every beat of her heart. One of the elders, the highest organizational leader on a congregational level, was a serial pedophile. Apparently, he wasn't the only one. The rage Rhebekka felt was as overwhelming as a flash flood in a canyon. For the first time in her life, Rhebekka thought she might be capable of taking a life. *Give me strength, Lord. I know this isn't your will, and these weren't your servants.*

Ellie pulled back slightly and wiped her eyes. "I think it's why I kept making horrible relationship choices before Siobhan. I don't know what I was trying to prove to myself, but I refused to let that experience define me and take away my ability to connect with someone on a sexual level."

"No one has a right to take anything from you, not then, not now. You don't have to carry this alone."

"I think I just shoved it in a drawer and locked it away. Watching that documentary jerked the drawer open and spilled everything out onto the floor."

"Buddha said that three things cannot long be hidden, the sun, the moon, and the truth."

Ellie scoffed. "There are those in power that do their damn best to hide the truth."

Rhebekka picked up their joined hands and squeezed her sister's fingers. "Then it's our job to shine a light into the darkness so there isn't any place they can hide."

A single tear ran down Ellie's cheek and found its way to her lip. She wiped it away with the neck of her T-shirt. "Did I ever tell you you're my hero?"

Rhebekka smirked. "Are we having a *Beaches* moment?"

"You ass." Ellie snorted and smacked Rhebekka's shoulder.

"But it made you laugh."

"It definitely did. You're the best sister ever, Bek."

"Nah, you sewed that title up years ago. Now, serious question. What do you want to do about what happened?"

Ellie gave her a quizzical look. "What do you mean do about it?"

Rhebekka knew there were many things they could do, given their notoriety and wealth. "What I'm asking is do you want to pursue holding Tom and Dave Broader accountable, or do you want to let it go?"

The younger sister sat back in the seat and stared out the window. For a few long minutes,

Ellie said nothing. When she finally did speak, it was in a soft but clear voice. "If I do nothing, the cycle likely continues, doesn't it?

"It's impossible to know, but with the organization enabling them the way they do, then I'd say the chances are good that one or both are still involved in the sexual abuse of others."

"How do we even start?"

Rhebekka turned to her. "The first thing is that you write down everything you can think of, and I'll enlist the services of our talented Daniel. If they have an online footprint, he'll uncover it, no matter how deep they've buried it. I don't have to explain his special skills."

"No, you don't. So, what happens once we gather the info you're looking for?"

"My next suggestion is we find out whether Carrie is still a practicing Witness and if she's willing to corroborate what happened. Can I assume you witnessed what they did to Carrie and vice versa?"

Ellie nodded.

"You were both minors at the time. That made what they did to you and Carrie statutory rape. We contact the authorities and see if there are any statutes of limitations on the crimes committed. As far as the congregational elders, the fact that you and Carrie suffered this together means they can't deny it based on their own judicial rules from Deuteronomy. 'A matter must be established by the testimony of two or three witnesses.' By their own rules, joint testimony is powerful and biblically binding."

Ellie balled her fist up. "Or just deny us all together like they normally do."

Rhebekka eased her sister's hand open and gently stroked the white knuckles. "If we can convince Carrie to testify, then they are bound by their own internal guidelines to investigate the incident. Let's see if Carrie has a social media account. If so, feel out whether making contact and friending her will be a way to break the ice."

Ellie grew quiet again, staring out at the white expanse. "Damn that documentary. I don't know if I'm strong enough to survive dredging this all up, Bek. I buried this inside myself so I didn't have to feel the guilt and shame ever again."

Rhebekka lowered her voice and forced her sister's gaze back to her own with a gentle tug of her chin. "First of all, you were not, under any circumstances, responsible. There is zero guilt on your part. Secondly, the shame lies with the individuals that took advantage of a young girl who couldn't defend herself. Again, zero responsibility on your part. It takes courage to hold someone accountable. Nothing will take as much courage as this in everything we've done, and I'll be right by your side."

Ellie grabbed the door handle and climbed out of the Land Cruiser. "I need some air. I'm okay. I just need to clear my head. Stay here."

"Ellie, I—"

"Please, Bek. I just need a few minutes." Ellie shut the door and walked near the guard rail surrounding the overlook.

Rhebekka gripped the steering wheel so tightly that her hands ached. The smooth, wooden surface made a squeaking noise. She knew they'd get through this, but it was Ellie that had to decide how they would proceed. Her painful past would have to be revisited, not Rhebekka's. It was Ellie's innocence that had been stolen, not hers. As badly as her blood boiled, she knew that Ellie would have to be the one to sit on the witness stand and face the people who had abused her. Rhebekka knew, from years of ministering, that it was far too common for someone in power to use religion as a weapon of control. In this case, they used it to silence and abuse the victim with impunity. "Lord, keep me from doing something I'll need your forgiveness for."

It was hard not to let hatred consume her for the people who had hurt her sister, Carrie, and anyone else the father and son had preyed on. Rhebekka watched her sister pull her coat tighter around her shoulders against the ever-present breeze and tried to think of something comforting to say. She searched for words of wisdom to offer, but none came to her. Naomi was so much better at the nurturing part. Watching her wife with Lucian, Rhebekka saw a totally different side of the woman she'd married. She'd only glimpsed this protective caregiving by watching her with Ellie.

A few more minutes passed. Ellie raised her face to the sky. It looked as if she was asking for help from a higher power. She turned to the vehicle and nodded once before she got back inside. She stared out the windshield. "I don't know where this will lead, but if I don't speak up, it will only continue."

Rhebekka reached out and pulled Ellie's cold hand into her own. "I agree. Let's get in touch with Daniel and let him get started finding the Broader family, including Carrie. I looked up a group called Silent Lambs. Let's sit down together and contact the administrators. That should give us advice on how to proceed. I'll be with you every step of the way."

"You know Mom will never believe us."

Rhebekka ground her teeth, the squeak making her wince. She could feel the pounding in her temples and the ringing in her ears getting worse. "She couldn't disown us any more than she already has. We all make choices in our lives, Ellie. We'll see if she chooses to let the truth set her free, or if she chooses to stay imprisoned behind the bars of a lie."

They left the overlook in silence. As they headed back to town, they began to hum, then sing "Secure Yourself," their escape anthem. The harmonies they rolled through resonated deeply in Rhebekka. This was how they'd survived. They'd found a harmony and a rhythm together and had used it as a path forward into the lives they now led.

"When will Siobhan be home?"

Ellie's smile crept onto her face. "She's there now. She and the triad were practicing in the studio."

"It's nice to see you so happy, little sparrow."

"She's the best thing in my life. I can't imagine her not being in it now, especially now."

"Siobhan is the rock you can lean on. Let her comfort and protect you. Other than Naomi and myself, there isn't anyone I trust more with your well-being. How about we call your best half to come over to my place? We'll stop by Karmen's, pick up something decadent, and crash with Lucian to watch a movie. He and Naomi should be back soon from shopping."

Ellie slapped her shoulder. "My best half? I thought I was the best half, traitor."

Rhebekka quickly looked at her sister, only to see her squinting and smiling at her. "Just kidding."

"No, you're right. She is the best part of me."

Rhebekka shook her head. "I was kidding about that, but I do know she's perfect for you. Go on, call her."

While Ellie called Siobhan, Rhebekka pulled up in front of Karmen's and got out. Her phone rang with a call from Naomi. She answered it as she walked in the door. "Hey you, perfect timing. I'm picking up some sweets from Karmen's for a movie marathon. What would you two like?"

"You know my favorites. Lucian, do you have any sweets preferences?" Naomi asked.

Rhebekka could hear Lucian mumbling something and Naomi trying to encourage him. "Let me talk to him."

"Hey, Bek." Lucian's voice was small and tentative.

"Hey, bud. How was shopping?"

"Naomi bought way too much. It'll take me forever to pay you guys back."

Rhebekka rubbed her forehead. "Lucian, we talked about this over breakfast. I trust Naomi in all things and hope that you will trust both of us to look after your best interests. So, I need you to trust that it was out of love and concern if she bought something for you. Now, what kind of cookies or pastry would you like? I'm bringing home enough for Ellie and Siobhan to join us, so what will it be?" She waited, knowing this was a small thing, but the emotions behind it were much more significant than something like a cupcake.

"I like anything lemon," Lucian finally said.

"Oh, you and Naomi have more in common than you know. She's a sucker for iced lemon cookies. That's already on my list to get."

"Cool."

"Okay, put Naomi back on for a minute. And Lucian?"

"Yes?"

"See you at home."

Lucian chuckled. "See you at home."

Naomi came back on the phone. "All set?"

"Ellie and Siobhan are joining us. Want me to pick up pizza as well?"

"We must be on the same wavelength, because I already ordered three larges from Sirianni's. They should be ready for pickup in ten minutes. I was going to call and tell you I'd ordered enough for everyone."

"Got it. How much beer is in the fridge?"

"Plenty. There are two unopened growlers. See you when you get here."

"Love you, Naomi. See you at home."

"Love you, too."

Rhebekka hung up and approached the counter, where Zandra stood. "Hey, Z. Karmen roped you into front of the house operations again, huh?"

Zandra took a deep breath and let it out slowly. "It's better for me to be here than back there. I can't cook to save my soul, and I wouldn't know a pinch from a gallon."

"Why do you think Karmen fed me for all those years before Naomi came to save me from my attempts at poisoning myself?"

"She really needs some help. Business is booming, and our one part-timer is graduating from high school and headed off to college. What can I get for you?"

Rhebekka cupped her chin and looked at the display case. "I need a dozen chocolate chip cookies, two dozen raspberry kolachis, a dozen and a half of the lemon-iced cookies, and a death-by-chocolate cake."

Karmen came out of the back room, wiping her hands on her baker's apron that was covered with what appeared to be brightly colored swipes of red, blue, and green icing. "Is there a party at your place that we haven't been invited to?" She walked from behind the counter and kissed Rhebekka's cheek. "Good to see you."

Rhebekka kissed her back. "No party, just a movie marathon. You two are welcome to come, though I don't know what the subject will be. Knowing Ellie and Naomi, it will be a Sandra Bullock romcom."

Karmen giggled. "Those two do have a thing for that woman. Anyway, I'd love to, but we're so short on help here that I'm trying to get a jump on tomorrow's orders. Unfortunately, that sign in the window doesn't seem to be attracting many potential employees."

Rhebekka squinted as her mind whirled a bit. "What are you looking for in an employee?"

Karmen fell heavily onto a stool and sighed. "Someone dependable and willing to show up on time first off. It's pretty hard to find someone who is willing to be at work by five in the morning."

Rhebekka nodded. "Okay, what else?"

Zandra offered her opinion. "Someone who can follow directions and have some people skills. Retail experience would be helpful but not necessary."

Karmen snapped her fingers and pointed to Zandra. "Exactly. It has to be someone who can work independently. I need to be able to show them what to do a few times, then rely on them to do the job."

Rhebekka remained silent for a minute before mentioning their new house guest. "You know that Lucian is staying with us for as long as he wants. He's already said, more than once, that he wants to be as independent as possible. We insist that he finishes high school and explores a trade or college. What if he comes in and applies for the job?" She watched as Karmen looked at Zandra.

Zandra held up her hands. "It's up to you. You need the help, and Lucian needs a job. It sounds like a pretty good fit. He's five minutes away." She smiled at Karmen and pointed to Rhebekka. "He seems to come with good references."

Rhebekka patted her own chest. "That he does. Lucian needs to have a support group and some stability in his life where he has some semblance of control. He needs a place to live, a source of income, and a group of family and friends. Being trans hasn't been easy for him at the children's home. I think this might be just what he needs."

Karmen smoothed down her apron and placed her hands on her hips. "Have him come in and fill out an application. Let him get this on his own. That will allow him independent decision-making and responsibility."

Rhebekka pulled Karmen into a hug. "I know you didn't have it easy growing up. You'll recognize that tough kid grit in him, the same one that made you successful. I love you, Karmen, for much more than keeping me well fed before Naomi. I can never thank you enough."

Karmen hugged her, then held Rhebekka at arm's length. "You took care of me just as much. We're family. Let me get your order packed up. Send him down here."

Rhebekka watched one of her best friends bustle around the store with Zandra, gathering the order. Karmen had waited years for someone who would see the amazing woman she was. Rhebekka thought for a minute about her family of choice and how many of them had found happiness. *God's grace knows no end.*

Chapter Seven

NAOMI SNUGGLED INTO RHEBEKKA'S arms and sighed at the feeling of utter contentment she found there. She'd had a great day with Lucian.

"You seem a million miles away." Rhebekka kissed her forehead.

She lifted her gaze and captured Rhebekka's lips. "No, I'm right here. I'm reliving the day with Lucian. It was so hard for him to let me buy him anything. We didn't buy anything he didn't need."

"He has very little but his dignity. It means a lot to him. I felt the same way when we first left home. I spent every dime I made to buy a car to get Ellie away from our situation. I had to tell my parents I bought it to go out in service while Mom was working. Ellie and I made a plan that would get us away from the hell we were living in. We put everything we had into that chance at independence, and we wouldn't let anyone take that away from us. I imagine Lucian feels something similar."

Naomi kissed her chest. "I'm sure he does."

"I think I might have a solution that will give him some of the independence he craves and keeps his dignity intact."

Naomi leaned back and looked at her. "Do tell."

They lay there, as Rhebekka told her about how overworked Karmen was with no help and the job opportunity.

"All he has to do is go apply."

Naomi thought back to the conversation with Lucian on the ride home. Lucian had earnestly expressed that he didn't want to be a burden to them. He'd even asked if she knew of any jobs he might be able to apply for. "He mentioned taking a walk today to see if anyone was hiring."

"Then maybe instead of pointing him to Karmen's place, we let him discover it on his own. I'll give Karmen a heads-up to watch for him. That way, there is a sense of accomplishing this on his own."

Naomi ran a finger under the hem of Rhebekka's T-shirt, touching soft skin. She smiled at the low groan that escaped. Her wife was so responsive to her touch. Naomi recognized anticipation of her touch with every rise and fall of Rhebekka's chest. She snaked her hand under the T-shirt and found the swell of Rhebekka's breast. "Stay very quiet," Naomi whispered in her ear.

"Mmm," came Rhebekka's muffled response.

The T-shirt had become a barrier to how Naomi wanted to touch Rhebekka. She sat up and removed her own, depositing it off the side of the bed. Rhebekka scrambled to sit up and mirror her actions. They removed anything else they wore that would prevent them from being skin to skin. They were kneeling on the bed, face-to-face. Their mouths crashed together, and Rhebekka wrapped Naomi in her strong arms. They lay back with Naomi on top. Typically, Rhebekka took charge of their lovemaking. Naomi was also aware of how her wife craved to let go.

"I love you so much." Naomi kissed along her jaw, stopping to nip at her earlobe. The action brought the expected reaction, as Rhebekka's body arched into her. She continued her path, intermittently nipping, sucking, and biting until she reached Rhebekka's breasts. The nipples she found were already erect, waiting for her touch. Naomi looked up at Rhebekka, who stared at her with hooded eyes. "What do you want?"

Rhebekka groaned and guided Naomi's head to her breast. "Please?"

Naomi ran a hand across a tight nipple and teased by squeezing it between her fingers. The jerk of Rhebekka's hips was all the encouragement she needed. She leaned down and tasted slightly salty skin. She took the nipple in her mouth. With each suck and nip, Naomi built Rhebekka's arousal. She could smell the heady scent of desire emanating from the woman she loved. Her tongue circled the nipple and felt it grow ever harder. She switched to the other nipple, not wanting any part of Rhebekka to lack her touch. Her hands wandered Rhebekka's hard body, skimming over each rib and settling on a hip bone that wasn't nearly as definable as it had been when they'd reunited. She marveled at the feel of Rhebekka's body under her fingers. "So soft."

"You're killing me."

Naomi kissed down her stomach, over the hollow near the hip bone, and finally nuzzled the soft patch of hair above her target. "You'll die happy. Now quiet."

Naomi kissed down her thigh, giving equal attention to every sensitive spot she'd discovered in their time together. Her fingers sifted through the damp curls at the juncture of Rhebekka's thighs. The smell of her lover's need was strong and drew her in like an oasis in the desert. Nothing in the world turned her on like making love to Rhebekka. She was aware of her own wetness and the tightening of her center. Touching Rhebekka, tasting Rhebekka, was an aphrodisiac like no other.

Rhebekka fisted handfuls of the sheets, her body trembling with desire. The whispered plea came softly but urgently. "I need you."

Naomi didn't waste another second before she moved Rhebekka's legs farther apart and settled between them. She looked up at Rhebekka with all the raw passion she could express. "And I need you." She dipped her head and buried her face in the liquid silk she knew would be waiting for her. The heat of Rhebekka's need did her in as she inhaled deeply, then swallowed the ambrosia that flowed across her tongue.

Rhebekka opened and closed her fists on the sheets and bucked at every touch of Naomi's tongue. She reached down, seeming to frantically search for connection.

Naomi threaded her fingers through Rhebekka's as she lapped at her clit, circling it with her tongue, then delving in. There was a bond between them that had only grown stronger. She increased her attentions and locked eyes with Rhebekka as she pulled her clit into her lips and sucked. She ached to make her lover climax. Rhebekka's body began to shudder and buck, making it difficult to keep Rhebekka's eyes in view. Once again, Naomi found the connection and tightened her grip on Rhebekka's fingers. With one steely glance, she issued her silent command for Rhebekka to come. The order was obeyed with a stiffening of Rhebekka's body, as she bowed up off the bed. Naomi struggled to stay with her and keep the strokes of her tongue rhythmic and on target. As Naomi's mouth flooded with the evidence of Rhebekka's climax, she shifted until Rhebekka's leg was between her own. She clenched her center tightly against the connection she found and followed Rhebekka over the edge. It might have been seconds, minutes, or hours. Naomi had no idea. They rode the wave of their shared silent pleasure until only slight aftershocks remained.

Rhebekka pulled on Naomi's hands until they lay skin to skin, their chests heaving, their bodies damp with sweat. They lay quiet for a long time. Rhebekka kissed Naomi's forehead. "I love you."

Naomi looked up and kissed her. "I love you too. Go to sleep." She felt Rhebekka mumble something she could barely understand. She glanced at the clock and understood. *Yes love, two is better than four.*

* * * *

Rhebekka stretched and enjoyed the languid feeling that still thrummed through her body from last night's intimacy. She immediately recognized Naomi was not in bed with her and rolled over and folded her hands behind her head on the pillow. *Five bucks says she's making breakfast.* She could smell coffee and looked over at the clock. It was seven in the morning, and she had little doubt that Naomi was in the kitchen staring into the refrigerator. Her wife was an early riser, unlike her sister Ellie had been all those years ago.

Since she and Ellie struck out on their own, she'd always risen around the same time, even with the late-night tour schedule. She'd fall asleep around four and wake no more than four hours later unless she'd been on a bender. Sometimes she caught a nap during the day, but her system was accustomed to the routine. With Lucian in the house, last night's lovemaking had been different but no less intense. The connection she and Naomi shared proved that words sometimes weren't needed. Even without the passionate declarations, her orgasm had been all-consuming.

She rose and grabbed her crutches before entering the bathroom and turning on the shower. She still smelled like sex, and that wasn't something she wanted to embarrass Lucian or herself over. The floor glistened as she hopped in and turned on the water, grateful they'd installed a small bench for her to stabilize her remaining limb on. She was more thankful for the instant hot water system. *I guess Naomi felt a shower was necessary too.* She soaped up, feeling the tenderness in her nipples from last night's activities. It made her smile, remembering the command to stay quiet. She poured shampoo into her hand before vigorously scrubbing her hair. She watched the soap run down her arm and across the realistic tattoo of a guitar bursting from her forearm. *I need to remember to call Roman's.* Naomi held the towel she sought. "Peeping Tomasetti." Rhebekka watched her wife drink in the entire length of her body before holding out the towel.

Naomi leaned against the bathroom door frame and grinned. "You're like a walking art gallery. I always see some new detail. Can I help that I'm a big fan of Roman's artistry?"

Rhebekka toweled off before hopping out of the shower and draping the terrycloth across her shoulders. "Look all you want. You bought the lifetime ticket to the exhibit."

Naomi stepped forward and kissed her. "Good morning." She reached out and grabbed the mug on the vanity. "Thought you could use this."

Rhebekka took it, kissed her cheek, then sipped greedily. She leaned against the marble vanity and eyed Naomi. "You are an angel."

"Or the devil, depending on what time of day it is."

"Definitely an angel of mercy, either way."

Rhebekka sipped the coffee before handing the cup back to Naomi and making her way back to the bed with her crutches. Naomi followed and gave her the tightly fitting sleeve that covered her residual limb. Naomi threw jeans and a T-shirt at her before leaning down and kissing her.

Rhebekka drew her in and tumbled them both back onto the bed. "I love you."

Naomi settled between her legs and drew a finger down Rhebekka's cheek. "The feeling is very mutual."

"Lucian up?" She kissed Naomi's chin and then nibbled down her neck.

Naomi pushed up on her palms and looked down at Rhebekka. "Behave, and yes. He's fixing us breakfast."

Rhebekka squinted at her. "Can he cook?"

Naomi chuckled and stood. "I think he can manage scrambled eggs and toast. He offered, and as you said, his dignity is important to him. I know you'll put ketchup on them no matter how they taste."

Rhebekka threw her shirt at Naomi. "Smart ass." She put on the rest of her clothes and locked her prosthesis into place. She stood and took Naomi into her arms. "Let's play it by ear this morning about mentioning Karmen's job opportunity. If he asks, we'll tell him some places to go. If he doesn't, we'll let him wander down the street and find it."

Naomi nodded. "Christmas break will soon be over, and we'll need to figure out what he's going to do about school. I did a little research this morning, but I want to call the board of education and see if they offer a remote learning program to allow him to finish out."

"That would be perfect. I seriously doubt he cares much about the pomp and circumstance of graduation, but if he wants to attend, we'll make that happen. I'm sure Chance will also call today about the sexual assault case. The people that hurt him have to face justice."

Naomi melted deeper into Rhebekka. "That's going to be a tough thing for him to face. I can see unrest in him, something deep and dark. I can't tell yet if it's pain or anger."

"Both, I'd say. I think he needs to talk to Siobhan." Rhebekka rested her cheek on the top of Naomi's head.

"You think Siobhan will be okay with opening up to him?"

"I think it's one of the things that's helped Ellie deal with what happened when she was young."

Naomi sighed. "What's your plan forward with bringing the elders to justice?"

"That's another coffee can of razors I'm trying to climb out of. There's a group called Silent Lambs I've been chatting with. They've been helping former Witnesses hold the organizational leaders accountable for years. I hate this for her, but like Lucian, Ellie needs to see justice before there can be true healing."

"Let's hope the outcomes are slightly different than how Siobhan got justice."

"It scares me to think we might never have known her."

Naomi kissed her chin. "Enough of these thoughts. Let's go eat breakfast. At the very least, I need another cup of coffee before we save the world."

Rhebekka put an arm around Naomi's shoulders as they walked. She would shed light on what others wanted to keep hidden in blue envelopes and incidents that went unreported out of fear. A verse from John popped into her head. *'Everyone who does evil hates the light...'* *Time to shine a little light on what far too many want to keep hidden.*

* * * *

Rhebekka chuckled as she watched Lucian shovel the last bite into his mouth. He grabbed his dishes and theirs before taking them all to the sink and loading the dishwasher, then turned to look at them.

"I'm going to walk around town and check the job openings. Maybe I can find something close, so transportation won't be an issue. Maybe I could go a little farther if I had a bicycle."

"Marvin is downstairs on the peg. You're welcome to use it whenever you'd like. There's a spare helmet there as well." Rhebekka sipped her coffee.

Lucian cocked his head and squinted. "Marvin?"

Naomi laughed. "That lime green monstrosity at the bottom of the steps."

"The Salsa Mukluk fat bike? That thing is wicked."

"Marvin and I have traveled many miles together." Rhebekka tapped her leg. "I don't ride as much as I used to. My therapist said I'd need a different prosthesis, because the ankle movement necessary is different than walking."

"If you ever do, maybe we can ride together," Lucian said with a hopeful look.

Naomi put her hand on Rhebekka's shoulder. "I think that's a great idea. We could go hit the trail as a family this year."

Lucian's smile was all the incentive Rhebekka needed. "I'll check with the doc and see what it will require. We have some of the best trails anywhere up here."

Lucian clapped his hands and looked at the clock. It was just after nine. "Well, wish me luck."

Naomi hugged him. "I'll do that and say a little prayer too."

Lucian blushed. "I can use all the help I can get."

Naomi put a hand on his shoulder. "Do you have your phone with you?"

He patted his pocket. "Yup. I know, call if I need anything. I got it." He walked to the door and grabbed his coat off the hook.

Naomi came back to Rhebekka's side and slid under her arm. Lucian turned to look at them. "I wish I could say thank you a thousand times, and it wouldn't be half enough to tell you how much I appreciate everything you two are doing for me. It's nice to be part of a family again. I haven't had that since I was twelve. It's strange, but in a really good way." He ducked out the door.

They listened to his quick steps down the stairs and the sound of the door closing. Rhebekka turned Naomi in her arms. "How'd you get him to accept a phone?"

"I made a deal with him. I promised I wouldn't constantly try to keep close tabs on him if he checked in regularly on the phone. I explained what happened to you and how terrified I was that I couldn't reach you. I think it made an impact, but the proof will be if he calls in. Do you have your sermon ready for tomorrow?"

Rhebekka nodded. "I want to make sure I give him a personal invitation. This week, we start back to our youth group after the Christmas break. I will make some calls and give the kids a heads-up in case Lucian wants to join them. I think he'll get a kick out of ArchAngel. I tailored my sermon around compassion and instances where compassion was shown even when it was frowned on."

Rhebekka let Naomi slip from her arms and grabbed her guitar. She strummed as she watched Naomi go to the kitchen and begin to pull items from the pantry. *How did I ever survive without her in my life?* Her mind swirled around Christ and how he treated people, both Jews and Gentiles. She thought about the story of the woman at the well, the healed lepers, and even the compassion shown to those hung on the cross alongside Christ. All were shown extraordinary grace. *What a world it would be if those who professed to follow those teachings actually did so with their actions more than their words.*

* * * *

As the pastor of a non-denominational church, Rhebekka had no governing body, bishop, or supervisor. This allowed her to welcome any and all to House of the Rising Son. Rhebekka answered to no general assembly or synod about who attended her services or what she shared with the congregation. She did have a board, elected by the congregation, to advise her. Sydney Parker, Kristi Ryker, Franklin Middleton, and Tom Roland made up the donation committee of that board. The group was meeting to set the intention for the year's first quarter donations. They met in the sanctuary to consider donation requests and congregational suggestions.

"You all have been trusted with my true identity and how I fund House of the Rising Son with my income from that career. Today, we meet to determine where our funds will go. I'm open to suggestions."

The group sat around in the sanctuary. As usual, Rhebekka had a guitar in her hands. She strummed through various hymns, never settling on just one, but combining several into something she planned on playing at Sunday's service. It helped her think, and her group enjoyed it.

Sydney raised a finger. "I know this is a little self-indulgent, but could we do something for veterans? A group I work with helps female veterans. Some don't qualify for VA assistance for one reason or another. My friend, Barbara Nice, is on the board, and they always need funds. This group helps with homelessness and unemployment. They also try and offer services to deal with the mental health aspects. Some women have suffered military, sexual trauma, while others suffer PTSD."

Tom Roland sat up straight and nodded. "I'm a veteran myself, and I can say that there will never be enough we can do for those who took the oath to defend freedom. Women serving in my day were often treated terribly. I have no doubt it's never gotten better."

Sydney took a deep breath. "I make no secret that after my injury on my last deployment, I've never been the same. There are some things we can't forget and things we pray we will always remember. Maybe we can research other veteran's groups to consider as well for our future choices. Does anyone have objections to our first quarter donations going to A Promise Kept?"

The group shook their heads and voted to send the donations to the group. Rhebekka thought about Kierlynn and made a mental note to introduce Sydney to her.

Rhebekka watched them climb into their cars, then smiled at Lucian walking down the street. She held the door for him. "Well, how goes the hunt?"

Lucian's face lit up. "I got a job! Three days a week at the place we had those awesome cookies from the other day."

"Karmen's?"

"Yeah. She hired me on the spot. She said she's really needed someone for a while, and with my retail experience, she thought I'd be a good fit."

Rhebekka rubbed her hands together. "Is she going to pay you in cookies?"

Lucian chuckled. "No, but she did say I could deliver whatever you ordered. I start at five on Monday morning."

She stopped and put her hands on Lucian's shoulders. "I'm proud of you. How would you like to jam up at Redemption's Road with Naomi and me tonight?"

"Really?"

"Really. I'm the house entertainment several times a month. Sometimes I can get Naomi to play with me, but mostly I'm solo. If you can handle some bass, I think the audience would enjoy it. You can meet my friend, Tank, and her sister, Kierlynn."

They walked up the steps, and Rhebekka smiled when Lucian ran to tell Naomi the news. Naomi thanked him for calling in and congratulated him on his new job. Rhebekka sat on a stool and watched as Naomi's eyes danced at Lucian's excitement. Her wife was a beautiful soul and a natural giver.

Lucian washed his hands and gathered bowls as Naomi cut thick slices of bread she had pulled from the oven. The kitchen smelled of potato soup and homemade bread.

"Bek said I could come and jam with you two tonight."

Naomi turned to Rhebekka and smiled. "She did, did she?"

Lucian nodded.

Naomi filled a large bowl for Rhebekka and set it in front of her. "Then I say we'd better get in a little practice this afternoon." She put a second bowl on the bar for Lucian.

Rhebekka bowed and prayed before she spooned up a bite and moaned at the cheese and bacon flavor. "This is so good. You put even more bacon in it this time."

"I listen to requests, and who doesn't like more bacon?" Naomi spooned up some soup, dragging it across the edge of her bowl before eating it. She pointed to her bowl. "Not too shabby."

Lucian chewed a big bite of bread, chewed quickly, and swallowed. "Between working in the bakery and your cooking, I'm going to put on ten pounds."

Naomi pointed her spoon at him. "You could do with a little more meat on your bones. A good wind might carry you off."

The three of them bantered back and forth until the meal was completed and the dishes washed up. They headed to the sound booth and grabbed an instrument of choice. The black Fender bass Lucian played when they jammed down in the sanctuary looked good in his hands as he swung the strap over his neck. Rhebekka grabbed her grandfather's guitar and ran through her tuning routine. Naomi was the calmest of the three sliding her Fender into place.

"What are we going to play?" Lucian ran his hands over the frets, bouncing with nervous energy.

Rhebekka winked at Naomi, who broke into Heart's "Barracuda" without hesitation. The next two hours found the three of them jamming to anything that came to mind. Lucian easily followed along with his own unique bass tones.

Naomi moved to the keyboard and began to sing Brandi Carlile's, "The Joke." Rhebekka noticed Lucian watching while Naomi played and sang about ignoring all the negativity from others. The three people in the room understood how much rejection hurt. Two of them knew it was possible to get beyond it and find true happiness. Together, she and Naomi would ensure Lucian had someone to guide him as he found his place and path. Offering refuge in a storm was something intrinsic to their faith. Naomi plowed through the chorus and hit the big note as Rhebekka and Lucian played on. It might not have been the most significant concert she'd ever played, but it was one of the most satisfying.

* * * *

The ski resorts were in full swing, and Redemption's Road was the place to be after a day on the slopes. Rhebekka sat at the bar while Naomi introduced Lucian to a few people they knew. Many in the crowd were tourists interspersed with regulars and locals. The Confluence was the biggest indoor music venue in the area. The three of them had already done one set, and she was enjoying the way Lucian basked in the attention. There were always jerks in the crowd, but the fact he was in Naomi's capable presence seemed to ground the young man.

"Hey, Tank. Good crowd tonight." She clasped Tank's hand and met her firm grip.

Tank sat a mason jar in front of her and looked around. "Yeah. The snow has been good, and that's good for all the businesses. Thank God for Kierlynn. She's been phenomenal help here. She's even interested in becoming an assistant brewmaster. I figured I'd talk with you about it tomorrow after the service."

Rhebekka looked over to see Kierlynn gathering up jars from the bar top and filling customer orders. "She looks pretty comfortable behind the bar. You know you have my permission to hire as you need it. If you think she's looking to stick around, hire her full-time and teach her to brew. My life seems to be getting a bit busier every day." She turned round to see where Lucian and Naomi had disappeared to just as a rowdy group of tourists entered and grabbed an empty table. Lucian came through the door from The Confluence and walked over to Rhebekka. One of the men watched him, leaned over to his buddy, and pointed.

Rhebekka turned back to the bar. "Tank, we might want to watch this group."

"Already ahead of you, boss. Hey, Lucian. Would you like a soda or anything?"

Lucian shoved his hands deep into his pockets. "How long before we do another set?"

Rhebekka looked at her watch. "Another ten minutes or so. You okay?"

He put his head down. "Yeah, I feel better when I have a guitar in my hands. I'll take a Coke if you have one, Tank. Thanks."

Rhebekka thought about the meaning behind what Lucian said. It felt like he used the guitar as a shield between him and the world, something he could hide behind, something others could focus on beyond the individual with their fingers on the strings. She smiled at him. "I'm glad you came with us tonight."

The door to the bar opened and Harley Kincaid stepped in. She held it open for her daughters, Megan and Lindsey. It was rare to see the three of them out for an evening, but Rhebekka smiled when Megan held Lindsey's hand. Redemption's Road wasn't billed as an LGTBQIA+ bar, primarily. It was merely a safe space that accepted all, as long as respect was shown.

"Hey, Rhebekka. Good to see you, Tank. Looks like the place is hopping tonight." Harley stepped up to the coppertop bar and pulled out her wallet. She watched as Megan and Lindsey made their way through the crowd and settled at a table.

"Harley, nice to see you out and about with the girls. We're honored." Rhebekka held out her hand for Harley to shake.

"It's a rarity for all of us to be off at the same time, but it's Megan's birthday, and Lindsey is still on Christmas break from school. Good to see you. Hey, Tank, can I have a Sprite and two Savior's Reds?"

Tank pointed at her and turned to the taps. "Coming right up."

"We'll be back on stage in a few minutes. Do Megan and Lindsey have a special song?" Rhebekka jerked her thumb in the young couple's direction.

Harley seemed to ponder the question. "They danced to "I Choose You" at their wedding."

"Sara Bareilles?" Rhebekka sipped her beer.

"I'm not good with knowing who sings what. I just remember there is a line about telling the world they got it right." Harley paid for her drinks.

Lucian smiled. "That's definitely the song."

Rhebekka put her hand on Lucian's shoulder. "Harley, this is Lucian Altovice. He's the newest member of our family and one hell of a bass player."

Harley shook Lucian's hand. "Nice to meet you, Lucian. You couldn't be in better company than the reverend here."

"I agree." Lucian's smile was timid but present.

Rhebekka looked at her watch. "We'd better make our way back to the stage."

A prickling feeling crawled up her neck. The pull was overwhelming as she turned her head toward the crowd, her eyes instinctively looking for Naomi. One of the men from the group they were concerned about was leaning heavily on his hands, using his height and hands to trap Naomi against the wall. Naomi's eyes hardened as she planted her hands on her hips. Rhebekka tapped the bar top to get Tank's attention and jumped up from her sawhorse.

Tank stiffened as she trained her eyes on the area Rhebekka indicated. "You want me to take care of it?"

Rhebekka shook her head. Naomi was a capable woman who'd taken some Krav Maga self-defense classes from Sarah Ryker with Jax, Lindsey, and several other women in the community. She was not someone to be messed with.

The next few seconds seemed to happen in slow motion as the man slid his hands down the wall and grabbed Naomi's arms. The instant he clasped Naomi's biceps, she stiffened.

There was a roaring sound in Rhebekka's head. She lunged forward but was still ten feet away when Naomi swung her arm from her hip straight into his groin. The man doubled over but still held on. Naomi used a secondary move landing an opened-handed palm to his nose.

"Back off!" Naomi's shout pierced the room.

Rhebekka made it to Naomi's side at a run, sliding between her wife and the man lying on the ground holding his nose and groin. Naomi's hands were up, her stance wide. Rhebekka put a hand behind her against Naomi's abdomen. "I'm here. You're okay."

Tank had her knee on the man's chest and a phone in her hand as the rest of the man's friends rose in a feeble attempt to come to his aid.

Siobhan quickly joined Tank and pinned the man's legs with her knee as he struggled. "What the fuck do ya think yer doing, ya gobshite? Yer lucky she didn't kill ya. Lay still."

Harley, Megan, and Kierlynn moved between Rhebekka and the table of men.

"I'd sit down unless you want to suffer the same fate. I'm Sergeant Harley Kincaid, and this is Trooper Megan Kincaid of the West Virginia State Police. There are other officers on the way to this location. Unless you'd like to join him in the jail cell with an ice bag between your legs, I suggest you stay out of it."

The three men slowly sat down and stared at their friend lying on the floor. Rhebekka turned to see Lucian at her side as well. She turned and pulled Naomi into her arms. "Are you alright?"

Naomi trembled against her chest. "I am now."

Rhebekka kissed her forehead. "I'm right here. You're safe now. What happened?"

"I was visiting with a few tables around the room and this guy offered to buy me a drink over in The Confluence. I refused. He cornered me when I came back through the door to find you for the set. Told me he hated to see a pretty lady by herself and that he'd like to get to know me. He then described in detail how he planned to do that. I told him I was married and pointed you out at the bar. That's when he started pouring it on, telling me he could change it with one kiss. Then he put his hands on me. I'd had enough." Naomi wiped at a few tears.

Rhebekka turned her head as the door clattered open and Daniel Ryker walked in with his K9 at attention. A trooper with him addressed Harley immediately.

"Sarge, looks like you've got things under control. What do you need from us?" Daniel rested one hand on his gun and the other on his radio.

"That seems to be the case. First, you'll need to take a statement from the victim, Naomi Deklan, and determine if she wants to press charges." Harley rubbed a hand across her chin.

The man on the floor groaned and tried to sit up. "What about me pressing charges against the bitch for breaking my nose?"

Rhebekka knelt down and rested an arm on her knee as she looked the man in the eye. "The woman you just referred to as a bitch is my wife. I watched you put your hands on her. She repeatedly told you she wasn't interested in your offer. She felt threatened and defended herself." She stood and waved an arm around the room. "You're from out of town in a local bar with plenty of witnesses who will gladly give a statement about what you said and did."

The man sighed. "I'm sorry."

Rhebekka cupped her hand to her ear. "What was that you said? I couldn't quite hear you."

The man groaned as he was helped to his feet by Daniel and the trooper. "I said I'm sorry for offending her. It won't happen again."

Tank stepped forward. "You're damn right it won't because you and your group are banned from these premises permanently. If my staff or I ever see you in here again, you will be arrested for trespassing." She turned to his table of friends. "Do I make myself clear?"

The men nodded. Daniel stepped toward Naomi.

"Do you want to press charges, Mrs. Deklan?"

Rhebekka interlocked her fingers with Naomi's. "It's completely up to you, honey."

Naomi took a shaky breath. "If he agrees never to come back, then I won't file charges."

"Are you sure?" Harley asked.

Naomi stepped closer to Rhebekka. "I am. They need to leave now. We have a set left to do and an audience that came out to hear some music."

Daniel tipped his hat and turned to the table. "You heard the lady. It's time for you all to go. Let's step outside, and I'll get your information before we send you on your way."

The three other men grabbed their coats and helped their limping friend out the door.

Rhebekka watched them go, then drew Naomi into her arms. "Are you sure you're okay?"

Naomi grasped at Rhebekka's back and spoke softly into her neck. "I am. We need to keep an eye on Lucian. This is going to stir things up with him." Naomi turned to him. "Come on, Lucian. We have a set to play and people that want to be entertained by something other than barroom drama."

Lucian looked to Rhebekka, then back to Naomi. "Are you sure?"

Naomi straightened and reached for Lucian's hand. "Definitely. Come on."

The three of them took the stage and picked up their guitars. Rhebekka took a deep breath and leaned into the mic. "Well, folks. We've had a different kind of excitement tonight. Here at Redemption's Road, we do our best to make sure everyone is welcome. The color of your skin, your gender, where you're from, the God you pray to, or who you choose to love doesn't mean a damn thing to any of us. So, respect the person and their pronouns to the right, left, in front of, and behind you. If we all did that, the world would be a better damn place. So let's lighten the mood a bit. There's a song by The Highwomen that seems appropriate. This song is called *If She Ever Leaves Me*."

That crowd clapped and whooped, bringing a smile to Naomi's face. She leaned into the mic. "There are only a few things that don't fit with me about the most perfect lesbian country song." She held up one finger. "I do have tattoos." She indicated the tattoo under her wedding band, then held up a second finger. "And it took me far too long to get her to marry me to ever think about leaving her." She turned to Lucian and started the count. "One, two, three."

Rhebekka started the song's melody, then rolled into the lyrics. She loved the punch line to the title and sang it with gusto. She looked directly at Naomi, who added the harmony with the same amount of enthusiasm. It wasn't that she was making light of what happened in the bar. Far from it. She needed to state that everyone's choices should be respected.

Megan and Lindsey took the dance floor beside Ellie and Siobhan. Lucian was happily thumbing out the bass line. Rhebekka was sure there would need to be a conversation with the young man about what happened. *Plenty of time to talk. For now, we'll let it go in the music.*

Chapter Eight

SUNDAY MORNING, RHEBEKKA PACED the stage and smiled at the background music Naomi provided to her sermon. This particular Sunday was Epiphany, the day when Christ was revealed as fully human and fully God through the visit of three gentile kings from the East. "The Magi followed the star and were greeted with a physical manifestation of a promise to unite the entire world, not just the Jewish people. This was the day you and I became part of the bigger picture, the grander plan of a loving God."

She turned to look at her congregation of friends and family. These precious souls were children of God, exactly as they were. Lucian stood in the back, his head slightly down. Her heart ached for him as he struggled to believe he was worthy. She and her sister had felt the same at a very different time in their lives.

"The God I believe in created each and every one of us. No matter what we look like or what we seem to be to someone else, God knows our hearts. We were the most beautiful part of the grand plan, created in God's image. To believe that a loving God doesn't want a perfectly crafted creation to be happy makes no sense to me."

She began to sing a song she'd written for Naomi after meeting her. The first verse spoke of a tiny flicker of light shone into the darkness. That flicker grew into a flame, as each person joined their own light with that of another until the light shined so brightly that there was no more darkness. Her congregation knew the song well. It fit the moment. When the verse ended, she sat down on the edge of the stage and strummed her guitar. Her congregation had grown in size, but they still appreciated the shorter format followed by the open forum to ask questions.

"Okay, folks. What burning subjects would you like to talk about today?" Naomi came to the edge of the stage and sat down beside her. Rhebekka strummed *We Three Kings* in keeping with the Epiphany theme.

The congregation often commented on how being able to freely seek guidance from someone who was as much friend as pastor made them feel equal and included. Rhebekka smiled as Hunter came and sat down between her and Rhebekka. He placed his hand on the backside of her guitar and smiled. He could feel the music more than he could hear it. That thought made Rhebekka's heart swell. She looked out at Chance and Jax, who sat close together, holding hands.

There were whispers, as everyone settled in. Finally, Penny spoke up. "Pastor, can you speak about grace?"

Penny's topic was one very close to Rhebekka's heart. It was something you couldn't buy or win. "Grace is forgiveness of our sins, freely given, and not earned by our own works. If grace could be earned on our own, we wouldn't have needed Christ's sacrifice. No matter how much good we do in the world, it's only through that supreme gift that our passage into heaven is guaranteed. We are imperfect and sinful people. Our tab was paid for by someone free of sin. Grace is the love of God given to us without any if, and, or but type of conditions. We would never be worthy of it on our own, but I'm grateful every day it's afforded to me. In turn, we should show grace to those around us, help those in need, and love one another as we have been loved. There is no greater grace than to be compassionate people following Christ's example."

Laura raised her hand. "Does that mean people shouldn't be held accountable for their actions?"

Rhebekka shook her head. "No, grace doesn't mean someone can do whatever they want without consequences. I'm just not of the belief that a loving God has created a fiery hell that he will condemn his creation to. There is always a reckoning, though that judgment is in God's time and way. The second greatest commandment is to love one another as we love ourselves. If we follow that simple edict, we'll never do anything we'd be afraid to stand before God and explain." She felt Hunter scoot in closer and rest his head on her arm. She leaned over and kissed his head.

She began to sing *Amazing Grace* and was quickly joined by Naomi, filling in the harmony. Her spirit lifted as the congregation joined them. Their voices joined together like those tiny flames of light that forced out the darkness. It was during moments like this she felt closest to God. She was grateful for the ability to share her faith with others in a way that was far more meaningful than her door-knocking childhood ever could have been.

* * * *

Late Sunday afternoon, Naomi looked into the oven at the lasagna as Lucian sliced a loaf of bread he'd brought home from the bakery. She sensed something was on his mind. "Want to talk about it?"

Lucian stopped mid-slice before shrugging his shoulders. "Not sure there's much to say."

Naomi wiped her hands on a dishtowel and leaned back against the counter. "Lucian, the one thing you'll learn about me is that I'm persistent. If you don't believe me, ask Rhebekka how long I can wait. I can see the wheels in your head turning and the questions you want to ask."

"Is that so?"

Rhebekka walked into the kitchen and kissed Naomi's temple. "Take my word for it, Lucian. She can wait years. After lunch, I'm running out to Chance and Jax's. You two want to come along?"

Lucian yawned. "I think I'm going to take a nap. Getting up at the buttcrack of dawn will take some getting used to. I'm going to have to go to bed a little earlier to work with Karmen. She had that big order for this evening that she had to finish up before the service this morning. I don't know how she does it, but she's a worker, that's for sure."

"Karmen built that store from the ground up, but with Zandra's marketing and advertising, it's gotten too busy for her to handle by herself. She told me you're a fast learner, and she's so grateful you came to work for her."

Lucian's face lit up at the compliment. "I'm learning a ton. She's very patient with me, but she can work my butt into the dirt."

Naomi chuckled. "Karmen came from a rough home life and was determined to never live in poverty again."

"I'm grateful for the opportunity. I think I'll eat and pass out for a few hours." Lucian covered a yawn.

Naomi moved to get plates from the cabinet. "Then let's eat and let you go to sleep."

Everyone grabbed something and headed to the table. Rhebekka reached out and clasped Naomi's hand, as she held her other one out for Lucian. "You never have to pray with us if you don't want to, but you're part of this family. We never want to leave you out."

Naomi watched Lucian war with his emotions. "Faith is something personal, and however you believe, or don't believe, is okay with us."

Lucian fiddled with his spoon. "I used to go to church with Nan when I was little." He looked at Rhebekka and Naomi, then slowly held out his hands until they both grasped his in theirs.

Rhebekka softened her gaze at him. "In this house, you are free to believe or not believe. I would never force anyone into the position I grew up in. Thank you for trusting me enough to pray with you."

They bowed their heads and Rhebekka offered a short prayer of thanks for the meal and their family.

Naomi picked up her knife and slathered the bread with the soft Amish butter in the middle of the table. She took a bite and moaned. "Lucian, this is fantastic. Did you make this bread?"

Lucian beamed. "I did. It was my first try, so Karmen said I could bring it home to see what you thought."

Rhebekka spoke around a mouthful of bread. "I'd say you've got it down pat. Well done."

They ate, chatting about Lucian's new job and the planned pie night at the Parker's next Saturday. Naomi smiled at the conversation around her table. She'd dreamed of days like this, though she never thought she'd have to wait almost half her life to get it. They finished eating and clearing the table.

Lucian leaned against the counter and yawned. "I'm gonna go crash." He rubbed his eyes. "Is there anything else you need me to do?"

Naomi came over and hugged him. "No. Go to bed. I'll check and see if you want anything when we get back."

Rhebekka brought Naomi's coat and helped her put it on. "You've got our numbers programmed into your phone, right?"

Lucian grinned. "I do. Go, you two. Say hi to Hunter for me."

"We'll be back in a few hours. Take your partners in crime with you to keep you company." Naomi pointed to the cats rubbing against Lucian's legs.

He reached down and scratched both of the girls. "They're both snuggle bunnies. Okay, you two go do your thing. I'm going to examine the inside of my eyelids for holes. Wake me when you get back."

Rhebekka saluted as they turned and walked toward the door. "Without fail."

* * * *

Jax handed Naomi a glass of red wine. "Oh, thank you. I rarely get the opportunity to share a good glass of wine. It's never been Rhebekka's drink of choice."

"For as different as Chance and Rhebekka are, they share many similarities. Both are women of extraordinary character, have had more than one career, are very protective of their family and..."

Naomi filled in the last point. "Big fans of beer."

Jax touched her nose and laughed. "Ding, ding, ding. To be honest, I rarely think about drinking wine. Sometimes it brings up memories better left buried."

Naomi knew precisely what she was talking about. Jax's ex came from a long line of winemakers and grew up on a vineyard. "Has your last bit of trouble settled yet?"

Jax took a slow drink. "Unfortunately, no. As of now, I will still be required to fly to California to defend myself against something I had nothing to do with. The date keeps changing. One more mess Lacey has dragged me into."

"Will she even consider settling?"

Jax huffed. "I'm sure her lawyer is trying to do everything but that. The Montgomery family isn't known for admitting defeat. Had it not been for Lacey's grandmother, I'm not sure I'd have gotten through my divorce without bloodshed."

"I guess I never realized how fortunate I was in my divorce. Aaron and I knew we weren't happy and that it was time to move on. We split things amicably and hugged after we signed the final paperwork. I wished him the best, and he did the same for me."

Jax smiled. "It's hard to imagine you with anyone other than Rhebekka. You two are so perfect together. If you haven't figured it out, my son is in love with both of you."

"The feeling is very mutual. There is no better feeling than when he crawls on the stage between us to feel the music. He's come so far since he's been with you and Chance. You've been so good for him."

Jax shook her head. "It's Hunter who has enriched our lives. I never thought I'd be a mother. Lacey had zero interest, even when her brother had a child. I thought I'd lost my opportunity until I reconnected with Chance. As much as I love my godson, Jace, holding him woke up a part of me I thought was dead and gone. He made me want to be a mother."

Naomi sipped her wine, recognizing those feelings all too well. It made her think about the years she and Rhebekka had missed. If she admitted it to herself, Lucian's presence in their lives had dramatically reduced the empty feeling. He wasn't a baby, but he was definitely in need of a mother figure. She was more than willing to be whatever he needed.

"Lucian seems to have settled in with you like he's always been there."

Naomi couldn't hold back the smile. "He's incredibly gifted in so many ways. He started a part-time job with Karmen the other day. He made it clear to us that he wants to make his own money."

Jax leaned forward and placed her hand on Naomi's arm. "I'm sure it's difficult for someone in Lucian's position to become dependent on anyone."

The two women sat side by side on the couch, staring into the crackling fire. Naomi was grateful to have someone to confide in who could understand.

"It took Rhebekka and Ellie years to lean on anyone but each other because of how they grew up. Lucian's trust has been broken so many times. I expect that's why he learned to rely only on himself. We're always going to be there for him, no matter what road he chooses. He may not have grown up with a family, but he has one now."

"That's what matters. You and Rhebekka are like family to us. If you ever need a shoulder to lean on, I've got two good ones right here." Jax crossed her arms and patted her own shoulders.

"The feeling is mutual. I wonder what our wives are up to?"

"Besides enjoying a good beer? I think Chance wanted to ask her the same thing I'm going to ask you. We're working through Hunter's adoption process and wanted to know if you'd agree to be character witnesses for us."

Naomi clasped Jax's hand. "Of course. That goes without saying. I have no doubt I can speak for Rhebekka as well when I say whatever you need. Hunter is a lucky little boy."

Jax wiped a tear from her eye. "We're the ones who are lucky."

"God works in mysterious ways. Hunter may have lived a tragic life before you two, but now he has a wonderful opportunity to grow up healthy and happy."

"Someday, he'll have questions about his birth mother. I'm not exactly sure how I'll explain it."

"You'll find the words. There will be sadness, but also an understanding of how loved he is, even in the pain of losing someone he'll never get to know."

Jax sighed and took another sip. "From your lips to God's ears."

They sat in companionable silence with their heads resting against the couch. No more words were needed, just the comforting presence of a good friend and an excellent bottle of wine.

* * * *

Rhebekka frowned as she looked out the window at the snow and sipped her beer. "What time do you want to take him over for his interview?"

Chance stepped up beside her. "Settle down, Momma. Your cub is stronger than you think. The trooper wants to interview him on Tuesday. I was thinking maybe before we do that, we can retrieve the things he left at the group home."

"I don't want him to go to that interview alone. Can Naomi and I come?"

"That's up to Lucian, but I have no issue with it. He's eighteen and can give his permission. I talked with Harley about who we should ask to speak with. It will be up to the trooper on how he chooses to conduct the interview."

"Chance, we told him we'd protect him in every way and I fully intend to keep that promise. He's been through enough."

"I promised him the same. Whatever we need to do, those responsible for his assault need to be held accountable."

Rhebekka paced the spacious kitchen. It was obvious the family spent a great deal of time in this room. A pair of Hunter's snow boots sat by the door, one on its side. There were dog toys in a box on the floor and a shelf full of board games. This was a home, something Lucian hadn't had since his grandmother died. "You and I both know they're going to try and make him uncomfortable. Once he's back inside those doors, they have one more opportunity to take a swipe at him. They can't be allowed to cause him any more trauma."

Chance stopped Rhebekka on one of her trips and smiled at her. "Sit down a minute before I have to replace my floor."

Rhebekka took a deep breath and sat down at the bar beside Chance. "I'm sorry. There isn't a guitar for me to take out my frustration on. Naomi's used to it. Do you really believe some court is going to believe Lucian?"

"Rhebekka, I believe in the justice system. If I didn't, I couldn't do my job. Harley pointed me in the direction of a trooper with a sister who is trans. If anyone will understand, he will. These crimes are becoming all too common. These instances will continue with impunity if we don't stand up for the marginalized."

Rhebekka slowly turned her beer bottle on the bar, the condensation leaving a ring on her coaster. "He's just getting his bearings. I don't want to take his feet out from under him."

"I don't think you're giving him enough credit. He found a way to survive brutally cold weather while avoiding detection for weeks. I think he's much tougher than you think."

Rhebekka stood and walked to the sliding glass doors looking out onto the deck. "Even tough people hurt, Chance."

Chance joined her. "I won't argue that point. How about I stop by tomorrow after he gets home from his new job? I'll have a talk with him. You can be present, and we can work out a plan on how to handle what's coming."

Rhebekka leaned against the door frame, staring out into the darkness. Zeus came and put his nose under her hand. She smiled and stroked his alert ears. "Hey, boy. I'm okay, thank you."

"He's incredibly perceptive. I'm surprised to see him. He's normally glued to Hunter, especially after he's gone to bed. Good boy, Zeus."

Rhebekka watched his tail wag. She wished she knew the right thing to do. The reality was the choice wasn't hers; it was Lucian's. All she and Naomi could do was support him through whatever was to come. "Okay. I trust you, Chance."

Chance put a hand on her shoulder. "Now that we agree on that, I have a favor to ask."

Rhebekka beamed. "Name it."

* * * *

Naomi watched the clock. The ticking grated on her with a constant reminder of what was coming. Pen in hand, she put her feelings down on paper.

> *Rhebekka's been on pins and needles all morning. She played late into the night after we got home from Chance and Jax's. I had to drag her upstairs around three and spent another hour massaging the cramps out of her leg. She never knows when to quit. Chance is coming by today to interview Lucian, and he's as nervous as Rhebekka is. It seems Lucian and Ellie both have things they'd rather not discuss. Lord, give me the compassion to help see this family through the minefield of painful memories that threaten the path to the future.*

Naomi went to her wife and wrapped loving arms around her from behind. She kissed Rhebekka's shoulder. "He'll be okay."

Lucian came down the hallway wearing a pair of black jeans and an oversized gray T-shirt. His dark hair was still dripping water onto his shoulders. "She's right, Bek. There isn't anything they could do to me that would be any worse. I'm eighteen. Chance said that makes me an adult." He smiled. "It's not like they can take my birthday."

Naomi smiled against Rhebekka's shoulder. "Smart guy right there. Listen to him."

Rhebekka relaxed in her arms. "I know. You're both right. It just pisses me off."

"Better to be pissed off than pissed on." He winked. "It's going to be okay." He ran his hands through his hair, finger-combing his thick bangs to the side of his forehead.

The doorbell rang, and Rhebekka checked the camera on her phone before unlocking the outside door. "It's Chance and Zeus." Rhebekka put her phone back in her pocket.

Naomi held Rhebekka tightly. "Lucian, will you let her in the loft door?"

"You bet." Lucian crossed the floor and greeted the sheriff and her K9. "Hi, Sheriff. Come on in."

Chance was a formidable woman in uniform, who left little doubt about who was in charge. Naomi walked over and hugged her. "Nice to see you again, Chance. Can I get you something to drink?"

Chance took off her jacket and her Stetson. "A hot cup of coffee would hit the spot. I've been standing out in the cold directing traffic around a group of tractor trailers stuck on Backbone Mountain. You'd think, somewhere in their driver's training, they would have been taught how to put chains on."

Naomi chuckled to herself as she went to the kitchen for the coffee. She placed filled cups on a tray and followed everyone to the dining room table. Chance's sentiment was a common one around the county in the winter. In the summer, truck drivers following their GPS ended up on roads that appeared to cut time off the route. The reality was that they often got stuck in sharp bends on roads not intended for large trucks. It cost drivers time and money to call a tow service to get them turned around and back onto the main roads. "How bad is it out there?"

Chance accepted a cup from the tray as she sat down. "Icy in places. The snow is still coming down pretty steadily."

Rhebekka took her cup and kissed Naomi in thanks. "The kids were bummed that school was canceled, because that meant kids' club was canceled as well. I had a special treat for them that Daniel created as a Christmas present."

Chance ran a hand through her hair. "The whole region has been hit pretty hard with this storm. Half of Randolph County is without power." She knocked on the wooden table with her knuckles. "So far, we're good here in Tucker County. Does this place have a generator?"

Rhebekka nodded. "Indeed, it does. During my first year here, I was still deep in renovations. The power went out for four days after a giant storm. The only heat I had was from an old, sketchy fireplace. I was too cold not to use it. After that, I installed a whole-building, natural gas generator."

Chance sipped the coffee and looked at Naomi. "Oh, that's good. TipTop?"

"You know your coffee, Sheriff. We're pretty addicted to it. There's more in the kitchen if you want it. I'll even send you out with a full thermos."

Chance nodded to her. "Much appreciated." She turned to Lucian. "I wanted to talk to you about tomorrow. We have two things to accomplish." She counted them off on her fingers. "One, we need to go get your belongings. I'll be right with you. I've already arranged for us to do that at eleven." Another finger went up. "Secondly, we have an interview with Trooper LaMount. I've worked with him before and found him to be a stand-up guy. Trooper Kincaid recommended him for his experience with the trans community."

Naomi scooted her chair closer to Lucian and placed her hand on top of his tightly clenched fist. "You don't have to do this alone, Lucian. We can come with you. It's your choice, and we'll do whatever you like."

Lucian wiped angrily at a stray tear. "Why do we have to go there? I didn't leave much behind that I need. Can't they just mail it to me?"

Chance looked directly at Lucian. "They have some things you wouldn't have had access to, like your birth certificate and social security card. You have nothing to worry about. We'll be with you. Ms. Laura will also be there. The last administrator has been placed on leave, and someone else from the main organization wants to do an exit interview with you."

Lucian shoved his chair back, the legs squealing against the hardwood floor. "Fuck them. I don't owe them one damn thing. No one, besides Ms. Laura, gave a damn about me there. I won't take any more of their shit."

Naomi rose and went to him. There was genuine anger and something else in his eyes. She could see the terror behind the anger. He was close to a panic attack, something she had seen in Ellie more than once over the years. Slowly, she moved her hands until they rested on the sides of his head. She forced his eyes to hers. "Lucian, breathe with me. It's just you and me. One breath in." She exaggerated an intake of breath and slowly let it out through pursed lips.

Lucian trembled beside her as tiny beads of sweat formed on his upper lip. His breathing was short and rapid. His pupils were dilated. He clasped her forearms as she continually directed him to take a breath in and slowly release it. There was no doubt in Naomi's mind that he was in fight or flight mode. If she didn't get him calmed down, he'd hyperventilate.

"In and out, Lucian. You are in no danger. You are safe and loved. We will not let anything happen to you. In and out. That's it. One more time. Rhebekka, get me a bottle of water and a cold cloth." Naomi sighed with relief as Lucian released the death grip a bit. He was following her directions and breathing with her.

Rhebekka approached with an uncapped bottle of water and the cold washrag. Naomi took the cloth and ran it across Lucian's brow. He relaxed even more as she continued to wipe his face. "I'm right here with you, Lucian. Slow your breaths. Breathe with me." She looked into his eyes as they slowly returned to normal.

"There you are. I'm right here." Naomi held her hand out for the bottle of water. She brought it to his lips, and he clumsily tried to take a drink, spilling some on the floor.

"I'm sorry." Lucian's small voice cracked with emotion.

Naomi reached out for Rhebekka's hand and brought her closer. "You have nothing to be sorry about. We're here for you." She clasped Lucian's hand and Rhebekka covered both of them with hers.

Rhebekka placed her other hand on his shoulder. "We are your family, and this family protects its own. No one will ever lay a hand on you that you don't allow. You won't be staying one minute longer than you have to. You also will not have to be alone with anyone."

Naomi smiled at him. "Take another drink and let's sit down. You're okay, and I'm right here with you."

He collapsed into Naomi's arms, his sobs filling the room with such sadness.

"It's okay, I've got you. We love you so much, Lucian. Let it out. Let it go." Naomi soothed him with everything she had. She could feel his legs going out from under him and turned to Rhebekka, who instantly recognized what was happening and helped lower them both to the floor. Naomi sat holding him as he cried, with Rhebekka's strong arms around both of them.

Naomi began to sing *You're Not Alone* by Allison Russell. The lyrics reminded them that no matter what sorrow surrounded them or what was to come, they would never be alone again because they were family. She held him tight and felt Rhebekka pull them closer to her, joining in perfect harmony. As helpless as she felt, she knew that this was exactly what a mother would do, comfort her child. She kissed the top of his still damp hair and thanked God for prayers answered, even when they didn't come in the expected form.

Chapter Nine

NAOMI WATCHED RHEBEKKA PUSH her breakfast around her plate. *Yesterday was an emotional rollercoaster, and today will be even worse.* Rhebekka and Lucian had spent the rest of the day with guitars in their hands. Each seemed to be purging the anger and frustration with every chord. They'd only stopped when she called them to the dinner table. The two of them choked down a few pieces of pizza and returned to the instruments. Naomi had sat in with them and finally pulled the plug on the jam session at ten when she noticed Lucian's eyes starting to droop. She'd woken this morning, determined to start their day on a positive note. So many thoughts swirled around her brain. She needed to get them out. She turned to her journal.

> *Today is going to be incredibly hard on my family. Lucian endured so much inside and outside those walls. I can only pray that, by bringing this all out in the open, it never happens again. It breaks my heart to see what many LGBTQIA+ kids go through in typical family settings, let alone those institutionalized. I can't imagine how hard it has to be when you feel like everything and everyone is against you, without a single person on your side. There has to be something better out there. If not, someone needs to develop protective and supportive policies. These kids deserve so much more than they get. Lucian has us now, but how many other kids like him have no one?*

She put her pen down and covered her wife's hand. "You don't have to eat if you don't want to."

Rhebekka put down her fork and clasped her hands as if in prayer. "I hate this."

"We all do." Naomi leaned over and kissed her cheek. "Now is the time for us to be strong for him. He needs to look at us and know we can withstand any storm. Today, he's like Daniel walking into the lion's den. Daniel knew that God would protect him. Lucian doesn't know God like that, yet, but he knows us. Our faith in him is what will get him through."

Rhebekka wiped at the tears streaming down her face. "Is he still sleeping?"

Naomi nodded. "I think he rolled around most of the night. I peeked in at him about thirty minutes ago. Both cats were snuggled under the covers with him." Naomi ran her hand through Rhebekka's black hair, fringed in crimson. "You, on the other hand, didn't sleep more than an hour."

Rhebekka sighed and used her thumb to wipe at a water stain on the table. "Sorry, honey."

"There's nothing to be sorry about. It's my job to care about your well-being, and I do love my job."

"This is going to be one fucked-up day."

Naomi nodded. "Most likely, but we will do everything we can to make sure Lucian has no doubt that we are firmly in his corner."

"I'm so angry. Their job was to protect him, and they did anything but!"

Naomi put her fingers to her lips. "Shh." She turned and looked back toward where Lucian slept. "We all know that, but we have to remember that we didn't fail him. Chance will make sure those responsible will answer for their crimes. That's not our job. Our priority is to make sure Lucian feels safe now. He starts virtual school in a few days, and he'll be able to graduate. That's our next priority. Right now, he has a safe, warm home and people who care about his welfare. That has to be enough for now. There will be more to come, and we have to make sure we are ready for every hurdle he'll face."

Rhebekka shook herself and wiped away the rest of the tears. "I'm afraid."

"Honey, what are you afraid of?"

"Failing him. I don't know how to be a parent."

Naomi laughed. "Is that so?"

Rhebekka looked a bit angry. "No, I don't. I've never had a kid."

"How old was Ellie when you got her away from your parents?"

Rhebekka protested. "That's not the same."

Naomi turned until she was looking directly at Rhebekka. "I think it's very similar. Answer a few questions. Did you remove her from a bad situation? Did you feed and shelter Ellie? Did you look after her health and her emotional well-being? Did you lose sleep worrying about what would happen to her?"

"Yes, but—"

"No buts. That's what a parent does. You didn't give birth to Ellie or Lucian, but you care and worry about them in a parental way. Ellie is my sister-in-law, but she's always been like a daughter to me as well. Parenting isn't about DNA. It's about love. Our family might not be conventional, but we are a family, without a doubt. Now answer my questions. Did you look after Ellie like a mother would?"

Rhebekka nodded. "I guess so. I just didn't have good role models in that department."

Naomi kissed her cheek. "I know. I think it's well past time for you to make peace with your childhood. Your father is gone. He used the power granted to him by their religion to be a dictator. The reality is your mother is brainwashed. She's unable to see her religion and elders for what they are, a control monger that instills fear of God for very selfish reasons, instead of teaching about the God of love we know. You and Ellie need to find a way to forgive her. I understand you might not ever be able to forget the many ways she didn't protect you the way she should have. You still suffer from her mistakes, but you no longer have to answer for them. We talk to our flock about the gift of grace. When you learned about it, your life changed forever. Today isn't the day to get into it, but you and Ellie need to face the elephant in the room. Your mother is just as worthy of grace as any one of us. She needs someone to peel back the curtain and expose the great Wizard of Oz for exactly what it is, an organization that subserviates women for their own purposes."

Rhebekka's lip trembled. "What if I fail him?"

Naomi put their foreheads together. "I won't let you. We're a team, and team Deklan doesn't fail." She heard the sound of a toilet flushing. "Game time."

Rhebekka got up. "I'm going to go wash my face."

Naomi nodded and let her hand linger in Rhebekka's as she walked away. She closed her eyes and folded her hands together. *Please, Lord, pour your strength and grace on all of us today. We will need you close.*

She rose from the table, took Rhebekka's uneaten breakfast, and scraped it into the garbage. *We need something sweet.* The fluffy crepes Siobhan had taught her to make would do the trick. She worked to create a stack and heard Lucian and Rhebekka enter the kitchen as she flipped another one.

Lucian put his nose in the air. "Are those crepes?"

Naomi took a plate down from the cupboard. "They are. Do you want cream cheese or strawberry preserves in yours?"

In unison, Lucian and Rhebekka answered, "Strawberry."

"So much alike. You two set the table. I'll bring them over." She listened as the two of them followed her instructions, chatting about music as they did.

Lucian placed silverware at each place setting. "It's after nine. How come you guys didn't eat earlier?"

Rhebekka huffed. "She tried to get me to. Although, in my defense, she didn't offer me crepes."

Lucian poured himself a cup of coffee. "Sorry I slept so late."

Naomi cupped his cheek. "You didn't sleep much."

"Too many things screaming in my head. I couldn't shut them up. I finally put my earbuds in and turned on my music to drown it all out."

Naomi slid the last crepe onto a plate and turned off the stove. She quirked an eyebrow at Rhebekka. "Sounds like someone else I know, though that one tends to prowl around at all hours with headphones attached to a guitar."

Lucian took the serving plate to the table while Rhebekka grabbed the strawberry syrup and found her seat. Naomi sat between them. Lucian looked at them for a few long seconds before stretching his hands to them and dropping his head.

Naomi grasped his hand and looked to Rhebekka, who closed the circle. Rhebekka finished the prayer, but Naomi held on for a few more seconds, letting God's peace wash over her. *Watch over your children today, Lord. Only through you will all things be made right.*

* * * *

Naomi reached out and held their hands as they pulled up to the front of the children's home. Chance had pulled in just before them. She and Zeus went inside to meet Ms. Laura. Naomi could feel the dampness of Lucian's hand as she turned to look at him.

"Lucian, look at me. Sing with me." She needed to ground him, and few things could do that like music. She started the chorus to "Lean on Me." The song spoke of everything she wanted him to know. He could rely on them, even when he didn't feel strong. By the time they'd made it through the chorus a second time, his bounding vein in his neck had settled to a normal pulse. "Better?"

Lucian nodded and took a controlled breath. "Yeah, thanks."

His hands were still damp but no longer trembling.

Rhebekka turned to him. "There is nothing in there that we will let hurt you. Words are painful, but stop and consider the source. We'll be right beside you as you do this."

Chance knocked on the window, and Naomi opened her door. Laura stood looking at Lucian with a timid smile on her face. He climbed out and gave her a small wave.

"Hi, Ms. Laura. It's good to see you."

She put her hand on his shoulder. "It's really good to see you, too. I promise this is going to be okay. The gentleman you'll be speaking with today will make things right. I think you'll be a little surprised when you talk with him. We've arranged it so Naomi and Rhebekka can be with you, though the questions will be directed to you. Just be honest and detailed. Can you do that?"

Lucian sought out Naomi's eyes. She watched a myriad of emotions cross his face. She stepped forward. "I have faith in you, Lucian. Tell the truth. That's all you have to do."

He took a deep breath and straightened his back. "Let's do this."

They entered the children's home and walked to the administration office. The whispered conversations were nearly deafening to Naomi. She watched as Lucian nervously cracked each knuckle on both hands.

The painted walls may have once been a cheery yellow, but now resembled a dirty tan more than anything. Duct tape seemed to be holding more than one table or chair together. At the end of one hallway, a group of older boys slouched in several well-worn chairs. Upon seeing Ms. Laura and Lucian pass, the boys made several lewd comments that stopped Naomi in her tracks. Anger swelled within her, as they made obscene gestures and grabbed themselves suggestively. Chance stepped to her side with Zeus at attention.

"Is there a problem here, gentlemen?" Chance's voice was a register lower than her usual tone.

Most of the boys sat up straighter, except for one. He rose to his feet and stepped forward while grabbing his crotch. "Well, well, if it isn't dykes on parade. You can't do shit to me. I'm a minor."

Chance stepped into his personal space and used all six feet of her frame to loom over him. "Minor or not, I will cite you for indecency and juvenile delinquency. If that doesn't work, I'll call every trooper within a five-county area and give them your name and particulars. You spit on the sidewalk, and you'll find yourself facing juvey. Mr. Jones will no longer be here to cover up your indiscretions."

"Fuck you. Mr. Jones will kick your ass. He'll be back next week and put that fucking freak in her place." The boy took a step toward where Lucian was standing with his fists clenched, rage written all over him.

Naomi adjusted her stance and moved between them. There was no way this kid was getting an inch closer to Lucian.

"Nathan! That's enough!" Ms. Laura rushed back into the room. "Go to your dorm room." She pointed when he didn't move. "That wasn't a suggestion. Now!"

"Mr. Jones will come back and take care of your attitude, too," Nathan sneered.

A man with close-cropped, dark hair stepped into the room and walked straight up to Nathan. He took command in a suit and tie tailored to his form. "I'll handle this, Ms. Laura. Thank you, Sheriff. Nathan, you don't know me, but I'm well above Mr. Jones' pay grade. He no longer works here. As of today, I am the new supervising administrator in this facility. I won't tolerate any of this behavior. A member of staff has issued you an order. If you can't understand the simple order, let me clarify it. You are in violation of the code of conduct. All your social or extracurricular activities are nonexistent until a committee of staff has evaluated your status. Any attempt to circumvent this order will result in the permanent removal of these privileges. Do I make myself clear, Nathan?"

Rhebekka had joined Naomi, moving between her and the insolent teenager. They watched as he ground his teeth, turned, and left the common area. The man shifted his attention to the other boys with Nathan.

"As of now, you are all under evaluation. I expect residents of this group home to respect all visitors, especially those in law enforcement. Boys, a famous line says there is a new sheriff in town. It's best if you understand I'm not talking about the one standing in the uniform. See yourself to your rooms."

He turned to Rhebekka and Naomi, holding out his hand. "I'm Asher Shannon, the new administrator. I'd hoped to meet you under different circumstances. Unfortunately, as you can see, I've got my work cut out for me." He looked Lucian square in the eye. "Nothing that has gone on here for the last few years is acceptable." He took a few steps closer to Lucian, stopping at a distance that indicated he was no threat. "You and I have more than one thing in common. We both grew up in the system, and our birth certificates didn't get everything right. If you're willing to talk to me, I hope I can make significant changes here. I realize you're now eighteen and under zero obligation to do so, but I'm asking for a little blind faith between you and someone who has walked in your shoes."

Lucian stepped forward and held out his hand to Asher. "I'll give you a chance because the only staff that ever gave a damn about my well-being is standing in this room asking me to. I'll give you a chance because the other people that came with me took a chance on me when no one else would."

Naomi melted into Rhebekka and fought the tears that threatened to fall. She closed her eyes and said thank you to the God that shut the mouths of the lions.

* * * *

The rest of the day had been draining. Mr. Shannon took down a detailed account of the attack, the assault, and the failure to act on the part of the staff that were aware of what had happened. Lucian identified Nathan as the ringleader the night he'd been assaulted. Asher handed over a file to Lucian with his paperwork and important documents. All his belongings he'd left behind had been retrieved from a locked space. The interview with Trooper LaMount had gone as expected, professional but no less agonizing. Rhebekka had nearly chewed a hole in the inside of her cheek by the time they finished. More than once, she asked God for the strength to not go after every person who had failed Lucian. She watched in the rearview mirror as Lucian turned Mr. Shannon's business card over and over in his hands.

Naomi slid her hand into Rhebekka's and turned to the back seat. "We're very proud of you, Lucian. That was incredibly difficult, but you handled it with great courage."

"I didn't feel courageous. I wanted to punch Nathan for the things he said. He's always been able to get away with whatever he did."

Rhebekka wanted to put a good ending on their afternoon. She drove through familiar streets in Elkins, making her way to a place she hoped would bring a smile to Lucian's face. "There's someplace I want to stop before we head home."

They pulled into the parking lot of The Wright Note, the store where Lucian had worked. A quick glance at the rearview mirror revealed a slight smile on Lucian's face, as his bright, nearly golden eyes stared back at her.

Rhebekka parked and turned slightly in the seat. "Mr. Wright wanted to see you, and I want to pick up a few things."

Lucian brushed at a tear. "He was nice to me."

Naomi reached back and put a hand on his knee. "He speaks very highly of you."

They exited and walked toward the small shop. A tall man with a boyish grin and a head of strawberry-blond hair quickly came from behind the counter to greet them.

"Lucian, it's so good to see you."

"It's good to see you too. I'm sorry I didn't get in touch sooner." Lucian tentatively took Stephan Wright's outstretched hand.

He engulfed Lucian's hands in his. "I was quite worried when I heard you'd gone missing." He tilted his head slightly. "Would your disappearing act have anything to do with why you turned in your resignation?"

Lucian dropped his head and nodded. "I didn't want to just walk out on you. You were a good boss to work for, and I wanted you to have time to find someone to replace me."

Stephan released Lucian's hand and put an arm around his shoulders. "Lucian, I could find another employee, but there was no replacing you." Stephan put out his hand. "Thank you for bringing him by. I was grateful to get your call, Rhebekka. Nice to see you, Naomi."

Rhebekka patted him on the back. "It's always a pleasure. Were you able to get the things in that I asked about?"

His face lit up. "Indeed. Follow me."

They made their way to the counter, past the guitars hanging from the wall. Rhebekka watched Lucian look over each instrument. His eyes stared a minute longer at the black Fender bass that hung there. She smiled to herself. *He's going to freak.* The glass counter had a display case with a multitude of guitar accessories. Three bar stools offered them each a seat while Stephan stepped into the back.

"Here you are." He stepped out and placed a handful of Earnie Ball Slinky strings, of varying gauges and metals, on the counter. Lucian was distracted by the replacement strings, which enabled Stephan to place the Fender bass in front of him, unnoticed. A second later, Lucian did a double take, seeing the guitar without taking in its significance. Rhebekka held her breath for a moment that seemed like hours. Stephan had told her that this was the bass Lucian played most often, the one he'd been saving up for.

Lucian turned his head toward Rhebekka and Naomi. "Did you order a new guitar?"

Naomi stepped down from the stool and came to stand close to Lucian. "I did. This"—Naomi pointed to the glossy black instrument—"is our birthday and Christmas gift to you."

Lucian raised his hands as if to touch the Fender, then put them back in his lap. "I can't accept this. I know what this costs. It's too much."

Stephan came around the counter and put his hand on the guitar. "It's from me too. I know how much you wanted it. Please don't offend me by refusing our gift. It's something the three of us wanted to do." He picked up the guitar, plugged it in, and placed the strap around Lucian's neck.

Lucian sat there, the emotions playing out all over his face. His eyes were glassy, and he swallowed hard. It took a few more minutes of warring with himself, before he adjusted the neck strap and took the guitar neck in his hand. His right hand trembled as he reached for the ever-present pick Rhebekka pulled from her back pocket.

She laid it in his palm and closed his fingers around it as she looked deep into his eyes. "I remember what it was like when Grandpa gave me my first guitar. There was a feeling, something that could only be compared to the happiest moments in my life, as I held it. With that guitar, I could express all my thoughts without saying a word. I could take that guitar and create something no one had ever heard before, something that could reach out and touch the hearts and souls of the people that came to hear my band perform. I know the bass is your instrument of choice, so it's time you have your own. When I called Stephan, he told me this was the one you had your eye on. We're giving you the same gift that someone gave us, a chance to play your feelings out, without ever having to ask for permission."

Lucian put his arm around Rhebekka's neck and hugged her tightly.

Naomi wrapped them both in her arms and pulled them even closer. "Lucian, we are your family now, and this family gives the gift of music."

Lucian wiped at another tear. "I don't know how to thank you."

Stephan stepped behind the counter. "You pay us back by giving to someone else if you're ever able. My grandfather started this store almost fifty years ago. He gave music lessons for free, whenever he had a promising student that couldn't afford to pay. My dad continued that tradition when he took over the store. As a result, several students became musicians and music teachers. They all credit my grandfather and father for being someone who cared enough to take a chance. I'm just doing the same thing they did. You're a natural, Lucian. All we're doing is giving you the tool to use your talent."

Lucian looked at Stephan. "That's why you let me work here and play, isn't it?"

He nodded. "You are one in a long line, though you are the most talented I ever had the chance to help. I have little doubt, with the help of these two, I'll see you on the stage someday, if that's what you want."

Rhebekka prodded his foot with hers. "Come on. Play for us?"

Lucian cleared his throat and shook out his hands, before putting them in place and picking his first chord. He began playing the bass line from one of Regal Crimson's older songs, *Out of the Ash*. It wasn't their most popular, but the bassline was killer. Stephan handed Rhebekka a Gibson. The two began to jam, and Naomi sang the lyrics. Rhebekka and Lucian joined in, their voices blending smoothly, as if they'd sung together many times before.

"Out of this burnt-down life, I will let go of all this strife. I will escape the past, right out of the ash."

Chapter Ten

NAOMI WIPED DOWN THE counter and checked on the Mexican casserole she'd put in the oven. Homemade tortillas chips were waiting in a warming dish. The smell of chili powder and black pepper wafted throughout the kitchen the minute she opened the door. Cheese and tomatillo sauce bubbled in the glass baking dish. *Perfect. I hope this tastes as good as it smells.* She sat down and opened the journal she found she was writing in more and more these days.

> *It's been a long time since I've been as angry as I was yesterday. To see the egregious way Lucian was treated by the others at the children's shelter was infuriating. To know those boys felt empowered in their misogyny, because an adult had encouraged it, tells me all I needed to know about why Lucian ran. His scream last night tore my heart out. He was gasping and thrashing around in his bed, fighting the sheets he was tangled in. I knew he had to be reliving what happened to him. I held him for hours while he sobbed. I will ensure that he never has to feel that kind of terror again if it's the last thing I do. On the other side of that coin was watching him visit the music store. He was obviously at home there, and Stephan was kind to him. Probably one of the only people in his life who was. The look on Lucian's face when we put that Fender in his hands was priceless and just one of the many happy memories I hope we will make with him.*

Rhebekka's arms encircled her from behind. Naomi relaxed into the embrace, and Rhebekka brushed a kiss across her shoulder. "You think he'll be okay?" Naomi asked.

"Only time will tell." Rhebekka sighed. "Karmen said he did fine at work. As hard as yesterday was, there were a lot of good things that came out of it. Hopefully, he gained some closure. He now has someone else who is trans to talk with. Asher can help him navigate the waters in a way we can't. I'm introducing him to Daniel next week. Above all that, he has us. I'd say that's a hell of a new start."

Naomi turned and rested her head against Rhebekka's chest. "He looked so happy in the music store when we sang together."

"He was. We need to remember that he's still trying to get his footing. There will be days when he doesn't know where he fits in, and he'll run up against more than one bigot. The kids in our group welcomed him with open arms. They celebrate differences as much as anyone. What he'll have now is something he hasn't had for a very long time, a firm foundation with us that won't go away. I'm hoping once Siobhan talks with him, he'll have one more ally."

"I know you're right. I just can't help wanting to protect him."

"It's completely understandable. All I ever wanted were parents that supported me for exactly who I am, parents who would be there no matter what."

Naomi pushed back a little and looked into Rhebekka's eyes. "I know it still hurts that they were so hard on you."

Rhebekka led her to the living room, where they sat on the couch. "It's more than that. They didn't protect Ellie. I could deal with my lot in life. What happened to Ellie still affects her. If it wasn't for Siobhan, I'm not sure if she'd ever have a healthy relationship. I think it would be good for Lucian to talk with Siobhan."

Naomi curled into Rhebekka's side. "She can certainly relate. What Siobhan lived through was horrific. What time are they coming over?"

Rhebekka checked her watch. "They should be here any minute. I told Lucian that Siobhan wanted to talk with him."

Lucian came into the room with his new bass. Like a typical teenager, he plopped onto one of the soft, leather couches surrounding the fireplace. He swept his dark bangs out of his eyes and began thumbing out familiar riffs.

Naomi smiled and enjoyed seeing his comfort in their home. He'd changed into the baggy sweatpants and the loose hoody he preferred. His feet were bare and tapped in time with the song he was playing.

The door camera alerted them to visitors. Naomi checked the display that sat on an end table. "It's Ellie and Siobhan." She hit the buttons to let them in.

Ellie's blond locks swept around her shoulders as Siobhan helped her remove her coat. Rhebekka got up and hugged her sister while knocking knuckles with Siobhan.

"Hey, you two." Naomi rose to hug them both. "I miss you guys. You need to come over more. Ellie, there are times when I feel like I saw you more when I lived in Colorado." Naomi held her at arm's length and eyed her critically as she assessed her for any sign of illness. Relief washed over her when none were apparent. It seemed that Ellie was managing her post-thyroid cancer life without complications and thriving in her new position as a producer. Naomi drew her in for a tight hug.

"I miss you too. The best thing is that we live in the same town, and I don't have to take a plane to see you. We need to pick an evening for a weekly dinner and TV binge watching. I thought my schedule would lighten up since I wasn't touring."

Naomi put her arm across Ellie's shoulders and walked into the kitchen. "I agree with you that we need a family night. The only evening we're occupied is the monthly Salvation and Libations."

Ellie snickered. "Only my sister would bring beer and the Bible together."

"She's just following Jesus' example. Think about how many times wine is mentioned in Christ's ministry."

"Very true." Ellie raised her nose and sniffed the air. "Whatever that is smells heavenly."

Naomi opened the oven and pulled out the casserole. "One of my former congregation members gave me the recipe. It's one of Rhebekka's favorites." She pulled the foil off to allow the cheese to brown and returned the pan to the oven.

Ellie grabbed plates out of the cabinet and headed to the table. "Have I told you how happy I am with you two back together?"

Naomi closed the oven door and set the timer. "About a million times, but I'll never get tired of it. I hate how long it took, but all that matters is she finally got over herself. Have I told you how happy I am that you found Siobhan?"

Ellie returned and opened the silverware drawer. "I could hear that about a million times, too. She grounds me in so many ways. When I was touring worldwide, I was constantly disoriented. I didn't know where I was from day to day. Daniel used to send me three texts daily with our location to keep me oriented. I still needed it written on my arm when I stepped on stage. Now I wake up in Siobhan's arms in the same bed every morning. I didn't know losing my career would bring me my greatest joy."

"Siobhan thinks the sun rises and sets in you. I'm so happy for you. You think the two of you will ever make it official?"

"I promise that you two will know right after we do. That's as much as I'll say." Ellie winked. "For now."

"Tease."

"Hey, I waited a very long time for you two to get your shit straight. You'll just have to wait a little longer."

Naomi pulled glasses off the shelf and added them to the table. "As long as I know it's just a matter of when and not if, then I can wait as long as necessary." Sounds of a video game filled the loft. "I'd say they found something to keep themselves occupied while we get dinner ready."

Ellie pointed into the living room. "I heard Lucian playing bass when we came in. He has a lot of talent for never having taken professional lessons."

Naomi nodded. "Some people are born with God-given talent."

"I might ask him if he wants to do studio work with a few of my acts."

Naomi smiled and clapped her hands. "He'd be so stoked. He's working with Karmen at the shop in the mornings. He has to finish high school with some virtual learning classes, but I know he'd be excited about the opportunity." The timer went off. "Go round up the troops. Supper is ready and I'm starved."

Naomi took the main dish to the table and gave thanks for the good things in her life with the words of Psalm 145:16. "You open your hand and satisfy the desires of every living thing." *I certainly have been blessed beyond my measure.*

* * * *

Rhebekka snuggled closer into Naomi's side. Lucian added a few more logs on the fire before settling down in what had become his spot on one of the other couches. Siobhan reclined against the stone hearth on the floor as Ellie lay with her head in her lap. The light from the flames cast a soft glow around the room, dancing off the walls and objects near them.

"That was one of the best meals I've ever eaten." Lucian patted his gut. "Between your cooking and the bakery, I need new pants again."

Naomi pointed to Rhebekka. "You have nothing to worry about with the way you run around. Wait until summer when she gets you out with her, mountain biking on every trail she can find."

Rhebekka saw Lucian's eyes stray to her residual limb. Naomi had encouraged her to take off her prosthesis while relaxing in the evening. She tended to leave it on far too long and overdo it. After dinner, she'd removed it and replaced it with the knee walker sitting on the side of the couch. Naomi constantly reminded her not to let the skin break down and form an open wound. "I ordered a different limb for when I bike."

Lucian adjusted his position. "I don't know if I could deal with it as well as you do."

"The things that have happened to us should never have the final say in our choices," Rhebekka said. "I refused to let what happened to me dictate what I can and can't do."

"You're just braver than I am." Lucian stared up at the ceiling.

Rhebekka looked at Siobhan and cursed herself for how she was about to ruin this idyllic evening. It was too good of an opening for what Siobhan had offered. Rhebekka hadn't gone into detail with Siobhan, as she felt it was Lucian's story to tell. "Learning to live with a prosthetic leg isn't nearly as brave as what you and Siobhan have lived through."

The confusion on Lucian's face was apparent as Siobhan sat forward and pulled the bracers from her arms. She ran her fingers over the red corded scars that circled her wrists. She took a deep breath, then looked directly at Lucian.

"In 2013, I was part of the Irish Defense Forces deployed to Africa. As part of the European Union mission, we provided a variety of training to the Malian armed forces. Ma role was to teach hand to hand combat at the Koulikoro Training Camp. Let's just say not many men care to be put on their ass by a woman, multiple times. So one night, out in the field, I woke up as I was drug out of ma tent by ma feet." She stopped and cleared her throat.

Ellie scooted closer and wrapped her arms around Siobhan's waist. "I'm right here, baby."

Siobhan leaned back and kissed her temple. "I'm so lucky to have ya... Anyway, one of them put his hand over my mouth, while another put loops of cable around my wrists. I felt the metal bite inta ma skin." Siobhan rubbed her scars and looked at Lucian again.

Rhebekka watched, her heart breaking for them both, as the young man sat riveted to every word Siobhan said. Her anger continued to boil against those who sought to take what was not offered.

Siobhan began again, her voice stronger. "I was chosen for that mission for a reason. I've trained men and women all over the world ta defend themselves with and without weapons. I bit the hand covering ma mouth until I tore a chunk of flesh away. I let ma body go slack, making it harder for them ta carry me. Thanks be to God that it worked, and I ended up on the floor. I scrambled to ma feet and kicked the shit out of them both with every bit of strength I could muster with ma hands tied. The ruckus brought ma mates out of their tents. They witnessed an ass-kicking by one of Ireland's finest. One of them is navigating prison in a wheelchair, and the other is navigating hell."

Lucian sat with his mouth agape, his eyes as big as the face of the clock behind him. "You killed him?"

Siobhan took a deep breath. "I took no pleasure in taking his life, Lucian. I did what I was trained to do. Survive."

Lucian dropped his head and clasped his hands together. "I tried to fight. I did. There were just too many of them."

Siobhan lifted his chin. "The point is, ya didn't give up. I'll teach ya how ta take care of yourself."

Lucian perked up. "You will?"

Siobhan sat forward and grabbed Lucian's hands. "Aye."

Rhebekka watched a bond of trust and respect being forged between the two. The details of Siobhan's experience were far more harrowing than she'd shared with Lucian. The bracers she wore on her arms weren't to cover the reminder of her near abduction. They were more to shield her from the memory of being forced to choke away a man's life with the cables he'd bound her with. There were times when Siobhan's flashbacks were severe. Rhebekka had only witnessed one, but the sight of the near-feral fear was something she wished she could forget. She hoped Lucian could find a kindred example of survival and success in Siobhan.

Naomi wiped tears away. "We love you, Lucian. Remember that you can turn to any one of us for anything. Together, we'll find a solution to any problem."

A slow smile crept up on Lucian's face. "Could we find a solution to my need for a bowl of ice cream?"

Rhebekka laughed as she rose and pulled Naomi to her feet with her. "As it says in Matthew, 'Ask and it will be given to you; seek and you will find; knock and the door will be opened to you.'"

There would be difficult days ahead, problems that would seem too insurmountable, and solutions that were fleeting. Tonight, the problem of a sweet tooth was easily solved.

* * * *

"Okay, everyone. Let's finish the homework and you'll have some time for ArchAngel." Rhebekka grinned at her youth group, as they scrambled to get their work out of their backpacks. Lucian stood at her side with a small laptop under his arm. "You, too. Naomi told me you have an English assignment due in the morning."

Lucian yawned and nodded his head. "Yup."

He looked around for a space and sat near Holly, who was waving him over. Rhebekka had introduced Lucian to the group and turned it over to them. Each of them did as Rhebekka had expected by introducing themselves and welcoming him in with open arms, completely aplomb when Lucian relayed his preferred pronouns. Holly had become accomplished on the fiddle with Siobhan's help. The small band she formed with Alton and Amanda the previous year continued to play together. Rhebekka had spoken with Holly over the phone, asking if she would take the lead in making Lucian feel welcome.

She returned to the video game room and dialed Daniel on her cell phone. She put the phone on speaker as she began to type commands into the dedicated computer that housed the scriptural-based video game. The hero, a sword and shield wielding ArchAngel, was the purveyor of good over evil. She donned her virtual reality headset and watched her character, Vulgate, fly onto the screen. The ancient, winged book sporting a steampunk theme, requested by the kid's club and designed by Daniel, had been a gift after her accident. Daniel answered the call.

"Hold on, Bek." Daniel started yelling at someone. "You fucking guys are killing me. This is a simple issue. Figure it out! Sorry, Bek. What's up?"

Daniel always had a slight edge to him when he was multi-tasking, but this seemed out of character for him. *Kill him with kindness, Rhebekka.* "I called to say thank you for the upgrades to ArchAngel. The new graphics are sick. The kids will see it for the first time in about an hour." Rhebekka wanted to cheer him up. "You know you could be pulling down big bucks for this game. The kids eat it up."

Daniel grumbled. "If only adults were as easy to please." There was a long pause before he continued. "Ignore me. I've had a really shitty day."

Generally, only two things put Daniel in a tailspin. Even an impossible-last-minute-technical glitch in an arena filled with eager fans couldn't freak him out. Daniel's anxiety, typically, surrounded either his parents or a woman. She didn't think he was currently in a relationship, so she was betting on the first. "What did your parents do this time?"

Daniel sighed audibly. "I went home for their fiftieth wedding anniversary. We had relatives in from Florida, and Mom couldn't stop telling Aunt Tonya about how well her daughter, Daniella, was doing in the music business. And no, she hadn't gotten married and had 2.5 kids yet. I'm so fucking sick of it. I transitioned fifteen years ago. Fifteen fucking years, Bek!"

"You are perfect as you are, Daniel. You are now exactly as you were intended to be. I've learned, through experience, that there are no magic buttons to making others see the truth. What you need to know is that you are never alone, ever. I think it's time you made a trip to the mountains. I know Ellie would love to see you, and I've got a young man I think could use someone else he can relate to."

"How is Lucian doing?"

"He's had a rough few days. The trooper is investigating his assault and will let us know if there is enough evidence to file charges. The good news, Lucian is enrolled in virtual learning here in the county, and can finish high school and get his diploma. Siobhan is setting up a schedule to teach him some self-defense. He's gainfully employed and one hell of a bass player."

"I'd like to meet him. Let me look at my schedule and see when I can get a break. To be honest, sometimes I'm afraid I might never want to leave if I come up there."

"And that would be a bad thing how? You always have a home wherever Ellie and I are. If it's employment you're worried about, you know Ellie will hire you in a minute for your soundboard skills."

"Bek, it's not the money. I have game patents that allow me to live however I want. I'm still working because I need to be busy, not because I need the money."

Rhebekka was well aware of Daniel's financial security. He could have sponsored their tours with the interest he accumulated in three months. Daniel desperately wanted to be needed and a part of something. In music and the gaming world, he'd found a purpose. "And your computer doesn't work unless you're in New York? I promise you we have internet, and Ellie has some up-and-coming acts. She'd love your help in making their dreams come true."

"Let me think about it. I can't do anything for a bit because of my current commitments. Anyway, if you didn't see it, the lion's den challenge you asked me to create is in there. Once they realize they have no weapons, they need to rely on their powers of prayer to increase their faith bar. That offers them the protection to keep the lion's mouths shut."

Rhebekka laughed. "You are brilliant, my friend. Thanks for the upgrades."

"You're very welcome. ArchAngel is one of my guilty pleasures. Give my love to Naomi and Ellie."

"Look at that schedule. I want to see you sooner than later."

Daniel chuckled. "I promise. Later, gator."

"After a while, crocodile."

Rhebekka hung up, lifted her goggles, and stared at the wall with the kid's gear. She smiled at the new sets she'd purchased and the added one with Lucian's name. She walked back into the gathering room and looked around. The kids were milling around, their bookbags all zipped up and placed near the door. She clapped her hands. "Everyone done?"

Expectant eyes turned to her, and affirmative nods confirmed their answer. She gestured behind her with both thumbs. There was a mad scramble toward the AV room, with Lucian bringing up the rear.

Rhebekka bumped his shoulder. "Quit worrying."

He jammed his hands deep into his pockets. "What if I'm not any good at it?"

Holly came back and grabbed his arm. "It won't matter. You're playing yourself. I sucked when I first started."

Rhebekka's heart swelled at Holly's kindness. She'd taken her role to heart. Lucian grinned and picked up his pace. *He's going to be okay. Things are going to be just fine.*

* * * *

"And then this freaking lion put its head right on my shoulder! I swear I could feel it panting on my face." Lucian threw a handful of popcorn in his mouth and stared at Naomi with wide eyes.

Naomi chuckled. She'd never seen him quite so animated. Her heart warmed. "It sounds like you had fun."

Lucian's full mouth necessitated a head nod answer.

Rhebekka grabbed a handful of popcorn from Naomi's bowl. "Daniel has outdone himself with the new headset he designed. It gives the gamer something close to a 4D experience with scents and air movement. I told him he needed to market ArchAngel. By the way, I invited him for a visit. It sounded like he needs his family of choice."

Lucian's mouth dropped open. "You know the dude that created that game?"

"We do. Daniel used to be Regal Crimson's production manager. He handled all the logistics involved in the audio-visual packaging of the tour. That's him in the picture with the pyrotechnic display." Naomi pointed to a framed photo on the wall of Daniel with his arms across Rhebekka and Ellie's shoulders.

Lucian stared at the photo for a moment. It looked like he was studying it intently, before he shook his head and turned back to Naomi. "If it's okay with you guys, I'm going to Ellie and Siobhan's after I finish my schoolwork tomorrow. Siobhan promised to start my self-defense classes."

Naomi swallowed a mouthful of popcorn. "Will you be too tired? I know you have to work in the morning."

"I should be okay. I'm headed to bed here in a little bit."

Rhebekka looked over at him. "You feeling okay?"

"Yeah, yeah. I'm fine." He stood and covered a yawn as he stretched. "I can never thank you two enough for all you've done for me. I never thought I'd ever find a place I could be myself."

Naomi stood and put her hands on his shoulders. "Lucian, we wouldn't want you to be anyone you're not. This is a safe space and always will be."

He wrapped his arms around her and dropped his head to her shoulder. "Thanks."

She hugged him back, swallowing the tears that wanted to pour down her cheeks. "Go on, off to bed."

"Night." He tapped his hand against his thigh. Both cats jumped off the back of the couch and followed him down the hall.

Naomi sat back down and snuggled into Rhebekka's arms. "He seems like he's doing okay."

"He's finding his way. All we can do is try and give him the tools to navigate the world by his compass." Rhebekka shifted, giving Naomi room to lie in her arms.

Naomi began to twist a lock of her hair, her mind contemplating a thousand things at once.

"What are you thinking about?"

Naomi shifted so she could see Rhebekka's eyes. "There are so many kids out there just like him, just like Daniel. The other day, I read that there are over four million homeless kids in the United States, and over 40 percent of them are LGBTQIA+. Few people step up to give them the stability we're trying to give Lucian. A growing percentage of

151

kids like Lucian are aging out of the foster system. That's over a million and a half kids with no place to go."

"I know how that feels. Ellie probably didn't think much about being bisexual when she was young, but I damn sure knew I was a lesbian. The only way we still had a home was to deny the real us."

Naomi turned to look at Rhebekka. "You cleared a path for Ellie to become whoever she wanted to be. No matter what, she had you to turn to."

"We had each other."

"But what if she hadn't had you? Ellie could have been out on the street, homeless and vulnerable."

Rhebekka shivered. "I don't even want to think about that."

Naomi pushed back and looked at the woman she loved. "What if we could do something about it, even on a small scale?"

Rhebekka tilted her head. "What do you have in mind?"

"What if we looked into becoming a foster family? Or figured out a place they can go when they age out."

"Like a transition home?"

Naomi tipped her head from side to side. There was a pause in their conversation as Naomi laid back against Rhebekka's chest. "Something like a house of refuge when they reach this technical age of majority. These kids have already been dealt a bad hand. How many are truly prepared to care for themselves without assistance?"

"Hell, I'd been planning it for years and wasn't prepared."

"Exactly. What if we helped form a safety net? Work with our friends for some vocational training. We know people in the music industry, social services, emergency services, ministry, childcare, and even—"

Rhebekka began to chuckle. "Slow down there. I'm not sure we can fit all those kids in the same room with Lucian. We only have so much space."

Naomi pinched her. "I didn't mean all at once, goof." She stopped for a moment, unconsciously twirling her hair again.

"You're thinking again."

"What if we got a bigger place?"

Rhebekka leaned down so that they were eye to eye. "You mean move out of here?"

Naomi sat up. "Not right away. I think there are many things we'd need to get in place. We'd have to find the right house, check the regulations, and make pertinent connections with the groups that would know who needs help. That's just a few things that would have to be done before we ever opened the door."

Rhebekka pulled her back into her arms. "This is an important idea. If we can provide even a few kids a better step into their futures, we'd be fulfilling the second greatest commandment."

"Love thy neighbor as thyself," they said in unison.

Naomi snuggled under Rhebekka's chin. Her thoughts were on Lucian and all the kids like him, who just might have a fighting chance if her idea became a reality. She hoped whatever house they found had neighbors who liked rainbows.

Chapter Eleven

RHEBEKKA SLID ONTO THE couch in the office at Redemption's Road. Tank handed her a cup of coffee. A million things were running through her mind. She was constantly worried about Lucian and Ellie. *Now figure out how to fulfill Naomi's desire to provide a safe landing spot for kids like Lucian.*

"What's bouncing back and forth inside your head between your ears?"

Rhebekka grinned at her old shadow. "So many things. I can't even quiet my mind with music."

"I'm not sure if I ever remember you saying that. What's got your thoughts in a margarita blender?"

Rhebekka looked around the office. She stood and walked over to a picture of her, Tank, and Ellie. Tank had just started with the tour in security. Over time, she'd become Rhebekka's second skin, closer to her than her own shadow, which is exactly how she earned the nickname. Rhebekka tapped the picture. "We were so young."

Tank laughed. "Young and stupid with dreams too big to fit into the box everyone tried to keep putting us in."

"Where would we have been if we hadn't found our way to each other?"

Tank ran a hand through her disheveled hair. "Hell, if I know. It's way too early in the morning for me to get this philosophical."

Rhebekka took a sip of her coffee and sat back down. "What would you say if I told you Naomi and I want to try and put together something that would offer kids like you, like Lucian, a place to go once they leave foster care or the system in general?"

"Lucian just moved in with you. You need something else to keep you busy? I can put you to work here at the brewery." Tank laughed, then sighed. "When I turned eighteen, there wasn't a check coming anymore for my keep. That made the foster family less accommodating, and they put me out on the street with my clothes in a garbage bag. I had a letter to report to Camp Lejeune for basic training, a bus ticket to Florida, and a wallet with one hundred and seventeen dollars."

"Ellie and I had a beat-up Subaru and about a thousand dollars tucked into a guitar that held our hopes and dreams."

Tank gestured between them with her coffee cup. "We turned out okay. I'm all for you and Naomi giving a kid a better jump-off point than we had. You know Amy and I will do anything to help."

Rhebekka grinned. "That's good news, because if we find a house to handle what she wants, I'm betting it will need renovations." She stopped and thought for a minute. "If we move out, would you and Amy be interested in the loft?"

The chair squeaked as Tank leaned back. "I'd need to ask Amy, but it would solve one issue. Amy and I have been spending more time at her apartment to give Kierlynn space, since I told her she could stay with me. With your offer, we could move into your place, and she could stay at the brewery apartment. It's something to think about anyway."

"How's it going with Kierlynn? I've been so busy with Lucian that I haven't had a chance to check in."

"We're still finding our footing. She's carrying a lot of baggage from her tours in Afghanistan, so we're taking it one day at a time. Amy found her a female veteran's group over in Deep Creek."

"That reminds me, Sydney might have other resources to help her. She suggested a new charity for us to support, involving veterans."

Tank nodded. "At this point, I think anything might help." She looked at her watch. "Come on, it's time to get the new batch of beer started. I've been working on a new formula, playing off Eden's Ale with a fruit twist. I'm thinking of calling it Forbidden Fruit."

Rhebekka nearly spit coffee all over the place. "Nice. Okay, brewmaster, let's go to the garden and pick some apples." She stood and squeezed her best friend's shoulder on their way to the supplies.

Tank had come a long way since her obsession with Ellie. Self-consciously, Rhebekka rubbed her cheek where Tank had landed a punch the first time she saw Ellie with Siobhan. Their friendship had survived, though it had been touch-and-go until Rhebekka's accident. *Amazing how almost dying puts so many things into perspective.*

Kierlynn was a quiet but fast study. She seemed able to anticipate what Tank would need next. Rhebekka spent the rest of the morning helping the two load ingredients into the giant vats. At noon, she bid them goodbye.

She stopped at Karman's store on the way home and texted Naomi as she walked in the bakery door. Karmen's partner was covering the counter. "Hey, Zandra, long time no see."

"Good to see you too." Zandra shook Rhebekka's hand. "We need to have dinner together, soon."

Rhebekka smiled at the woman who had brought such happiness into Karmen's life. "I like that plan, especially since you and I get to eat far too much good food with our best halves cooking. So, how's the new employee?" She craned her neck to see through the windows in the double doors that led into the kitchen.

"He's working out fantastic. I can't tell you how much pressure it's taken off Karmen. The kid shows up ready to work and almost has to be ordered to take a break."

Rhebekka didn't doubt Zandra's words or Lucian's work ethic. The job had given Lucian a sense of control and empowerment to make decisions for himself. "Can I get a couple of chicken salad croissants and potato soup to go? I'm sure Lucian will eat lunch here, but I'll take a treat home to Naomi."

Zandra leaned through the doors. "Rhebekka's here with a lunch order. Can you come and fill it, Lucian? I've got a customer coming in to pick up those cookies in a few minutes."

Rhebekka heard a muffled answer. Lucian sported a broad smile as he pushed open the door. He went to the small sink and washed his hands before donning server's gloves to put the order together.

"I'd have delivered these if you'd called. Karmen told me to knock off early to finish an English assignment." He started packaging up the food.

"Well, then go ahead and pack some of each for yourself too. Naomi went to the post office to mail a birthday present to her mother. She should be back by the time we get there."

Lucian nodded. "The sheriff was here just a little while ago. She'd called in a take-out order for Jax and the other staff at the animal hospital. She asked how I was doing and gave me a little update. From what she said, Asher has shaken the place up."

Rhebekka watched him diligently packing her order. There didn't seem to be any distress over the news. This simple fact put Rhebekka's raw nerves slightly more at ease. Lucian was finding his footing on the solid ground they were trying to provide. Her heart swelled that she and Naomi had been able to offer him a safe haven. *How many kids are desperately treading water in an ocean of humanity's callous indifference? What would happen if just one of them were offered a life raft?* She was reminded of King Lemuel's words in Proverbs. *'Speak up for those who cannot speak for themselves, for the rights of all who are destitute. Speak up and judge fairly; defend the rights of the poor and needy.' A house of refuge we will be.*

* * * *

Her stomach full, Rhebekka drove to Ellie's. The time had come to pass on the information about Tom and Dave Broader. Daniel had unearthed contact information and so much more they could turn over to the authorities. He'd called her right after lunch. She replayed their conversation as she drove.

"What's up, technogeek?" Rhebekka tossed the remnants of their lunch in the trash.

"You might want to sit down."

"I don't like the sound of this, Daniel."

"Nothing's wrong. I wanted to tell you that I located Tom and Dave Broader. They've moved about six times. Both currently live in the Alexandria, Virginia area and attend a larger congregation than the one you grew up in. Tom is a widower in his seventies and is serving as something called a district overseer. Dave is in his fifties. I'm not sure if Dave serves in any position in the hierarchy. It looks like Tom's wife, Betty, died almost ten years ago."

Rhebekka rubbed her forehead and moved over to her small desk. "What about Carrie? Were you able to find her? Is she still an active witness?"

"Oh, she apparently flew the coop after graduation. The whole family moved about a year after you and Ellie took off. Carrie's been married three times and now owns a small restaurant with her current husband, in Arizona."

"Arizona? It sounds like she moved as far from them as she could."

"From everything you've told me, are you surprised?"

Rhebekka sighed. "Not in the slightest. Tell me more."

Nothing Daniel revealed after that was beyond what she'd expected. One interesting tidbit he'd told her was that Dave had been charged with child abuse at one point. Child services had been called by the school about bruises on his daughter. Daniel had somehow hacked into the file and found that the child was uncooperative, and Dave's wife explained the bruises away as nothing more than an accident. Rhebekka drove with anger boiling in her gut. She felt certain Dave was likely physically and sexually abusing the child, especially when she found out he wasn't the biological father. Bastard.

She parked in front of Ellie's and shut off the truck. Her head was pounding, and she let it fall forward until it rested on the steering wheel. "Lord, I've long relied on you to guide my hands and feet. Help me expose the evil done in your name. Be with Ellie and me as we shine a light in the darkness." Rhebekka ended the prayer and looked up to see Ellie watching her from the second-floor window. She pulled the keys from the ignition and opened the door. *Your will be done.*

* * * *

"It's not your fault, Ellie." Rhebekka clasped her sister's hands in hers. "Look at me." Ellie's eyes were tear-filled when they met hers. "They're sexual predators who used their influence to make a child believe she had to protect God by being silent about their abuse. First, it wasn't God that molested you, and second, the Almighty doesn't need our protection. That's just a lie they perpetrated to keep you, Carrie, and whoever else they've done this to, quiet. The only way to bring them to justice is to expose them for what they are."

Ellie leaned forward, resting her head on Rhebekka's shoulder. Her words were difficult to understand through the sobs. "This is so fucked up."

Rhebekka pulled Ellie into her lap, enveloping and cradling her as she'd done so many times when Ellie was little. "It is. They can't hurt you anymore. The power is in our hands now."

"It's the reliving it, Bek. I have nightmares every time we bring it up. If it wasn't for Siobhan, I don't know if I'd be doing as well as I am. She's the only thing that drives the darkness away."

Rhebekka wiped Ellie's tears. "In John, it says, 'Light has come into the world, but people loved darkness instead of light because their deeds were evil. Everyone who does evil hates the light, and will not come into the light for fear that their deeds will be exposed.' That's why there is no doubt that Tom, Dave, and hundreds of others just like them, who stand as governing bodies in every Kingdom Hall, are not godly men. Nor are they servants of the true God. We'll shine a light so bright, no shadow will exist for them to hide in. No corner will be dark enough for them to cower in, and no shade will offer comfort from the heat of the spotlight."

"Bek, I don't know if I'm strong enough to turn on that light." Ellie's voice was trembling as she clung to Rhebekka.

"I hope we won't be the only ones with our finger pressing the on button."

Ellie sat back and wiped at her tears. "What do you mean?"

"Daniel found Carrie."

Ellie sat up straight. "Carrie Broader?"

Rhebekka nodded. "She's in Arizona, slinging hash at a 50s diner with husband number three. From everything Daniel can find, she hasn't stepped foot in a Kingdom Hall since she ran away with husband number one. I've got plane tickets to Flagstaff in the morning to see if she's willing to help us turn on the sun."

Siobhan leaned over and rubbed Ellie's back. "I think ya should go. Rhebekka showing up alone won't be near as convincing as having the one she suffered with in silence standing there reminding her that there is a reason ta come forward."

"On the testimony of two witnesses, or on the testimony of three witnesses, the matter should be established. She'll remember, Ellie. She'll remember." Rhebekka covered Ellie's hands in hers.

Ellie looked back and forth between her and Siobhan. Rhebekka wasn't sure what her little songbird's answer would be, so she fell back on an elemental connection. She started to sing,

"This little light of mine, I'm going to let it shine..."

Ellie smiled and joined in. "Let it shine, let it shine, let it shine."

* * * *

It was deep into the first hours of the morning and only a few hours before she and Ellie would board the plane in Elkins that Rhebekka had chartered to take them to Pittsburgh. They'd discussed flying private the entire journey, but decided neither was in the mood for eleven hours on a small plane. Their anxiety level was already pinging off the charts, and it seemed a bridge too far for Ellie.

"I can feel you thinking." Naomi's voice broke the quiet. Rhebekka pulled her closer. "You always were good at feeling things I didn't say..." The gentle touch of Naomi's finger tracing patterns on her skin soothed her soul. "How do you think Carrie is going to react when she sees us?"

Naomi kissed her chest. "I'm sure it's going to be a shock. Did you think about calling instead of just showing up?"

"I thought about it, but it would just be an opportunity to pretend it never happened, if she even took the call. When the truth is staring you in the face, it's much harder to ignore. I know it will be a difficult reunion. Seeing Carrie will be just as hard on Ellie. It's going to remind both of them of so much pain."

"I wish I were going with you, but Lucian."

Rhebekka kissed her head. "Lucian is our priority. He's not a minor, but I don't want him to think we would abandon him because of something we needed to do. It's all too fresh right now. Ellie and I will be fine. You're right where you're supposed to be."

Naomi leaned up on an elbow and looked into her eyes. "You'll call me?"

"I will, as soon as we land." Rhebekka shifted until Naomi was beneath her. She kissed a spot just below her lover's ear. "Until then, how about I give you something to remember me by until I get home?"

"Oh, I'm liking the way you think more and more." Naomi tilted her head and spread her legs, and Rhebekka gladly settled between them.

Rhebekka groaned, then sat back on her knees and pulled Naomi into a seated position to remove the threadbare Regal Crimson T-shirt she was sleeping in. As Naomi's arms went over her head, Rhebekka leaned forward and captured an erect nipple in her mouth. Naomi's soft gasp of pleasure motivated her to continue her exploration. She brushed her lips across the other nipple, as Naomi's head cleared the neck of the T-shirt. The last remnants of clothing between them were removed. Skin to skin, they found the rhythm of music only two bodies in love can create.

Rhebekka's fingers softly traced across Naomi's ribs, her thumb floating across silky skin until it rested in the hollow just inside Naomi's hip bone. She let her lips find Naomi's as they melded together into one, bodies rising and falling in a wave of pleasure. Her tongue delved in, meeting an equally anxious one that swirled around her own. She loved Naomi with every cell in her body. Nothing, not even music, had ever called to her and claimed her so completely as this woman who now wore her wedding ring. She cupped Naomi's hip and pulled it tightly into her own body.

Naomi's hands cupped her face as they kissed. With each thrust of her hips, Naomi's eyes would involuntarily flutter shut before opening again to lock on Rhebekka's gaze. *Such a gift she is.* Rhebekka's back arched into blunted fingernails that raked up her back, dragging a passionate moan from her core. As much as she wanted to feel Naomi all along her length, she wanted to taste her more. A trail of heat radiated from each fingernail Naomi had scratched along her skin. Moving down Naomi's body, she left a trail of wet kisses at the base of her throat, across each breast and rib, and settled in the soft hollow near her hip that her thumb had explored earlier. She lingered there, sucking and nipping at the soft flesh that pebbled under her touch.

Naomi bent her knees, and Rhebekka settled between them, nearly quaking with the need to taste her. She leaned on her elbows, breathing deeply of cocoa butter lotion and the sweet musk of Naomi's desire. The pads of her thumbs ran along the creases where Naomi's thighs met soft curls. She was dripping with need, and Rhebekka could no longer restrain herself from tasting her. She dipped her head and breathed deeply as her tongue touched fevered flesh. Desire took over her focus and she drank Naomi in. *So sweet.*

Naomi's fingers slid into her hair, tightened, and held her in place. Rhebekka licked and sucked the tender flesh. Though her wife nearly begged, she held back from touching Naomi's clit. She delved her tongue inside, darting in and out. Naomi's hips rose off the bed, forcing Rhebekka to curl her arms under her lover's thighs to hold her in place. Naomi's body began to tremble, signaling it was time for Rhebekka to change tactics. *I need her to come.*

She gazed up to watch Naomi's chest heave with each lick. The sensitive bundle of nerves that crested Naomi's center deserved her attention. Rhebekka gladly lavished it with various broad strokes and tiny grazes of her tongue. Naomi's body surged toward the ceiling as Rhebekka latched onto her clit, sucking and humming into her flesh until Naomi finally released her head to clutch at the bed sheets instead. Naomi's boneless body fell back to the bed, and Rhebekka drank in the sweet completion of Naomi's climax.

Moments later, Rhebekka left a wet trail of Naomi's essence as she kissed back up her wife's body, then covered panting lips with her own. Nothing, not even thousands of screaming fans, could compare to how she felt in these private and intimate moments with Naomi. A passionate kiss met her as she covered Naomi's body again. Naomi was her touchstone, the one person in this physical world who grounded and centered her.

Naomi lay beneath her, recovering and using her fingertips to trace invisible patterns on Rhebekka's back. She thanked God every day for Naomi's stubborn determination to break down every barrier Rhebekka had created between them. *How did I ever survive without her, without her touch?* She'd asked herself these questions a million times, but there were never any answers. The truth was, she hadn't survived, she'd only existed. *PIMO.* The acronym frequently referred to Jehovah's Witness members. *I was living day to day, physically in, but mentally out. A black-and-white world devoid of the colors of true joy and connection.*

"What are you thinking about so hard?"

Rhebekka lifted her head. She shifted down slightly and rested her chin on her hands, steepled on Naomi's chest. She could stare into those eyes for eternity... but there had been a question. "You."

Naomi furrowed her brow. "Me?"

Rhebekka leaned down and kissed the valley between Naomi's ample breasts. "Yes, you. I was thinking about how much better my life is with you in it."

Naomi cupped Rhebekka's face. "That street goes both ways, love."

"There are days it's so hard to forgive myself for what I put you through. I get angry at all the time I forced us to miss."

Naomi rolled them over until she was resting on top of Rhebekka. "How would you counsel a congregation member if they had this same burden?"

"What do you mean?"

"If Jax came to you and said she couldn't forgive herself for not making her way back to Chance sooner, what would you say to her?"

"Oh, that's not fair."

Naomi chuckled. "Maybe, but it's as close of a comparison as I can find in my post-orgasm bliss."

Rhebekka pulled her in tighter, tucking Naomi under her chin. "Well, I guess I would tell her that looking back prevents us from seeing what's in front of us."

"It's always harder accepting the spoonful of medicine in our mouths than being the one holding the spoon."

"Oh, that was good."

Naomi rolled her hand as if taking a bow before an audience. Rhebekka laughed.

"That's one of the things I truly love about you. You have the uncanny ability to force me to get out of my own way."

"It comes from loving you the way I do." Naomi kissed the side of her neck and nestled back into place. "I wish I could go with you today."

Rhebekka sighed. "I do too. This will be painful for Ellie, and Carrie for that matter."

Naomi yawned. "Be as gentle as you can be. Bringing up those memories will be like cutting through scar tissue to open up a wound that never truly heals."

She held Naomi closer and kissed the top of her head. "I'll try. Go to sleep. We have to get up in a few hours. I just want to hold you."

Minutes later, Rhebekka felt Naomi's body completely relax and her breathing even out into the rhythm of sleep. The sun would rise soon enough. For now, she'd live in this moment with the woman who kept her world bright with color and chased the black and white into the shadows.

* * * *

Rhebekka felt Ellie startle as the wheels of the plane touched down on the runway. The pilot had tried to avoid a storm that blew in over the desert. "All over now. How's your stomach?"

Ellie pushed her hair behind her ear. "It will settle soon. You'd think we'd be used to it, with all the years we've flown."

"I never did care to fly, but in this case, it was better than spending days in the car."

Ellie looked out the window as they taxied in. "Are you sure this is a good idea? I mean, I haven't seen Carrie in years."

"Only one way to find out. An in-person meeting is harder to ignore than a phone call, songbird. All she can do is tell us no. Even if she does, we're going forward. It may change our strategy but not our purpose. We have to speak up for those still suffering at the hands of those who hide behind their position with threats of dishonoring a God they use for their own sick purposes." Rhebekka took a deep breath and held Ellie's hands in hers. "Do you remember what I said about them perverting the verse from John?"

Ellie nodded.

"In this case, the truth will set you and Carrie free. It will also ensnare them in the lies they've told for decades."

Flying the longest leg of the trip in first class had made the journey slightly more bearable, but they weren't done yet. They still had a thirty-minute drive to Williams. They taxied to a gate, where a ground crew met them to deplane. Luggage in hand, they headed to the car rental counter. Less than an hour later, they were on their way to their hotel in Williams. They were too tired to approach Carrie immediately. They chose to go to the diner in the morning for breakfast.

A small taqueria and a convenience store offered them everything they needed for the trip and their stay. It had already been a very long day and they were both exhausted. Rhebekka glanced over at her sister, who looked out the side window, chewing her fingernails. She reached up and pulled her sister's hand into hers.

"Sorry, Bek."

Rhebekka rubbed her thumb across the rough edges of the mangled nails. "You haven't chewed your nails this bad since we ran away from home."

"Fuck, Bek. Do you know how hard I worked to bury all this shit? Yet here I am, drudging all this up. If Carrie is anything like me, the last thing she wants to do is remember what they did to us. Are you sure we're doing the right thing?"

Rhebekka pulled off to the side of the road and put the rental car in park. She closed her eyes for a second before turning to Ellie. "Songbird, I question every single thing I do when it comes to this. In my desire to bring them to justice, am I causing you more trauma? Will stirring all this up make any difference at all? How can three people make even one small dent in an organization of that size? So no, I don't know if we're doing the right thing. Unfortunately, I know this will get worse before it gets better."

Ellie dropped her head. "I'm sorry, Bek."

Rhebekka leaned across the console and pulled her sister toward her until their foreheads touched. "I can only tell you that if we do nothing, they continue to get away with it. They continue to have the opportunity to hurt someone else. That's something I'm not sure I can live with. I asked you to come on this journey, but you don't have to continue. You don't have to come and talk to Carrie. I can put you back on a plane."

Ellie wiped at the fat tears running down her cheeks. "I know I don't have to, but that won't stop the nightmares. It won't stop Tom and Dave."

Rhebekka shook her head gently. "No." She kissed her sister's forehead and sat back in her seat. "What do you want to do?"

They sat there for a few minutes, staring out into the desert. Rhebekka had done all the pushing she intended to do. This had to be Ellie's decision.

"I hope she's happy to see us," Ellie said as she twisted the top off her iced tea and took a long drink.

Rhebekka put the car in drive and pulled back onto the road. "Only one way to find out."

* * * *

Naomi looked at the clock on the wall. She'd talked to the girls when they'd landed in Flagstaff. Tension and anxiety ran thickly through their conversation, and Naomi said a small prayer.

"Hey, Naomi, can you help me with something?" Lucian came into the kitchen and went to the refrigerator for a Coke.

Naomi smiled at the simple action that said so much. It told her Lucian was beginning to truly see this as his home, because he no longer asked if he could get something to drink. "Sure. What do you need?"

Lucian reached into his back pocket and pulled out a few score pages. He handed them to her.

She unfolded and smoothed the pages on the counter. For a few minutes, she looked over the notes, letting the melody play in her head as she hummed the tune. "I love the bridge. When did you write this?"

"It's something I'd been tinkering with when I worked at the music store. It was in the things we picked up from the group home. It didn't seem important to take with me when I split. I took things to help me survive."

Naomi held the pages in one hand and took one of Lucian's hands in the other as she led him to the piano. "Well, you have plenty of time to think about it now. Let's see what it sounds like." She sat down and patted the bench beside her. She put her hands on the keys and began to play. There were dark and broody measures, while the chorus was noticeably upbeat and hopeful. The transitions could be smoother, but that was an easy fix. Naomi turned to Lucian when she'd finished what he had written so far.

A sheepish grin crept over his lips. "What do you think?"

"Lucian, this is incredible. You have more talent than you give yourself credit for."

He dropped his head and fiddled with the tab on the Coke can. "It's just something I've been tinkering with."

Naomi put her hand under his chin and raised his eyes to her. "Lucian, I married into a family of incredible musicians that have toured the world. I'm not in the habit of blowing smoke up anyone's backside." She pointed to the sheets. "This is really good. If Rhebekka were here, I have no doubt she'd say the same."

"Is there anything you think could improve it?"

"Well, let's break it down and see." Naomi picked up a pencil that lay on the music desk.

Lucian's smile brightened. "Naomi?"

"Yes?"

"If I ever forget to say it, I want you and Rhebekka to know how grateful I am for taking me in. I don't know where I'd be without you two."

Naomi felt tears prick her eyes. She put her hand on Lucian's cheek. "We feel pretty lucky to have you with us, so let's call it even."

"Not even close. Okay, enough mush. How do we fix this song?"

Naomi wiped the corners of her eyes with her thumbs before she put her hands on the keys. "Go get your bass, and let's run through it together."

He nodded and got up. She watched him walk away, before closing her eyes and thanking God for sending Lucian to them. *Your mercy is great.*

* * * *

The following day, Rhebekka watched the steam rise from the strong cup of coffee she wrapped her hands around. Her nerves were on edge, and a thousand butterflies turned cartwheels in her stomach. Ellie picked at her waffle, seemingly as uninterested in eating as Rhebekka was. Both had slept fitfully until around one in the morning when Ellie had come crawling into bed and cried herself to sleep. They'd had another long talk and called Naomi and Siobhan for guidance, again, before coming down to breakfast. They wanted to try and time their arrival after the breakfast crowd but before the lunch rush. In a family owned restaurant, Carrie would likely be an integral part of the operation.

Rhebekka reached out her hand, and Ellie clasped it. "Whatever happens, it's going to be okay."

"I wish I could believe that as much as you do."

"I saw an instrument store at the one end of town. Do you want to kill some time? I've been picking out a new song. Maybe you can help me put lyrics to it." Rhebekka squeezed her hand.

"Music is always your go-to when you're stressed. I'm game if you are. I certainly can't seem to eat."

Rhebekka held her hand up for the waitress. She ordered two coffees to go and paid the bill, leaving a generous tip. She handed one of the cups to Ellie as they left. The streets looked nearly deserted, but she didn't think that unusual in a tourist-trap town during the off-season. A bitter cold wind swept under her coat as she unlocked the car. Ellie buckled in and pulled back the plastic tab on the cup lid before wrapping her hands around its warmth. Rhebekka started the car and cranked the heat. For a few minutes, only cold air blew from the vents, making her shiver. She waited a bit before she pulled out onto the street. "We'll probably be there before the warm air ever starts."

"That's one thing we never worried about in that Subaru of yours. At least the heater worked. Air conditioning was typically sketchy, but we never froze."

"The miles that car saw."

"Yeah, and your back seat saw a few things too." Ellie chuckled.

"Hey, I was a baby dyke stretching my wings. Could I help it if girls fawned all over me? The more girls there were in the audience, the more tips we took home."

"You were a cute, baby dyke. I used to laugh at how many of them wrote their numbers on the bills they threw into our tip case."

"There were only a few I ever hooked up with. It just wasn't my style."

"I think having your sister share a one-bedroom apartment hampered your style more than anything."

Rhebekka let out a hardy laugh. "Maybe, but I could have gone to their place. I wasn't a saint, that's for sure. I didn't look forward to trying to find my clothes in the middle of the night to get out of there. It was about the music for me."

"Sure, and the girls were just a bonus."

"Smart ass. There's the store. The sign says open." Rhebekka parked out front and exited with her coffee cup.

Inside, there were bins of vinyl records stacked in alphabetical order. They browsed the titles and pulled out vintage albums to look at the cover art. Rhebekka read the musical credits on Joni Mitchell's album *Blue*, with Carole King's *Tapestry* tucked under her arm.

Ellie walked over to her with a stack of albums in her hand. "Siobhan is going to be so excited." Ellie held up the Queen album. "Freddie Mercury's vocals will hold up to the test of time. He was a gay artist who died far too soon. Queen is her all-time favorite."

Rhebekka smiled. "She's got excellent taste, Queen the band, and her very own queen."

Ellie blushed. "Stop."

"Not a chance."

A woman approached. She looked to be in her early thirties. "Good morning. I'm Sandy. Is there anything I can help you with?"

Ellie nodded to the albums in her hands. "Can you ship these for me? I really don't want to lug them back on the plane."

The woman smiled broadly. "Certainly. Would you like me to do the same for you?" She pointed to the albums Rhebekka held.

"Yes please, though I'm not quite done." She noticed Sandy was nearly vibrating with energy. If she was a serious music lover, she'd already identified who was in the shop.

Rhebekka slid Blue under her arm to join Carole's album and held out her hand. "Rhebekka Deklan. It's nice to meet you."

The woman shook her hand, then squinted a bit as if trying to work out the details. "It's nice to meet you, Rhebekka. Has anyone ever told you two that you are dead ringers for Bek and Ellie McNally from Regal Crimson?"

Ellie chuckled and held out her hand as well. "A time or two. That would be because we are Bek and Ellie. I take it you know our music?"

Sandy nodded enthusiastically. "I've been to several of your concerts with my dad. No one put on a show like you two."

Rhebekka felt the blush spreading across her cheeks. "We did try to give the fans their money's worth. I'm so glad you enjoyed it." Rhebekka looked around the shop. "This place is great. Vinyl is making a huge comeback."

Sandy's smile seemed even bigger than before at the compliment. "My dad started this business about ten years ago. There isn't a huge demand within the area, but we do a great online business."

Rhebekka nodded. "I can see why. I don't know what it is about holding an album jacket that feels so different than an electronic version." She browsed a bit and found the album she was looking for. Fleetwood Mac's Rumors was an enduring favorite she could listen to, over and over.

"My dad said the same thing. It's why he started the store. Well, that and his love of music. He will never believe you two were in the store."

"We could take a picture with your storefront for him." Ellie shifted the albums under her arm.

Sandy blushed. "I wouldn't impose on you like that. Most big musicians want to be left alone."

Rhebekka laid a hand on her shoulder. "A lot of those musicians forget that they weren't always the big stars they are now. The best artists remember and celebrate the people who made them big in the first place. We'd be nowhere without our fans. This is a simple way to give back."

"My dad would love it. He's a fan as well."

Ellie handed her the albums, and the three of them worked their way to the counter. "Really? What's his favorite song?"

"He's always told me that *Out of Ash* got him through the adjustment of coming back home from overseas at the end of his military career."

Rhebekka looked around the shop at the instruments that hung from special racks around the room. She put her albums down on the counter and looked up at the Martin guitar that hung nearby. She pointed to it. "May I?"

Sandy was wide-eyed. "You want to play here in our store? I'd be thrilled. Dad will lose his mind once he hears about it. He had to make a run to Phoenix to pick up a load of new records early this morning."

Rhebekka put the guitar strap over her head and headed to an area where a few stools sat arranged in a semicircle. She pulled the pick out from her back pocket and sat down. "How about you find your cellphone and video this for him? What's his name?"

Sandy grabbed her phone off the counter. "That would be awesome. His name is Keith Smith."

Rhebekka considered Ellie as they sat down. "I'll take the lead if you want to carry the harmony." She knew Ellie was still dealing with the loss of her formerly powerful voice. The harmony in this song was subtle, lending itself to Ellie's abilities.

Ellie nodded and smiled. "I'm okay, Bek. I promise."

The next few minutes reminded Rhebekka of their early days. Ellie had been so unsure of her voice, always choosing to sing harmony until Rhebekka had left the band. It had taken some time for Ellie to come into her own and find the confidence to take the lead. Regal Crimson hadn't missed a beat after that and won many more awards.

Rhebekka sang about the mythical bird that would burst into flames before rising anew from the ashes. The lyrics led them through the forest floor after a wildfire and the rebirth of life out of the scorched earth. Her sister's harmony ran strong and true beside her voice. This had always been one of Rhebekka's favorite things to do. Singing with her sister was a gift she would never take for granted.

The final note rang out on the guitar as Rhebekka looked up and pointed to the cell phone. "That's for you, Keith Smith. Thanks for letting us explore your awesome, vintage vinyl and play these quality instruments. A big shout-out to your fantastic daughter, Sandy. She was more than welcoming and helpful."

Sandy stopped the video and ran her hand through her hair. "He's going to shit himself."

Rhebekka chuckled. "Feel free to use that as a promotional item in your advertising. Thank you for being so hospitable to two sisters that needed to kill a little time."

They moved back to the counter to make their purchases and gave the shipping address of Ellie's studio for the albums.

Sandy finished up the sales slips and looked a little sheepish. "Would you take that storefront picture for me? I'd like to print it off and give it to him for his birthday next month."

"Ellie and I will be happy to do that. We'll take a few with you as well. When will your dad be back?"

Sandy looked at the clock. "He left early this morning. He should be back by four."

Rhebekka followed her through the store and out the door. "No promises, but if we have time, we'll stop back to let him get his picture with us. That is if you think he'd want that."

Sandy nearly choked laughing. "If I think he'd want it? If he knew you were here, he'd crawl back from Phoenix. He's going to be so jealous I got to spend this much time with you."

They took the pictures they'd discussed and headed back to the car. They hadn't worked on any new material, but playing music together had steadied them. It was time to face the music in figurative terms. What they were about to do would be far less pleasant than singing together.

"You ready?" Rhebekka put her hand over Ellie's.

Ellie stared out the windshield. "Not really, but I don't think I ever would be, given why we came here."

Rhebekka nodded. She understood that dredging up these memories was painful. She only hoped that, in doing so, they would rip off the Band-aid quickly so the healing could begin. *Be with us, Lord. Help us do the right thing. May what they've done in the name of protecting you be brought to light.*

Chapter Twelve

RHEBEKKA PULLED THE CAR into a spot across from the diner. They sat in silence, watching a few people move about. The café resembled a chrome train car with a few bar stools at a counter and some scattered tables. The breakfast rush seemed to be over, and they were resetting for the lunch crowd. They were too far away to see faces, but each person wore a white apron.

"We probably won't get a better time. Let's go do this." Ellie opened her door and stepped out.

"I'll be with you the entire time. You aren't alone, Ellie." Rhebekka closed and locked the doors.

"I'm grateful for that. I hope she's still the girl I knew. I also know what happened to us changed us forever."

They crossed the street and Ellie took Rhebekka's hand as she pushed open the door. The smell of fried food and strong coffee hit Rhebekka immediately. The place was clean and well cared for. It was the quintessential 1950s diner, complete with the female servers in rolled pants, Mary Jane shoes, white cotton blouses, and a large bow holding their hair in a ponytail. The men were in white T-shirts and rolled jeans. The sign said for them to seat themselves, so they did. One of the servers approached them in just a few moments, with a coffee pot and two cups on a tray with cream and sugar. She put the tray down and pointed to the menus stuck between the salt and pepper.

"Can I get you started with a cup of coffee, or would you prefer something else?" She pulled an order pad from her apron pocket and grabbed for the pencil stuck through the top of her ponytail.

Rhebekka pointed to the cup. "Coffee's fine. Ellie?"

"It's probably too early for a gin and tonic, so coffee will have to do for me as well."

The waitress poured steaming cups for them and waited as they looked over the menu. Rhebekka pointed to the dessert section. "Do you have pie ready at this time of the day?"

The waitress nodded. "All day, every day. It's one of the things we're known for. My mom makes amazing pies. The only one I don't care for is raisin, but that's because I think they're gross."

Rhebekka knew this was her opening. "Your mom works here?"

The young girl grinned. "She owns the place with my stepdad."

"Well then, I say we support a family owned and operated business. I'll have the chocolate silk pie. Ellie?"

She put her menu down and faced the young waitress. "I'll have the strawberry."

The waitress finished writing their order down. "I'll leave the coffee pot with you and be right back with your pies. Here's the cream and sugar."

The young girl left, and the sisters fixed their coffee to taste.

The clinking noise from her spoon broke the silence in the empty diner as Ellie stirred her coffee. "No doubt who she belongs to. She looks exactly like Carrie at that age."

Rhebekka nodded as she took a sip of the dark brew. "Uncanny."

The kitchen door swung open, and the person they'd come to see stopped abruptly, nearly spilling the pies. She reached out her hand to catch the tilting tray. "Ellie?"

Ellie nodded slightly. She rose and took the tray from Carrie. "It's me."

"What are you doing here?" Carrie's eyes shuffled back and forth between Ellie and Rhebekka.

Rhebekka stood and took the tray from her, then guided Carrie into the booth. Ellie sat across from her, sliding over to make room. Ellie and Carrie looked like rabbits ready to bolt at any minute. Rhebekka decided to take the lead for a bit. "It's nice to see you, Carrie. Sorry for dropping in so abruptly without warning."

Carrie clasped her hands together on the table. Rhebekka set the tray down and reached out to cover the trembling hands with her own. "I can tell you that Ellie was just as apprehensive when I suggested we find you."

Rhebekka could see the scared, timid girl Carrie used to be. "You and Ellie were very close as kids."

Carrie nodded. She turned to stare blankly out the large, picture window. It was several seconds before she turned back to them. "We were. I always considered her the sister I never had."

A tentative smile crossed Ellie's face. "I always looked at you as a part of my family too. I hated leaving you behind when we took off. If I could have figured out how to take you with us, I would have."

Carrie nodded. "I didn't stick around too long after you two left. I spent a few years making a mess of my life, relying on the wrong people." She glanced over at their waitress. "My daughter is the only good thing that came out of it. About five years ago, I met Eddy, and we moved west to take over his parent's restaurant."

Rhebekka gestured around the diner. "It looks like it's going pretty well."

"My husband is pretty handy on the grill, and I seem to have a knack for baking. My daughter, Paula, is an excellent waitress and the best damn thing I ever did. How she turned out the way she did is a mystery. I think she raised me instead of the other way around."

Ellie patted Carrie's hands that trembled on the table. "I'm happy for you. It looks like we both did pretty well for ourselves."

Carrie smiled. "I'd say you two did more than pretty well. I've kept up with your career. I was sad to see you'd retired."

Ellie shrugged her shoulders and swallowed a bite of her pie. "Sometimes, we have to face hard truths. My hard truth was that thyroid cancer changed my voice. It was time to retire that dream and find another. So now I produce upcoming young acts."

"And she's done incredibly well. Many have already cut their debut records and are making their way up the charts." Rhebekka took a sip of coffee.

"What did you end up doing after you retired from the band, Bek?" Carrie signaled for Paula to bring another cup.

Rhebekka nearly snorted. "You won't believe it. I'm a non-denominational pastor at a small house of worship I started."

Carrie laughed and covered her mouth. "You've got to be kidding me. I figured you'd be like me and never have anything to do with religion again."

Rhebekka tipped her head from shoulder to shoulder. "I spent a lot of years running as far from religion as I possibly could. We had the band, and that was all I needed."

"Of course, that's when she met the love of her life." Ellie grinned and brought another bite of pie to her lips.

Carrie looked down at the ring on Rhebekka's hand. "You got married?"

"Not immediately. I almost lost everything out of stupidity. Somehow, she never gave up on me. She helped me see that there is a saint in every sinner. We are all worthy of grace. When I finally accepted that fact, I could also accept Naomi's love."

Carrie poured herself a cup of coffee. "She, huh? I'd never have guessed that all those years ago, but you certainly look happy. How about you, Ellie? Did you get married?"

Ellie shook her head. "No, at least not yet. Siobhan blew into my life when I least expected it. I'm happy to be secure in what we have right now. If something more is in our future, I'll embrace it with arms wide open."

They sat there for a moment in silence until Carrie cleared her throat. "As happy as this unexpected reunion is, I know you two didn't come all this way just for a piece of pie."

Rhebekka bit the inside of her cheek and shook her head. "It is pretty good pie, but no... Not long ago, Ellie and I watched a documentary called *The Witnesses*. It triggered some things in Ellie. Her memories are things I'm sure you don't like to think or talk about."

Rhebekka watched as Carrie glanced over to the doors to the kitchen; she waited a few seconds before she began again. She didn't want to cause Carrie pain, but this was important.

"Carrie, I've been in contact with an organization called Silent Lambs. They give voice to the victims. They focus on formulating a plan to bring to justice the pedophiles the organization tries to hide. They are experts on the particular statutes involved from state to state."

Ellie reached out and held Carrie's hand again. "What happened to us was wrong. What's worse was they both blamed us. The truth is your father and brother abused us, then threatened us with congregational discipline for tempting them. If that wasn't enough to silence us, they said it would bring shame on God and his chosen. All of that was bullshit."

Rhebekka picked up where Ellie left off. "As children, we were taught not to question them. We were to have implicit trust in them. They violated that trust. They shouldn't have gotten away with it back then. If those who were harmed continue to stay silent, it makes it that much easier for them to do it again to some other child. What would you do if it had happened to Paula?"

Anger crossed Carrie's face. She dropped her gaze, and tears fell onto the Formica table. Ellie moved over to Carrie's side of the booth. She wrapped her arms around her and rocked her gently.

Rhebekka knew this had to be extremely painful. The memories had likely been buried for years, shoved down into places rarely exposed. "Carrie, I honestly don't want to cause either of you more pain. You and Ellie suffered this indignity together. I think it's time that you find the justice denied to you both."

Carrie wiped a hand across her eyes. "I don't know if I'm strong enough. Until recently, my life has been a mess. Before Eddy came into our life, Paula and I barely got by. Do you know how it feels to worry about where your next meal comes from or when someone will show up at your door with an eviction notice?" Carrie wiped angrily at her tears. "As successful as you both have been, I doubt you could understand."

Rhebekka stiffened, doing her best not to get angry. She sat back and looked at Carrie. "Yes, I do. The only difference was that you were worried about your child. I was worried about my sister. We had a hand-me-down guitar, a used Subaru, and a few dollars to our name when we left. We were sure our father would find us and drag us back. We drove for days, living on day-old bread and a jar of no-name peanut butter. We lived in cheap hotels and played for tips. Other than being pregnant, we know exactly what you went through."

Rhebekka took a deep breath and tried to calm her growing indignity. "Carrie, we didn't show up here to blow your world to shit. We came here to try and offer you an opportunity to stop the cycle. I'm betting you know your brother has children. Do you think he and your father have changed so much that they are truly sorry for what they did to you and Ellie? Do you think they've stopped abusing children?"

They sat there for a few minutes in complete silence. Rhebekka had no idea what was going through Carrie's head, but her silence spoke volumes. Finally, she rose and pulled money from her pocket before sliding bills under her half-empty mug. "I'm sorry, Carrie. Coming here was probably a mistake. I should have listened to Ellie and left this alone. Forgive the crusader in me that believes that far too many people have used God as an excuse for the atrocities perpetrated on children. I'll find another way."

Rhebekka walked out of the diner and stood on the sidewalk with her fists balled and her face to the sky. *Tell me what to do. If I'm on the wrong path, show me the error of my ways and lead me in the path of righteousness.* Her pocket vibrated and she pulled her phone out. *Naomi.* She answered. "You've always had perfect timing."

"I missed you and thought you might need a friendly voice. First things first, I love you. Second, do you want to talk about it?"

Rhebekka sighed and leaned against a streetlamp as the voice of the woman she loved soothed her ire. "Not sure there is much to talk about, but I am so thankful you love me."

"I'm guessing the meeting with Carrie didn't go well?"

She shifted her position. "It was for a while. I don't think Carrie is ready to confront the past. Hell, Ellie barely is. I'm not so sure this was a good idea at all."

There was a moment of silence long enough for Rhebekka to check her phone to ensure the call hadn't dropped. Eventually, Naomi spoke.

"When I showed up at your hotel door, how long had I waited for you to come to your senses?"

Rhebekka dropped her head and held the phone so tight that the edges cut into her fingers. It was a rhetorical question. Naomi always had a way of making her see things through a different lens. "I get it. Everyone comes to their truth in their own time."

"Whether Carrie decides to join you and Ellie or not, you're not powerless. You have a platform, and nothing in the world stops you from shining light on things others try to hide in the shadows. Come home. Lucian and I will be waiting on you."

Those words were all Rhebekka needed. She had a family that supported her in every way. Ellie had firsthand knowledge of the evil that existed. With or without Carrie, they would shine a light so bright it would rival the sun.

Ellie came out of the diner with Carrie by her side. The two of them had very determined looks on their faces.

"I think our light is going to get a whole lot brighter. I'll call you in a bit." Rhebekka ended the call and looked at the two women before her.

Ellie spoke up. "The three of us have some planning to do."

Paula came out of the diner, a confused look on her face. "Mom?"

Carrie held out her hand to her daughter and looked at Rhebekka. "If what happened to us ever happened to Paula, I'd stop at nothing to have them thrown in jail. They'd be lucky if I didn't castrate them myself." She pulled Paula close. "There are things I haven't told you. Things that aren't pleasant and will probably explain why our lives were so screwed up for a long time."

Paula looked at her mom. "You are the strongest person I know. You're my hero, Mom, and nothing will ever change that."

Ellie wrapped her arms around both of them. "Your mom and I used to be the very best of friends. She's a pretty amazing person, and I'd like very much to get to know the daughter she brought into this world."

Rhebekka knew this was only the first step of many, but it was a step forward. That was all that mattered. They'd figure it out, and in the end, she'd make sure the three beautiful women before her would be as whole as they could be.

* * * *

Naomi held her phone to her chin. It was hard to imagine how difficult it had been for Ellie and Rhebekka to face the unpleasant memories from their past. Their childhoods had been anything but idyllic. Ellie and Carrie had been violated, and their childhoods were stolen. Rhebekka had been beaten, and all of them indoctrinated to believe that women were inferior, not capable of choosing their own paths in life. She was grateful that Rhebekka had been strong enough to plan and execute their escape. She was sure it was part of why Rhebekka was so good with Lucian. *He dared to escape the hell he lived in, just like they did.*

She looked over the living room toward the studio, where Lucian stood with headphones on, his bass hanging across his shoulders. The look of pleasure on his face warmed her. *He's safe and happy. I know we can offer that same security to others just like him.* The studio door clicked open, and Lucian headed to the refrigerator and pulled out a can of soda. He crashed onto one of the sofas near her and pulled back the tab, releasing the characteristic sound of compressed air escaping. After a long drink, he wiped his mouth with the back of his hand.

"Did you hear from Bek yet?"

Naomi nodded and gestured with her phone. "Just a few seconds ago. They made contact with Carrie and are working through things."

He shook his head. "That has to be hard."

"It is, but as you know, the best way to fix something is to face it head on."

Lucian fiddled with the pop tab. "I'd never have been able to do that without you guys."

Naomi moved over beside him and wrapped an arm around his shoulders. "I'm glad you agreed to let us help you. There are far too many kids in your situation with no one looking out for them."

He nodded slowly. "I know a couple of them from the group home are still trying to find their way, and they've been gone for a few years."

"Friends?"

He raised his shoulders halfheartedly in a shrug. "Kind of. Miles is a few years older than me but is way more feminine than I ever was. He used to get the shit beat out of him regularly. I'd see him around Elkins after he split. He'd find his way into the music store to check on me. I'd try to give him money if I had it, but he wouldn't take it."

Naomi was grateful Lucian was opening up to her. "Did he age out, or did he run away?"

"He aged out. He could have stayed for a few more years if he'd tried to go to college or something. The last time I saw him, he'd tried to get into a beauty college in Clarksburg. Hard to do when you don't have any money."

Naomi took a deep breath. The idea she'd mentioned to Rhebekka, about having a place for kids like Lucian to go to after they turned of age, seemed even more critical. "You know, I've had an idea I've been bouncing around. There isn't anything concrete, but Rhebekka and I are open to exploring the possibility. Let's pretend you hadn't had the issues at the group home you did, but you aged out of the system. What would you have done?"

He was quiet for a while, finishing his soda and crinkling the empty can he held. "I honestly don't know. They don't automatically throw you out when you hit eighteen, but there are conditions you have to agree to. I can't imagine I'd want to have stayed, even if those asses hadn't tried what they did. It's hard to be the gay kid in that situation."

"Rhebekka and I have talked about seeing what it would take to create a transition home. A place where kids like you and Miles could go to after managed care, until they got on their feet."

Lucian cleared his throat. "Are you wanting me to leave?"

Naomi's heart clenched and she put a hand on Lucian's arm. "Not even for one second." She put her hand under his chin and raised it until his eyes met hers. "This is your home for as long as you want it. That won't change, understand me?" She waited when he didn't answer her. "Lucian, you are part of our family, meaning we want you with us indefinitely. Is that clear?"

He took a deep breath and rubbed his hand down his black jean-clad leg. "Yes."

She cupped his cheek and kissed his forehead. "Okay. Now, what I was trying to explain was that others like you may need a landing spot after they grow old enough to leave state care. If we could find a house large enough to accommodate a few more people, we could help those who feel they don't have anywhere to go."

"Like a halfway house?"

She rocked her hand a bit. "Sort of. This would be a place where kids, who fall into the LGBTQIA+ spectrum and are aging out of the foster and managed care system, can live as they figure out what they want to do. I'm assuming there are grade-point stipulations and other prohibitive languages in some of the options in the system. My idea is a house of refuge, where they can be who they are and figure out their next steps without pressure."

"I've never heard of any place like that before. I'm sure Miles would have jumped at an opportunity like that. If I'd had a place like that waiting for me, I might not have chosen to run and end up living in your garage loft."

Naomi leaned back on the couch. "It's just an idea, but maybe you and I can go looking at places we might be able to renovate into what we'd want."

Lucian looked around. "Does that mean we'd be leaving this place?"

"Eventually, but that's down the road. For now, we look for something suitable, work on a plan, then put things into motion. What you need to know is that, at any time, if you feel uncomfortable or overlooked, we stop and reevaluate. While we want to help others, you are our first priority. We are a family, and this family takes care of each other."

Lucian didn't say anything for a few minutes. He looked at her with a hint of apprehension. "Can I ask you a personal question?"

"Lucian, you can ask me anything." Naomi tried to soften her voice to ease his tension.

"You can totally tell me it's none of my business."

"Okay, but I'll try to answer whatever it is."

"How did you meet Bek? From what I know of you two, you came from such different worlds."

Naomi smiled. The question was similar to one she'd asked her parents when she was young. "We were from different worlds, and I'm a bit older than she is. I was the pastor of my own church in Colorado. One day, this tall, broody, leather-clad, hungover woman straggled into my Sunday service."

Lucian's eyes grew wide. "Seriously?"

Naomi raised her hand as if swearing an oath. "Scouts honor. I knew who she was, but I didn't let on how aware I was that the lead singer of one of the most successful metal bands was slunk down in one of the back pews. There was something haunted about her. She sat there behind dark sunglasses and never said a word."

"You knew who she was?"

"Oh, honey. I'd been to more than one of her concerts before she wandered in. She was a star in every sense of the word. Of course, you know, firsthand, her guitar skills, but you've never heard anything like her playing and singing to a crowd of thousands."

Lucian grinned. "I've watched tons of videos about them on YouTube. I can't imagine what it would have been like to see them live."

Naomi pulled her feet up beneath her on the couch and leaned on one arm to look at Lucian. "I've done that a few hundred times myself, but nothing compares to how she and Ellie could wind up a crowd and have them all singing along. It was mesmerizing."

He was quiet for a few seconds before continuing his line of questions. "So, she magically ends up at one of your sermons and, poof, turns into the Rhebekka I know now?"

The question made Naomi laugh. "Not hardly. It took her years to become the person you know now, though I've loved every version of her."

"You two seem so perfect."

She put a hand on his shoulder. "We're far from perfect, and there was a time when we lost each other."

"No way. I can't even imagine you two not together."

Naomi grew quiet. Those five years had been pure torture. She'd run the gambit of emotions from anger to desperation. "I never gave up on her, even when she gave up on herself."

Lucian ran his hand through his hair. "It blows my mind to think of her giving up on anything, and I can't believe she walked away from you."

Naomi sighed and paused to gather her thoughts. "Rhebekka spent most of her life not believing she was worthy of anything good. She was born into a family with religious beliefs that taught her the very natural feelings she had were an abomination. Her entire childhood, she was fed lies that being gay would lead to losing her eternal life. Like someone trying to force a square peg into a round box, she had to lose parts of herself to fit in. The fact that she and Ellie ran as soon as they could was life altering for them. She never believed she was worthy of my love or God's grace. She was no angel when I met her. Drugs and alcohol clouded her judgment."

"Sounds like one of those television shows about fallen rock stars."

Naomi nodded. "It almost was. She made a horrible mistake for which she couldn't forgive herself, even though I did. It took the death of her father to bring us back together."

"And somehow, in all this, she becomes a minister?"

"Something like that. Rhebekka was so very lost and searching for redemption. Somewhere in the process, she realized she had the gift to share God's grace with others, something she was denied her entire childhood. She also can reach kids like no one else I've ever seen."

Lucian pointed at her. "I've witnessed that for myself. The after-school program is pretty unique. The kids love her."

"It's one of the reasons she was so determined to find you. I can't remember if we ever told you how long she walked in the deep snow looking for you."

Lucian sat up, alarm in his eyes. "With her bionic leg?"

Naomi stifled a laugh. "Well, it's not exactly bionic, but yes. She was nearly hypothermic when I picked her up. There have only been a few times I've ever seen her that scared. She was worried sick about you."

Lucian got up and threw away his pop can. "I never meant for her to get hurt. I never even knew she was looking for me."

Naomi rose to meet him, putting her hands on his shoulders. "We know that. You did what you had to do, just like she did when she and her sister ran away. I only tell you this to make you understand what a priority you are to her."

Lucian wiped at a tear. "I haven't had a family since my gran died."

Naomi cupped his cheek. "I wish we'd been able to know her. She seems to have given you a great foundation."

Lucian leaned into the touch. "She'd have liked you guys. She was pretty awesome and never made me feel like a freak. Gran always called me a tomboy, but I was okay with her not understanding that it was more than just how I acted. It was who I was, who I am."

"I think she would have been fine with it, no matter the terminology. Now, I have an important question for you."

"Okay."

Naomi grinned. "Pizza or chili with cornbread?"

"Oh, now that's a tough choice. I've got a question back. If I say chili, will you teach me how you make it?"

Naomi cupped her chin and looked at him as if she were contemplating a challenging task. "One condition."

"Name it."

Naomi put her arm around his shoulder and led him toward the kitchen. "You have to chop the onions."

"I'll happily be your sous chef."

"Then chili it is. I'll even teach you to make cornbread in a cast iron skillet." Naomi led him into the kitchen. She never thought she'd have the opportunity to teach her grandmother's cooking skills to her child, but she was very grateful to have this young man in her life to do just that.

* * * *

Rhebekka sat in their hotel room with a phone to her ear, talking with Andres from Silent Lambs. The last time they'd spoken, Andres had told Rhebekka that he'd start the groundwork for their next steps after they'd contacted Carrie.

"It's a class four felony for anyone eighteen or older to have sex with a minor between the ages of thirteen and fifteen. From what you've told me, this would be multiple counts against both men. The penalty is five years to life."

Rhebekka grumbled. "One lifetime isn't enough for what they stole from my sister and Carrie." She wiped her hand down her face. "Okay, what now?"

"The first thing we need to do is have Ellie and Carrie meet with our attorney, who specializes in cases against the Witnesses. He'll have Ellie and Carrie file police reports. We can only do so much until they are indicted."

Rhebekka looked around the small but comfortable hotel room. She rose and went over to the coffee maker. "Carrie and her husband run a diner here, and it won't be easy for her to get away for long periods. Her daughter Paula works with them."

"Our attorney can come to her for most of the preliminary things. I can't guarantee you that the prosecutor will do the same. There will be interviews and depositions that will most likely have to be done in Virginia. We have some funds to help victims travel if that's a problem."

Rhebekka held the phone to her ear with her shoulder as she poured a cup and added powdered creamer to the brew before stirring it with the tiny, red-plastic straw. "Money isn't an issue. I'll take care of Carrie's expenses. I want to make sure Tom and Dave don't get to hide behind some privacy crap. I want their names known."

"We've got to get them convicted first. The fact there are two victims will make this much easier. They can back up each other's testimony to the events, but Rhebekka, you have to remember that this will be painful. The Witnesses will do everything possible to smear them both and make them seem like liars and unreliable witnesses. Are they prepared for that?"

Rhebekka paced the room, blowing across the Styrofoam cup. "I don't know that anyone could be prepared, but they are ready to do what's necessary."

Ellie returned to the room, her phone to her ear as well. She kicked off her shoes and crawled up on the bed.

"Andres, Ellie just came in. I'll call you when we're back home. Until then, do whatever is necessary for us to move this along. Now that the ball is rolling, I want the momentum to steamroll right over them."

"I'll send an email of what our next steps are. Try to impress on Carrie and Ellie that their combined testimony is what will put the nails in the coffins. Thank them for being brave enough to move forward with this. I know I don't have to say this, but with your and Ellie's notoriety, this will get some press coverage."

Rhebekka drank slowly. She knew he was telling the truth. "I realize that, and I know what they'll do to try to use that same notoriety against us. No matter what, the truth has to come out. Talk with you soon." She disconnected her call and went to sit on the bed with Ellie.

Ellie held her cell phone in her hands. "Sounds like everything is okay at home. Siobhan said Lucian came by after he'd finished at the bakery for another self-defense lesson."

"I'm grateful to her. Lucian seems more confident than before he started. She's been very good for him. How're you doing, little sparrow?"

Ellie pushed her hair behind her ear. "Horrible, but coping. So many memories that I worked a lifetime to keep buried continue to make their way to the surface."

Rhebekka set down her coffee and took her sister into her arms. "I know how horrible this is. I wish I could spare you this pain."

"What do they say at the gym? No pain, no gain? I can only hope there is a big gain when we're done."

Rhebekka kissed the top of her head. "I hope so too."

Ellie snuggled in closer. "You know, Mom is going to flip her shit."

Rhebekka nodded. They sat there in silence for a few minutes. She knew Ellie was right. Rhebekka wished her mother would be angrier at the men who had violated her daughter more than that her daughters were bringing reproach on an organization she believed in, heart and soul. "I'm planning on calling her tomorrow. The one thing I don't want to do is blindside her. Once I explain everything, it will be up to her who she puts her faith in."

Ellie sat back, angrily wiping her tears. "Like she'd believe me."

Rhebekka rubbed her back and reached for a tissue from the box beside the bed. She handed it to her sister. "It will be harder to deny, given Carrie's account will match yours. Remember why we came out here. Both of you giving testimony to the same thing meets their organizational requirements for the burden of proof. That's how we demand accountability and justice."

Ellie sniffed and wiped her eyes with the tissue. "You know they'll still try to deny it."

"Oh, I expect them to. I expect them to circle the wagons and label us apostates, as if they haven't already. It doesn't matter. We'll use what celebrity clout we have to get this into the public's eye. Think about how we felt watching that documentary. It moved us to action, and I pray our efforts will move others. I hate what you and Carrie will have to go through."

"I can see it now. TMZ will be all over this, trying to figure out how to spin the scandal into a privileged celebrity trying to seek attention."

Rhebekka cupped her jaw. "Honey, we are trying to get attention. I want them to face the consequences of their actions. I also want the organization that elevated them into leadership positions to answer for their actions. I want Tom and Dave Broader to spend the rest of their lives in prison, where they can't hurt another child."

"I have to believe that's possible. If they're acquitted, it will feel like a lot of pain for very little return." Ellie chewed on her thumbnail.

Rhebekka took her sister's hands into hers. "We have Carrie back in our lives. In my mind, that's something very positive. No matter how this turns out, we will know we tried everything we could."

Ellie took a deep breath and curled into her sister's arms. "This sucks."

Rhebekka slowly nodded as she held her sister. "It definitely does, but it will get better. We've faced bigger obstacles, and we've always come out on top. I'll do everything I can to ensure this isn't the exception. Tomorrow, we'll head home to the people who make life so much less sucky."

Chapter Thirteen

NAOMI DROVE ALONG THE narrow streets of Thomas. She was evaluating the homes with For Sale signs in the yards. It was going to have to fit their specific needs. Lucian was with her, and she valued his opinion.

"What time are they getting back?" Lucian stared out the car window.

She turned onto Douglas Road. "Their plane gets into Pittsburgh at three. They'll take a private plane back to Canaan Valley's airstrip from there. If all goes well, we'll pick them up around five."

Lucian pointed. "What's that?"

A stately home with large stone columns sat up on a bank. The wrought-iron fence that surrounded the yard was in need of significant repair. "I'm not sure." She pulled over and grabbed her phone to look at a map of the area. "According to this, that house once belonged to the Buxton and Landstreet Company Store owner. I know the realtor."

"Wonder if there is a way we can look inside?"

"The listing agent is Chance's mom. I'm sure we can call her and ask." Naomi continued to scroll on her phone. "There are a few pictures. The inside looks huge."

Lucian leaned over and looked at the pictures with her. "The place is a little rough. It doesn't look like anyone except the squirrels have lived here for a long time."

"Nothing a little elbow grease and a good contractor couldn't fix. Let's keep this on our list of possibilities and continue our quest."

"I'm game as long as you promise to make that taco casserole for dinner."

Naomi rubbed her chin, then pointed at Lucian. "You drive a hard bargain. That means we've got to stop by the grocery store. We have another hour to look around and get back home in time to cook the homecoming feast. I'll tell you a little secret. It's one of Rhebekka's favorites too."

"Then let's get a move on, because you're going to have to make two pan's worth."

The grin on Lucian's face filled Naomi with joy. "Deal."

She put the vehicle in drive and turned around at the old company store, now a local artisan gallery. One thing Naomi enjoyed was feeding her family. It was one of her greatest pleasures, and she loved making them happy. In just a few hours, her family would be complete again.

Dark days were coming. She could feel them the same way others could feel a storm coming in their bones. She also knew that their faith would sustain them. A familiar story came to mind. The disciples were fishing from their boat when a storm overcame them. Jesus slept, unconcerned. The disciples were terrified the boat would sink and pleaded with him to save them. He rebuked the wind and the waves until calmer seas prevailed. He questioned the disciples about their absence of faith. Naomi knew how strong her faith was, even with the gathering storm, and she would use that faith as a rudder to steer her family through the rocky weather ahead.

* * * *

Rhebekka waved to the pilot and wrapped Naomi in a hug. "It's good to be home. I missed you like crazy."

"I missed you even more." Naomi kissed her, then turned to Ellie and pulled her into a hug.

"Good to have you back." Lucian bumped his knuckles with Rhebekka's. "I'll put your bag in the car."

"I appreciate that. Thanks for coming to meet us."

Lucian grinned. "Isn't that what family does?"

Rhebekka smiled and nodded. "Absolutely." She watched with relief as Naomi soothed Ellie. Her wife was a sister and a mother, all wrapped up in one beautifully compassionate package. She put a hand on Siobhan's shoulder and nodded at the two who stood deep in conversation. "This was a rough trip. Necessary, but it dragged us all over the coals a bit."

Siobhan nodded. "Aye. She's like a green sapling. She bends with the storm but will always come back ta true center."

Rhebekka thought about Siobhan's analogy. She was right. The winds of Ellie's life had battered her to near breaking. "I'm more than grateful for you, my friend. She leans into your strength, and you brace her up. I can never tell you enough how thankful I am you're in her life."

"Yer sister is precious to me. I'll always be here to catch her. I'm guessing this isn't finished."

Rhebekka shook her head. "In some ways, it's just begun. The difference is our voice will be stronger with our friend Carrie able to validate our accusations. She's going to need you more than ever."

Siobhan shifted Ellie's bags into one hand and unlocked her new jacked-up Jeep Wrangler. The panel beneath the tire mount swung out of the way, and she hefted Ellie's bags in with little effort.

"You are deceptively strong, my friend. I've carried one of those bags the last few days, and I swear one of my arms is now longer than the other." Rhebekka cupped a hand on Siobhan's shoulder.

"Years in the service will do that to you. Now I do it because I like ta stay ready for anything."

"And my sister thinks it makes you very hot." Rhebekka laughed at the blush that rose in Siobhan's cheeks.

Siobhan kicked the toe of her boot into the snow. "Well, there is that too."

Rhebekka pulled Siobhan into a one-armed hug. "She loves you, and we're thankful to have you in our family."

"I hope, someday, ta be worthy of making her a permanent member of ma family."

"Ask her."

Siobhan took a deep breath and watched Naomi and Ellie embrace. "I have. On multiple occasions."

Rhebekka's breath hitched. This was news to her. "And she said no?" She was incredulous.

Siobhan rocked her head back and forth. "More like not yet. This demon that haunts her needs ta be gone. She has this ludicrous notion that she's broken. I'll spend the rest of ma life putting every small piece back together, even if she never marries me."

Rhebekka lifted her arm and let Naomi slip under as Ellie joined Siobhan. "You two go home. This journey has just begun, and we have many miles left to go. Recharge your batteries for a few days until I can make some arrangements. I'll contact our attorney so she can move forward with the plan we have in place." She cupped Ellie's cheek. "It's going to be okay, little songbird. It will be worth it."

Ellie wiped at a tear. "Mom's going to shit."

Rhebekka put her hand under Ellie's chin and gently brought it up until they looked directly at each other. "Don't add that to your worries. I'll handle our mother."

Ellie moved until she could hug Rhebekka. "Don't let her guilt tactics put one more dent in your heart. Promise me?"

Rhebekka let go of Naomi long enough to wrap her sister up tightly in an embrace. She kissed the top of her head, then rested her chin there. "I promise." They stood like that for a second. Rhebekka squeezed her again, then let her go. "Always forward. I love you."

Ellie rose on her tiptoes and kissed her cheek. "Put it in drive, Sis. Love you too."

* * * *

"I'm stuffed." Rhebekka sat down on the couch and put her feet up. She patted her stomach with one hand while opening her arm for Naomi to tuck in. It was rare for them to be apart these days, and it always felt strange not having Naomi by her side. "I can't tell you how much I missed you."

"That street goes both ways, honey. Some might say that it's good for us to spend time apart. Those are also the people that don't know our history and how much time we've already spent apart. I'd be happy to spend every day of the rest of our lives like this." She snuggled in closer. "The reality is, there will be times we have to be apart."

"I know. I just don't have to like it."

"Well, you make it up to me in some pretty fantastic ways."

They lay together on the couch, watching the flames dance inside the fireplace. Lucian came into the living room with a laundry basket full of towels.

He sat down and began to fold them. "We're almost out of laundry soap, and I used the last dryer sheet." Marley jumped off the back of the couch and tried to snuggle down in the basket full of warm towels. "Oh no, you don't. I have enough cat hair in my bed. I don't need to try and dry my face with a towel full of it."

Rhebekka snickered. "I've experienced that a few times myself, compliments of JJ and Marley."

Lucian stroked down Marley's back and scratched under her chin. "I give them a hard time, but I like hearing them purr. JJ usually sleeps above my head, and Marley tucks herself behind my knees."

Naomi smiled. "They are cuddle bugs."

Lucian finished folding a towel and placed it back in the basket. "I think it's awesome that you rescued both of them. You guys are good at that."

Rhebekka furrowed her brow. "Good at what?"

He smiled as he folded a hand towel. "Giving animals, and people, a home when they don't have one."

Naomi held up a finger. "Speaking of which, Lucian and I went out and about today before we picked you up. We think we might have found a candidate for our plan."

Rhebekka sipped her mug of hot chocolate. She was slightly confused about what plans Naomi meant. Finally, it dawned on her after another sip. "Really, where at?"

"Down on Douglas Road, part of the Buxton Landstreet estate," Naomi said.

"I didn't think the company store was for sale. They have several businesses in there."

Lucian added more detail. "Not the company store. Before that building, there's a great big house behind a set of monster, wrought-iron gates."

Rhebekka realized the property they were talking about. "No one has lived in that place for as long as I've been around. Tank might know. The last time I drove by there, it looked like it needed a complete overhaul. Are you two sure it's even for sale?"

Naomi pulled up the real estate website on her phone. "This says it is."

Lucian stood with the laundry basket. "I'm going to go play for a bit, then head to bed. I've got work in the morning, and Karmen has a big catering job we're prepping for. She said she'd need me tomorrow night to serve." Both cats walked along the back of the couch. Marley jumped on his shoulder.

Naomi chuckled. "Looks like your groupies would like a private concert. Let me know if you need anything. I'll see you when you get home from work."

"Will do. Glad you made it home safe, Bek. If I haven't said it lately, thanks for trying to save more than my soul."

Rhebekka looked quizzically at him. "You're welcome, but it isn't necessary. It's what family does."

"I'm slowly learning that. Night." He let JJ jump into the laundry basket and carried them both out of the room.

She pulled Naomi to her. "Who's handling the sale? Someone local, or an out-of-state company?" Rhebekka asked.

Naomi scrolled through her phone to the information on the sale. "It's Maggie's agency. The land alone is worth more than the house. Some developer will likely tear it down and build condos if we can't get it."

"That would be a shame. Look at all that woodwork. I wonder how many bedrooms there are?" Rhebekka stopped on one of the photos. "The kitchen is almost the size of something commercial."

"I think we need to call her tomorrow and see if it's possible to look at it. There's a huge stable area off the back. We don't have any horses, but you know that Ellie will eventually need more space for her production company. That old stable could be renovated into a badass recording studio. Hell, with as much room as the property has, she and Siobhan could even build a house there."

Rhebekka thought about it. "All we can do is try. Let's get a look at it first. I'd rather renovate than do a new build." She pointed to the screen. "This place has character."

"It won't be cheap."

"The best things in life never are." Rhebekka kissed the top of Naomi's head. "Good thing I invested my royalty money well."

They sat looking at the pictures one by one, pointing out things they found interesting. Rhebekka's mind wandered from subject to subject aimlessly. Naomi must have noticed. She covered the photos with her hand.

"How are you feeling about your trip?"

Rhebekka sighed. "It was difficult to watch them relive such painful memories. They've been through hell, and what comes next will be just as hard. If I could, I'd change places with either of them."

"Ellie knows that. I can't speak for Carrie. We need to talk about the elephant in the room. When are you going to tell your mother?"

"Not until I have to. I thought about calling her tomorrow. I don't want to blindside her, but the last thing I need is for her to warn them that her prodigal daughters are coming after them. She might not think there is anything we can do to touch them, but it's not just us. We have Silent Lambs on our side, and Carrie's testimony will solidify our position." Rhebekka took a deep breath. "I know how this is going to go down. Given how she acted at my dad's funeral, I know what side of the gallery she'll be sitting on. Her cuts will be deeper than even Daniel's imagination could design with all the technology available."

"I've witnessed many things in my life. A woman who chooses an organization above her children is something I have a hard time reconciling."

Rhebekka sighed. "She thinks she's choosing God."

"I'd beg to differ with her if it'd do any good."

"It wouldn't. My mom clings to the Witnesses like oxygen, as if she'd wither and die without them in her life."

"And that is why I'll never understand her. Lucian isn't my child by birth, but there is nothing I wouldn't do. God wouldn't ask me to choose an organization over my child."

There were many things that Rhebekka couldn't understand about her mother. Sometimes she believed her mother saw herself as a modern-day Abraham, sacrificing Isaac in the act of ultimate devotion. She felt Naomi's fingers rubbing her jaw.

"Stop that. You're going to break your teeth one of these days. This muscle jumps like crazy when you grind your teeth."

Rhebekka sighed. "Clenching my jaw is better than yelling silently inside my head. A migraine is the only thing that accomplishes."

Naomi leaned over and kissed her temple. "Grinding your teeth does the same thing. Let's set that aside for the night. We have a busy weekend ahead. We're supposed to play at Redemption's Road tomorrow night. There's also your Sunday sermon. Did you have any ideas?"

Rhebekka felt self-disappointment settle in. "I'm not sure I have a message in me. My head and heart are so jumbled up that forming a coherent thought beyond breathing almost seems to be out of the question. Sometimes, I feel like I am the last person that should be trying to teach anyone about grace, when I still struggle with it."

Naomi ran her hand through Rhebekka's hair. "Paul said that he was the worst of sinners and that he was shown mercy so that we could see Christ's perfect patience. Paul persecuted Christians until he was humbled and stripped of everything. In his letter to the Corinthians, he said, 'But by the grace of God I am what I am, and his grace to me was not without effect.'" Naomi stepped back and made contact with her eyes. "You continue to believe that everyone deserves grace but you."

Rhebekka was having a momentary lapse of confidence. It felt like she was walking through a thick, wet fog of doubt. "Some days, my faith feels as fragile as a spider web."

Naomi leaned in and kissed her. "Spider silk is deceptively resilient. Did you know that it's five times stronger than the same size steel and can be stretched four times its original length without breaking? Your faith is just as strong."

"You always know the right thing to say. It's why you're a great pastor."

Naomi tapped her chin. "Oh, honey. I'm far from being a great pastor, and you are far from being a poor one. How about I handle the sermon on Sunday? We'll pull out the old hot-seat session at the end."

"I still think back to your days at Open Door. Your congregation hung on your every word. Your ability to reach your audience was unmatched." She raised her hand. "I can personally testify to that. At that point in my life, I wanted nothing to do with religion, and you single-handedly changed that."

"I appreciate the compliment. My words wouldn't have touched you if your heart hadn't been open to the message. What do you want to do about our set at Redemption's Road? If you aren't up for it, I can easily see if one of Ellie's acts would like to fill our set."

Rhebekka pulled Naomi into her lap and pulled her close. "No. We've been on the schedule for weeks, and I know Lucian has been looking forward to it. The music and the atmosphere may be just what I need."

The grandfather clock chimed ten times. Rhebekka leaned forward and languidly kissed Naomi, enjoying the slide of her lover's soft lips and the smell of her perfume. She was torn. Part of her itched to pick up the guitar and rid herself of the anxiety that coursed through her like poison. The stronger part longed to lay down and make love to the woman who had fought so hard to be with her. She refused to let her head be so clouded with doubt about her faith that she missed the joy of being with her wife. "I think we need to move this to our bedroom."

Naomi met her kiss, then ramped it up. With all the grace of a dancer, Naomi stood and held out her hand. "No arguments here."

Rhebekka joined their hands and followed her.

* * * *

Naomi led them to their bedroom sanctuary and flicked on the lights, only to dim them to a soft glow. Behind the closed door, she hoped to give Rhebekka a moment's respite from thoughts of the past. She pushed her down on the bed and straddled her lap, kissing her deeply. Her hands roamed Rhebekka's jaw, letting her lips follow her fingertips as she slowly unbuttoned her wife's denim shirt. She kissed her way down until her teeth grazed the muscle at the juncture of Rhebekka's neck and shoulder and smiled as her touch elicited a small intake of breath. Her lover shuddered at the contact. She pushed her hands inside the shirt and slid it down over muscled shoulders.

Tattooed skin revealed itself as the shirt fell off. She was grateful Rhebekka rarely wore even a sports bra and grazed her fingertips across the erect nipples. She moved until she was sitting in a position to admire Rhebekka's back, tracing the angel wings with the tip of her fingers, before leaning over and kissing the wing of the demon. Inside her lover existed a saint within the sinner, light within the darkness, and joy within the sadness. She was a dichotomy of contradictions that blended into the woman her wife had become.

"I love you, Rhebekka. No matter what lies before us, this love binds us to each other with an unbreakable armor."

Rhebekka leaned into Naomi's touch, reaching back and pulling their heads together. "You are my anchor in every storm."

Naomi reached around her lover and cupped her breasts, kissing along the strong muscles that trembled at her touch. She let one hand slide down Rhebekka's side, feeling each rib as she moved. She grazed her fingertips along the seam of the jean-clad legs and, one by one, released the buttons of the fly. "Lift your hips."

Rhebekka did as asked, and Naomi slid the jeans down to expose her heated skin and let the denim fall to the floor. She knelt to release Rhebekka's prosthetic leg and remove the sleeve. She motioned for Rhebekka to move fully onto the bed. Naomi stood and slipped out of her pants and sweater before climbing on top of her lover. Her fingers sensually traced the detailed line of each tattoo depicting the many layers of her lover's soul. Naomi had left on the deep, emerald-green lingerie that had been carefully chosen for Rhebekka's pleasure.

Rhebekka reached up and touched the silk. "My favorite."

"I had to remind you what brings you back home every time."

"That's something I never forgot, even when you weren't with me. You were seared into my heart."

Naomi leaned over and kissed the spot where her name was branded into Rhebekka's skin. "I never wanted you to endure a pain like this for me."

"That pain was so temporary to what it felt like to lose you. The skin healed, but the heart didn't until you were back in my arms."

Naomi leaned over and kissed her, tasting the bitterness of the hops from the beer they'd enjoyed with dinner. Rhebekka unclasped the bra as Naomi sat up, allowing Rhebekka to draw it down her arms. When Rhebekka's warm hands covered her breasts, she arched her back in pleasure and gasped when those hands wrapped around her and flipped her onto her back. Rhebekka stared down at her with a deep hunger in her eyes. Naomi realized Rhebekka wanted to feel in control, not lost. "Make love to me."

"With pleasure, Mrs. Deklan." Rhebekka covered one of Naomi's nipples with her mouth and sucked it gently before grazing it with her teeth.

The pleasure that shot through Naomi's core was intense. She grew wet with anticipation. Soft lips and a warm tongue traced under her breasts and left a heated trail as Rhebekka made her way down. She clasped Naomi's bikinis with her teeth and slowly pulled them over her hips and down her legs. Rhebekka nestled in between her thighs and kissed each hip bone.

"Don't tease. I need you," Naomi panted. She felt her legs moving over Rhebekka's shoulders and gasped as Rhebekka latched onto her clit and sucked hard. Her back arched as her lover slid two fingers inside her, driving them deep until she trembled. The strokes came fast and hard as the skillful tongue destroyed what remained of her control.

The crest approached her like a car headed straight into a dead-man's curve at a hundred miles an hour. The orgasm enveloped her like a tsunami crashing onto the shore, forcing her back to bow off the bed. It was some time before she felt like she had floated back into her body. Hazel eyes stared back at her when she forced hers open. Naomi traced a dark eyebrow with her fingertip. "It's good to have you back home."

"No place I'd rather be."

Rhebekka crawled up her body and nestled into her chest. She held her close and waited. The kind of release Rhebekka needed wasn't sexual. Instead, it was an emotional one surrounded by safety. That Naomi could provide and would for the rest of her life. She felt heated tears drip onto her skin. The subtle jerk of Rhebekka's body indicated she was quietly sobbing. Naomi pulled her tighter, willing Rhebekka to feel the security of her love. She knew Rhebekka, always wanting to appear strong, rarely shared this side of herself. "Let it go, baby."

They lay there in their faintly illuminated bedroom. The streetlights softly threw shadows on the wall. Naomi smiled with pleasure as the sobs quietly ended. The steady rise and fall of Rhebekka's body indicated that she'd cried herself to sleep. In these moments, she could feel Rhebekka's love in a completely different way. They had complete trust in the family they'd finally built. *There's a violent storm coming with fierce wind and rain. I'll make sure my heart is her shelter and our family, the rock she's anchored to.*

* * * *

Naomi poured two cups of coffee and scrolled through the pictures of the property they wanted to see. Rhebekka walked into the room yawning, her hair strewn in every direction. The low-slung pajama pants revealed gorgeous glimpses of warm skin. She was very proud of herself that Rhebekka hadn't left the bed after they'd made love. From the looks of her, she'd actually slept. *I wonder how many more years before I permanently change her bedtime.* Naomi handed her the cup and kissed her. "Good morning."

Rhebekka grinned. "Morning. Sorry I fell asleep on you."

"Makes me feel pretty powerful that I can put you to sleep after we rock each other's worlds."

"I used to play the guitar to tire myself out. Now I play your body instead."

Naomi wrapped her arms around Rhebekka's neck. "I'm certainly not complaining. Have I told you how much I enjoy going to bed with you and waking up spooned into you?"

"I love being the big spoon." Rhebekka picked up her coffee and sipped. "What's on our agenda today, beautiful?"

Naomi moved to the stove and began cracking eggs for omelets. "The first thing I want to do is call Maggie and see about the property. After that, I'd like to go check in on Jax. She has that court date in California coming up, and I think she's really disturbed by it. She called and invited us to lunch. I told her I'd check and see how you're feeling after your trip."

"I'm game. I need to call Daniel sometime today. The last time I talked with him, he was so unhappy."

"He needs to come for a visit."

"About that. If we get this house, what would you think about offering for him to come and stay with us for a while? Longer if he wants. He has no family that supports him, and helping us with this transition home for kids like him might give him a new purpose."

Naomi thought about the slight young man with immense technical skills and laughed. "I think it's a great idea. Do you think we have the bandwidth he'll require to do his normal techno-wizardry?"

Rhebekka sat at the bar and cradled her coffee cup. "I have no idea. The broadband in this area was upgraded over the last few years, but I couldn't even begin to understand what he needs. I know Daniel well enough to believe he'd be able to construct his own network if he had to. He's that damn good."

Naomi pulled the robe's tie a little tighter as she added a dash of heavy cream, salt, and pepper to the eggs, before whisking them together.

"Let me help." Rhebekka moved to the sink and washed her hands. She picked up the knife and diced up the peppers and onions waiting on the cutting board.

Naomi added the vegetables to a small pan to sauté separately before adding them to the omelet. *She's come a long way from reheating things in the microwave. I love when she offers to help.* It was these mundane moments of domesticity that warmed Naomi's heart. She'd dreamed about a life like this with Rhebekka for so long. Sometimes, she had to pinch herself to remember this was her reality. Their life wasn't always easy, but more than worth it.

"Let's eat and call Maggie." Naomi plated the omelets and carried them to the bar while Rhebekka refilled their coffee cups.

They joined hands as Rhebekka said a small prayer of thanks. "I'm sure the property has a reserve. If we see it and want to proceed, we need to find out if they are taking open offers. We'll need to call my financial adviser to figure out how to liquidate some things to make that large of a purchase."

"I have some investments we can use as well."

The breakfast conversation revolved around the steps needed to make it work. Naomi was sure there were regulations they would need to follow. With the last plate placed in the dishwasher, they headed to the living room. Naomi pulled her phone off the side table and dialed the number to Maggie's business. A receptionist answered the phone and asked where she could direct the call.

"Hi, this is Naomi and Rhebekka Deklan. Would Maggie Fitzsimmons be in today?"

"She is. Please hold for a moment and I'll see if she's free."

They listened to an instrumental version of *House of the Rising Sun*, and both women chuckled.

Rhebekka leaned over and kissed her cheek. "Maybe that's a good sign of things to come."

"From your lips to God's ears."

Maggie came on the line. "Good morning, Naomi and Rhebekka. It's great to hear from you. Don't tell me you've grown out of that fabulous loft you renovated."

Naomi laughed. "About that. We have a bit of a radical idea, and we think you're handling a place that may just be the perfect fit. What can you tell us about the property down in Douglas, near the old Buxton and Landstreet Company Store?"

"The place behind the wrought-iron gates that hasn't had anyone in it for years," Rhebekka added.

"Wow, when you two make a change, you do it in a big way." Maggie proceeded to tell them about the property and the buildings. "The place is a wreck inside. The only inquiries I've had want to bulldoze it for the property. The owner wants to sell, but part of the deal is that the house can't be torn down. It's not on any historical registry, but she is adamant that the history of the place not be lost. Most people don't want to take on that much financial obligation on top of the purchase price. There are plenty of developers banging on my door to try and convince me they can offer enough money to get that clause removed, but she is adamant."

Naomi high-fived Rhebekka. "Well, that's a point in our favor then. We don't want to tear it down, but renovate it enough to provide a type of transition house for LGBTQIA+ kids coming out of the care system. A place to find their footing before making any life-changing decisions."

"I'm intrigued. How about I show you the place this morning before you get your heart set on it? I'm not kidding when I say it's a mess," Maggie said.

Rhebekka gleefully rubbed her hands together. "What time?"

Naomi watched her lover with so much admiration. When she'd come up with this idea, she'd been concerned about how much it would change the life she and Rhebekka were only beginning to build. As she watched her lover's eyes dance, she cursed herself for ever doubting that Rhebekka would be solidly on board. *My broken angel might finally be ready to heal those damaged wings.*

* * * *

A little after ten, Rhebekka jammed her hands into the pockets of her leather jacket and stared through the rusty gates in front of her. The house's stone facade was covered with enough moss to carpet a forest floor, and the marble steps leading to the front door were dull and weathered. "Are you sure about this place?"

Naomi looped her arm through the crook of Rhebekka's elbow and squeezed. "Look beyond the neglect. What did the opera house look like before you remodeled it?"

"In comparison, this place looks like a palace."

"And now it houses a congregation of people who can find and exercise their faith. It's also a home full of love." Naomi pointed to the enormous house. "This place is waiting for someone to give it the love and attention it deserves and a family to make happy memories."

Maggie pulled up and got out of her vehicle. "Good morning, you two. Let me unlock this gate, and you two can ride with me. Leave your truck right where it is." She stopped to hug them both before using an enormous key to unlock the heavy gate.

Rhebekka stepped forward. "Let me swing them open. I'll pull them closed behind us if you don't want anyone else in." She marveled at how much Chance resembled Maggie. When Chance's father died in the line of duty, Maggie stepped in to raise her brother's child. She and Dee proved that you didn't have to give birth to someone to be a parent.

Maggie handed her the key. "I appreciate it. I'm not as young as I used to be, and these things are damn heavy. The rust on the hinges doesn't help."

Naomi climbed inside Maggie's full-size pickup as Rhebekka pulled hard on the gates. They groaned open, and she waited until Maggie pulled through before she closed them and climbed into the back seat. "If we buy it, that's the first thing that needs to be fixed. I'd pull a shoulder out of socket if I had to do that daily."

Maggie nodded. "I have one of our maintenance guys scheduled to come over and put some rust buster on them. I'm too damn old to be straining that hard."

Naomi put a hand on her shoulder. "Pretty soon, your grandson will be old enough to open whatever you need."

They parked the truck and Maggie got out, dabbing at the corner of her eyes. "Oh, how we love that little guy. I can tell you that being a grandma wasn't on my radar, but I love every minute of it. Dee is like a big kid around him."

Rhebekka rubbed Maggie's back. "We love Hunter too. What a blessing for everyone to have him come into our lives."

Maggie flapped her hands. "Let's look at this place before you two turn me into a blubbering idiot." She went on to tell them the particulars of when the house was built and who had originally lived there. Inside the front entrance, the scope of how ignored the place had been became very apparent. A blue tarp flapped at the ceiling, where a corner had come unmoored and dangled inside a two-by-two-foot hole in the roof. Bits of wood and plaster lay on an intricately tiled floor where the ceiling had given way from the constant siege of rain, snow, and ice.

"Time has not been a friend to this beautiful place." Naomi moved farther into the entrance.

Maggie shook her head. "Sadly, no. From what I understand, during one of those storms we had over Thanksgiving, a giant limb broke off that tree out front. Workers found it had completely crashed through the roof. I'll have to get someone to secure that tarp. If not, the floor will be ruined. The current owner is very elderly, ninety-five to be exact, and is being cared for in a nursing home. Her mind is still sharp."

Rhebekka looked around the foyer. Wide, crown moulding outlined the ceiling, and a matching trim board joined the walls to the floor. Some of the wallpaper curled down as if it had become too tired and lonely to stay in place. A thick banister framed a grand staircase, gently curving its way to the second floor. "She sounds like a character. I'll bet this place was fantastic in its heyday."

"I've seen pictures from when the coal mining company held grand balls for the stakeholders and politicians. It's heartbreaking to see it in such disrepair. As for Claire Buxton, she is definitely a character. Let's move on to some of the other rooms. The dining room is through here, and the kitchen is beyond that."

They followed Maggie through each room as she described what her inspectors had found was wrong and what would never be allowed in a modern renovation. Rhebekka could see the wheels turning in Naomi's head. Her wife was biting her lower lip as she walked around the kitchen with Maggie.

"I'm guessing the original owners had staff, because I can't see this being a family kitchen." Naomi ran her hand across the butcher block island.

Maggie nodded. "They were very wealthy. There's a small servant quarters off a back room where the cook and gardener lived as part of their employment. It has a separate entrance from the outside as well. The last keepers passed away about fifteen years ago."

Rhebekka walked to the impressive six-burner gas stove, with two large ovens underneath. "I'm glad you know how to use all this stuff." She put her hands on the counter about two feet apart. "Put me a microwave right here, and I'll be fine."

Naomi walked over to her and slipped her arms around her waist. "Good thing you married someone who can cook. I thank God you had Karmen to feed you every day before you saw the error of your ways."

Rhebekka held her tight. "So very true. Let's see the rest of this place."

Maggie walked them around the kitchen, pointing out the wide plank flooring. "Many prominent homes still had practical flooring in the areas mainly occupied by staff. Most people today couldn't afford wood like this in the main areas of their homes. From what I've discovered, the wood that makes up the flooring throughout the house was milled right here within the county. Another interesting fact is that much of the stone was cut from a local quarry."

"This place seems to be an industrial history lesson. I'm still amazed it wasn't on the market before now."

Maggie led them to the grand staircase. "It wasn't on the market because Claire refused to sell. I've known her for some time, and I will tell you that when she's set on something, the matter is settled. Her greatest fear was that it would be torn down, and the land used to turn out characterless condos for the tourists coming to ski. That's why I think your idea will intrigue her."

"If we move forward with this, is there a way we can talk with her? I want to ensure we honor as many of her wishes as possible, within reason, of course." Naomi slid her hand into Rhebekka's.

Rhebekka looked around at what a colossal undertaking everything would be. She was very thankful she had a great money manager that had invested aggressively when the market was right and moved things into safer options when the market was volatile. The woman now managed Ellie and Naomi's investments. Daniel had done exceptionally well with the same adviser. "This place is huge. I know it looks big from the outside, but I had no idea how big it was on the inside. These bedrooms are more like suites than a place to lay your head."

Maggie nodded as they stepped into one of them. "This is the smallest, and I think it's still bigger than Chance's first college apartment." Her phone pinged. "If you two are okay looking around a bit by yourselves, I need to step out and make a call."

Rhebekka waved at Maggie. "Go ahead. We'll be here." They walked around, stepping off the space for size. Rhebekka turned to Naomi. "I wonder how hard it would be to put at least a small bathroom in each of these spaces?"

Naomi shrugged. "It has the room for sure. That would give each one the privacy they desperately need. Lucian told me that he always felt so vulnerable trying to bind his chest."

"There are so many just like him. If we can pull this off, we need to talk with him about things like this and get his input. It's one thing to think you know what someone needs. He could tell us what would have made him more comfortable."

"I love how your first thought is to include him."

"This is going to be his home too. He has valuable insight that we'll need if we're going to make this a successful endeavor."

Six large bedrooms circled the staircase, each in a varying state of disrepair. Some of the lath and plaster was cracked, and some ceilings showed water damage from leaks. The place was freezing. Several windows were broken and missing pieces of glass.

Naomi pointed above each of the doors. "Check those out."

"Oh, those are so cool."

"That is one of my favorite parts of this place," Maggie said as she rejoined them. "It's a rare treat to find even one intact, stained-glass transom. This place has six. I often find that they've been pulled out or covered over. They served an important role before modern air conditioning. When opened, they allowed for ventilation while maintaining some privacy. They also helped bring in natural light."

Naomi clasped her hands together. "I love them. My grandmother's house had one. It wasn't stained glass, but it worked."

"I want to show you the other rooms downstairs, and then we'll head outside to the other buildings on the property." Maggie waved them toward the stairs.

"This place really is huge." Rhebekka held Naomi's hand as they made their way down.

Naomi nodded. "For what we envision, we'll need that kind of space."

Maggie led them into a large room with floor-to-ceiling bookcases and a library ladder that ran on a rail. The books were gone, but it was easy to see the former glory of the room. "Every room has a fireplace, and I think she had all new double-walled flues put in many years ago. We'd need to get them inspected. It reminds me of Chance and Jax's library, though this is on a much grander scale."

Naomi spun around. "This place is unbelievable. Can you imagine studying in here for classes?"

Rhebekka chuckled. "I see the wheels turning, Mrs. Deklan. Maggie, I don't think we need to see anything else. If the outbuildings are in the same general shape as this place, I think I understand what would need to be done." She pulled Naomi close and nodded at her wife's wide smile. "When could we meet with Claire?"

Maggie pulled out her phone. "I can set something up today, if you'd like. Do you want to call any home inspectors in before we start talking prices?"

"I want to bring in an inspector, but only to lay a roadmap for the most critical needs. We don't have to do it all at once, but the ground floor rooms and at least two-bedroom areas would need to be renovated first. I think I'm safe in saying Naomi and I would like to make an offer."

Maggie dialed and held the phone to her ear. "Then let's get you an audience with Ms. Claire."

Rhebekka held Naomi in her arms and looked around the once-grand dwelling. In this place, they would build a home and rest it on the rock-solid foundation of their faith, love for each other, and commitment to their family with Lucian. *'The rain came down, the streams rose, and the winds blew and beat against that house; yet it did not fall, because it had its foundation on the rock.'*

* * * *

They had an appointment with the seller at two. Rhebekka and Naomi contacted their financial advisers when they returned to the house. It would take about a week to liquidate enough investments to produce the cash needed for the offer they wanted to make.

Naomi watched Rhebekka walk around the house, her Fender strung low on her hip. "I like that song. Keep it in."

Rhebekka nodded. "I want a little different playlist for Friday. Something totally upbeat. Ellie and Siobhan will be there too. I can guarantee she needs it as much as we do."

"Can we convince Siobhan to play a few of Trad's Irish songs?"

Rhebekka shrugged. "I don't see why not. I'll add Bob Seger's 'Old Time Rock and Roll.'"

Naomi grabbed a wooden spoon and pretended to use it as a microphone as she sang and danced around the kitchen. The song was iconic, and it made her happy to see Rhebekka smiling at her antics. She sang a few verses and the chorus before putting the spoon back in the ceramic crock it came from.

Rhebekka moved her guitar behind her and wrapped her arms around Naomi's waist. She pulled her close. "I love you with every cell in my body. When I look back on my life just a few years ago, it pales in comparison."

Naomi kissed her and looked deep into the eyes she'd been lost in from the moment they met. "And I love you right back. Do you think this idea is crazy?"

"No, I don't. I think it's a natural progression of what we are supposed to do. The scriptures speak of caring for widows and orphans. We may be trying to fulfill that assignment uniquely, but we will fulfill it. That is, if we can persuade Ms. Claire to sell to us."

Naomi thought about the monumental task of repairing the mansion. "How long do you think it would take to make it livable?" The issues were far deeper than the cosmetic fixes of a good cleaning and fresh paint.

"We'll have to get an inspector there who can tell us what is critical to fix first to stop any deterioration and make it safe. The roof will certainly need to be replaced. The tree that busted through it opened the rafters to the brutal weather we get around here. On top of that, unless someone did lead and asbestos abatement sometime in the last twenty years, I'm positive we'll be required to bring in specialists. I had that issue with this place."

Naomi put her head against Rhebekka's chest and found comfort in the steady thump-thump of her heart just under her ear. "Do you think we're biting off more than we can chew?"

"These are all things that will take time and money. We happen to have both. I'm still writing songs, and the royalties from Regal Crimson will be coming in for years. We can't do it all at once, but I'm confident we can do enough to make a home for a few who need it until we can do more. We can also fundraise. Ellie and I still have enough contacts in the business that we could do a benefit concert or something. For now, we have enough money to get started if the price isn't too steep."

Naomi's phone chimed an alarm. She reached over and silenced it. "There's no time like the present to find out. It's almost time to go. I'm going to change into something that isn't splattered with red sauce."

"I think you look perfectly delicious with red sauce splashed all over you."

"You say that because you're happy I'm making stuffed shells for everyone at Salvation and Libations tonight."

Rhebekka bit her lip and held her finger and thumb close together. "Maybe just a little bit."

"Go put away your toys. I'll be ready in ten minutes."

"It will cost you."

Naomi turned and grinned. "Name your price."

Rhebekka pulled her close again. "One kiss."

"Only one?"

"One that lasts a lifetime should do."

"If I do that, we'll be late for our appointment. So here's a peck as a down payment. I'll pay in full after we get home tonight from taking everyone home."

Rhebekka sighed. "I'll take this deal, only because I plan to hold you to it with interest."

Naomi leaned in and brought their lips together in a feather-light kiss filled with enough tenderness to express her love before pulling away. "Denying you more is just as hard on me."

An exasperated huff left Rhebekka as she dropped her arms and pulled the Fender over her head. "If I must."

"I'll be back in a few minutes." She made her way to the bedroom and slipped out of her yoga pants. She hoped the jeans, turtleneck, and belted sweater she'd worn earlier to see the house would be presentable. She ran a brush through her long, dark hair and applied a light coat of plum-colored lipstick. *Lord, be with us today. If this is your will, help us find a way to make this happen.*

Naomi made her way to the door and stepped into her calf-high, fur-lined boots before sliding into the coat Rhebekka held open for her. "Thank you, baby. Let's go buy a house."

* * * *

They met Maggie in the visitor's parking area at the nursing home. Naomi reached for Rhebekka's hand as they walked to the entrance doors. "Did you get something to eat?"

Maggie patted her stomach. "I did. Jax made soup beans and cornbread. We ate while Hunter explained his latest drawings to us. He's very good for his age."

Naomi chuckled. "He is the cutest little guy. How's his speech coming?"

Maggie wagged her hand back and forth. "Slow, but with Julia's help, he's doing better all the time."

Rhebekka chuckled. "I love how he leans in and touches the piano to feel the vibrations."

Inside, they signed the visitor's book. Maggie walked them down a hallway. "I reserved a small area where we can sit and talk. Claire will be comfortable, and we can have some privacy." She pointed to a room ahead.

There were several ruby-colored sitting chairs. Some of them were in an odd upright position. Naomi recognized them as lift chairs that helped those in need stand up without strain. Her mother had broken her hip several years ago and required one during her rehabilitation. Swallowed up in one of the chairs was a tall, slender woman with a head full of silver-white hair.

Maggie led the introductions. "Claire, these two wonderful women are Naomi and Rhebekka Deklan. I showed them your property this morning." She turned back to them. "Naomi and Rhebekka, may I introduce you to the remarkable Claire Buxton. Once you make her acquaintance, she's someone you'll never forget."

Naomi stepped up with an outstretched hand. "Claire, it's a pleasure for us to meet you.

Claire smiled back at them. "Pleasure's mine. I don't get many visitors anymore. Everyone who knew me well has been gone a long time. My body's worn out, but my heart runs like a Timex. 'Takes a licking and keeps on ticking.'"

This brought a round of chuckles from the group. Maggie pointed to the chairs. "Let's sit down and talk for a bit."

Claire sized them up. "Tell me about yourselves and why you're interested in that monstrosity my daddy built."

Naomi nodded. "We'll be happy to. I'm originally from Colorado, where I was a music teacher turned non-denominational minister. I started a house of worship serving those often turned away or turned off by traditional religion. I spent years ensuring those who felt left behind understood they were children of a gracious God."

Rhebekka spoke up. "I ended up being one of those she captured in her net of kindness and love. I grew up in Virginia and left home once my sister graduated. We had a long and successful music career until I felt a different calling. I was a complete mess and absolutely broken. It sounds corny, but she showed me the light." She pointed to Naomi.

Naomi reached out and covered Rhebekka's hand with her own. "Your brokenness let the light in. I just made sure you weren't standing in the darkness."

Claire spoke up. "Unless I miss what these old eyes are seeing, you two are a couple."

Naomi stiffened slightly, preparing for the blow that might be coming. "Yes, Rhebekka and I are legally married."

Claire sighed and looked into the distance as if she remembered something. It was a few minutes before she spoke again. "Sometimes I wonder if anyone recognizes how fortunate they are to be living in a time when your relationship won't get you thrown into jail. Hell, nowadays, the law actually allows you to get legally married. When I was barely out of school, I was expected to marry some man, even if I didn't love him. After that, I'd tend to a home and the five kids he'd decide we were to have." She visibly shivered. "What I wouldn't have done to be born in a different time."

Rhebekka threaded her fingers through Naomi's. "It's a constant battle to hold on to those hard fought rights. At every turn, someone is trying to take them away. I grew up in a religion that didn't approve of who I truly was or who I was attracted to. It's one of the reasons it took me so long to accept the grace Naomi showed me I was worthy of."

Claire steepled her hands. "We'll come back to this, but you know, even if you buy the house, you can't tear it down. So tell me why you're crazy enough to want that giant place with all the stipulations I've got on its use."

Naomi's heart pounded in her chest. Whatever she said next could make or break their plans. *God, if this is your will, give me the words.* "Not long ago, Rhebekka and I took in a young man who had grown up in a group home after his grandmother died. Lucian had run away from the home because of the abuse he suffered. This young man was being abused because of his personal belief that he'd been born into a body that didn't reflect who he truly was inside. He wasn't the only one at the home whose sexuality would have made them a target. Lucian was aware of others hiding their sexuality to avoid the harassment and physical violence he was suffering."

She took a deep breath before continuing, to give Claire time to absorb what she'd said. Naomi had no idea how Claire would react, but she pushed on. "There are far too many lesbian, gay, bisexual, transgender, questioning, intersex, and asexual kids in the foster system. When they age out, they have few options for safe housing while they go to work or school. They need somewhere to help them transition into the adults they are, not who someone else says they should be. The worst-case scenario is they end up on the streets."

Rhebekka picked up the discussion. "Our idea is to create something akin to a sanctuary house for these vulnerable kids. While staying there, they can seek employment, higher education, or a trade that will help them support themselves. In addition, we can help them get counseling and medical care as it's needed. These kids, or young adults, need someone fully in their corner. A community that supports and accepts them exactly as they are, not who someone wants them to be."

Naomi sat back and watched Claire steeple her fingers at her lips. She didn't note any distress or anger at what they'd proposed, only serious contemplation. For being ninety-five, the woman was remarkably graceful. Her silver hair fell slightly into her eyes. Steady fingers pushed it back and smoothed it into place as she began to speak.

"When I was growing up, there were expectations. Young women in my circle were expected to be seen and not heard, to grow into women of grace that married and reared children at home while recognizing the man was the head of the household, no matter what." Claire stared into some middle distance before she spoke again. "That was so far from who I was. My mother always said I had a mouth on me and was too headstrong, but my daddy..." She trailed off. "My daddy was an influential man in the community. He employed hundreds of people in the company's heyday. He encouraged me to learn accounting practices for business and sent me to school. I worked for the company for fifty years and did so without a husband." She raised a finger to emphasize the point.

"That's remarkable, even by today's standards. I'm sure you showed many women they could make their way." Naomi leaned forward. "How did the community feel about it?"

Claire smiled slightly. "Oh, I was considered the old maid by the time I was twenty. Later I was just considered a spinster. That's what they called unmarried women in my day. I had a brother that died in the war and a younger sister that died in childbirth. The baby didn't make it either. My parents were devastated, but we carried on. As they aged, I cared for my parents until they passed. I'm the last of my family, and that house is all that's left standing of who we were."

Rhebekka nodded. "It's a beautiful place. Even with the things that need attention, you can see how important it was to your family."

"It was a good place to grow up. My siblings and I ran those grounds and climbed every tree on the property. Our staff was like family to us, and I took care of them long after they were unable to work. They never wondered where they would live. I can't imagine Tip not having a place to go."

"Tip?" Rhebekka questioned.

A slight blush came over the thin skin on Claire's face. "Tip was Harold and Sissy's daughter. She was as strong as any man I ever knew and worked most of them into the dirt. She lived with her parents until they passed right there in the quarters attached to the house. I'm not sure how I'd ever have made it without her. She was a sight."

Naomi's senses tingled. *Could Claire and Tip have been a secret couple?* "Tip sounds like she was pretty incredible."

Wistfulness came over Claire's face. "Oh, she was. Tip was ten years younger than I was. When she was little, she followed my siblings and me everywhere. She had a lot of suiters that would come calling, but she never gave any of them the time of day. She always told me the sun rose and set in my smile." She blushed again. "There was no one like her in my life, I can tell you that. I lost her fifteen years ago, to a stroke." She wiped gently at the tear that trickled down her cheek.

Naomi reached out and placed a hand over the frail one that rested in Claire's lap. The skin felt like silk but as delicate as crepe paper. "I'm so sorry for your loss. It doesn't matter how long you have someone you love in your life, losing them takes a huge part of our hearts when they go."

Maggie handed her a tissue. "When Dee had her heart attack, I didn't know if I'd survive if I lost her."

Claire accepted the tissue and dabbed at her eyes while she held Naomi's hand. "Tip loved me in a way no man ever would have. She understood when to push and when to back off. Oh, she was a terrible tease, but when she said she loved me wholeheartedly, I knew she meant it. I'm sure people in this town knew what we were to each other, but to most, we were just two old spinsters prattling around in that giant house. None of it mattered to us. We had the finances to take care of ourselves, and we didn't need much beyond a handyman now and then. I thought I'd go right with her when she died, but I'm still here and wishing I wasn't."

She turned and looked directly at Naomi and Rhebekka. "What I wouldn't have given to be able to live as you two do. I know exactly who you are. I may be old, but senile, I am not. Maggie can attest to that as well. You two have made for lots of interesting eavesdropping when people have thought I couldn't hear or wasn't listening. Turning that house into what you two want it to be will take a fortune. Yet here you two are even knowing the stipulations I have. I won't budge on those. The house must stay and be restored. An irrevocable trust is associated with it, and my lawyers have ensured it's iron clad. I'd rather see the house fall and go back to the earth than see those characterless condos be crammed into every square inch of the property."

Rhebekka handed Claire a set of papers. "I had a good career before becoming a pastor. That career afforded me the ability to invest. I still have a songwriting career and royalties that will live long past my lifetime. I didn't know what I wanted to do with my finances until Lucian came into our lives, and my wife came up with this idea. I don't want to insult you with an offer that won't reflect what you think the property is worth. I hope you'll see this as a good-faith first negotiation."

Claire took the papers and slipped on the glasses that hung on a gold chain around her neck. She read carefully, asking clarifying questions before folding the papers and placing them on her lap. "My doctors have made sure to carefully document my mental status and health. I have a monthly checkup to ensure that whatever I decide to do can't be called into question for mental capacity. My body may be failing me, but my mind isn't. Now, with that said, I'm going to make you an offer you can't refuse. I've turned down more money than you have on this paper because no one has come to me with a plan to do something that would mean any more to me than what you propose. Tip and I could never be open outside the walls of our home, but you two can make those walls into a home for the next generations of Tips and Claires. Your offer assures me that you can afford to restore what Tip and I so lovingly cared for. I have enough money to be comfortable here until I join Tip in the great hereafter, so I will give you the house and grounds for one hundred dollars. I'll have my lawyer draw up the transfer to make everything legal. All I ask is that you stop by every once in a while to show me the progress, as I'll not likely see the completion in my limited time here on earth."

Naomi sat back in complete shock. This was not what she'd expected. She looked over at Rhebekka and saw the same emotions playing across her face. "Claire, that's an incredibly generous offer, but that's not what we expected. We want to pay you a fair price. One hundred dollars is far too little."

Rhebekka echoed the sentiment and pointed to the paperwork. "I'm fully prepared to pay you that amount or more. You deserve to do whatever you want with the money."

Claire scrunched up her brow. "And if I tell you two what I want to do is support your plans, would you presume to tell me I'm not in my right mind or not entitled to do as I please? If that's your assumption, then I'm dealing with the wrong people." Claire folded her arms across her thin frame.

Naomi raised her hands, imploring Claire not to take offense at their concerns. "Claire, that in no way is what we are implying. Rhebekka and I have worked hard for the things we have. No one has given us anything. We've had to fight tooth and nail against what would tear us apart and destroy what we have tried to build and what we stand for. Your offer is beyond generous. Frankly, it's overwhelming, and we would, in no way, want anyone to believe we're taking advantage of someone who has lived this long."

Claire nodded. "Very well, one hundred and one dollars and not a penny less."

Rhebekka howled with laughter. "Maggie told us you were a corker, but you are much more than we expected." She gestured between herself and Naomi. "To most people, what we're proposing would be looked at with scorn and disdain. We were worried to death that you'd be some ultra-conservative homophobe that would send us out of here with our tails between our legs."

Naomi wiped at her tears of laughter. "Imagine our surprise to find out we were talking to someone who enjoyed a love like ours. It's more than we could have ever imagined."

Claire uncrossed her arms and chuckled. "I understand. You need to know that I do not require a single dollar more to live exactly as I do. No million dollars will make me young again, and it won't bring Tip back. I have more than I need. I wanted to ensure that what my daddy worked so hard for wouldn't be destroyed in the name of progress. I already have a contractor on standby to fix the roof and make some repairs. I didn't want to fix everything so someone would look at my home as an easy grab and flip. The repairs will be done before you take ownership."

She leaned forward. "There will be no arguments, and all this will be in writing by tomorrow afternoon. This is the last thing on my plate, girls. I've been waiting for someone like you to come along and answer my prayers. Now, if you believe in God's will as strongly as I assume, you'll let an old lady die happy. Tip is up there smiling that someone else won't need to hide who they are just to have a place to live. Tip might have been an older version of this Lucian, had we lived in a different time. She'd be proud of this, and so am I." She tapped her hands on her knees. "Since we're still in the winter months, expect to take ownership late spring or summer. That will give my contractors time to fix what needs to be done. You need to understand that this money had been set aside for decades and won't affect my finances to live as I'm accustomed to, not even in the slightest. I want to do this, and since I have an encyclopedia full of documentation that says I am completely of sound mind, I can do what I want."

Naomi melted into Rhebekka's arms, crying tears of joy. "Claire, I don't know if you believe in angels, but you are certainly one here on earth."

Chapter Fourteen

RHEBEKKA SPOKE WITH HER attorney in New York three weeks after they'd signed papers with Claire for the house. They'd filed a lawsuit against the Witnesses' parent organization, The Watchtower Bible and Tract Society in Kings County, New York. So much was going on that it was hard to keep up. "Justine, what's our next step in the case?" She heard papers shuffling and the clicking of computer keys over the line.

"I've filed several discovery motions for documentation. We've also worked with Silent Lambs and several other organizations to produce deposition-worthy testimony about the systematic coverup of the sexual abuse and sexual assault former members endured," Justine replied.

Justine Recht was an imposing figure. She stood a mere five foot five, but her presence in the courtroom was that of a giant. A true force of nature with a head of bright-red hair, she was the lead on the team that was suing the Witness organization on behalf of nearly 200 women and men with claims of abuse. Ellie and their friend Carrie were two of those claimants.

Justine was also handling Ellie and Carrie's civil case against Tom and Dave Broader. "According to the Charlottesville Police Department, the sexual abuse charges against both of them would have had to have been filed within a year of Ellie and Carrie becoming adults. There are other charges they will take to the prosecutor with no statute of limitations. I know this is hard, but we need to file whatever we can. In doing so, you never know who else will step forward. Has Carrie been able to get in touch with her sister-in-law?"

Rhebekka ran a hand through her hair and made some notes. "She did, but the woman wouldn't speak with her. Interestingly enough, their daughter no longer lives with them. She's not even in the same state. Carrie's niece, Lisa, married a man in the military and moved to Alaska right after she turned eighteen. Nothing says fuck you like marrying a worldly man outside the organization who pledges allegiance to a government they don't believe in."

"On top of that, they moved about as far away as possible from the family. I don't think any of that's a coincidence. Carrie is trying to make contact. When she talks to her niece, I hope she finds out nothing ever happened, but my gut screams differently."

"Keep me updated on that. I'll have our investigators look into the CPS investigation on file. How are you holding up under the media scrutiny?"

Rhebekka thought about the local and national reporters that had shown up at House of the Rising Son the previous Sunday. They'd made a royal ruckus when Sheriff Fitzsimmons asked them to put down their cameras and stop disrupting the service. She chuckled remembering how adamant Chance was about throwing Mya Knolls out if she tried to interview one more person during the service. Chance's ex-girlfriend was certainly doggedly persistent. "Carrie and I have already spoken to CNN, ABC, CBS, and MSNBC. I know this will make your jaw drop, but we even heard from Fox News. We've put out the statement of our intentions."

"You were careful, right?" Justine asked.

Rhebekka had been schooled, repeatedly, by her attorney about the language to use, what to say, and what not to say. "Per your approved press release, yes."

"It's important to remember that they are a global organization with attorneys of their own looking at how to wiggle out of anything they can for any reason. If they can try to destroy you in the process, then that's a win for them."

Rhebekka grew angry. "They already tried that years ago. I'm far older and stronger now."

"That's my girl. We'll talk soon. I have a meeting with my team in a few minutes. We've got them dead to rights, Rhebekka. We just need to stay the course. I promise to fight like a momma lioness all the way to the verdict."

"Thank you, Justine. The lambs can be silenced no more."

Rhebekka had no more hung up with Justine, when her phone rang again. She looked at the caller ID. She'd been expecting this call and was surprised it had taken this long. "Mom, what can I do for you?"

"Rhebekka Lynn McNally, how could you do this? You continue to bring reproach on Jehovah's name. Do you have no decency in you at all?"

Decency? That's rich. She let a few seconds pass as the forest fire of rage burned over her.

"Rhebekka Lynn, did you hear me?"

"Did you know?" Rhebekka's tone was icily cold, lacking the emotional tidal wave crashing over her. The next words out of her mother's mouth could irreparably sever their relationship.

Her mother scoffed. "Know what? I know that this isn't the way to handle things. The elders know Jehovah's wishes and how to handle it."

"They certainly know how to hide it to protect the organization while not giving a damn about the children irrevocably damaged. Did you know?"

"I knew you hated the organization, but do you hate me this much?" Irene McNally tsked.

Rhebekka annunciated each word slowly and clearly, asking the question again. "Did you know?" Her mother grew quiet, and Rhebekka was sure she heard sobs on the other end of the line. "For the last time, answer my question. I warn you to think hard about your answer, because what you say will have long-reaching consequences. Did...you...know?"

"Did I know that someone was sexually abusing my child? Did I know it happened repeatedly? Is that what you are truly asking me? You must really think me to be a monster. Of course, I didn't know! As Jehovah is my witness, I would have never let her go over there. I encouraged her to go visit Carrie to get your father to stop screaming at her. I trusted them. Tom was an elder, for heaven's sake."

"Exactly, Mom. He was in a perfect position to abuse a vulnerable little girl looking for anyone to show her kindness and understanding because the man responsible for our birth beat us whether we needed it or not. I also want you to know that elder taught his son to follow in his footsteps as an abuser."

Her mother's sobs nearly broke her, but Rhebekka's anger was riding right beneath the surface of her inked skin and threatening to burst through. The horrible things Ellie had endured fueled her rage. For the next ten minutes, Rhebekka let it all out. The pain of her childhood, the resentment that her mother placed an organization above her children, and her disgust at her mother's blind allegiance to that came rushing out of her like a river overflowing its banks and ravaging everything in its path. "All the evidence in the world will never change your mind that these are not men of God. Their truth, as you refer to it, is far from that. They are men of evil and serve only themselves. Despite your beliefs, Jehovah's Witnesses aren't God's chosen organization. God loves people from all religions, backgrounds, and walks of life. Jehovah's Witnesses wall themselves off and claim to be living a Christian life while harboring pedophiles and rapists and hiding it from the authorities. And for what? Do you really think God needs our protection? It's not God doing these abhorrent things, but man. How did Jehovah's Witnesses come to believe that they are so self-important that only they have the true way? Go back and really look at what your precious organization does to protect those who hurt the most innocent."

Rhebekka barely caught her breath before opening both barrels on her mother. "How many times do you think there are two witnesses present during the crime of sexual assault on a child that would offer your precious elders enough evidence for them to actually do something about it? Do you know what their directive is when the crime does meet their criteria? Do they turn that person over to the authorities? No, they further traumatize the victim by making them describe, in detail, what happened to them. They do this in a room full of other men with the perpetrator present. In the overwhelming majority of cases, they tuck it into a blue envelope and sweep it under the rug like it never happened. They frequently fail to warn the next congregation that there is a pedophile moving into their midst. When it happens again, they take no responsibility."

Rhebekka lowered her voice to her most menacingly calm version. "An elder in your congregation raped his own child and your daughter. That elder's son, a ministerial servant, raped his sister and your daughter, repeatedly. These men abused my sister, your daughter, over and over again. How in your twisted brain can you believe these are God's servants? In case you didn't know, they are currently serving in another congregation and likely doing the same damn thing. Oh yes, I can certainly see how these men are capable of protecting God's reputation. Cling to them, Mother, hold on to the belief that only they can lead you to paradise. Keep believing God despises people like me but loves men like that and trusts them to lead his sheep. My God is, without a shadow of a doubt, completely different than yours. I'm done, Mother. Goodbye."

Rhebekka clicked off the call. She stared at her phone and did something she'd never done before, not even in the years she'd spent out on the road. With a single stroke, she blocked her mother's number and removed the contact information from her phone. It was mostly a symbolic gesture. Her mother would know how to find her. Rhebekka knew her mother could use several other numbers to get in touch with her. She made the impulsive gesture purely out of self-preservation. Irene McNally's name would no longer light up her cellphone screen or burn through her heart. *That's not the God I know. My God doesn't need the protection of mere human beings. A woman that chose an organization over her children isn't a mother I want anything to do with.*

Naomi's perfume wafted all around her. Hints of coffee beans and vanilla filled her senses, as delicate arms wrapped her up. "I'm sorry, baby."

"I just can't do this dance with her anymore. Despite overwhelming evidence, she still clings to her version of the truth and a God I'll never believe in or understand."

Naomi kissed the side of her head. "I think it's beyond understanding, honey. The lie is so ingrained that it's distorted her world in the way rose-colored glasses do. No matter how hard you try to see things right in front of you, it always has the tint and distortion of the glass you're looking through. Her lenses are like those sunglasses they give you after cataract surgery, with thick blinders on the side. That kind of lens only allows in the amount of light they chose for you."

Rhebekka took a very shaky, deep breath. "More like the blinders they put on horses to keep them in line." Her chest felt tight, and her head was pounding with such ferocity it rivaled the rock concerts of her past. She held her hands out and watched them tremble with anger-filled adrenaline. She turned them over and stared at the tattoo of her grandfather's guitar bursting through her skin. There were only two ways to purge this poison from her mind, music or sex. Angry sex had never worked for her and Naomi. It felt all wrong. She let her head fall back on Naomi's shoulder. "I need to play."

Naomi squeezed her tightly. "I know. I was going to suggest it. Go downstairs, because I know you need room to pace. I have a few calls to make. Don't be surprised if Lucian joins you in a bit. You know he loves to jam with you."

Rhebekka picked up her head and nodded. "I'd welcome a good shred session with him when he gets home."

Naomi came around to look her in the eyes. "I'll be coming down to bring you some water and to check your hands. If you think you're going to ignore your bleeding fingers, think again."

Rhebekka kissed her softly. "I don't even feel it when it starts to happen. You'd think, after playing all these years, the callouses would prevent it."

"They might, but there is a limit to everything's endurance. Go play. I love you."

"And I love you."

She walked over to the studio and grabbed both her grandfather's Gibson and her Fender before making her way downstairs. Naomi was right. She needed ample space to pace. When she played in the sanctuary, there was a peace she didn't find in most places. In this space, she found God's ear. Melodies flowed from the thoughts in her head, down through her heart, and out through her fingers on the strings. *Lies and deception all designed to keep us in line.* She raked the pic across the Fender strings. *Puppets. We were all puppets. Marionettes connected by invisible wires that forced us to dance on command, in the name of a God that offered no grace and no compassion, on a stage for the world to see.* Rhebekka scowled as she squeezed the neck of the guitar harder. She settled into Metallica's *Master of Puppets* and let the raw emotion of the heavy metal music wash through her veins. This was where she found her peace. Every note she played was a conversation with God.

She played harder and faster, losing herself in the music that purged the toxic thoughts and feelings from her mind like steam in a sauna does for the body. Notes reverberated off the walls, bouncing back to her like an echo while the vibrations made their way through the hardwood floor. Those vibrations penetrated her feet and climbed her legs until they joined with the guitar that created them. Rhebekka played on through the tears that rolled down her cheeks and neck to be absorbed by the collar of her T-shirt. *Help me understand, God. I'm begging you.* The bass of Lucian's guitar joined in and matched her note for note, adding the framework for each song she led them into. No words needed to be spoken, as the tears continued to pour down her face.

There was no sense of time. She added thousands of steps to the worn finish of the stage. The heavy curtains surrounded her with safety, like the embrace of a loved one. She played on without conscious thought of time, until her arms began to feel like rubber. She felt a hand on her shoulder.

"That's enough, my love. It's time to stop. You're limping and shaking." Naomi lifted the guitar off Rhebekka's neck and handed it to Lucian. "Let's go take a bath. I need to hold you."

Rhebekka nodded. She looked at Lucian with more love than she could have imagined for anyone beyond Naomi and Ellie. Her hand trembled as she cupped his cheek and felt him lean into it.

Lucian stepped into the touch and wrapped his arms around her waist. "You taught me who God is and what it is to know the love and grace of a higher power. You and Naomi have given me a family. No matter what happens in my life after this, I will have known these things because you two showed me what it means to have people care about you. You and Naomi will always be my family. I love you both."

Rhebekka pulled him to her tightly and brought Naomi into the group hug. This was the family she wanted and needed. If it was the last thing she did, she would be the mother she wished she could have had. This young man would know love without conditions from those closest to him. She vowed that Lucian would know the love and protection of a family.

* * * *

Naomi directed Rhebekka into the bathroom. "Let's get your leg off." She watched as Rhebekka toed off her boot and unbuckled the wide, black belt snugged around her slender waist. She brushed Rhebekka's hands away and unbuttoned the worn jeans riding low on her wife's hips. She smiled at the bare skin that revealed itself as the denim slid over Rhebekka's hips and landed around her thighs. "I so love that you go commando." Naomi leaned in and kissed her hip bone.

"You know me, rebel to the marrow of my bones."

Naomi pointed to the edge of the tub. "Sit. I'll take your prosthesis off."

Rhebekka nodded and sat down as instructed. She pulled her T-shirt off over her head. "You're too good to me."

Naomi tenderly removed everything until Rhebekka was down to only what she'd been born with. "That's not possible. Go ahead and get in. I'm going to get us a drink. Light the candles on the ledge, please." She leaned over and kissed Rhebekka.

"Quickly, because I need you."

"Quick like a cat," Naomi quipped.

Lucian was in the kitchen when she entered to get the wine. She pulled two stemless wine glasses from the cabinet and watched Lucian pour himself a glass of chocolate milk.

"I turned all the lights off and put the guitars on their stands in the studio. Will Bek be okay?" He took a sip of the milk.

"Thank you. She'll be okay. It's very hard on her to realize that, after all these years, her mother still doesn't value the children she brought into this world. Not the way she should, anyway. As a pastor, the God Rhebekka knows would never want to be associated with those who hide the abuse of children." She pulled the wine from a rack on the countertop and uncorked it.

"That's part of the reason I stopped believing God even existed. How could the most powerful being in the universe let anyone hurt children? I understand it's not God's fault, but sometimes it's hard to understand why a being that powerful wouldn't stop it."

Naomi thought for a moment about how to respond. The sad part was she didn't have an answer other than the free will God gives humanity over their choices. Judgment over those choices was not always immediate. *No one knows the day or the hour when God says enough.* "I wish I had a good explanation beyond saying there are many things we don't know or understand. I have to believe there is a plan and an end to the wickedness humankind perpetuates on others. All we can do is try and show everyone the perfect love poured out on us when Christ died, by being examples of his love. Beyond that, it's in the hands of a much higher power."

Lucian sighed heavily and finished his glass of milk. "I appreciate you trying to explain it, but it still doesn't make sense to me. I'm going to bed." He put his empty glass in the dishwasher and stopped to kiss her on the cheek. "Love you, good night."

Naomi smiled. "Love you too. Night." She watched him walk down the hallway, avoiding the cats trying to slalom through his ankles. She grabbed the glasses and the bottle before making her way back to the bathroom. Rhebekka had slipped into the water and was resting with her head leaning against the back of the tub.

"Is Lucian okay?"

"He loves you and hates to see you all torn up."

"I'm sorry for worrying you both."

Naomi undressed and accepted Rhebekka's hand as she stepped into the tub. She poured the wine and offered Rhebekka a glass before leaning back against her chest. "There is nothing to be sorry for at all. Your feelings and emotions are a vital part of you. They make you who you are. Hiding that would only force you to be something you're not."

Rhebekka sipped the wine. "No matter how many times I try to make sense of it in my head, I can't jam the puzzle piece in place without beating it to death. I have faith in a God of grace, but that doesn't mean that God agrees with what happens."

"Lucian and I were discussing why God doesn't stop the evil. There have been enough books to fill a giant library on why, and the question will be around as long as humankind walks this earth."

She felt Rhebekka's weary sigh. "As pastors, we teach others about a loving God, yet even with all our experience and knowledge, there are questions that still elude us." Naomi wrapped an arm around Rhebekka's leg and sipped at her own wine.

"I never got a chance to tell you about Justine's call." Rhebekka filled her in on the plan for their attorney's multipointed legal plan.

They talked for several minutes, until the water began to cool. Naomi climbed out and dried off. She slipped on a robe, then helped Rhebekka out of the water and onto the side of the tub. It had taken Rhebekka a long time to accept help without guilt. Naomi dried her lover off with a soft towel and handed her the knee walker. She corked the wine and left the glasses on the vanity as she followed Rhebekka to bed.

"Now that you're good and relaxed, turn over on your stomach. I'll give you a massage." Naomi went to the dresser and found the cocoa butter.

Rhebekka leaned in and kissed her. "I like the sound of that."

Naomi removed her robe and straddled Rhebekka's butt. She squeezed a generous amount of lotion into her palm and warmed it with her hands before running them from Rhebekka's lower back up to her shoulders. She smiled at the groan of pleasure at her touch. Her hands glided down the inkwork that covered her wife's back and arms. *Roman outdid himself on this.* She ran her thumbs down Rhebekka's spine, which displayed an inked depiction of the burnished wooden cross Rhebekka still wore around her neck. The detail was incredible. As her hands worked on the knots she found, the memory of fastening that cross around Rhebekka's neck came back to her.

"I always want you to remember this as the day you realized and accepted you are absolutely worthy of the grace Christ's sacrifice offers." Naomi smoothed her hand down the small piece of artwork dangling from the braided leather choker.

Rhebekka touched it and smiled sheepishly. "I'll always be a work in progress. I still don't feel that worth you speak of in the way I should. Every year, on what they called the memorial, the bread and the wine were passed on a tray, from hand to hand, through every member of the congregation. We were repeatedly told that there were a finite number of people who were the chosen ones. They were the only individuals that partook."

Naomi hugged her. "I'll never understand how any human can withhold from anyone what a divine being offered as a sacrifice for all. Somewhere they missed the direct words of Jesus that said 'do this in remembrance of me.' That didn't mean to just waft it under your nose as a tool of control or a means of punishment. Who does that to a woman starving for grace?"

She held the cross in her hand, brushing against Rhebekka's breastbone. "When we take in the sacrament, we commune with the sacrifice freely given. We recognize and acknowledge that gift. That an imperfect human could decide another's worth of that sacrifice is far from Christ's intentions. You, my love, are worthy of it all."

Rhebekka pulled her tight. "I would never have known what grace was if it weren't for you."

"We are both 100 percent saint and sinner, Rhebekka. Inside you, all the things that describe love exist. You are patient, kind, able to bear all things, believe all things, hope in all things, and endure all things. Find your peace in the perfect love that grace can bring."

Naomi ran her finger around the outline of the demon wing, reading the words of the verse embedded there. She kneaded Rhebekka's shoulders and drew a moan from the woman beneath her.

"That feels so good. You have magical hands."

"It's a labor of love. Every time I look at this work of art, I see something different." She rubbed across Rhebekka's shoulder blades. "I can see every tiny feather on this wing and every scale on the other." She leaned forward, letting her lips linger on the warm skin as she kissed it.

"Like you always tell me, the saint within the sinner."

"Perfect in our imperfection. Turn over, please." Naomi lifted enough to allow Rhebekka to roll onto her back. She moved down to Rhebekka's foot and warmed more lotion in her hands before digging her thumbs deep into the arch. She smiled when Rhebekka's toes curled.

"Remind me to return this favor. I forget how good a massage feels when your body and soul are bone weary."

"I'll take you up on that." Naomi looked around their bedroom as her hands continued to knead. Since moving in, she'd made changes to create a place of respite in their private space. The soft grays and darker charcoals Rhebekka had chosen for herself had been accented with velvety turquoise pillows and stunning artwork. Together they'd shopped local stores for paintings and wooden carvings from the area's artisans. These small touches had turned the once sparse room into a peaceful sanctuary.

"What's going on in that beautiful head?"

Naomi chuckled as she rubbed up Rhebekka's calf. "I was thinking about how comfortable our home is, particularly this room."

"The loft became a home when you walked through the door for the first time. Before that, it was a place I spent time, hung my clothes, showered, and walked the floor with a guitar around my neck. Now it's the place I find peace and love because you're here."

"And now you even sleep a few hours."

"More than I ever did when you weren't in my arms."

"Not something you ever have to worry about again." Naomi worked her way up Rhebekka's calf to her thigh. She watched her wife close her eyes and arch her neck in pleasure. She moved to the other leg and examined the surgical scars on the residual limb. She tenderly kissed the skin before gathering more lotion and gently massaging the area. "Is it still sensitive?"

"It's a strange feeling. Sometimes when I first wake up, I forget it even happened. When I'm on it too long, it lets me know."

Naomi moved to the calf and worked the corded muscles. She let her hand wander higher to the inside of Rhebekka's thigh, eliciting a groan from her love. She could feel her own desire climbing and moved to straddle the muscled thighs beneath her and rubbed lotion across the defined abdominal muscles. "All those hours on the bike definitely show."

"It was one of the things I missed most while I recovered. Marvin and I put many miles behind us on the trails over the years. You do know you're driving me crazy, right?"

"Somehow, I'm betting you can tell how much touching you affects me as well." Naomi ran her palms across erect nipples and felt Rhebekka arch into her in pleasure.

"Fuck, baby."

Naomi leaned over, took one of them into her mouth, and sucked hard. The reaction from Rhebekka's body left her no doubt that it was time for a very different kind of massage. She looked up at hooded eyes full of need. "I'm dying to touch you."

"Not nearly as much as I'm dying for your touch. You've wound me up and I'm ready to explode."

"Then it's time for me to light the fuse." She moved until her naked flesh and Rhebekka's hot skin melded together. She brought their lips together in a scorching kiss and rolled Rhebekka over until she looked up at the gloriously tattooed body above her.

Rhebekka moved her hands into Naomi's hair and met her with the same fervor. Their tongues battled as they arched and undulated against each other. Naomi moved her hand between their bodies and sought Rhebekka's center. Copious wetness covered her fingers as she slid them through the silk.

"It's always so good with you, Rhebekka."

In a breathy voice, Rhebekka echoed the sentiment. "Nothing like it in the world."

Naomi touched and stroked, gently brushing Rhebekka's clit sparingly, saving a concentrated assault for the moment Rhebekka would move up her body and position herself above her mouth.

She reached up with her free hand and pulled at a hard nipple until Rhebekka gasped. "Join me."

Rhebekka tweaked her own nipple in time with Naomi's touch, driving Rhebekka higher and higher. When trembling thighs began to vibrate the bed, Naomi urged her up and smiled as Rhebekka grabbed the rail of the headboard. *Time to take it up one more notch.* She tilted her face up and brushed her lips through the dark curls above her. "So wet." She darted her tongue out and dipped into wet flesh. The slight touch made Rhebekka twitch and jerk with pleasure.

Naomi slid her arms around Rhebekka's hips and guided her down until she could securely hold Rhebekka in place and taste her fully. She delved her tongue deep inside Rhebekka's center and delighted in the gasp she drew from her lover. She languidly licked at the sweet and salty flesh. The trembling began again as she latched onto Rhebekka's clit. So close, my love. Let go. She drew her nails across Rhebekka's lower back and looked up into eyes full of desire. This had always been their pattern. Rhebekka craved control and rarely conceded to anything except when she felt out of control. In these intimate moments, she laid herself bare to Naomi.

Rhebekka let go of the railing and put her arms behind her back. Naomi moaned as she clasped Rhebekka's wrists in her hands and crossed them, holding them tightly. She increased her suction and added quick flicks of her tongue across the engorged clit. She watched Rhebekka arch her back and open her mouth in silent ecstasy with the powerful orgasm that ripped through her, flooding Naomi's mouth.

Rhebekka's neck tendons corded with the strain as a second orgasm crashed over her. Naomi drank it all in and rode the waves with her.

When Rhebekka's body began to slump, Naomi urged her to lie down on top of her. She pushed back the dark, copper-tipped locks and kissed her love's damp forehead. They lay there for several minutes, holding each other. "You are so beautiful in your release. Did you know that?"

Rhebekka pulled in a deep breath and chuckled. "I've never watched myself in that moment, so I'll take your word for it. Woman, you have just rocked my world."

Naomi pulled her in tighter. "Like a hurricane? That was my entire plan, to make you forget everything."

"Your simple act of being in my life accomplishes that."

"Thank you, baby. This takes it to another level, something we uniquely make together."

"In my wildest dreams, I couldn't have imagined the life we have now."

"I know why. There is no way to fully imagine pairing the similarities and differences of two people into a dance of give and take. We balance each other. When you're afraid of the rocks of the coast in a storm, I'm the lighthouse that guides you around them. When I feel lost in that same sea, you are my north star that guides me home. This family we've created is our house of refuge, our safe harbor to ride out the storm." She kissed Rhebekka's forehead again and used her fingertips to trace an infinity pattern on Rhebekka's back. She'd discovered it entirely by accident, but it worked nearly every time. "Sleep now, shut down your rambling mind, and find peace in the safety of my arms."

Naomi knew there was so much more pain and sorrow to come. Lord, please cover them with your mercy and shelter them in your grace, because I know this is far from over.

Chapter Fifteen

RHEBEKKA WALKED INTO ELLIE'S studio. The glossy black and chrome motif of the reception area gleamed. She smiled at the face that greeted her. "Hey, Amanda. How are you?" The young woman from her youth group had come so far from her days of being a sullen teenager with one parent in the military and one at home carrying the load.

The almost eighteen-year-old senior was involved with a work-study program through the high school. From one in the afternoon until three, Amanda did whatever Ellie's crew needed. Some days, she worked the front desk, fielding phone calls and taking messages. On other days, she was learning to run the sound board as they recorded one of the signed artists.

"Hi, Pastor Rhebekka. It's nice to see you."

"It's always a pleasure to see you as well. How's the family?"

"You know my moms. They're both busy planning out my future college prospects."

"I saw the list of schools you're considering. Pretty impressive, if you ask me."

Amanda blushed. "I really like what I'm doing with the studio work. I want to pursue it as a career."

Rhebekka smiled at her. "Then you couldn't be in better company. My sister has some great contacts. Is she around?"

"It's my place, Bek. I'm always around." Ellie walked up and put her arms around her sister. "It's good to see you."

Rhebekka hugged her back just as tightly. "It's good to see you too. I thought I'd come by and hang out with you in the studio for a bit." Rhebekka had a surprise for Ellie arriving within the hour.

"Wonderful. You can listen to Strings and Silk cut Storm Shelter. That song fits them and their skills. They love that we offered it to them."

Rhebekka began to hum the tune they'd written together earlier in the year. "I'll bet. Martina and Myranda's harmonies have to be killer on it."

Ellie nodded. "They remind me of us when we started, minus the running for our lives feeling." Ellie turned to the desk. "Amanda, do you need anything?"

"Nope, but I have three messages for you. Two are interview requests, and one is from someone claiming to be your mom. She demanded to speak to you, but I told her our policy was to take a name and number." Amanda handed her the slips of paper.

"Thanks, I'll take care of them. You're doing a great job. Tomorrow, we'll do some mixing, if you're interested."

Amanda was nearly vibrating in her seat. "If I'm interested? Is there anything about me that makes you think I wouldn't be?"

The sleek reception area filled with laughter as they continued to joke and visit with Amanda.

Rhebekka noticed the slips of paper were crumpled in her sister's hand. "Let's go listen to the girls sing our masterpiece. Good to see you, Amanda."

"You too, Pastor Rhebekka."

Rhebekka wrapped an arm around her sister's shoulders as they made their way down the hall to the sound room. Ellie threw the message slips in a trash can and slid an arm around her sister's waist. "How many times has she tried to call?"

"I stopped counting after the first two dozen."

"I had it out with her this morning. She continues to believe I am the personification of the devil in worldly form and my main ambition is to defame her beloved organization."

"I'll bet she said something like how could you do this to Jehovah." Ellie made air quotes with her fingers.

"Winner, winner, chicken dinner. I blocked her number and took her contacts out of my phone. This time, I'm really done. You can lead a horse to Blackwater Falls, but you can't make it drink."

"It depresses me, so let's forget about it for now. Let's go see the girls."

Rhebekka squeezed her sister in a side hug and followed her down the hall into the recording studio. Inside the room, a small sound crew watched through thick glass into the live room as two striking, auburn-haired women pressed their headphones to their ears and leaned close to the pop filters in front of the microphones. Rhebekka was transported back in time. Though she and Ellie didn't resemble each other anywhere near as much as the twins did, she could see the two of them standing in a booth similar to this one.

The music and lyrics they'd created together came through in delicate harmonies. Rhebekka closed her eyes and fingered the chords she'd written for the song. As the notes filled the room, she couldn't help but marvel at the girls' personal spin on the song. They were bringing it to life with their style. "I love it. This takes me back."

Ellie smiled and wrapped her sister up in a hug. "It's like déjà vu for me, more times than I can begin to say."

Rhebekka looked around. "Minus all the spilled beer and pop on the floor. I always had to wash my shoes after we left that by-the-hour studio we started in."

"Remember how nicotine stained the walls in the control room? It ran down the walls in nasty streams when it was humid because the damn air conditioner didn't work."

Rhebekka laughed. "The good old days."

"Can we try that again? I was a half beat off on that last line." Martina asked from inside the booth.

Ellie leaned over and pressed the intercom button. "We can, but you worry way too much. Rhebekka and I were standing right here, and it sounded great."

Rhebekka motioned the girls while pressing the intercom for her turn. "You two are bad ass. It was awesome. Believe in yourself."

Martina bent her head but smiled widely behind the hair hiding her face.

Rhebekka and Ellie sat through another few takes before the girls took a break and joined them in the control room to listen to the playback. Rhebekka felt her phone vibrate and checked the text message.

Pulling into Thomas.

Ellie turned to her. "Do you need to go?"

"Nope. Naomi's on her way and bringing you a present."

Ellie's eyes grew comically saucer-like. "Is she bringing me food?"

"Probably." She patted her own gut. "She certainly has changed my eating habits. Lucian loves to cook with her."

"I'm proud of you, Bek."

Rhebekka turned and looked at her quizzically. "For what?"

"Everything you've accomplished. Honestly, think about where we came from, what we went through."

She grabbed her sister's hand. "What we went through."

Ellie nodded. "Yes, what we went through, but you got your shit together long before I did. You walked through the gates of hell, gave the devil the middle finger, and walked back out smoking one of his cigars with your hair on fire."

"Very dramatic."

"Did someone say dramatic? I've yet to see it. I expected a banner with my name in three-foot letters saying 'Welcome, Daniel.'"

"Daniel!" Ellie squealed in excitement and jumped into his arms. "What are you doing here?"

The joy Rhebekka saw in Ellie's greeting made her heart soar. She lifted her arm for Naomi to slide under. Anytime she could do something to make her sister happy, it brought her a wave of peace. Daniel was one of Ellie's dearest friends. The three of them had traveled the world together before Rhebekka retired. Daniel had promised to stay on, even after Rhebekka left the band, and he fulfilled that oath.

Daniel hugged Ellie and set her down before shaking hands with Rhebekka. He turned back to Ellie. "I'm hoping you might have an opening for a techno whiz. I'm pretty tired of all the traveling. Your sister here tells me she has a grand plan."

"It's good to see you, man. It's not just me. We have a plan." She gestured to Naomi. "How about we all head to Redemption's Road and discuss this plan? Ellie, can you get away?"

Ellie nearly vibrated. "That's the good part about being the boss. I make my own hours. Give me twenty minutes to wrap a few things up and I'll meet you there. I'll bring Daniel, since I don't plan to let him out of my sight for at least a few days." She did a little wiggle in pleasure.

Rhebekka pointed at her. "Call Siobhan and have her join us when she can. What we have planned will take a village."

Ellie came over and drew her into a tight hug. "I love you, Bek. You always seem to know what I need when I need it. Best surprise ever."

"You're welcome, little sparrow. I'm just doing what Grandpa did when he wanted to build a barn—he called the family. That's what I'm doing now, gathering the family."

* * * *

Rhebekka walked through the door at Redemption's Road. Tank and Kierlynn were sitting at the bar looking over a pile of paperwork. "Afternoon, folks. Might a thirsty woman find a tasty beer in a joint like this?" She held out her fist to her longtime friend.

Tank bumped knuckles with her as Kierlynn rose and ducked under the bar. She grabbed two mason jars. "What'll you have?"

Naomi pointed. "A Forbidden Fruit for me, and she'll have a Savior's Red."

Kierlynn nodded and turned to the taps. "You got it."

Tank joined them at a small table near the fireplace. "What brings you two in here on a non-music night?"

Rhebekka looked at Tank. "Daniel's in town. He's over at Ellie's studio with her right now. They'll be joining us in a bit." Rhebekka watched for any change in Tank's demeanor and saw nothing. Ellie still wouldn't come without Siobhan, but Tank's relationship with the good doctor had gone a long way to bridging the Grand Canyon that had developed from Tank's former possessive tendencies.

"Daniel's here? That's awesome. What's he up to?"

"I told him, some time ago, that Lucian needs some role models that have walked in his shoes. Mr. Shannon, from the group home, calls to talk with him at least once a week. That gives him someone to ask questions we wouldn't have the answers to. He and Daniel have talked about music and gaming several times, but I hope Daniel will stay for a while and be like a big brother. He's gone through the full transition and can help Lucian navigate those waters if that's what he chooses to do."

Naomi leaned into Rhebekka. "No matter what he decides, we'll be by his side. We're his family."

Tank watched Kierlynn bring a tray with their beer on it. "I didn't have a soul to call my family until I met you and your sister. Now I have Amy and a sister I didn't know existed."

"Kierlynn, can you grab me a clipboard with some paper with the drinks?"

She gave a thumbs-up and brought everything to the table. When she'd passed out the drinks, Kierlynn started to head back to the bar, but Rhebekka stopped her. "Sit with us. This will involve you as well. You're part of this extended family, as far as we're concerned. We need all hands on deck for this gig." Rhebekka patted the chair beside her when Kierlynn hesitated.

Naomi rose and pulled out a chair for Kierlynn. "Please, join us."

Kierlynn blushed but took the seat. "I haven't had a family since the army. It's taking some time to get used to. What can I do to help?"

Rhebekka rubbed her hands together. "It's a long list, but nothing we can't handle if we work together."

They round-tabled a list of things that had to be addressed to turn the property into the type of home Rhebekka and Naomi described. Kierlynn and Tank had a great deal of insight into communal living, having been in the armed services.

"Privacy was a rare luxury when you lived in the barracks. What you are proposing is a safe space for a queer kid. The fact that they will

229

have safe common areas and private quarters they will control will be incredibly freeing." Kierlynn crunched a piece of ice from her glass of Coke.

Tank added to her statement. "The barracks offered very little of that. As a woman in the military, it was rare to feel safe anywhere."

"That's why we want every one of our rooms to be more like an efficiency apartment. Not necessarily for cooking because that would require an entirely different set of permits. Each will have a bathroom, a small sitting or study area, and a sleeping area. There are enough rooms to knock out walls and create what we want." Naomi wrote a few ideas on the papers.

"We're talking with a safety consultant to help us meet codes for sprinklers and fire escapes. Right now, we think we can create four suites and our living quarters."

Tank studied the list. "What about Lucian? Will he stay in one of the suites, or has he decided to attend college?"

Rhebekka drank the last of her beer. "He hasn't made any decision about college yet. He will have the option of what he wants to do, but our living area will have room for him with us. If he decides he wants a suite, that will be fine too."

Naomi nodded. "He hasn't had a family since his grandmother died, and the group home was certainly anything but nurturing. Unless I miss my guess, he'll stay with us."

Rhebekka sat watching Kierlynn take it all in. "Do you have any thoughts on things that could make it better?"

Kierlynn sighed. "I know this is going to sound odd, but rules. Not the Ten Commandments, but at the very least, house rules. These kids will need to understand this is an opportunity, but not a free ride. Things that are expected and things that aren't allowed. Everyone should have house chores that aid the group and requirements to keep their personal suite reasonably clean. No one will do that for them if they were on their own unless they paid for it."

Tank pointed to her sister. "I'll agree with that. Some of the kids you're talking about will crave the normalcy of it, and the structure will help them bring their own life into balance. It doesn't have to be overbearing, but a simple set of boundaries and expectations, early on. It's not a frat house with a house mom. It's an opportunity to create community and responsibility. The military did many things I can't forgive them for, but they did teach me to be responsible for myself."

Naomi leaned over the table and put her hand on Tank's forearm. "This is why we want you involved. We want to mentor these kids, help them further their education, or find a trade. You've had the communal living experience we will need to draw from." Naomi turned to Kierlynn. "Both of you have."

Rhebekka sat back and watched the ideas roll out. The people of her chosen family never saw obstacles in times like this, only opportunities. She was grateful for the input and the enthusiasm. *This just might come together better than I thought.*

* * * *

Naomi turned as the door to the bar opened. Ellie came in with one arm wrapped around Siobhan and one linked with Daniel's. Tank rose and greeted Daniel like the old friends they were and headed behind the bar.

"It's good to see you, Daniel. What would you like to drink? Siobhan, Ellie, anything for you?"

How far we've come in a little over a year. I wouldn't have believed it possible, but here it is right in front of me.

Tank introduced Daniel and Kierlynn, and then poured a round for everyone. Kierlynn rose and helped get the order. Naomi motioned for them to all move to the larger table in The Confluence. "We'll have more room for everyone."

Rhebekka wrapped an arm around her wife. "They had some great ideas."

"That's the idea of the village. Each brings something a little different to the table, and together, it helps us form a more rounded plan."

They all took seats as Tank and Kierlynn passed out the drinks and joined them. For the next hour, they bounced ideas off each other.

"I could teach them to wait tables and bartend over at Beanders. I think it's important that ya require them ta either be in school or have a job. We know enough business owners between us to start a list of jobs, even if they're part-time," Siobhan offered.

Ellie agreed. "I could put some to work in reception, because I want to start showing Amanda more in the production room. Eventually, she'll be headed to college."

Rhebekka nodded. "I'm betting Karmen could use more part-time help. That would allow her to start the delivery service and expand her catering."

"Did someone say my name?"

They looked up to see Karmen and Zandra joining the group with Lucian on their heels.

Naomi scooted over to make room for Lucian beside her. He smelled of powdered sugar and chocolate as he sat down and kissed her on the cheek. "It's good to see you. How was work?" she asked.

He pushed his dark hair out of his eyes. "It felt like we made enough brownies today to cover a football field. I'll be seeing mixing bowls in my sleep."

Karmen brushed some flour off her forearm. "I certainly couldn't have taken on an order that big by myself. I'd be lost without him."

Pride beamed warm and bright from Naomi's heart as she watched Lucian blush. She patted him on the back. "I'm glad you could join us. We're brainstorming ideas for the new place." She looked back to Karmen. "When we get everything up and running, we'll check with everyone about possible employment for the family members we take in. No obligation, just something to consider if you need more help."

Karmen pointed to Lucian. "If they are all as willing and dependable as he is, I'll be happy to teach them the ins and outs of the bakery and café."

Rhebekka reached across and clasped Karmen's hand. "I would have starved if it hadn't been for you."

Naomi knew that Rhebekka rarely cooked. She also knew that before their reunion, Karmen had fixed most of Rhebekka's meals. These people were a family that she was forever grateful she'd been privileged to join.

Rhebekka clasped Daniel on the shoulder. "Lucian, I'd like to introduce you to someone. This is Daniel Montoya. He was the technical production manager for Regal Crimson and the inventor of...."

Lucian stood and held out his hand. "And the badass creator of ArchAngel and a dozen other of my favorite video games. I'm stoked to meet you."

Daniel grinned from ear to ear as he nodded to Lucian. "The one and only. Rhebekka tells me you're one hell of a bass player. Maybe you can lay down some bass tracks for one of my games."

Naomi grinned when Lucian turned a dozen shades of red. She knew he and Daniel were about to become fast friends. She turned to Lucian. "Okay, you two can discuss all that techno-wiz stuff later. Lucian, this project came about because we want to offer others like you a safe home to get on their feet after foster care. There are also kids who have been kicked out of their own homes because of who they are or who they love. We want you to have a major part in how this all comes together. Do you have any suggestions on what we should do?"

He studied the list of things they'd written down. "I know this will sound weird, but everyone got the same sheets, bed spread, and generic things in the group home. On laundry day, if you didn't have your name written on everything, you never knew that what you got back was yours. It would be nice if everyone had a choice, something representative of their style or personality. Kind of like what you did for me when I moved in with you and Rhebekka."

There were nods around the table. Naomi looked at him with wonder. She'd never consciously thought about how he'd perceived things as they'd shopped and purchased things for his room. It seemed natural for her to do, but it had obviously meant a great deal to him.

Naomi smiled at him. "That's a great suggestion. We'll have a set for when they first move in. Then we'll go shopping for the individual things they would like."

He continued. "Maybe we set up a dinner night where everyone comes together to check in on how we're doing, issues, or suggestions."

Rhebekka nodded in her agreement. "I love that. When we find out there is an issue, we don't let it fester. We get it handled. I want to work to have access to counselors and other resources as well. It may be a small project in the grand scheme, but for those we can help, I want it to make a difference."

"They just need someone to care about them, exactly as they are, without someone wishing they were different. We had so little say in our lives. We came from different situations, but they shoved us into cookie-cutter molds regardless of what got chopped off in the process. It was like being in jail, and we hadn't done anything wrong to get there other than lose everyone important to us."

Tank laughed. "Sounds a lot like the military, wouldn't you say, Kierlynn?"

Her sister quickly nodded her concurrence. "I understand why the military does it, though. They train us for battle and hope when the real thing presents itself, we follow that training to a predictable outcome. For us, the uniform was supposed to bind us as a team. I know that's not what happened to you, Tank, but overall, that was my experience."

Tank nodded. "No, my experience was more like Lucian described. The minute they found out I was something outside the red, white, and blue lines they created, they handed me a set of dishonorable discharge papers."

Kierlynn turned to her. "I think that's something that needs to be revisited. It might not mean anything other than clearing your record to be labeled as discharged, but at least it wouldn't contain the stigma the dishonorable one does."

Tank put a hand on her sister's shoulder. "I appreciate the thought, but that's ancient history and I only look to the future now. I have something better, a little sister."

Naomi reached out and clasped Rhebekka's hand as she listened to the chatter and ideas flow back and forth about their endeavor. In her heart, she knew this idea was stretching its wings, just like Lucian.

* * * *

Rhebekka looked at the big clock behind the bar and leaned back in her chair. Each person sitting around the table appeared to have a vested interest in seeing this plan come to life. The ideas rolled out so fast that she could barely keep up writing them down. She'd finally tasked Lucian with helping to capture it all. She knew that Tank and Kierlynn would need to prepare to open the bar to the public.

"I think we've put together a great list of things we think will help this project get off the ground. I want to put these ideas into a document to help us determine what will be needed to implement the plan and what to do first." Rhebekka looked at the expectant eyes around her. "I know you all are worried about the psychological repercussions of the lawsuits and what cutting our mother out of our lives will do to Ellie and me." She got up, walked to Ellie's chair, and placed a hand on her sister's shoulder. "We're going to be okay. This process has to play out. From Psalm 82, we know that God requires judges to defend the powerless, to deliver them out of the hands of the wicked. If they don't, they will answer to God. The abuse would have continued if we did nothing to expose those who do these heinous things. If we help one child, then it's worth everything we have to go through to expose it."

Ellie took a deep breath and leaned back. "It wasn't something I wanted to do, but if not me, then who?"

Naomi reached across the table and pulled Ellie's hand into her own. "'If God is for us, who can be against us?'"

Rhebekka looked over her gathered family of blood, friendship, and love. *Who can be against us, indeed?*

The group scattered to the wind. Rhebekka, Naomi, and Lucian climbed into the Land Cruiser. "I think I'm in the mood for pizza. How about you call in a pie to Sirianni's, and we'll run over and pick it up before we head home?"

"I like that idea," said Lucian. "I'm dead on my feet after baking all those brownies."

"That sounds heavenly. I want a salad too. Anyone else?" Naomi pulled her phone from her pocket.

"No. I don't want to ruin my unhealthy eating habits. Pizza is its own perfect food. It has all four food groups in one bite. No plates, no utensils necessary."

Rhebekka caught Lucian's grin reflected in the rearview mirror. She made a fist and swung it into the backseat for Lucian to bump it. "I'm with you, dude."

Naomi shook her head. "Thanks for the commentary. There's nothing wrong with adding variety to your diet. One cannot exist on pizza alone."

"I disagree." Lucian and Rhebekka said simultaneously.

"You two." Naomi placed the order while Rhebekka drove.

In less than a half hour, they were back home lounging on the couch, watching the reboot of *Fantasy Island* with Roselyn Sanchez playing a female hostess. The white-attired Elena Roarke followed her great-uncle's footsteps. She granted the guests fantasies while teaching unexpected lessons, just like the iconic role Ricardo Montalban played in the 70s cult classic.

"She's freaking hot," Lucian said around a bite of pizza.

"Agreed," Rhebekka said.

Naomi grabbed another slice. "I loved this show as a kid. When Tattoo would ring the bell and yell 'de plane, de plane,' I'd get so excited."

The trio watched the show and commented on the different character's fantasies.

"If you could go back and change something in a fantasy, what would it be?" Lucian took a sip of his soda and scratched JJ's ears.

Rhebekka chewed and thought about the question. What would she go back and change? Her childhood? Her career? She had only one major regret because it had been totally in her control. "I'd only go back and change one thing." She looked at Naomi. "I'd never make the same bad decisions I did when we broke up years ago."

Naomi gave her a slight smile. "It cost us a lot of years, my love, but it's all water under the bridge. We have each other now."

Rhebekka nodded. "I know that, but I could have had more. Instead, I hurt the one person, besides Ellie, that believed in me unconditionally."

"I think you punished yourself more than I ever did. In doing so, it tore out my heart. I choose not to think about those days because my life was so empty without you. Now, I have the family I'd always dreamed of. If going back meant that we wouldn't have Lucian with us or had not landed here, it's hard to say if all the empty spaces inside of me would have been filled."

Rhebekka pulled Naomi close and kissed her temple. She looked at Lucian. "I won't argue with any of that, though I wish I'd never hurt you."

Naomi rested her head against Rhebekka's cheek. "You've more than made up for it, baby."

"I hope I meet someone that loves me the way you two love each other," Lucian said, holding his crust for Marley to sniff.

They all laughed when Marley snatched it from his hand and bounded off the couch.

Rhebekka chuckled. "I told you she's a thief."

"Hey, random question for you, Naomi. What's your middle name?"

Naomi tipped her head at the out-of-the-blue question but answered openly. "My mother's maiden name was Brandt. Her father's, my grandfather's, first name was Regen, which is rain in German. That's why I was named Naomi Rainelle. Why do you ask?"

"Oh, no reason. I heard Ellie call Bek by her full name, Rhebekka Lynn, and I just wondered about your middle name. I'm going to head to bed." Lucian stood and walked over to them and kissed them both on the cheek. "For what it's worth, if fixing anything in my past would have made me miss meeting you both, I wouldn't change a thing. I can't imagine where I'd have ended up. Goodnight."

"Ellie only calls me that when I'm on her last nerve." Rhebekka ruffled his hair while Naomi kissed his forehead. "Right back at ya. Love ya."

They continued to watch the show without him. Naomi's yawn was timed perfectly with the theme song's start.

"Let's go to bed. I know you'll end up either in the studio or the sanctuary, but for now, let's go lie down."

Rhebekka rose and held out her hands for Naomi to clasp. "I'd be content just holding you, even if I don't drift off for a while."

Naomi groaned as she left the couch. "I'll clean up tomorrow."

Rhebekka grabbed the remnants of their supper. "Honey, it's two empty beer bottles and a cardboard box. I think I can handle it. Go get ready for bed. I'll be in shortly."

She carried everything to the kitchen and poured out the liquids before breaking down the box and throwing it in the trash. Her eyes scanned the room. Framed photos of their wedding, candid shots of their friends, and captured moments of the start of their relationship adorned the walls and shelves in their home. Rhebekka walked over to one. She picked up the shot of the two of them on stage, taken about two years into their relationship. She felt Naomi's arms wrap around her from behind.

"You were so damn sexy in those leather pants."

Rhebekka covered Naomi's hands with one of her own. "They were hot as hell. You know what I remember about this picture?"

"That I was scared to death to be on stage with you?"

Rhebekka pulled Naomi's hand to her lips. "No," she laughed. "I remember seeing you make your way onto the stage and thinking that my world was complete with you by my side. It didn't matter what we were doing, you were the key to my happiness."

"We were so young, or at least you were."

"A head full of dreams and a hand full of wishes." She picked up another photo. This one captured the moment she slipped Naomi's wedding ring onto her delicate finger. "This moment was the answer to my most fervent prayer. May she be mine for the rest of my life."

"Wish granted, my love." Naomi walked her over to a photo that hung, pride of place, on the wall. "This one is in my top five of all time."

The recent photo showed Naomi, Lucian, and Rhebekka on the stage at The Confluence. Lucian's bass hung around his neck as he leaned into a mic. Naomi was smiling ear to ear, her lips inches from the mic. Rhebekka was slightly in front of both of them, her grandfather's Gibson slung over her shoulder, eyes closed in song.

Rhebekka was surprised. "Why this one?"

"I was standing on the stage with the love of my life and the child I dreamed of having with you. We were singing Lady Gaga's *Born This Way* in three-part harmony. It was one of those snapshot moments I'll never forget."

Rhebekka chuckled. "It was a pretty cool moment. It was one of the first times Lucian agreed to do more than play bass in the background. The lyrics meant something to all of us, even though they don't all fit perfectly. My mother would never say I was born to be any kind of star."

"Definitely her short-sightedness. What's the saying? God doesn't make junk. Come to bed."

Rhebekka walked with her hand in Naomi's and stopped momentarily for one last look before switching off the lights and following her down the hall to their sanctuary.

Chapter Sixteen

WEDNESDAY, RHEBEKKA SAT IN the after-school space with Daniel. She was giddy with anticipation at introducing him to the kids who begged, every day, to play ArchAngel. She watched him look around the space she'd created for playing his game.

"What do you think?" She leaned forward in her chair and rested her elbows on her knees.

"This place is rad. You certainly didn't spare any expense on equipment." Daniel looked at the VR goggles hanging on the wall.

"It's like buying a Ford Fiesta. It will get you where you want to go, but the experience would be totally different if you'd bought a Corvette."

Daniel chuckled. "Agreed."

"I know you came to visit, but I hope you consider becoming a permanent member of this tribe. There is enough land with the house we've purchased for you to build whatever you want on it. You could do so much for the kids around here. But hell, I'm going to be honest. I have selfish reasons. I've missed you, and I know Ellie feels the same. You are part of our family, and without you, there's a hole."

Daniel ran his hands over the picture that hung in the VR studio. That day, the kids had introduced the steampunk version of Rhebekka's ArchAngel flying book character. "It was so much fun working with the kids on your character, Vulgate."

"You shocked the hell out of me that day."

"I had a lot of help. When Naomi called to connect me with the kids, it was one of the first projects I'd enjoyed working on in a very long time. To see how much those kids loved you absolutely warmed my heart. Not one of them was a blood relation to you, but you'd never have known it by the way they talked about you. They chose to be family with you. The only time I've ever felt that way was when I was touring with you and Ellie. He sat hard in one of the chairs and heaved a huge sigh. "I'm tired, Bek. If you all want me here, I'll be happy to plant myself and put down the roots I've been avoiding all my life."

Rhebekka got up and hugged him. "There is no doubt we want you right here with us. I can barely keep up with the technology these kids use in school. We could use a volunteer coordinator to help teach coding and other techno-geekery magic to these kids. I know Ellie will be thrilled to have you in the booth helping promote her new artists."

"Thanks, Bek. I think this is what I've been searching for."

"Daniel, my brother, welcome home."

* * * *

Life seemed to be flying by at a maddening pace. It seemed like only days ago, she and Rhebekka had signed the papers to purchase Claire Buxton's family home. Naomi stared at the plans splayed out on her dining room table. The architect they were working with had taken all their suggestions and tried to find ways to incorporate them into what was actually possible. She ran her fingers over the section of the home that was to be their private living quarters. She smiled at the size of Lucian's room.

Rhebekka kissed her shoulder. "I wanted to make it bigger, but he didn't want it to feel like an apartment. He said any bigger, and it would feel like it wasn't part of our home."

"I won't disagree with him." She swept her hand over the area with the suites. "This area should have a totally different feel than our section. Not to separate us from them but to give Lucian the home he's never had. I don't want him feeling like he's growing up in a hotel."

"Miles had some great ideas about making the suites feel like individual homes while blending the common areas to feel like it all fits together. I know he talks about going to cosmetology school, but he has a real eye for interior design. Karmen says he's working out great at the bakery."

Naomi sipped her coffee and walked to the living room. "I'm happy he agreed to let us help him find temporary housing until we finish this. When our new place is finished, he'll be the first resident. I still can't believe how much work our construction crew has gotten done in less than a month. The roof alone was a bear, but they are already moving on to remodeling our living area."

Rhebekka sat down and opened her arm in invitation. "Remind me to thank Sydney for recommending Q Construction through our veteran charity. They are ex-military and either part of the LGBTQIA+ family or strong allies. The company owner wanted to ensure these former soldiers could be gainfully employed at a company accepting them for who they are. They believe in this project, and that goes a long way."

Naomi snuggled in close and chuckled. "I'd say hiring Karmen to cater lunches for them hasn't hurt either."

"While on tour, I learned that a hungry crew couldn't perform at peak level, night after night. Ellie and I made sure to give them something more than cardboard pizza. Besides, I think Lucian gets a kick out of delivering the feast to them every day. It gives him a daily perspective on the changes."

Naomi sighed as she glanced around the living room. It would be hard to leave this place someday. It was the first long-term home she'd shared with Rhebekka. *We made love here for the first time after our five-year separation. Rhebekka proposed in this very room... These walls hold memories of Lucian becoming part of our family.* The pictures that dotted the shelves and walls chronicled their lives. She focused on one of Lucian with his driver's license standing in front of Rhebekka's Tundra. "He's come so far."

Rhebekka nodded. "He certainly has. For the first few weeks, I was so afraid he'd bolt. I even contemplated putting a GPS tag on that leather jacket because I knew he'd never leave it behind. Day after day, he came back."

Naomi smacked her. "Honey, that's just wrong, but very resourceful. My heart said he'd stay if we made a home for him that was too hard to leave behind. Parents who love and accept who you are, are a rare find. He fell into a family that encourages him to be exactly who he is. We give him the freedom to spread his wings and a soft place to land when things go wrong."

Rhebekka pulled her tighter. "Very true. I can't imagine how different things could have been for Ellie and me had we had the same."

"Speaking of Ellie, how's she doing after her testimony?"

"Siobhan finally convinced her to see a counselor. The nightmares of reliving it were becoming too overwhelming. Every time Siobhan sees her with the news on, she unplugs the TV. The news crews have been relentless."

"I'm glad they hired some security. Marlon was only too happy to come vacation in the mountains for a few months. It's amazing how much of a wall a sixty-year-old man can be."

Naomi nearly snorted coffee out her nose. "It also might have something to do with the man being almost seven feet tall and built like a linebacker."

Rhebekka laughed. "Well, there is that. He told her he hasn't had this much fun since our heyday when he had to throw rabid fans off the stage. I think Chance was just as gleeful to arrest Mya when she refused to leave Ellie's studio. Crashing a recording session in progress is expensive. Now that Marlon is there, that won't happen again."

"How about Carrie?"

"She told Ellie the story has made their business traffic pick up from people looking for the story, but it's a hassle when they show up at their home. Eddy isn't much smaller than Marlon, so he's been pretty good about being able to protect his family. I hired some security for them when they're out and about."

Naomi tucked her feet up underneath herself and pushed in tighter. "How does Justine think the trial is going?"

"She's trying to keep Carrie and Ellie hopeful, yet realistic about the outcome. She tells me privately that, if nothing else, it's put the organization's practices out in the open. Right now, they continue to say that neither Ellie nor Carrie gave them an opportunity to correct the problem because they remained silent for so long. Justine is establishing a pattern of inactivity even in the cases where someone came forward. Criminally, Tom and Dave are under investigation. None of us knows what will happen there, but Carrie said she hasn't given up hope in making contact with her niece in Alaska."

Naomi's heart hurt thinking about others that might yet step forward, and she hoped having someone else break the silence would help them do so. "Senseless. How could they ever call themselves men of God?"

"One of the mysteries of the universe. Let's talk about something else. Have you thought about a set list for tomorrow? When Lucian gets home, I'd like to practice."

Naomi reached back to the high table behind the couch and produced a long piece of paper with a list of songs. "I'm set on the first four."

"Oh, Lucian's creation is on here. He'll be stoked."

"He'll just be happy about the long, bass solo. The other three are actually his suggestions."

"All good choices. I think we can build an awesome set around these. Ellie said she wants to join us tonight."

Naomi turned in her arms. "That will be fun. She hasn't done that for a long time."

"She told me her voice feels really strong since she enlisted a vocal coach. I don't care if my little songbird ever sings another note as long as she's healthy and happy."

Lucian came through the door, threw his leather jacket on the hook, and put a box on the kitchen bar. He crashed like a heavy sack of potatoes on the couch. "What a day."

Naomi rose off the couch and headed to the kitchen to finish dinner prep for her family. It needed to be quick, so she chose a grilled chicken salad. It would fill them up but not cause their voices to get gunky, as Lucian liked to say. "Dinner will be ready in fifteen minutes. What made your day so hectic?"

Lucian sat up and turned toward them. "Karmen is running a special on cupcakes to get rid of some supplies. She's changing brands on a few things and wants the baked goods to be consistent. At a quarter a cupcake, we can't keep them on the shelf. Thank God, she hired Miles. There is zero way we'd be keeping up." He slashed a hand through the air.

"Hell, people buy them for two fifty a cupcake. A quarter is a steal." Rhebekka's phone pinged and she pulled it from her back pocket.

Lucian nodded. "Right? She sent me home with a dozen to get them out of the shop. By tomorrow, we'll be sold out. The new ingredients are coming in the morning, so Miles and I will be busy organizing everything at the butt crack of dawn."

Naomi pulled the chicken off the stovetop grill to slice for the salad. Lucian was animated as he spoke and imitated some of his customers. She wasn't sure she could be any happier. *Only when I'm sharing my day with many more just like him in our new home.* A local craftsman was building her dream table. She'd worked with Lucian to design a live edge hickory farm table with a resin progress flag in the middle, which would be a centerpiece in the house.

Lucian washed his hands and pulled a cutting board from the cupboard. He began to slice the vegetables Naomi had cleaned for their salads without being asked. "What did Bek think of the set list?"

Naomi smiled. "She loved it. We'll pick the rest during practice. I'm excited to sing your song."

"Ellie helped me with the lyrics. She even asked me if I'd consider letting Strings and Silk cut it as a single."

Rhebekka came back into the room. "I think it's one hell of a song and perfect for them. It's entirely up to you. I know how important first songs can be. They're a part of you because they come from some of your soul's deepest desires."

Lucian put the knife down and wiped his hands on his jeans. "About that?"

Naomi looked at him curiously. "About selling Ellie your song?"

He shifted from foot to foot. "More about something my soul desires. Can I talk to you two about something?"

Naomi put her hand on his shoulder and gently squeezed. "You can always talk to us about anything."

Lucian pointed to where Rhebekka was sitting. "Can you sit by Rhebekka? I have something to ask you."

Rhebekka pulled out a stool and held it as Naomi sat down. "There is nothing you can't ask us."

He rubbed his hands on his pants again and leaned on the counter. "I'd like to start my permanent transition. I think it's time to have more than just my first name reflect who I am."

Naomi had wondered when he would start to think about this part of being a trans man. She and Rhebekka had done research and spoken to a few experts on how to guide Lucian on his journey. "You know we'll do anything we can to help you do whatever you need to feel whole."

Rhebekka concurred. "Nothing is impossible."

Lucian nodded. "I've thought about starting the hormone treatments and eventually having top surgery." He tentatively looked up at them, as if to see if they were really listening.

"No matter what you decide, we'll be right with you every step of the way. All you have to do is ask." Naomi reached out and placed her hand on his forearm. He covered it with his other hand.

"When we got my driver's license, it irked me that the information doesn't reflect who I am."

Rhebekka pointed at him. "You are a young man named Lucian Altovice."

Lucian came around the bar and looked at them. "Lucian Altovice is who I was. Who I want to be is Lucian Rain Deklan. That would make me a part of both of you. If you'll agree to it." He stammered quickly, "It doesn't mean financially you are responsible for me in any way. I just want to—"

Rhebekka stopped him with a hand on his shoulder. "Take a deep breath." She waited until he had done so. She reached out and held Naomi's hand tightly. "I know that I can speak for Naomi when I say that we would be honored for you to be our son in name. You already are in our hearts."

Tears welled in Naomi's eyes. That he'd chosen to include part of her middle name as his own touched her heart in a way she thought only Rhebekka could. "You are my son, Lucian, with or without any changes, but this choice would make me so happy. We are a family, and our name should reflect that. If Rhebekka and I had chosen to have a child, he couldn't have been any more made for us than you are. You even have a love for music that matches ours. I'd say God has blessed us beyond measure with you."

Rhebekka kissed the side of Naomi's head. "She said it so much better."

They held out their arms, and Lucian leaped into them. He held them so tightly. Tears rolled down every face until they were all a mess.

Naomi's life had been a series of miracles that had surpassed all her dreams but one. Now, that wish had also been granted. *Give thanks in all circumstances; for this is the will of God in Christ Jesus for you.*

* * * *

The Confluence was always packed on the first weekend of June, and the crowd was exceptionally responsive this night. Rhebekka and Tank had decided to have a Pride party at Redemption's Road. No one was turned away, even if they weren't in the LGBTQIA+ community. They welcomed allies and friendly community members alike. She'd hired security to protect all who entered from those who might use the event as an opportunity for violence.

She looked out into the faces and saw many of their closest friends. Siobhan had a table right in the front, where Karmen, Zandra, Amy, and Daniel sat. Off to one side, at a larger table, Chance and Jax sat talking with Maggie, Dee, Kendra, and Brandi. They'd played through their first and second set before taking a break. When they returned, Lucian had blown the audience away with his original song, *The Other Side of My Mirror*. Daniel had cried and clapped so loudly that he'd likely bruised his hands. It was almost eleven o'clock and time for some special announcements and acknowledgments.

Rhebekka leaned into the mic and raised her hands to quiet the crowd. "Thank you all for coming out tonight for our Pride kickoff. The first Pride march happened on the first anniversary of the Stonewall riots. We owe much to those who came before us and the sacrifices they made. We also need to recognize our queer brothers and sisters in the military who have not often been welcomed as they served. I have someone extraordinary I want you to meet. Let me introduce you to Lieutenant Colonel Sydney Parker. Let's give her a hand." Rhebekka clapped as Sydney approached the mic.

Sydney waved for Tank and Kierlynn to join her. "Last weekend, we observed Memorial Day in thanks for those who have paid the ultimate price for our freedom. We honored those who have died in the service of their country. Unfortunately, others still suffer from unseen physical, mental, and emotional wounds. I want to thank all of you for your generous gifts that will allow us to donate $3,500.00 to a new program we've started. This group helps those LGBTQIA+ military veterans who suffer from PTSD, traumatic brain injuries, and those who have suffered sexual trauma in the military. The other group we are helping are some shelter dogs, many from high-kill shelters. These two groups will save each other as we put them together as a team."

There was a deafening roar of applause as Kierlynn took the mic Sydney handed her. "On a dark, snowy evening, I stumbled upon a box on the side of the road. Inside that box was this tiny, helpless, little terrier mix. She was nearly frozen when I picked her up and put her inside my jacket. Before she came into my life, I had one goal and very little hope of achieving it. I was looking for a sister I'd never met. I was so far inside myself that I couldn't feel anything but depression. Digie gave me a reason to get up, keep walking, and care about something outside my struggles. This program does the same thing for other veterans. With your help, we can give them a chance to feel that same purpose. I've been here for almost six months, and my life has changed dramatically. I found more than a new career. I found a family, and so many of you here are a part of that. Even if you're not a local, this place makes you feel like one. For that, I'm eternally grateful."

Tank hugged her sister and took the mic for a second before dropping it to her side and handing it back to Sydney. "You all have heard me bark, so I do not need that mic to say what I need to." The crowd laughed their agreement. She put an arm around Rhebekka's shoulder. "I have no doubt you know who these two incredible musicians are. Too many years ago to remember, they hired me to run security for their tours. I've done some crazy things in my life, but never as many as I had to back in those days. They became family to me. I grew up in the foster system here, and for all its issues, Tucker County was the only place I considered home. When Rhebekka settled down here, she offered me a new opportunity. She's always been a silent partner here, but Redemption's Road, The Confluence, and all you see here was her brainchild. She gave me a family and a life. Now, I have a blood sister, a family of choice, and a love I could never have imagined. For all this, Rhebekka Deklan, I owe you the world."

Rhebekka hugged her best friend. "You don't owe me a thing. You saved me as much as I saved you." She leaned in close. "Are you ready to do this?"

"I definitely am." Tank turned around and left the stage before dropping to one knee in front of Amy. The crowd fell silent. "Doc, I met you when I'd nearly lost some of the most important things in my life. You picked me up when I was as low as I'd ever been. I've never, ever been more grateful to have my ass kicked. Will you do me the honor of marrying me and spending the rest of your life making me eat low-fat food?" Tank pulled a velvet box from her shirt pocket and flipped open the lid to reveal a stunning diamond ring.

Amy covered her mouth and laughed. She nodded before leaning forward. "Yes! Yes, I'll marry you."

Tank slid the ring on her finger and Amy pulled her up before kissing her soundly. "Oh, thank God. I was afraid I was damned to a life of bacon cheeseburgers."

Amy smacked her on the arm and kissed her again. "Someday, lady..." Rhebekka strummed her guitar and began singing the couples favorite song, Bob Seger's *You'll Accomp'ny Me*. Several others joined them on the dance floor and sang along, until the entire room swayed along.

Rhebekka ended the song and pointed to Tank and Amy. "Let's have a round of applause for the newly engaged couple." She clapped along with everyone else. Eventually, the audience retook their seats. She motioned for Naomi and Lucian to join her and interlaced her fingers with her wife's. "I have a few announcements to make as well. I'm sure some of you have seen the activity up on the old Buxton property. Thanks to the generosity of the woman who grew up in that house, Naomi and I are planning a unique project. Tank and Lucian grew up in a completely unfair system, with no understanding of who they were. My beautiful wife, Naomi, came to me with an idea to offer LGBTIQIA+ kids who have aged out of the managed care system a safe place to land. We plan to create a group home for these kids or others forced from their homes because they're gay. Many of you have already offered your labor and your support. We are eternally grateful." Lucian stood with his hands on a cover board, hiding the mockup sign. Rhebekka pointed to him to reveal it. "I give you Tip'n Claire Haven."

If she thought the applause rocked the house before, it didn't hold a candle to what she heard now in support of their plans. Naomi folded into her arms and cried.

"I hope those are happy tears, baby." Rhebekka wiped the wetness from her cheeks.

"The happiest." Naomi's kiss was gentle and full of their love.

"This will be tonight's last song, but it fits. The first time I heard it on the radio, I couldn't get it out of my head. Once Naomi came up with this idea, I knew why that song wouldn't leave me." She started the intro to The Highwomen's, "Crowded Table" and was delighted when the crowd whistled their approval. Lucian picked up his bass while Ellie and Naomi joined in on the vocals. The three sang about sowing what you hoped to reap. Rhebekka believed that if you sowed the seeds of love and happiness, then that's what you could expect to reap. She and Naomi wanted more than anything to be the light that guided others home. For them, a crowded table meant a life filled with their friends and family gathered together. Their dream was to make that possible for those who had rarely, if ever, experienced family joy. *If it be your will, let it be so.*

* * * *

It was well after two in the morning when the remaining patrons left the bar. Tank had left a few lights on as she, Amy, and Kierlynn put the day's business to bed. The roll-up door was open, allowing a cool breeze to stir the malty fragrance of beer. Rhebekka sat with a yawning Naomi curled into her shoulder while Lucian sat beside them, thumbing his bass. Ellie sat in Siobhan's lap in quiet conversation.

Rhebekka turned to the young man she considered her son. "Lucian, your song was an absolute hit tonight. Did you see the way the crowd reacted?"

His cheeks colored, and the corner of his mouth curled into a small smile. "That was a trip. I didn't think anyone would like it."

Ellie disagreed. "They didn't just like it, young man. They loved it. Stop selling yourself short. Don't forget I'd like to help you produce it, whether you do it yourself or we work out a contract for the Moxie Belles."

"You think it's that good?" Lucian looked skeptical.

"I think we can make a few more improvements, but yes, it's that good. Trust me on this." Ellie sounded resolute.

Daniel walked back into the room. He turned a chair around and leaned his arms on the backrest. "You're very talented, Lucian. She knows what she's talking about. The lyrics gutted me, and I know I wasn't the only one."

"Thanks, everyone. You don't know what it means to me to hear that from the present company."

Daniel sat up a little straighter and gripped the back of the chair. "I have to say, folks, as someone who grew up in a home that couldn't adjust to who I was, I can't tell you what I would have done to have a place to go like you're offering, a place where I would have been completely accepted. As Lucian can attest, growing up in a body that doesn't reflect who you are makes it hard for you to thrive. It feels like the whole world is ganging up on you. Many years ago, you two gave me the chance to be Daniel. I can never repay you for that."

"There is no payment due, my friend. We love you. You're family to us." Ellie reached out a hand and took his in hers.

Rhebekka nodded. "She's absolutely right. We're a family that likes to help. We want you to know the grace we've been shown."

Lucian nodded his agreement. "This family doesn't know how to do anything but help. Rhebekka and Naomi have always talked to me about God's grace, something I didn't understand. They live their faith."

"The other thing I know is that they'll offer a place for these kids to find faith in themselves. When they explained it to me, I told them I was all in. It's why I've decided to move my computer graphics and video gaming company here to Tucker County. I plan to offer quality employment to the local community, including any of the residents of Tip'n Claire Haven that are interested."

Ellie jumped up and nearly knocked him out of his chair to hug him. He stood and had barely caught his balance when she jumped into his arms and kissed his whole face. "I've got my Danny boy for good!"

Daniel could only laugh as he hugged her tightly and pulled Siobhan into a group hug.

"She always told me ya were the little brother she never had. Welcome to the family."

Rhebekka laughed at them. "Looks like our table just got a little more crowded."

"Is it too crowded for a few more?"

Rhebekka knew that voice. She'd heard it from the time she was a child until she'd refused to listen to it not long ago. She wasn't surprised when Ellie turned her head as well. "Mom, what are you doing here?"

Eileen McNally stood in the doorway looking haggard. Her typically perfect makeup was streaked with what appeared to be tears. She had her hands on the shoulders of a young woman who bore a striking resemblance to Carrie Broader.

Who the young lady was became apparent when Carrie also stepped into the music venue. "Rhebekka, Ellie, I'd like to introduce you to my niece, Lisa Rivera."

Rhebekka watched as tears continued to stream down her mother's face. Despite all that had come between them, she didn't have the heart to be cruel to the woman who had given birth to her. Rhebekka rose and stood in front of Lisa and her mother. "Lisa, it's a pleasure to meet you. I apologize if my manners are lacking at this early hour. Carrie, it's good to see you as well." She let her eyes fall on her mother's face. "Mom?" She wasn't even sure what question she was asking, but her mother took the next step.

She visibly shook herself and looked Rhebekka in the eye. "I've found another silent lamb who needs to use her voice. I knew she'd need the support of some of the strongest people I've ever known. I'm also here to see if the bridge I burned is too far gone to cross or if I can lay the first board in a new one?"

Ellie came to stand to Rhebekka's left as Naomi joined her on the right. Naomi stretched out her hand. "Mrs. McNally, it's nice to formally meet you. I'm your daughter-in-law, Naomi Deklan.

The older woman's lip began to tremble, and Eileen brought her hand to her mouth before stretching it out to accept Naomi's greeting. "It's my understanding that I owe you a debt of gratitude for bringing such joy to my daughters' lives. Thank you for caring for them when I was far too blinded to see the error of my ways."

Naomi rubbed the small of Rhebekka's back. "I love them, and we're family, warts and all."

Eileen laughed slightly and looked at Ellie. "Ellie, I'm so very sorry. I didn't know." She choked up and covered her face with her hands as her body shook with sobs. "I'm so very sorry."

Rhebekka took a deep breath and silently asked God for the strength to be a living example of the grace and forgiveness that her faith required of her. *If I can't offer grace at this moment, standing in a place called Redemption's Road, then am I worthy of it in my own right?* She shook herself internally as she felt Naomi's hand close around hers. She softened her gaze toward her guests. "It's late, and we're all too tired for the long conversations required. For tonight, let's set everything aside and let grace be our guide tomorrow. You are welcome to come and stay at our home. There's plenty of room." She reached out for her mother's trembling hand and squeezed it gently. "'...for all have sinned and fall short of the glory of God, and all are justified freely by his grace through the redemption that came by Christ Jesus.'"

Her mother released a shaky breath and tried to smile. "It's a first step."

Rhebekka nodded and pulled her into a hug. "One of many to come."

Epilogue

NAOMI SAT AT A picnic table on the grounds of Claire's former home, reading the newspaper. She wiped at the bead of sweat that threatened to roll down her temple. It was late July, and the leafed-out trees were the only place that offered a brief respite from the unusual heatwave they were experiencing.

She put the paper down and pulled her long hair off her shoulders into a messy bun. Rhebekka sat beside her and kissed her neck as she put two glasses of lemonade on the table.

"Thanks, baby. I needed this. I just finished reading Claire's obituary. I'm so glad we could get her out here to see some of the progress before she passed."

Rhebekka nodded. "Me too. None of this would have been possible without her. The one good thing is that I'm sure she's been reunited with Tip. I'm sure they're watching over the progress. I'd like to believe we'll have another set of guardian angels watching over us."

"I still can't believe what she left us in the will." Naomi took a drink and sighed as the cool refreshment slid down her throat.

"It was a shock to both of us, but her attorney assured me that she'd taken all the necessary steps to ensure no one could contest her wishes. We weren't the only group she left money to. Now, we can do some things we hadn't planned on."

"Yeah, like the mother-in-law suite." Naomi shook her head and chuckled.

"That was something I would never have expected in a million years." Rhebekka looked up the hill and saw her mother trimming and tending to a flowering bush near the house's side door.

Naomi knew there was still a long way to go in repairing the relationship that had been so badly broken, but the mother and her daughters had come a long way since she'd last seen them interact at Wesley McNally's funeral. She watched as Eileen patted Lucian on the shoulder when he'd helped her work a dead branch out of the foliage. "Is she still getting calls and letters from the elders?"

"They are relentless when they know they are losing someone as staunch in her beliefs as my mother was." Rhebekka sipped her drink.

"Be honest with me. How are you doing with all this?"

Rhebekka moved the glass around the wooden table, making multiple rings with the condensation. "I'm not really sure. I know that, in order to move past it all, I have to be willing to let it go. Now that Ellie is in counseling, I think my worry over her reoccurring nightmares is settling. I know Siobhan will take care of my sister until the day she draws her last breath. The court case is still up in the air and likely will be for years. My feelings about my mother are evolving, but it's a slow process. God and I have a lot of talks about it on my bike rides."

"How's the new leg doing with that?"

Rhebekka chewed a piece of ice and answered. "It's taken some getting used to, but K-9 and I are doing just fine."

Naomi looked at her quizzically. "K-9?"

"Don't you remember Marvin the Martian's dog?"

Naomi chuckled. "You nut. Go, we have a group home to finish."

"Yes, my love." Rhebekka leaned over and kissed her before dropping an ice cube down her back and running away.

Naomi pulled at her shirt until the cube dropped out. "You ass. It's a good thing God and I love you."

She picked up her pen and returned to her journal.

> *To say things around here have changed drastically is far too much of an understatement. Rhebekka's mother is working very hard to rebuild her relationship with her daughters. Rhebekka says it reminds her of building this group home. We had to ensure that the foundation was sound before making any changes. I've had long conversations with Eileen about her deep-seated beliefs and why it's so hard to believe anything else. She and Rhebekka haven't broached the subject. I suspect that will take more than a conversation over coffee. Our son officially changed his name to Lucian Rain Deklan and is thriving with Daniel around full-time. A positive role model in his daily life has given him a great deal more confidence. The hormone therapy is dropping his voice and producing patchy hair on his upper lip and chin. He's thrilled! We've consulted with a plastic surgeon who specializes in helping transgender individuals. It's Lucian's decision, and we'll support him in whatever way he needs when he's ready.*

Tank and Amy walked up through the yard, hand in hand. Naomi waved them over. "Hey, you two. How goes the wedding planning?"

"Naomi, tell her a costume-themed Halloween wedding is an awesome idea," Tank whined.

"This genius wants us to dress like zombies for our wedding! My mother is already having a conniption fit that we're getting married on such short notice. She likes you right now, but you show up looking like you should be in a funeral instead of a wedding, and you'll need that prop casket from the brewery for real." Amy shook her head and crossed her arms. "Talk some sense into her, because I certainly can't."

"Tank is all yours to handle. I'm doing my best to talk Rhebekka out of us attending as Batman and Wonder Woman."

"Rhebekka always says be yourself, unless you can be Batman, then always be Batman. I tend to agree with her. Batman has the coolest toys." Tank couldn't contain a chuckle.

Naomi sighed. "And that's why you two are the best of friends. Can you imagine what people would think when you told them Batman officiated your wedding?"

"That is not going to happen. They will both act like adults. I promised my mother. The first time she met Rhebekka, she shot Mom in the forehead with a Nerf gun." Amy stared at Tank.

"Can I help it that Martha walked into the line of fire? It's not like they were aiming for her. Bek was teamed up with Kendra against Kierlynn and me." Tank held up her hand, palm up, trying to declare her innocence.

Amy put her head back and groaned. "Lord, help me."

Naomi nearly spit lemonade out on that comment. "I'll put in a good word for you."

Tank pulled Amy into her arms and kissed her cheek. "Very funny. Is Bek in the house?"

Naomi nodded. "She is. Go on in, love birds."

I'm so happy for Tank and Amy. I'm not sure I've ever been to a Halloween-themed wedding. If Amy has her way, this wedding won't have the chance to be my first. My bet is on Amy. It's incredible how Tank's life has changed. She and Kierlynn grow closer every day. Lt. Colonel Sydney Parker has been working with Veteran Advocacy Project, on behalf of Tank, to apply for a change in her official military discharge status. Tank spent almost twenty years in the Marines before being discharged for homosexual acts. The change on her official documentation could mean she will get the benefits she deserves.

Naomi looked toward the side of the house and saw Siobhan, Ellie, and Daniel looking over plans for the new studio. The three of them had big dreams. Daniel had already purchased a property in the industrial park to begin moving his graphics and gaming company. *Those three will change the world.* She returned her attention to her journal to make a few final observations.

My life is so blessed with people I call family. I'd always hoped Rhebekka and I would find our way back to each other, but I could never have imagined how full my life would be when that happened. I'm a mother, and if it's meant to be, I'll have that honor many more times within the walls of this house of refuge. We want that table to be very crowded and always have a place for one more.

Naomi closed the journal and set her pen on top. She looked up to see Lucian and Rhebekka, side by side, removing debris.

Lucian looked out the window. "I thought this was a family project, Mom."

Rhebekka joined him at the windowsill and nodded her agreement. "Yeah, I need somebody to boss me around."

Naomi's heart swelled until it nearly burst from her chest. "I'm on my way." *The rain came down, the streams rose, and the winds blew and beat against that house; yet it did not fall, because it had its foundation on the rock.* She pulled her gloves from her back pocket and headed inside, knowing the house the Deklans built would stand the test of time, forever and ever. "Amen."

About CJ Murphy

I began to create lesbian fiction after my wife suggested I write her a story as a personalized gift. I was privileged to be mentored by another published author who helped turn a raw manuscript, into an actual novel. Upon completion, she encouraged me to submit to Desert Palm Press. DPP offered me a contract for my first novel, *frame by frame* in 2017. My second novel, *The Bucket List*, was published in late 2018. I credit my storytelling ability to being an avid reader and having an adventure filled occupation for twenty-five years as a career firefighter.

Connect with CJ:

Email: cptcjldypyro@gmail.com

Facebook: CJ Murphy (Murphy's Law)

Blog: Murphy's Law Ink

Note to Readers:

Thank you for reading a book from Desert Palm Press. We appreciate you as a reader and want to ensure you enjoy the reading process. We would like you to consider posting a review on your preferred media sites and/or your blog or website.

For more information on upcoming releases, author interviews, contests, giveaways and more, please sign up for our newsletter and visit us as at Desert Palm Press: www.desertpalmpress.com and "Like" us on Facebook: Desert Palm Press.

Bright Blessings